LYNN KURLAND

THE PRINCE OF SOULS

A NOVEL OF THE NINE KINGDOMS

"Lyrical writing, brilliant mental imagery, richly descriptive magic, and larger than life characterization." —*The Reading Cafe*

Gift of Magic

"The exciting story line is fast-paced from the onset . . . Lynn Kurland spins another fabulous fantasy." —*Genre Go Round Reviews*

"A magical combination of action, fantasy, and character exploration that is truly wonderful! A journey well worth taking!" —*RT Book Reviews*

Spellweaver

"One of the strongest fantasy novels welcoming in the new year." —*Fresh Fiction*

"Kurland weaves together intricate layers of plot threads, giving this novel a rich and lyrical style." —*RT Book Reviews*

A Tapestry of Spells

"Kurland deftly mixes innocent romance with adventure in a tale that will leave readers eager for the next installment." —*Publishers Weekly*

"Captured my interest from the very first page." —*Night Owl Reviews*

Princess of the Sword

"Beautifully written, with an intricately detailed society born of Ms. Kurland's remarkable imagination." —*Romance Reviews Today*

"An intelligent, involving tale full of love and adventure." —*All About Romance*

To my girls

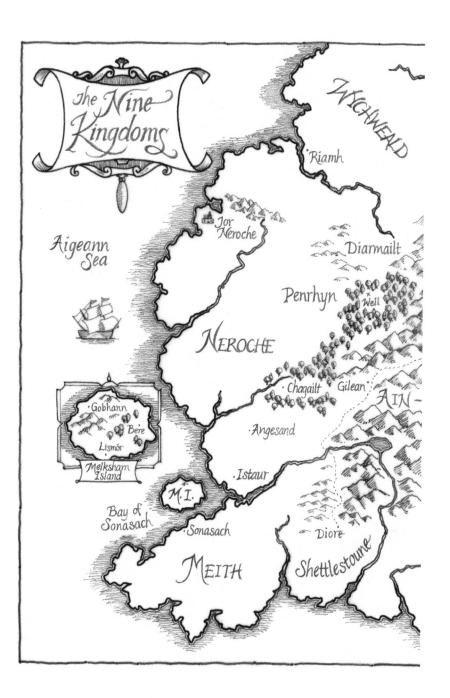

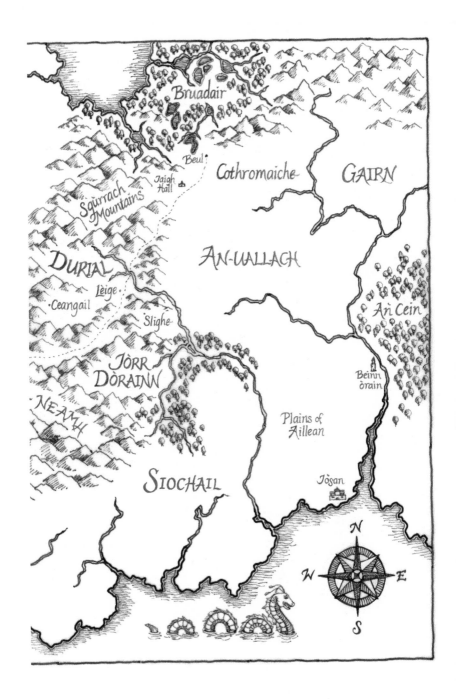

One

When a man was facing death, his mind naturally became consumed with questions of a profound and pressing nature, such as why pursuing his favorite things—murder, mischief, and mayhem—should result in the most fatal of the three being perpetrated upon his own poor self.

Acair of Ceangail leaned his head back against the weeping stone wall of a dwarvish dungeon, ignoring the alarming rattle in his chest, and wished he'd had the wherewithal to find the answer that question deserved. Unfortunately, his strength had been spent on numerous escape attempts, his voice worn hoarse from shouting demands that someone come release him, and his hands left bruised and bloodied far past the point where they might be acceptable at even the roughest of supper tables thanks to his banging them repeatedly against the invisible door of his cell.

He suspected he might be nearing his end.

That he might meet that end in the very last place he'd wanted to be, a kingdom ruled by a monarch he had endured innumerable humiliations to avoid encountering lest that selfsame monarch decide the time had come for him to indeed breathe his last, was almost more than he could bear. If the cold, vermin, and lack of food didn't finish him off, the irony of that likely would.

Such a terrible fate should have been impossible given the charmed nature of his existence. He had spent decades cutting a gleeful swath through the Nine Kingdoms, tossing himself with abandon into situations that would have given a lesser mage pause and extricating himself from the most impenetrable of strongholds with a wink and a cheery wave. Kings had ground their teeth, mages had hidden behind tapestries, and priceless treasures had leapt out of locked cabinets to take up residence in his pockets.

Why the course of his life had taken such a decided turn toward less desirable locales was —

Well, honesty was, as he reluctantly admitted to those he wasn't trying to rob or intimidate, his worst failing. If he were to be *honest*, he could pinpoint the exact moment when his life had veered off the smoothly paved path laid before his exquisitely shod feet and led him to a place that had been the beginning of the end for him.

It had been, if memory served, during the previous spring as he'd been going about his usual business of toppling thrones and attempting to pilfer the world's supply of magic. He'd been in the right place at the wrong time and found himself a reluctant witness to the sight of a very sharp blade coming directly toward a rather lovely if not perilously powerful maiden fair. His chivalry had risen like gorge, and he'd stepped in front of her to take the blade meant for her into his own black heart.

If he'd had even the slightest inkling how that colossal piece of do-gooding would begin the unraveling of the cloth of his life, he would have nipped off into the shadows and left the wench to fend for herself. But he'd jumped into the fray and the deed had been done. That act of selflessness—and lesson learned there, to be sure—had led to a series of events that had completely derailed his plans for the making of obstreperous hay.

Having his fine form restored to perfection by a piece of elvish rot had only been the beginning of the horrors he'd endured. Good deeds, polite smiles, fawning apologies he hadn't meant in the slightest: the list of what had taken up the subsequent months had been endless and endlessly trying. He had submitted to the indignities, though, because his freedom had hung in the balance.

Fate had obviously stepped in to take the helm only to set him on a collision course with the one soul before whom he had absolutely refused to bow and scrape, namely Uachdaran of Léige: maker of legendary swords, digger of priceless gems, and papa of one vexatious daughter with plans.

'Twas obvious to him now that he should have made an effort to clear up a few lingering misunderstandings between himself and the king of the dwarves. A rare bottle of elvish wine or an irreplaceable tapestry or two sent at just the right moment might have been the very thing to soften the king's heart and overcome any reluctance to share one or two of the kingdom's plentiful treasures. After all, dwarvish mines produced sparkling things he liked very much, and Durial was a place full of useful lakes and rivers.

If he'd helped himself to a handful of gems the king might or might not have missed, then used one—or perhaps several, the details escaped him—of the king's many rivers for his own purposes, who should have been the wiser?

Well, obviously the king had been, which was why he was rotting belowdecks instead of taking his ease in front of a roaring fire upstairs in the great hall.

Unfortunately for his hopes of luxuriating in fresh air again any time soon, he knew—and never mind how he knew—that not even the most creative of shapechanging would allow him past Uachdaran of Léige's containment spells. Worse still was knowing—and on that score he was all too happy to recount the ridiculous reason why he knew—that whatever the king's magic might leave of him after such an attempt, the fiendish spell currently sitting across his cell from him would certainly finish off.

He looked narrowly at that nasty piece of business that was definitely the cause for his being where he was at present and decided that reminding himself of exactly why that was might at least keep him warm for a bit longer.

There he'd been, less than a fortnight earlier, facing a formidable foe and limiting himself to a rudimentary spell of return, when things had taken a foul jog south. The words of his own spell had scarce left his lips before that damned thing presently glaring at him like a surly youth had leapt upon his mostly innocent person like a hound on a meat-covered bone and begun to chew. If it hadn't been for the intervention of a woman he loved but didn't deserve and the magical stylings of a prince he loathed but owed his life to, he would have definitely breathed his last.

He'd hardly managed to scamper off to safety with his lady before he'd run afoul of the local monarch who had popped him in a truly awful little prison and promised him a one-way journey to a spot in the East where the king had pointed out quite enthusiastically that Acair wouldn't be all that welcome.

He sighed as deeply as he was capable of at the moment. 'Twas all too soon for the business of endings. He had mischief to make, the world to save, a red-haired stable lass to woo. If he'd had any heart to break, that noise echoing in his soul would have been the sound of it. He would gladly have gazed upon Léirsinn of Sàraichte's lovely visage one more time, though he supposed having seen her that morning on the other side of the spell that guarded his door was the best he was going to manage.

Or had she been there yesterday? The day before that? He frowned, reluctantly conceding that it had become increasingly difficult to mark any distinction between dreaming and lucidity. Rousing himself to put events in their proper order, never mind attempting to marshal the strength to put the world back in its proper order, was simply beyond him. A little gloss of hopelessness over any piece of mischief tended to leave him rubbing his hands together with delight, but this was something else entirely. He could feel his breath slowing with every exhale, his strength ebbing with each heartbeat, his very will to live being pulled from him with every moment of imprisonment that passed. The thumping in his ears was likely what was left of his broken heart giving its all before —

He froze, which admittedly was done rather easily all things considered.

Were those footsteps?

He'd heard that sort of thing before, but usually those plodding boots belonged to some belligerent guard delivering his daily stew of things he absolutely refused to identify. A time or two the footfalls had been lighter and belonged to a spectacular woman who had come to keep him company in his hour of need.

Now, though, he honestly couldn't decide if he were hearing things or hearing actual *things*, if he could stir himself to distinguish between the two.

Aye, those were definitely footfalls. He closed his eyes and tried to identify the number of feet making them and if the cadence were pleasant or sinister. Before he'd even begun to come to any conclusion on the matter, the spell serving as the door to his hellish jail disappeared.

Before he could so much as blurt out a half-hearted, self-serving apology to whomever might have been responsible for the same, he was hauled to his feet.

"The king wants you upstairs," one of the two guardsmen there said curtly.

He imagined the king did and suspected the invitation had less to do with enjoying a robust pint of ale together and more to do with swinging all on his own from the nearest beam. Given the rather rustic nature of the king's lodgings, the old whoreson wouldn't have any trouble finding one of those.

Death it would be, then.

He indulged in a brief moment of regret that his legs weren't steadier beneath him. If he were to face the gallows, he would have preferred to have walked there with a swagger. He spared a brief nod of thanks to his spellish chaperon that appeared at his side and slung a shadowy arm around his shoulders. Enemy in life, friend in death.

He stumbled along between a pair of dwarvish guards he would have felled without so much as a twinge of conscience not half a year earlier and found it in himself to be grateful that his execution wouldn't happen below ground. Then again, for all he knew Uach-daran had invited several souls of note he might or might not have offended in the past to the event and didn't want them catching a chill. He could only imagine who might be on that list.

Please not Léirsinn. If he had to die, he didn't want her to watch. Not after what she'd put herself through to save him.

It took longer than it should have to make his way through the palace and out the front doors, but his guardsmen didn't seem anxious to rush off to other tasks. He finally limped out into the courtyard, then leaned over with his hands on his shaking thighs to catch his breath for a moment or two. When he thought he could manage it, he straightened. Perhaps his usual expression of sardonic amusement was beyond him, but he would meet his fate with his head held as high as he could manage.

The sun was inching up toward its mid-morning spot in the sky, but its pale winter light had done little to warm the air. That was no doubt why the courtyard was full of the satisfying smell of a hearty fire —

Or, perhaps not.

There, to his left, on the north side of the gates—he liked to keep those sorts of details straight in case the opportunity for flight presented itself—were the king's stables. He was surprised to see them wearing scorch marks.

Somewhat less surprising was the sight of the king himself standing but a handful of paces away. Acair attempted a polite bow. That sent him pitching forward onto his knees, which was perhaps better than landing straightway upon his poor visage though not by much. His guards hauled him back to his feet, then did him the very great favor of holding him up until he could stand there on his own.

He waited until the stars stopped swirling about his head before he nodded his thanks. The dwarves stepped away a pace or two, but no farther.

First things first. Though Léirsinn had told him the king had offered her a chamber, there was no sense in not making certain of it.

"My lady?" he asked pointedly.

"She is safely housed and recovering from her attempts to destroy my hall." The king leveled a steely glance at him. "I blame you for her misguided actions."

"As you should," Acair agreed, furiously calculating the amount of strength it would take to get both himself and his love out the front gates.

Though it galled him to admit as much, he knew it would take more than he had at the moment. The best he could do was keep himself free of the dungeon and recover a bit until the opportunity for escape presented itself.

He reached for his best expression of contrition, appalled by how easily it came to him, and faced the king squarely.

"I believe I feel an apology coming on."

Uachdaran folded his arms very slowly over his manly chest and lifted an eyebrow. "Do you, indeed."

"Perhaps more than one," Acair amended. "If there's time."

"I have all morning. Spew away."

Acair supposed the longer the apologies, the more chance to catch his breath, so he jumped in with both feet. "First, I would like to apologize for rushing off into the night with your middle daughter. If it appeases Your Majesty any, she almost killed me with a chair."

"I'll speak to her about leaving things undone when next we meet," the king said. "What else?"

"I apologize for making use of one—"

"More than one!" the king shouted.

"Several," Acair conceded. "Several rivers belonging to you that I appropriated for my own unsavory purposes."

The king looked at him for so long without moving that Acair began to wonder if perhaps all those sleepless nights he was responsible for might have done more damage than he'd suspected. The king was indeed a bit puffy about the eyes and he looked as if he needed a decent nap. Acair imagined his own visage didn't look any better, so perhaps 'twas best to let that observation lie.

"Insufficient," the king said crisply. He stroked his beard, encountered a few equally crispy ends, then pointed toward the stables. "Look at the damage there. Apologize for that."

Acair had already looked and wasn't sure he cared for a second viewing. "I didn't do that."

The king snarled a curse at him. Acair wasn't unfamiliar with the dwarvish tongue—it came in handy for knowing which spells to poach—so he understood precisely what the king was telling him to do with himself. He would have pointed out that he couldn't very well consign himself to Hell and engage in those sorts of activities by himself, but he imagined he didn't need to. With the way the king was looking at him, he wasn't entirely sure the king wouldn't be his escort and primary tormentor if given the chance.

So, instead, he chose discretion and kept his mouth shut. He would have attempted a look of regret, but he'd tried that a time or two in the past and found that sort of thing just didn't sit properly on his features.

He was made for sneers. It was his burden to bear, to be sure.

"I never said you lit the fire," the king said curtly, "though I'm guessing yours was the spell that was used."

"I don't imagine—"

"Shut up," the king said, turning away. "We'll go have a closer look and decide then. Follow me."

Acair didn't dare not, though it was rather a more dodgy business than he was comfortable with. He stumbled along behind the king, accompanied by a decent collection of palace guards, and tried not to dwell on the fact that he was within bolting distance of the gates. He also ignored the fact that at any other time he would have found the number of obstacles in his path toward freedom to be exhilarating not exhausting. At the moment, it was all he could not to weep with gratitude when the king stopped and turned to glare at him.

"Your lass, Léirsinn, said this morning that she wanted to do a bit of horse work. I agreed, because I thought it would keep her from trying to burn my house to the ground again."

Acair refrained from commenting on that. He'd heard all about that rather fiery adventure from the woman herself. It had been unsurprising, actually. She had recently acquired a bit of magic—something he still hadn't quite come to terms with—and her first act had been to set half a forest on fire. Red hair equaled a bit of a temper or so he'd heard, but he suspected that mentioning the same to her would only result in her turning her incendiary sights on *him*.

So many conversational topics to avoid. 'Twas enough to leave a man of quality reaching for ink and parchment in order to jot them down for reference.

"This," the king continued coolly, "is what your wee horse miss did earlier this morning after I refused to bring you upstairs."

"I can't imagine she would have burned a stable full of horses to the ground over that," Acair said slowly.

"She was aiming for *me*!" The king blew out his breath, accompanied by a curse or two. "My stables bore the brunt of her fury, though my own person is not without damage as well."

Acair thought it wise not to comment on the condition of the king's long, glorious beard, though that was where discretion ended. He considered, then gave his all to drawing himself up in his best imitation of a very dangerous black mage on the verge of dire deeds.

"You said my lady was well, but I have no proof." He gestured toward the stables. "That isn't proof."

The king's expression was enough to leave Acair wondering if the man was capable of sheering off parts of his mine with his glares alone.

"I do not harm women," Uachdaran said frostily. "Mistress Léirsinn is recovering from her exertions, as I said. I'm still considering whether or not I'll allow you to see her before I send you off to your well-deserved reward in Hell. You'll improve your chances by remaining silent."

Acair nodded, silently. He would have pled for a moment to enjoy his relief that Léirsinn was indeed safe, but dwarvish swords being loosened in finely tooled dwarvish sheaths were a chorus of reasons why he was better off not making any requests. He followed the king into his stables without comment and hoped for the best.

The truth was, the barn had only sustained minor damage and even that was only on the outside where Acair suspected the horses didn't find themselves troubled by it. He shuffled past pristine stalls until the monarch paused. He glanced to his left and was only marginally surprised to find his own horse housed there.

Sianach, that damned nag, had his nose buried in a bucket of something that smelled so much better than anything Acair had choked down over the last few days that he had to clutch the edge of the stall door to keep from swooning. He wondered briefly if his blasted horse would bite him if he tried to steal his breakfast. Sianach lifted his head, bared his teeth briefly, then went back to his grain.

The king grunted and continued on.

Acair walked until he simply couldn't go any farther. He grasped a post when it presented itself as something to be used in remaining upright, then blinked in surprise at the sight of a different horse sticking its rather distinctive nose over a stall door.

"Is that an Angesand steed I see in yon kingly accommodations?" he asked faintly.

"It is," the king said grimly.

"Lord Hearn is a good friend to send you such a valuable beast," he ventured, wondering why the dwarf-king seemed less than pleased with the gift.

"It isn't a gesture of friendship," Uachdaran said shortly, "'tis a bribe." He reached out and stroked the horse's nose. "And a tempting bribe it is. Hearn knows all too well that I've coveted this lad for quite some time."

The horse whickered in pleasure, then snuffled the king's hair. And damn Uachdaran of Léige if he didn't chortle a bit himself, looking as if he were a lad of ten summers facing his first decent mount and feeling the thrill of possessing the same.

"You have excellent taste in horseflesh, Your Majesty," Acair said. It was hard to go wrong with an Angesand pony, but they were equally hard to come by. That Hearn should relinquish one without a king's ransom being surrendered in return was unusual, indeed.

Uachdaran shot him a dark look. "Damned right I do." He pursed his lips, considered, then pulled a missive from out of a pocket. He looked as if he were considering chucking the thing into the nearest pile of manure, if such a thing could be found in such immaculate stables, then thrust it out without comment.

Acair had gained a healthy dislike for the written word over the past several months and suspected the current offering would be no more welcome than any of the others. But he was no coward, so he took it. Reluctantly, but there it was. He fully expected to find anything from additional questing tasks to pointed threats on his life scribbled there for his pleasure. He steeled himself for the worst, then unfolded the sheaf.

I need the bastard alive

Well, at least he didn't have to ask who had penned those words with such an aggressive scrawl. He half expected to see that the note had been sealed with manure and stamped with a horseshoe, but perhaps Hearn was trying to impress. He was vastly relieved to learn that the good lord of Angesand wanted him still on the job, as well as being enormously flattered that the man valued his services to the tune of a very fine horse.

Then again, perhaps that shouldn't have come as a surprise. Hearn had bluntly asked for aid in healing his son, Tùr. As had become habit of late, his own damnable propensity to spread joy everywhere he went had risen up like last night's bad beef to choke him and he'd agreed to add that to his list of Good Deeds To Do, a list that seemed to lengthen with every powerful soul he met.

The gods help him, he was going to finish his present business, retreat to his house on the edge of the sea, and lock himself in his study for at least a decade. He would never have any peace otherwise.

He handed the missive back to the king. "Interesting," he said casually.

"This is a heavy favor he asks of me," the king grumbled. "I would prefer to kill you."

Acair imagined he would.

"There is also the fact that your woman almost set my barn on fire," the king continued, "though knowing her love for horses, I must believe it was an accident. You need to teach her self-control." He paused, then snorted a mighty snort. "You, self-control. I can hardly believe those words came out of my own mouth."

Acair found himself in that same place more often of late than usual, but decided there was no point in admitting it.

"She's senseless at the moment, which I suppose leaves my hall safe."

Acair didn't imagine she'd been felled by anything she'd found at the king's table. Poison was not anything the man stooped to, and why would he? Uachdaran of Léige had a collection of spells and a reserve of power that any black mage worthy of the name would have happily investigated for as long as allowed.

He knew. He was that mage.

"I would say 'tis her magic that troubles her," the king continued. "I don't suppose I need to ask who succumbed to her foot-stomping and gave it to her, damn that weak-kneed lad from Cothromaiche. The only question is why she wanted the wretched stuff to begin with."

"I believe it was to save me," Acair said, finding it surprisingly difficult to say as much.

"You don't deserve her," the king said flatly.

Acair couldn't have agreed more. Soilléir didn't use his magic very often, or so rumor had it, so for him to have worked such a change in her was unprecedented. That Léirsinn had been willing to risk so much for his benefit alone was almost more than he could bring himself to think about.

Uachdaran pointed back toward his hall. "You'll attend that feisty gel in her chamber. A guard will be waiting outside the door, though I doubt you'll be much trouble in your current state."

Considering how desperately he wanted to lie down on anything that didn't slither about beneath him, he had to agree.

"I will apply myself to determining how I might slay you yet still keep that horse."

"It is a very fine stallion," Acair agreed.

"And you are not, so enjoy your breathing whilst it lasts."

Acair thought that might be best. He followed the king back into the hall, wishing he had the strength to check the path they were taking against his memory of the insides of the palace. The best he could do was note that they were headed toward the more exclusive guest chambers, not that that said all that much given that Uachdaran had very few guest chambers of any stripe. The man wasn't known for his willingness to entertain.

'Twas little wonder his middle daughter had wanted a life beyond the front gates.

The king stopped finally before a door, knocked, then stepped aside.

"My physick is inside with her. He is powerfully fierce, so keep that in mind if you think to escape."

Acair knew the king's physician and could say with certainty that the only thing Master Ollamh was equal to was clunking an intruder over the head with a bottle of tincture and hurrying off to hide behind a cabinet of herbs.

The door opened to reveal a well-appointed chamber with a large bed, an enormous hearth, and a table under the window that looked as if it might be holding up edible food. Acair found himself most relieved that Léirsinn was indeed safely tucked in.

Uachdaran nodded sagely toward the patient. "Such should be a warning to all who attempt essence changing, no matter the reason."

"I believe that in this matter, Your Majesty, we are in perfect agreement."

Uachdaran turned and started down the passageway. "Behave," he threw over his shoulder.

Ah, but that could apply to so many things. Acair supposed there was no point in assuring the king of things he couldn't wholeheartedly commit to, so he didn't bother. He walked inside, shut the door behind him, then swiftly crossed the chamber to the bed.

He took Léirsinn's hand in his own, hoping she would forgive him for his condition, and winced at the chill of her fingers. He had seen the results of essence changing a time or two and he had most definitely examined the remains of those who had surrendered their magic to his father—unwillingly, of course—but he wasn't sure what to make of the woman in front of him. If he'd been the sort to pray, he might have indulged. He would have been far more likely to sit down at a gaming table with some powerful being or other and do what he did best in return for a healing concession of some kind, but he didn't see any of those sorts of lads or lassies loitering in the vicinity.

The king's physician, however, was standing not far away, looking as if he currently found himself locked in a dungeon with a nest of vipers. Acair attempted a reassuring smile.

"I have no magic."

Master Ollamh considered. "None?"

"None that I can use," Acair amended.

The physick pulled up a stool and sat down on the other side of Léirsinn's sickbed. "One shouldn't change one's essence."

"On this, my good Master Ollamh, we agree completely."

"Have you ever seen the results of it?"

"My family tends to favor outright pilfering rather than messing about with alterations," Acair said, "if you know what I mean."

"I believe, my lord Acair, that I do."

Acair watched Léirsinn for a few moments, then looked at the king's healer. "Is there anything to be done?"

The man shook his head. "Time alone must do its goodly work."

Acair nodded, though he didn't agree at all. He'd seen what his father had left of mages whose power he'd taken and knew no amount of time would ever heal those lads.

That thought left him back where he'd been before, sitting in a dungeon and fretting over how quickly time was running out for him. There were mages at large with his death first on their to-do lists, he still had a damned spell dogging his steps with only one thing on its mind, and there was yet someone else roaming about the wide, vulnerable world whose goal seemed to be stealing all the souls he possibly could.

He himself was without the ability to use his magic, trapped in the hall of a monarch who wanted him dead, and the only thing standing between him and the gallows was the gift of a horse he was quite sure he would pay for down the road.

The single, faint ray of hope in the gloom had been a gloriously feisty, red-haired horse miss who could see things he couldn't and had saddled herself with powers she couldn't control to save his sorry arse.

Now, though, she looked to be nearer death than he was and he who had toppled thrones and brought terrible mages to their knees could do nothing at all to aid her.

He wasn't one to trust to time what he could see to himself, but at present, he thought he might not have a choice.

The sooner that changed, the better.

Two

✦

Léirsinn dreamed.

She stumbled through a forest full of fire, struggling to keep to a path that grew fainter with every step she took until it suddenly disappeared and she was left teetering on the edge of an abyss. She spun around only to find the path behind her gone and the trees obscured by heavy smoke that billowed toward her. There was no escape, no way out but forward into darkness.

She turned, closed her eyes and stepped out into nothingness —

Léirsinn woke abruptly and wondered if she'd been screaming. She shifted and deeply regretted it, for even that small movement sent a thrill of fever rushing through her. She felt as if her insides had been pulled out of her, tossed up into a whirlwind, then put back into her in the most painful way possible.

She had no one to blame for it but herself, of course, for she had been the one to make that desperate request to have magic so she might protect a man who had been tasked with saving the world from evil. She suspected, though, that the next time she was faced with the choice between traveling across the wilds of the Nine Kingdoms with a mage and becoming caught up in his madness or marching straight into the jaws of Hell with only herself for company, she was going to put on a pair of decent boots and start walking.

She lay still for another moment or two, then began to wonder if that choice had already been made for her. She didn't hear the shrieking of the damned, those poor souls who reputedly inhabited those fiery regions below the world, but her entire form felt as if she'd been standing too close to a Hellish bonfire. Even her eyes felt singed.

There was also an annoying buzzing that seemed to come and go in her ears and a smell that rivaled anything she'd encountered in the worst parts of the port town of Tosan.

She carefully moved her fingers against whatever she was lying on. She was more relieved than she wanted to admit to find the softness of a bed and not the rough stone of a dungeon floor. With any luck, her door would be unlocked and she would manage to free a certain lad of her acquaintance who was languishing in the dungeon, then escape with him before the dwarf king was the wiser. The sooner she was seeing to that, the better for them both.

She opened her eyes and stared at the canopy above her head. She thought she recognized it, but to be honest, she wasn't entirely sure. King Uachdaran had graciously given her the use of a guest chamber, but she hadn't spent very much time in it. When she hadn't been sitting outside Acair's prison door, she'd been either arguing with the king or worrying that Acair would be slain, their quest would fail, and she would never manage to free her grandfather from her uncle's manor.

When she absolutely hadn't been able to sleep, she'd allowed herself a moment or two to mourn the loss of an unremarkable existence in her uncle's barn, assuming she might have found her way back there and encountered anything but his sword in her heart. Then again, perhaps her uncle would think twice about bothering her now that she had the ability to spew out words and have them do something besides sound threatening.

She would have rolled her eyes if she'd had the strength to do so. The unfortunate truth was that she had no idea what to do with whatever magic Soilléir of Cothromaiche had given her, and her attempts to simply waggle her fingers and hope for the best hadn't gone all that well so far. She suspected she was fortunate that she hadn't completely burned the king's hall to the ground, though that at least might have prevented him from sending anyone else to his dungeon.

All of which brought her back to the point where she'd started: there was a man languishing in prison who had vowed to save the world and she was the one who had vowed to help him however she could.

She looked to her left to find a dwarf asleep on the sofa near the fire. She had a vague memory of him hovering over her with medicines, so perhaps he was the king's physick. His snores were formidable, which solved the mystery of the buzzing.

She looked to her right and discovered the source of the very vile smell she realized had been troubling her even in her sleep. It was an elven prince's bastard grandson, covered in dungeon leavings and listing so far out of the hard chair he was sitting on that she was half amazed he hadn't fallen to the floor already.

She sat up with a gasp. "You're free."

Acair startled himself awake so badly that both he and his chair went sprawling. She tried to catch him, but that only left her tumbling out of bed onto the floor next to him. She would have reached for him, but he held up his hand to hold her off.

"Don't let me ruin those lovely nightclothes of yours."

As tempting as it was to throw her arms around him just the same, he had a point. She had never owned anything so fine as the garb she was wearing, so ruining it with the grime *he* was wearing seemed a terrible waste. She settled for a deep sigh of relief.

"How did you manage it?" she asked, then she froze. "Should we run?"

"We're in the clear for the moment," he said with a faint smile, "so no need to hop out the nearest window and leg it before Master Ollamh wakes himself with his snores." He nodded toward the bed behind her. "Why don't you get off the floor so you don't catch a chill? I'll give you the entire tale once you're tucked back in."

She crawled to her feet, then righted his chair for him. "Let me at least fetch you some wine."

He heaved himself back up onto his seat, then closed his eyes and breathed lightly. "In a moment, when I think it will remain where I put it. I need to just sit for a bit, if you don't mind."

His condition was appalling, which left her suspecting he was very fortunate to still be breathing. She didn't think the king had left spells below to torment him, but obviously just being locked in that terrible place for so long had been enough to leave him half dead. She wasn't fully herself, which left her options for how to help him a bit on the thin side, but until he could eat, she could at least give him clean hands.

She walked over to a stand bearing a pitcher and bowl, leaning on various things on her way there when dizziness overcame her. She brought back what she needed, then set everything on the floor and found a footstool to use for a perch. She ignored his protests and washed his bruised and bloodied hands for him. She hesitated, then shrugged and dried his hands with one of the king's fine towels that would likely be fit only for the rubbish heap.

She set the towel and basin aside, then looked up at him. "Not much better, but at least you'll be able to eat without gagging."

His eyes were rather more bloodshot than they had been a handful of moments before. He was also seemingly speechless, which she imagined might have been a first for him.

"The fireplace smokes," she offered.

He cleared his throat roughly. "I'll be sure to pen a sharply worded complaint when I can toddle off to His Majesty's solar for ink and parchment."

She imagined he just might. She gathered up what she'd used, carried it all to the far side of the room where neither of them would have to look at it, then returned to sit on the side of her bed. She would have offered Acair her spot, but she had the feeling he wouldn't take it. A gentleman to the last.

"So," she said, "how did this all come about? I don't know if I'm more surprised to see you here or find myself here instead of winding up downstairs myself."

He settled back against his chair and sighed deeply. "I believe His Majesty is a little unnerved by your ability to burn things down and feared to anger you further."

"Surely not," she said, shifting uncomfortably. "Though I'll admit I did lose my temper."

He smiled faintly. "I'll choose discretion and refrain from making any comment about the color of your hair and what, if anything, that might indicate."

She would have glared at him, but she was honestly too unsettled by her actions to do anything but wish she hadn't been responsible for them. She had always prided herself on being in control at all times. It was part of what made her a good horsewoman, never mind keeping her alive when she would rather have told her uncle to go to hell.

With the king, though, she'd been overcome by a fury that perhaps exceeded what his flat refusal to release Acair should have warranted. She'd reached for a spell of fire-making Acair had insisted that she learn, confident that since it had come from him, it would have a bit of nastiness attached.

Certain that that would leave the right impression, she'd spat it out in the king's direction with a ferocity that would have alarmed her if she'd been able to think past the flames that had burned inside her—and apparently outside her as well. It would have been easier to believe she had memorized the spell amiss, but the truth was, it had gotten away from her in a way no bolting stallion ever had.

She found that she couldn't remember anything after that. Whether she had fainted because a guard had clunked her over the head with a sword hilt or she'd been overcome by the very foreign and unwelcome power that had rushed through her, she simply didn't know.

What she did know was that she wasn't sure she had any idea who she was any longer.

"We could talk about this, you know."

She pulled herself back to the present moment. "I don't want to."

"I mean—"

"I know what you meant."

He simply watched her in a way that was so reminiscent of the way his mother studied people, she almost flinched.

"Stop that," she said crossly.

"Can't help myself," he said with a shrug. "I like to look at you."

"You're not looking," she said, "you're coming to conclusions. There's a difference."

"There might be, but I'm honestly too tired to decide what that might be. I'll settle for simply looking at your fetching self without making any judgments."

She supposed she couldn't argue with that. She also imagined he didn't need to be told that he looked so thoroughly exhausted, she was half surprised he wasn't senseless on the floor. It was perhaps the worst thing she'd seen in days upon days of terrible things. Even in the dodgiest of locales while about the most dangerous activities, he had only ever looked as if he were on the verge of chortling before casting himself enthusiastically back into the fray.

Perhaps there had been a slow, reluctant march toward more serious expressions and viler curses, but in his defense, he'd been running from a mage of terrifying power he couldn't defend either of them against. The price for simply eluding that mage long enough to allow them both to escape had been very high.

"You should take the bed," she said. "You need it more than I do."

He shook his head. "The king would definitely slay me for daring the same, not that I would think to anyway. I'll pull up a scrap of floor later and be quite content."

"Then food, at least."

He hesitated, then nodded. "That would be very kind, thank you."

Weariness had also made him terribly polite. She rose, then walked over to the little table that stood under the window and sported a tray laden with tea and biscuits. She poured two cups of tea and carried them back across the room. Acair accepted one, though he didn't drink. She fetched a plate of biscuits and sat down on the bed, prepared to hand one to him when he looked like he could manage it. He still hadn't touched his tea.

"Not good?" she asked.

"I'm not sure yet. I think I might put it aside for now."

She caught his cup before he dropped it, then set it on the night stand for him. She took her time resuming her spot and wondered if perhaps waking the king's physick would be wise.

"I'm concerned," she said frankly.

"All I need is another hour or two of sleep, then I'll be back to my old self." He rubbed his eyes with marginally clean fingers, then shook his head sharply. "Let's talk about you instead."

She applied herself to her own tea until there was no more, then set her cup down next to Acair's and looked for something else to use as a distraction.

"Lovely weather we're having," she noted.

He leaned forward with his elbows on his knees and rubbed his hands together as if they ached. "It might be, but it has absolutely nothing to do with that other thing we need to discuss." His expression was very grave. "We'll have to eventually, you know."

"Not if I can help it."

"I'm very persistent."

That was true, but she thought that with enough effort she might be able to avoid the conversation completely.

After all, what was there to discuss? 'Twas bad enough that she had set aside her good sense and pride as she'd sat with him on the other side of his invisible but very functional dungeon door and attempted to memorize a few spells. The business of spewing out words into thin air and trying to convince herself there was anything but embarrassment to follow was naught but foolishness—and fraught with peril, as she had proven recently not only to herself but the king outside in his courtyard.

"Did you see the stables?" she asked, desperate to distract him, but realizing even that would bring them back round to things she didn't want to discuss. "They weren't completely ruined, were they?"

"Just a bit scorched," he said, "and you're hedging."

"Care for a biscuit?"

"Thank you, but nay, not yet."

She settled for a look of pleading.

He smiled briefly. "Very well, I'll leave you alone about it for the time being. Let's discuss something less personal, say the condition of His Majesty's beard. I think his having the same singed might be what turned the tide for me."

"I honestly didn't mean to," she said. "He wasn't being reasonable."

"He generally isn't," Acair agreed, "but you definitely made an impression on him. You saved me, which I appreciate greatly. Also compelling was a bribe made by an unexpected ally."

"Your grandmother?" she asked in surprise.

"Hearn of Angesand, rather, if you can believe it," he said. "There is an extremely valuable pony in the king's stables that has greatly improved the prospects of yours truly seeing spring. With any luck, we'll be on our way before Uachdaran decides he'd rather walk than ride."

She ignored the chills washing over her. Hot, cold, she hardly had any idea any longer what was amiss with her normally quite reliable form.

"Are you sure we shouldn't go today?" she asked.

"I'll admit I hesitate not to leave whilst the king is in such an accommodating mood, but I think another day of rest would serve us both well. I have a thing or two to investigate, if the opportunity arises."

She imagined he would create an opportunity where none existed, which should have worried everyone in the vicinity.

"You should rest as well," she said, "not make trouble."

"But I'm a first-rate troublemaker," he said smoothly. "Which you already knew."

"Acair," she said, realizing that she was coming close to begging. "Please don't snoop."

"I won't."

"You will."

He held up his hands in surrender. "I have no choice. There are doilies to rescue."

"Is that all?"

He paused, then looked at her seriously. "I believe there might be books of ours that need to be recovered as well, unless you have thoughts on their location."

She pointed over her shoulder. "Under the sofa cushion."

He closed his eyes briefly, then smiled at her. "We wouldn't want those getting lost out amongst the great unwashed masses—or my brothers, take your pick. There are things my grandmother jotted down that likely should have remained unwritten."

She suppressed a shudder at the thought. She hadn't had the chance to make a proper study of the book in question while they'd been in the middle of being tossed from his grandmother's solar, but she'd had an eyeful of Acair's expression after he'd glanced at what had been written in it. It was likely better to keep it tucked out of sight.

"Clever you for managing to hide it there."

"I stole the idea from you," she said, then she glanced over her shoulder at the physick lying there, still dead to the world. "Why is he here, do you think?"

"The king was wringing his hands over the possibility of my doing something untoward, so it seems he's here to guard you."

She smiled in spite of herself. "I don't think you have the energy to do anything untoward."

"Sadly I believe the only unpleasant thing I might manage at present is to shove him onto the floor and take his place on something not stonelike." He shrugged. "I generally prefer to put off mischief-making until after I've had a decent night's sleep and a hearty breakfast, so perhaps Uachdaran is safe for the day. You should also know that I never ravish maidens fair when they are indisposed." He leaned his head back against his chair and closed his eyes. "No amount of insisting will change my mind, darling, so don't even try."

She rolled her eyes, though she had the feeling more than one maiden fair had begged for his attentions. She pushed her pillow up against the headboard of the bed and made herself comfortable so she could keep an eye on him, nothing more. If it gave her a chance to watch him more closely than usual, so be it.

The inescapable truth was, that man there had been designed to be best admired by the light of a fire. It cast his appallingly perfect form into just the right amount of shadow, flickered rather lovingly along his chiseled cheekbones and jaw, and danced with daring abandon over his dark, rakishly windblown hair. Of course, sunlight did a better job of revealing his eyes that weren't quite blue, nor precisely green, but something altogether more spectacular.

She wondered just how indisposed a woman might have to be not to want his attentions.

"I could be persuaded to abandon my principles in a pinch," he remarked, opening his eyes and looking at her. "If you insist."

She imagined he could be persuaded to do quite a few things in a pinch, including leaving women swooning and everyone else running for cover.

"Good of you," she said, "but I wouldn't want to put you out."

"Definitely not in my current condition, but hold the thought for later."

She thought she just might.

"Still don't want to talk about magic?"

She shook her head. "Tell me instead what you did to make the king so angry."

"Besides being blamed for his daughter ruthlessly using me to escape his watchful eye and run off with one of my half-brother's cousins, a rather handsome but vapid elf from Tòrr Dòrainn?"

"Aye, that," she said, feeling entirely unsympathetic. "I have the feeling you didn't stop there."

"I'm flattered you have such confidence in my abilities," he said. He stretched his legs out and rubbed his knees as if they pained him. "To be honest, I might have slipped over the walls and helped myself to the odd, unattended spell whilst His Majesty was napping." He paused. "I may have done that more than once."

"Typical."

"Isn't it?" he asked. "I believe I've become predictable."

"I believe you're fortunate to be alive," she said seriously. "What else?"

He clasped his hands together and looked at them for a moment or two before he looked at her.

"I fear I may have indeed inconvenienced His Majesty with more than just the simple pilfering of a spell or two." He glanced at the physick still snoring happily on the sofa before he looked back at her. "'Tis possible that I may have used one or two of the rivers running deeply beneath the palace for my own nefarious purposes. Power and magic tend to travel more easily along water than land."

"Of course they do," she said, wondering if she were the one who should have been alarmed that such a thing was beginning to sound perfectly reasonable. "That was part of your plan to, ah —"

"Steal a goodly portion of the world's magic and trade it for spells and whatnot?"

She nodded.

"It was a complete miss, as I believe I've reluctantly admitted before. You would think that my failure in the same would have mollified our irascible dwarf-king, but apparently not. Perhaps he takes his rest more seriously than I suspected."

Apparently so if the king's anger had burned that brightly for so long. She wasn't entirely sure that he wouldn't reconsider any bribes sent his way, so perhaps they would be wise to be on their way while the winds were still favorable.

"We could bolt, you know." She paused, then looked at him seriously. "I could, you know . . . " She wiggled her fingers only to have him catch both her hands in his quickly.

"I think you shouldn't," he said. He released her and sat back. "I can't stop what you set loose, you know. Not at the moment."

"I didn't ask you to," she said quickly.

"And so you didn't," he agreed, "though you shouldn't be embarrassed by the same. Even the most pampered of Nerochian princes didn't work his first spell without some sort of mentor hovering helpfully at his elbow. But lest that prove to be an uncomfortable direction for our conversation, perhaps we should let that topic lie. We'll be safe enough for a day or two." He nodded at her. "You should rest."

"I'm not sure I can."

He smiled. "My visage is just that distracting, isn't it?"

It was, though she wasn't going to add to his arrogance by admitting as much. "I'm just worried we'll never escape," she said. "I'm not sure why I think that would be an improvement on our situation. Things aren't much safer outside the gates than inside them, are they?"

"Not much," he agreed, "but we must face that eventually. If I can keep myself alive here for a day or two whilst you're about your restorative sleeping, we'll make a dash out the front gates and see what's left of the world. You might distract what hunts us with the same sort of fiery business you used on our reluctant host."

"I was angry," she said. "The king was going to have you executed."

"Still would if it didn't mean forfeiting that very fine pony in his stables," he said. "And don't think I don't appreciate your defending me, for I do. I would wax rhapsodic about it, but then I would weep and that is a sight you definitely do not want to witness."

"Do you ever weep?" she asked.

"Over poorly cooked beef," he said. "Occasionally."

She had surprisingly vivid memories of waking to his tears on her face several days earlier. She looked at him and suspected he was revisiting that same moment.

"I thought you were dead," she said quietly.

"I know."

"I wasn't sure what else to do."

He closed his eyes briefly, then looked at her. "His Majesty needs to retain better staff," he said hoarsely, clearing his throat. "I vow my eyes haven't stopped burning since I entered the hall."

"You might have to write that missive after all."

"I might," he agreed. "But let's go back to your attempting to burn the king's stables to the ground. You were angry because he was no doubt going on about the horrible lengths he was willing to go to to inflict bodily harm on your humble servant."

She attempted a smile and failed. "I'm afraid I forgot most of what you taught me below."

"Well, what you remembered was a first-rate piece of work, my gel. That added to your insisting that I come pour your wine and King Uachdaran didn't dare refuse you."

She considered, then looked at him. "I'm not making a very good impression, am I?"

"I might not be the one to judge. There are impressions, of

course, then there are *impressions*. I prefer the latter, but I have a reputation to maintain. Before you attempt the same again, perhaps you should rest. A bit more tea?"

She nodded, though she wasn't at all sure that would do anything for her parched throat. It was as if that spell had scorched her insides right along with the king's beard and his stables.

She watched Acair push himself to his feet, sway, then walk over to the table. If his hands were unsteady as he poured from the pot he'd brought back with him, she wasn't about to comment. She rescued the cup he held out to her before he dropped it on the bed. The tea was cold, but not even that did anything to soothe either her mouth or her nerves.

Magic was a dodgy business, indeed.

But she had it and there was nothing to be done about it. She would have to learn how to master it just as she'd learned to master what had come through her uncle's stable doors. For all she knew, it was just that simple.

Perhaps if she continued to tell herself that while ignoring the fact that she felt as if she were on the back of a horse made directly from the fires of Hell, she might at least manage a few hours of sleep before she woke and had to face what her life had become.

"It will become easier."

She looked at him. "Do I want it to?"

"I would imagine," he said quietly, "that you don't. If I might offer an apology that I actually mean for a change, I'm sorry for it. It was generously done."

"Again, I didn't know what else to do."

"Ah, now that I don't believe," he said, smiling wearily. "I believe your purpose was to break what's left of my black heart, something you managed quite perfectly. I vow if I ever work a proper piece of mischief in the future, it will be nothing short of a miracle."

"Do-gooding does seem to be becoming a habit with you."

He snorted. "A habit I will cast aside like a cumbersome cloak the very instant I can. Then I'm back to the old business of wreak-

ing havoc and terrifying everyone I meet. Now, before I find myself
a patch of floor and have a nap, what can I do to make you more
comfortable?"

"I'm the one with the soft bed," she pointed out, "and I'll bury
my unease in sleep soon enough."

"Throw something at me to wake me if that changes," he said
with a yawn, "or if you feel unsafe. I'll trot out my harshest language
to defend you."

She watched him simply roll off the chair and stretch out on
the floor next to her bed. She imagined it was an improvement over
where he'd been sleeping for the past few days.

She stretched out and looked up at the canopy over her head.
The wood was intricately carved, no doubt representing heroic
scenes she knew nothing about. If that wasn't a perfect reflection of
her own life presently, she didn't know what was.

What she should have done when her life had become something unrecognizable was scamper back inside whatever barn she'd
been nearest to, saddle the first horse she'd come across, then escape
through the nearest set of barn doors before anyone had been the
wiser. With any luck it would have been a very unmagical pony who
would have carried her off into an equally unmagical sunset where
she might have found a different barn thoroughly free of mages
where she could have settled in for a lifetime of very ordinary, pedestrian horse work.

Instead, not only had she asked for the ability to work spells,
she had sat on the other side of an invisible doorway from a vile
black mage and learned spells from him so she might sally forth and
do damage with them. 'Twas only after that sallying that she realized
that using those spells was a bit like riding a spooked horse that was
bolting with her on its back, only this was a bolting horse that would
never be outlasted.

She half wondered if she would spend the rest of her life simply
trying to hold on and not be tossed aside to die a lingering, painful
death from having dashed her head against a rock.

"Things will look better after a rest, Léirsinn."

She would have answered him, but a quick look over the edge of her bed proved that Acair of Ceangail was either exhausted or had been talking in his sleep. She left him to it, then settled in for a bit of rest herself. To her surprise, she felt almost at ease. And all because a chivalrous black mage was within shouting distance.

Truly the world was full of things she had never expected.

Three

There were few things more inconvenient than a portly dispenser of strengthening draughts snoring comfortably atop a divan that hid under its austere cushions a book that would put a substantial rent in the very fabric of the world if it, as the rustics were wont to say, got 'round.

Acair leaned heavily against the footpost of Léirsinn's bed. As tempting as it was to give a little leap of joy over being free of the king's dungeon, he had to forebear. What strength remained him would likely be spent in overcoming the substantial obstacle that currently lay between him and the book he needed. Whatever Master Ollamh's virtues as a healer might have been, they were certainly outweighed, as it were, by the man's ability to nap through almost anything.

It wasn't as though he hadn't already made several attempts to interrupt his chaperon's slumber. He had cleared his throat with vigor, bumped a leg of the sofa—well, he'd kicked it deliberately, but who was to know?—and dropped a pewter mug on the hearthstone near the man's head. Léirsinn had woken at the latter, cursed him, then rolled over and gone back to sleep. Ollamh hadn't indulged in even the faintest grumble of annoyance. Short of physically rolling him onto the floor and liberating the goods from beneath yon sofa cushions, Acair supposed he would simply have to wait for the man to sleep himself out.

He forced down the brief flash of panic that rose up to choke him, an unaccustomed and certainly unpleasant sensation if ever there were one. The truth was, he was in a bit of rush to get things done. There were mages to identify and slay, shadows to disperse, and doilies to stuff into pockets—all things that needed to be seen to before some fool with more power than sense reduced the world to ashes.

He deliberately took a figurative step backward. Whilst escape out the front gates topped his list of things to do, Léirsinn needed a chance to rest from her attempts to reduce the king and his hall to cinders and he needed time to recover from his state of utter exhaustion. No harm would come to the world if he were to set aside his catalog of impossible tasks for an hour or two and soldier on toward things that were more easily done.

First things first and that was to pen a heartfelt note of thanks to Hearn of Angesand for having saved his own sweet neck. Admittedly the man had saddled him, fairly literally, with a horse that wanted to kill him, but that was surely just a bit of good-natured sport at his expense. If Hearn wanted his son to be healed from an encounter with a nasty patch of shadow, Acair was happy to attempt it. It was, he knew, the only reason he was still breathing.

He supposed he might understand the lengths to which one would go to save a loved one. Léirsinn had put herself in peril for her own reasons that might have had nothing to do with him.

But if she had done it for him because he meant that much to her—

He staggered mentally away from that thought with all the grace of a Slighian lad who'd spent the evening becoming overly acquainted with the local tap. Léirsinn had already watched him weep. He had no desire to reduce himself again to a blubbering mass of gratitude and embarrassment. Perhaps she was fond of him, or perhaps not. Best to concentrate on his list of Important Things To Do and leave more maudlin sentiments to Nerochian lads who used those sorts of displays to get themselves out of sticky situations.

He found ink and parchment and used it to heap praise on the good lord of Angesand's head for the gift of his life. He was halfway to using that ridiculous spell for hastening the drying of ink he'd pinched from Simeon of Diarmailt before he realized that using spells of any sort would make Hearn's efforts useless. He settled for blowing on the ink to dry it and paid the price in stars swirling around his head.

He reached for another sheaf, then hesitated. As tempting as it was to have all his correspondence taken care of, he decided that perhaps he would send a message to the king of Neroche later when he thought he could find the words to tell Miach that he'd lost his brother and hadn't taken the time to stop and look for him. That, he supposed, might tax even his own enviable powers of deflection.

He folded his note to Hearn and plopped a pot of ink atop it to keep it closed. He would seal it properly and find a messenger willing to go to Angesand later, when he felt more himself.

He walked back over to Léirsinn's bed and indulged again in a fond embrace of that sturdy footpost whilst he considered what needed to happen next. Perhaps he might do a bit of nosing about, then toddle off to the palace library for a friendly thumb through a book or two of spells. He might even manage a decent nap on a floor that was covered with something besides vermin.

But first a wee stroll to test his strength and give Ollamh a chance to finish what were no doubt delightful dreams about herbal concoctions. He straightened, swayed more enthusiastically than he was comfortable with, then shuffled over to the door. He put his ear to the wood, but heard nothing suspicious. He very carefully turned the heavy brass doorknob and peeked out into the passageway.

Three undeniably well-fed, obviously well-exercised guardsmen were leaning against the opposite wall, their eyes fixed on him. He smiled politely, then eased back inside the chamber and closed the door.

Damnation but Uachdaran of Léige was a suspicious bastard.

He put his hand on the wood to steady himself, then considered what else he could do that day with his strength at such a low ebb. He'd already addressed the easy item of a flourishy thank-you. More difficult would be fetching something he'd left stuck to the underside of Uachdaran of Léige's kingly seat. Retrieving his grandmother's prized doily—something he remained convinced was made from his grandfather's wails of terror spun into thread—from its place of honor on the king's side table was going to be the most difficult feat of all.

He needed the damned thing, though, so fetch it he would. It was one thing to have a mysterious mage with terrible power chasing after him, intending to slay him. It was another thing entirely to have his Gran setting off with the same idea.

A loud thump startled him, but he realized it was only Master Ollamh rolling off the sofa. He hurried over to offer the man assistance. If he happened to make a quick investigation of the underside of one of the sofa cushions, retrieve a small notebook, then drop it to the floor and kick it under Léirsinn's bed whilst he was offering said assistance, surely the king's healer wouldn't be the wiser.

"I believe, my good man, that you need a bit of fresh air," Acair said. "And look, there is a door conveniently placed in the wall for the setting off on just such a restorative adventure."

Master Ollamh looked equal parts confused and alarmed. "But I'm not to leave you here alone."

Acair helped the man over to the door—leaning rather heavily on him, true, but that wasn't to be helped—opened it, then gestured at the aforenoted trio of very burly guardsmen established against the far wall.

"Those lads there have me well in hand, wouldn't you agree?"

"But your magic," Ollamh said uneasily. "I know what you said before, but I've heard reports—"

"Which I would be delighted to either confirm or deny for you after you've taken a lengthy walk in the king's garden," Acair said. "I promise to keep all my spells unused and my tales untold until you return. Upon my honor."

"And the young miss?" Ollamh drew himself up and put on what he obviously thought was a stern look.

Acair refused to be offended, mostly because ordinarily the healer would have been thoroughly justified in his concern.

"I am on my best behavior," he said seriously. "Mistress Léirsinn is safe in my company."

Ollamh didn't look terribly convinced, but he did look as if he might soon lose whatever luncheon he'd ingested earlier. Acair shooed him out into the passageway, offered a friendly wave to his keepers holding up the far wall, then shut the door before they could offer any greeting in return.

He walked back over to the fire, knelt down to peer under the bed, and came as close to fainting as he ever had in his life. Finding himself sprawled rather suddenly with his face against the floor and his arse up in the air was an indignity he could have done without. It took more effort than he was happy with to retrieve Léirsinn's book from under the bed, then very gingerly ease himself back up to his knees.

He crawled up onto the divan with all the energy of a black mage properly breathing his last thanks to a lifetime of bad deeds, then had to simply close his eyes and wheeze until he thought he might manage to look at his surroundings and find them doing something besides galloping wildly around him.

No more dwarvish dungeons. His next stay in one was going to kill him.

He was grateful his hands were cleaner than they had been and refused to grow misty-eyed over the woman who had offered him such a tender service. The insults to the divan, however, were definitely going to be extensive. He likely should have been appalled by the condition of his clothing and what it would do to Uachdaran's furniture, but given that the man hadn't allowed him even so much as a quarter hour outside near a well, perhaps he had no need to be fastidious about his sofa-perching.

He waited until his head cleared a bit more, then turned his attentions to what he held in his hands. It was an unassuming thing, perhaps a bit bigger than his outstretched hand, just the size his mother preferred for her endless scribblings. He had the feeling the woman would choose an empty book over a last meal.

What made what he was looking at presently so desirable was the fact that his mother's mother had taken the time to jot down a few things she no doubt thought would unnerve him. A fair trade, perhaps, for forcing him to leave behind what he'd broken into her solar to steal. If he ever had the chance to scamper off with that *Book of Oddities and Disgusting Spells* his mother had advised him to acquire, he absolutely would and not suffer a single twinge of regret. He'd had a quick peek at its contents and wasn't quite sure he'd yet recovered from what he'd read there.

He'd also had a hasty glance at what he held in his hands, but he wasn't sure if he could trust his memory where its contents were concerned. If his grandmother had seen fit to share even a handful of disconcerting things, he would be penning her a flourishy thank-you as well. He took as deep a breath as he could manage at the moment, then opened the thin tome, prepared to give the scribblings there a proper study.

It hadn't seemed as if she'd been at her labors very long, but apparently he'd been more distracted by wondering how to escape her solar than he'd realized. Her notes were simply bursting with nastiness. If he hadn't been so damned tired, he might have indulged in a chortle of delight. Unfortunately, things were what they were at the moment and all he could do was drag in ragged breaths and try not to leave faintly grubby fingerprints behind as he continued to gingerly turn pages and shake his head over what he found there.

Spells were laid out, vile mages were listed—his name wasn't to be found anywhere on that roster which he supposed should have stung a bit—and a handful of oddities that apparently intrigued her had been jotted down for his perusal.

He sighed and turned another page, expecting to find that she would have nothing more to say to him save a wish that he speedily meet his end. Instead, he found himself facing a spell of reconstruction that left him almost recoiling, he who had spent the bulk of his life foisting vileness off onto almost everyone he met.

The thing was absolutely appalling, merciless in its workings and rather more permanent than what he was accustomed to using. It was something, he had to admit, that he might have hesitated to use unless absolutely necessary.

He reread the spell twice before it sank in what he was looking at. It wasn't essence changing in the usual sense, but it came as close as anything he'd ever seen. The idea that he might mold something into a shape it didn't particularly want to take and hold it there for far longer than a simple spell of reconstruction should have been able to manage was astonishing.

Ye gads, what was his grandmother about and why didn't she have better locks on her hidden cubbies?

He continued on past that thought before he had time to speculate on what his brothers might do with such a thing. He had his own way of taking bits of his own power and infusing them onto whatever talisman suited him, but that was less essence changing than it was essence slathering. There he was simply taking the same sort of energy he would have thrown behind a spell and more or less wrapping it around his chosen bits and bobs.

This, however . . . he took a deep breath. This particular spell made his own look like a village witch's charm. He could hardly stop himself from trying it out to see just exactly where its limits might lie. He looked to his right and found his ever-present companion crouched on the floor, peeking over the arm of the divan at him as if it might be suffering a bit of unease.

He understood. The spell was terrifying.

He memorized it without hesitation, of course, then repeated it silently, checking himself against what he was reading. He mouthed the last word and found himself rather glad, all things considered, that he'd memorized the bloody thing before the damned page caught fire.

He was so startled by that turn of events that he flipped the book up in the air and thoroughly failed at making a grab for it on its way down. It landed, quite fortuitously, face-down against the rug there. He supposed there was no sense in not smothering the flames by means of his boot placed gingerly atop the cover.

He waited until he thought a proper amount of time had passed before he picked the book up and turned it over, then swore when he realized that the whole business had been nothing more than the words having burned themselves off the page. The paper bore absolutely no sign of having recently been alight.

Theatrics. It ran in the family.

He ignored that damned spell next to him, squeaking as it hid, and considered what his grandmother's purpose had been in giving him something so dangerous. Even merely repeating the words in his mind set up a merry dance between them and whatever Cothromaichian spell Soilléir had used to bring him back from the brink of death. Perhaps Cruihniche of Fàs had simply wanted to make him miserable.

Essence changing or essence meddling. He could hardly wait to have the time to investigate the difference between the two.

He turned another page, fully expecting to find there a few words of comfort and encouragement.

Instead, he found a map.

He was, as it happened, not unfamiliar with maps. He was also not unfamiliar with the making of maps. He had taken his half-brother Rùnach's book of spells, removed those valiant attempts from inside the covers, then inserted a map of his own making in their place. That map had been a curious one, he had to admit, full of scratches that he'd made based on a few furtive glances over the shoulder of a very famous cartographer, Casan of Frith-rathad. The man lived far too close to Bruadair for his comfort, but it had been worth the fraying of his nerves to pose as a servant long enough to eavesdrop for a fortnight.

He didn't suppose it was a place he would venture again without very good reason indeed.

A furtive tap sounded against the door. He frowned, torn. There were things on his grandmother's map that he suspected he needed to investigate further, never mind that they left him feeling as if he might like a lengthy lie-down sooner rather than later.

But perhaps trouble was afoot. He heaved himself up from the sofa, paid the price in a robust sway that almost left him cracking his head against the footpost of Léirsinn's bed, then staggered over to answer the knock. He held his Gran's scribblings casually behind his back and opened the door, hoping it was someone with food.

It was instead someone with a book.

He didn't imagine that collection would be nearly as interesting—or as perilous—as what he currently held, but there was no sense in spurning something that might turn out to be useful. He recognized his guest as Eachdraidh, bard to King Uachdaran and guardian of the king's most perilous tomes. Master Eachdraidh also kept a history of the dwarvish kingdom, though why Uachdaran needed someone to jot down the happenings of his realm when the very stones of his foundation couldn't seem to shut up about the glory and riches of the same he didn't know.

He wasn't one to question those sorts of things, though—at least not within earshot of the local monarch—so he put on his most disarming smile and prepared to, as his mother would have said, make nice.

"Master Eachdraidh," he said politely, "what an unexpected pleasure."

The dwarf looked as though he considered the encounter anything but, though he held out a book just the same. Acair decided perhaps that rescuing it before it landed on the floor might count as his good deed for the day. He looked at the king's bard.

"A loan, I assume?"

Eachdraidh shook his head. "'Tis a gift," he said. "From the king."

Acair supposed Eachdraidh wouldn't make anything of his grandmother's scribblings, so he tucked them under the new acquisition and opened the latter to find a rather pointed title.

Good Riddance to Bad Rubbish

or

When Bad Mages Come to a Worse End

He would have laughed, but he knew he was still swimming in deep waters where the king was concerned. He nodded thoughtfully.

"Very kind," he noted.

"His Majesty thought you might find it, erm, instructive."

Acair imagined the king had been substantially less restrained about what he thought might be gleaned from said offering, but that was also something likely better left unsaid.

"Please convey my deepest gratitude to the king," he said. "I'm certain I will come away not only edified but properly warned."

"I daresay," Eachdraidh said nervously, "that such was His Majesty's intention."

Acair was utterly unoffended. He was, as it happened, free of the king's dungeon and still breathing. He was willing to endure quite a bit of abuse for the privilege. He held the door open and looked at Master Eachdraidh.

"Do you care to come in and take your ease by the fire?"

The dwarf looked as if he'd just been invited to hobnob with a collection of lads who likely had taken up a fair bit of ink in the book he'd delivered. He squeaked, shook his head quickly, then turned and hoofed it back down the passageway. Acair sighed, nodded to his guardsmen, then shut the door.

He rested his hand against the wood and considered the rest of what was left of his afternoon. He supposed Master Ollamh wouldn't return unless forced, which left him with nothing to do but stay out of trouble.

So difficult, truly.

He resumed his seat on the sofa, considered his reading choices, then opened the king's book. A cursory glance left him encountering many of the usual suspects, which was unfortunately uninteresting enough that he simply sat there, staring at nothing for far longer than he likely should have. The sad truth was he was just too tired to muster up any sort of enthusiasm for what he held in his hands. His robust apology surely should have earned him something more substantial, shouldn't it? It was almost as if that apology had been for naught—

He froze, then wondered what else might leave him dumb-founded that day.

He had *apologized* to the king. As noteworthy an occurrence as that surely was, it should have merited more than what would likely turn out to be a mere footnote in the record of the king's daily doings. He thought back to a conversation he'd had with a pair of meddlers in a tavern several weeks earlier, a conversation that was unfortunately still all-too-clear in his memory.

The choice is yours . . . no magic, or a visit to the king of the dwarves.

It had been that damned Soilléir to casually drop that fly into their conversational stew. But if no magic had been the price for no apology, surely now that the apology had been offered, his magic should have been within the grasp of his greedy, outstretched hands.

Surely.

He considered what he might try to test his theory and found himself suddenly nose-to-nose with that damned spell of death that dogged his steps. He drew himself up.

"What are you still doing here?" he demanded.

The spell only moved to take up a spot near the end of Léirsinn's bed, folded its arms over a spot where its scrawny chest should have been, and glared at him.

Acair felt his eyes narrow. There was obviously something more to the whole affair than what he'd been led to believe. If the apology he'd so fervently blurted out hadn't rid him of that bloody thing there, just what was its purpose?

There was something that didn't smell quite right and that wasn't just his dungeon-soaked garb.

Obviously the only way to discover the truth was to, as usual, be the one to do all the dirty work of looking for it. Unfortunately, until he could do more than sit on a sofa and wheeze, that search couldn't even begin. He put the king's book atop his grandmother's, pushed himself to his feet, then walked unsteadily around the foot of Léirsinn's bed, ignoring the spell of death keeping watch there.

He sat down next to the night stand where sustenance waited patiently to be consumed. He wasn't sure it would serve him very well, but he forced himself to at least partake of a biscuit or two and a few sips of tea.

That unpleasant task seen to, he leaned back and took a moment to simply watch that lovely woman there as she slept. He could scarce believe he was keeping company with a lass with absolutely no magic to her name who had bargained he knew not what for a bit of the same in order to save his sorry arse. He honestly couldn't remember the last time anyone had risked anything more serious than a spot at table for him. His mother did him the favor of generally not attempting to slay him when he arrived at her side door for a bite of supper and a bit of gossip, but someone who had no blood ties to him?

It was astonishing.

He listened to Léirsinn breathe for several minutes until he thought he had convinced himself that the rattle in her chest was merely from the chill of the chamber, not something more serious. If something happened to her . . . well, he would outrun that damned spell of death haunting him, find Soilléir of Cothromaiche, and bring him to Léirsinn on pain of death with a demand to heal her.

He thought he might understand more clearly than he wanted

to why Hearn of Angesand had been willing to bargain with him for the healing of his son.

A knock sounded on the door, which he had to admit was a welcome distraction from his maudlin thoughts. He didn't dare hope it was anyone more interesting than a servant bearing hot water for tea, but he wasn't going to spurn that. He rose, then hesitated. There was no sense in leaving dangerous things lying about, so he took the notebook with his grandmother's map and slipped it carefully under Léirsinn's pillow. That seen to, he got himself over to the door without undue effort, then opened it.

He found himself presented with a scene that left him thinking that perhaps all that do-gooding had served him well after all. Sometimes he could scarce believe how well things fell into place for him when his need was most dire.

Ollamh was standing there with his hands full of bottles, things no doubt brought to aid his patient. Next to him was a pair of lads bearing all manner of fine edibles. On the other side of the passageway were the same lads as before. The only difference was that they were now standing post with a slight slump to their shoulders, as if their duty had become just too tedious to keep them at their best.

Acair lifted the covering off what turned out to be a quartet of very fine appendages of some hearty bird or other. He didn't think, he merely liberated a pair, then walked out into the hallway, ignoring the squeaking of the physick.

"Just off to the loo, of course," he said smoothly. That excuse given, he handed the joints to two of the guardsmen with a wink. "Our secret," he assured them.

Perhaps 'twas unkind to take advantage of such rumbling tums, but he was a ruthless worker of evil spells and an unrepentant opportunist. What else was he to do?

He fixed a pleading glance on the third, patted his own belly, and tried to look a bit queasy. Sadly, the effort took far less pretense than he would have liked, but it had been that sort of spring so far.

"Down the passageway, if you please," he said, "then right back here for your own supper, my good man. The king will never know."

The guardsman looked unsure, something for which Acair couldn't blame him in the least. As he'd already admitted very reluctantly to himself, not much happened inside Durial's borders that the king didn't know about. Perhaps this, though, would be overlooked.

That was exactly what he hoped would happen for the sake of the senseless lad he subsequently stuffed into the loo only after removing the man's cloak and donning his helmet. Creases in his own locks were perhaps the least of his worries. Given how badly he needed a good soak in a tub, he thought he might owe his unwitting helper an apology instead of a strongly worded letter of complaint.

He had no doubts that Léirsinn would be perfectly safe in the care of Uachdaran's personal physick, so all that was left was for him to nip in and out of the king's throne room. He needed that damned spell of death stuck to the bottom of Uachdaran's chair as well as his Gran's doily if he could manage it. If he could blame the theft of both on an unnamed, never-to-be-found servant, so much the better.

Once he had one more night of vermin-free sleep behind him, he would face the more difficult problems of mages and shadows and places scribbled on his grandmother's map where he wouldn't want to go but would likely need to if the world were to be saved.

With a hearty but silent curse to keep himself warm, he strode off into the shadows to make mischief.

It was, he had to admit, his favorite sort of quest.

Four

Léirsinn woke to the sight of someone leaning over her. She shrieked and clouted him on the nose before she realized that it was simply Master Ollamh trying to hand her some sort of healing draught, not some foul mage trying to do her in.

She sat up and looked over the edge of the bed to where the poor dwarf had taken cover. She still had to hold onto the headboard to keep herself steady, but she wasn't pitching out of bed completely. Progress had definitely been made.

The healer's eyes were watering madly and he was protecting his nose with one hand, but his tiny cup of liquid had been spared. He crawled to his feet, holding his brew aloft as he did so. He handed it to her, waited until she'd drunk it, then took it back.

"How do you fare, mistress?"

She took stock of her poor form. The fires raging inside her had subsided from the enormous heat of a raging inferno to the toasty warmth of a small campfire, which was definitely an improvement. She wasn't sure she would ever be the same, but perhaps that was something to think about later.

She was trying to hit upon a response that didn't sound daft when it occurred to her that the king's healer looked very nervous.

He was taking an excessive amount of time to set his cup aside, which she supposed should have made *her* nervous. If there had been something vile in that draught —

She turned away from that thought before it galloped off with her to places she didn't want to go. She had never felt particularly at ease in her uncle's stables, but it had never occurred to her over the course of her time there that anyone would want to murder her. That she considered that more often of late than not was not a habit she wanted to begin.

She looked at Master Ollamh, prepared to thank him for giving her something that indeed left her feeling somewhat better, and realized that he was wearing the expression of a man who had tidings he didn't want to deliver. She braced herself for the worst.

"Is he dead?" she asked grimly.

The dwarf looked at her in surprise. "Lord Acair? Nay, not that I've heard. I am concerned about him, though. He hasn't returned."

Léirsinn felt the same panic rush through her that tended to accompany any news that Acair might have trotted off to do something he shouldn't have, only this time they were in a place where the local monarch had already kept him in the dungeon for days and likely wouldn't hesitate to return him there.

"How long ago?" she asked, wondering where she might start to look for him and if she might need to tack up her best spell of, well, something to use for, ah, something else.

Magic was, she was finding, harder to manage than even the most difficult stallion.

"He left quite some time ago to attend to, ah, certain needs." Master Ollamh paused. "I suppose 'tis possible he forgot the way back here."

She could easily imagine all the things Acair might be off attending to and knew they would have nothing to do with getting lost.

"I suspect," the king's healer said in a low voice, "that something foul might be afoot."

Of course something foul was afoot and his name was Acair of

Ceangail. She threw back the covers and motioned for the king's healer to get out of her way.

"No messengers have arrived boasting of having slain him?" she asked briskly, pushing herself to her feet.

Master Ollamh pointed with a shaking finger at a spot behind her. "Nay, just . . . ah—"

She kept herself from falling over Acair's chair thanks to Master's Ollamh's gallantly offered arm, then turned to look at the door to her chamber. She realized then that she had definitely crossed some sort of bridge that should have remained unassaulted. That she fully expected to see something dire—evil mage, feisty witch, powerful wizard with mischief on his mind—waiting for her there . . . well, if that didn't say more about her state of mind than she wanted it to, nothing did.

What she saw was actually worse. The spell of death that constantly attended Acair was standing with only its upper half inside the chamber, waving and hissing at her. That it was no longer nipping at its victim's heels could mean only one thing.

Acair was in trouble.

Well, he *was* trouble, but she suspected it was a bit too late to make that distinction. She was up to her neck in his madness with no way out but forward.

She limped across the chamber toward the door, then had to put her hands against the wall and rest for a bit. That at least gave her an opportunity to glare at Acair's magical chaperon.

"Did you lose him?" she demanded.

The fiend shook its shadowy head sharply.

"Then show me where he went," she commanded, reaching for the door's latch.

"But a dressing gown," the physick said from behind her. "Shoes, my lady!"

She didn't have time to look for slippers, and she was most certainly no lady, but she caught the heavy velvet dressing gown Master Ollamh tossed at her just the same. She shoved her arms through the sleeves before she wrenched open the door. Two burly dwarves stood there looking profoundly irritated.

"There were three before," Master Ollamh offered.

She imagined there had been and didn't bother asking what had happened to the third of their number. He was likely lying senseless somewhere, which would no doubt be a vast improvement over his condition once he woke from whatever had sent him into oblivion. She suspected that that something had been Acair's fist under his jaw, but she was slightly cynical when it came to the methods of the youngest son of the witchwoman of Fàs.

The shadowy spell led the way with merciless swiftness. Léirsinn tried to keep up with it, but even with all her efforts it continually turned itself about to snarl at her. She scowled at it and shooed it on, following as quickly as she could. It occurred to her after the third time she had to stop and rest against the passageway wall that it was a bit odd how protective that creature there was of Acair, but perhaps that was by design. There wasn't much point in having murder as the sole reason for one's existence if one's victim had scurried off into the night unnoticed.

She drew her hand over her eyes, reminded herself that those sorts of thoughts were not ones she usually entertained, then pushed herself away from the stone and nodded to Acair's magical keeper.

She wished absently that she hadn't refused shoes, but it was too late to remedy that. The chill of the stone beneath her feet inspired her to greater feats of speed, which was likely why she almost plowed into the king of the dwarves himself before she realized she had taken a turn right into his throne room.

The king was holding a candle aloft, though that was no doubt simply for effect. He glanced at her, then in the next moment the entire chamber burst into light that seemed to come from the very walls themselves, throwing the entire place into something that greatly resembled mid-day. She blinked a time or two until her eyes adjusted to the brightness, then she almost wished she hadn't.

Acair was standing next to the king's throne itself, delicately holding a doily between thumb and pointer finger and looking profoundly guilty.

"You!" Uachdaran thundered.

Léirsinn didn't stop to think, she simply bolted across the polished expanse of floor that separated her from the man she needed alive for various not-entirely-self-serving reasons. She would have flung her arms around him, but he was filthy.

"This is becoming something of a bad habit," he murmured.

She swore at him, then stood there, shaking, while she waited for either a sword or a spell to slam into her back. She was almost surprised to realize the only things flying in that grand hall were noises of disgust and anger coming from the monarch behind her. Given the revolting condition of the man she was protecting, she thought she might share in at least the disgust.

Acair, that damned rogue, seemed to find nothing untoward about the situation. Surely that was the only reason he took her hand and brought it to his lips.

"Thank you, darling —"

She released him, gave him a bit of a shove and a warning look on principle, then turned and faced the king. She ignored the undeniable fact that she was blushing and hoped the king would do the same.

"I need him," she said firmly.

"And I need him slain," the king said.

"You're supposed to leave me alive," Acair put in helpfully.

"I don't want a horse that badly!"

Léirsinn suspected the king might want to rethink that given the nature of the pony in question, but perhaps the current moment was not the proper one to offer that sentiment. Actually, she didn't imagine anyone would hear anything she had to say given the way the king was shouting at Acair and her would-be lover — there, she had admitted it, which she supposed would have satisfied his mother — was returning the favor.

Acair took her by the hand and pulled her behind him. She

didn't think to protest until she was standing there with her nose as close to his back as she could bring herself to put it. Either the man had lost his wits or he'd decided gallantry could replace his sense of self-preservation for the moment. She would have to compliment him on his copious amounts of the former the first chance she had.

Then again, perhaps she wouldn't, given that she realized that in the midst of that piece of chivalry, he had slipped something into her hand.

A spell of death.

Realizing that she knew what she was holding without having to look at it was the single most shocking thing that had happened to her in all the moments since she'd overheard her uncle plotting to kill her.

Knowing Acair, what she was gingerly holding onto was likely a rather elegant disk of gold infused with vast amounts of his power so that he needed to use nothing himself in order to use it on someone else. That she simply stood there and wondered where she might stash it for safekeeping instead of rushing screaming off into the night was . . . well, it was merely something else to add to that list of things that had never before been a part of her very sensible, magickless life.

She slipped the spell into the pocket of the dressing gown Master Ollamh had so thoughtfully insisted she put on, then leaned on the king's throne that sat directly behind her. She realized she'd knocked a helmet off the seat only after it clattered to the ground. Well, the mystery of where the third guardsman's gear had gone was at least solved. The noise didn't seem to distract the two men in front of her from their conversation.

"I could slay you and make it look like a terrible accident," the king growled. "It's been done before."

Léirsinn stepped forward and stood next to Acair. "But I would know the truth of it," she said. "You would have to slay me as well to keep it all quiet."

The king looked briefly as if that might not bother him over-much, then he sighed gustily and scowled at Acair.

"Your woman saves you for the moment, but trust me, that won't hold true if I get you alone. Now, put that damned piece of lace back where you found it."

"But it is my grandmother's—"

"Exactly," the king said crisply, "which is why I'll treasure it more than usual from now on. She'll hound you endlessly for it, which will give her something to do besides make a nuisance of herself on my borders."

Acair didn't move. "I don't imagine begging will sway you—"

"It won't."

Léirsinn listened to Acair sigh heavily, then make a production of returning the lace to its place of honor on a small round table near the king's throne. He smoothed it out, then patted it with a look of sadness that she supposed would have softened the heart of anyone watching him save the monarch still tossing vile curses his way. She watched Acair thoughtfully. While recovering his grandmother's doily certainly seemed a reasonable enough activity, she had the feeling that had been secondary to what he'd come for.

He'd been after that damned spell of death that was now in her pocket.

Acair turned and made the king a bow. "And all is put to rights, Your Majesty," he said. "My apologies for the intrusion."

"Your groveling needs work," the king said shortly. He pulled a rich woolen cloak out of thin air and held it out. "Wrap up in this, Léirsinn lass, and let's be off."

"To the dungeons?" Acair asked carefully.

"Kitchens," the king said shortly. "You've interrupted my slumber *again* and I need something soothing to allay the irritation. I'll consider a final spot for you after I've eaten."

"Your Majesty," Acair began carefully, "if I might—"

"Or you might not," the king said. "Dangerous to ask too many questions."

Léirsinn had to agree, though she didn't say as much. Acair sighed lightly, then started toward the hall doors, reaching for her hand on his way. She saw him hesitate and imagined he realized that he was holding the hand he'd put the spell into, but the spell was no longer there.

"Other pocket," she murmured.

He smiled at her very briefly. "Thank you."

"I'll keep it close."

"And unused, if I might offer an opinion."

She would have told him what he could do with his opinion, but she realized she'd been fingering the damn thing with something that might have charitably been termed preoccupation.

"*Very* dangerous," he added.

Well, if anyone would know, it would be him. She kept hold of utter destruction and walked into slippers that had somehow been placed in her path. Master Ollamh hard at work, no doubt. She accepted the cloak the king handed her with equal gratitude. His hall was warm enough near any sort of fire, but damned chilly everywhere else.

She glanced around herself as unobtrusively as possible but saw no one but the king striding on ahead of them. She leaned closer to Acair.

"No guards?"

"He doesn't need them."

She imagined that was true. She walked next to Acair, his spell trailing along behind them, and followed the king through passageways until they reached what she had to assume were the kitchens. If the king kept his distance from Acair, she understood. The dungeon had not been kind to him.

The king nodded to an older woman who came to stand in front of him. "Take this stinking lad here outside and throw water on him. He'll likely need something else to wear, but rags will do. I'm mostly concerned about his stench."

"Of course, Your Majesty," the woman said crisply. She looked

Acair up and down, then nodded briskly to him. "Come along, my lord. We'll have you smelling less foul in no time."

Léirsinn watched Acair turn a tremendously charming smile on the king's chatelaine and thought she might understand how he managed to have exactly what he wanted so often, no pilfering or spells needed. He made both her and the king a low bow, then marched off to meet his fate.

She followed the king as he led the way to a large wooden table set there before an enormous hearth. Perhaps he was a frequent visitor because apart from a trio of kitchen lads and lassies who gaped at him in awe, anyone else still awake paid him no special heed. His cook, if that's what the man was, seemed particularly unsurprised to see him.

"Ah, Your Majesty," the man said, wiping his hands on his apron, "what shall it be tonight?"

"Simple fare for three," the king said. "Hearty, though. The lad who'll join us will likely die tonight from the chill if luck is with me, so best send him off with a full belly. What have you left on the fire?"

"Beef stew, a loaf or two tucked back behind the oven to stay warm, a fine cobbler for dessert," the cook said, ticking those items off on his fingers. "Ale or wine?"

"Ale for three, if you please."

Léirsinn had heard rumors of the king's ale, but thought it best not to give offense by refusing a cup of it as it was set in front of her. She braced herself for something truly vile and wasn't disappointed. She also didn't attempt to look at the king until she was certain what she'd imbibed wouldn't come right back up and leave her spewing it all over the king's tunic. Then again, given her recent history with the monarch, perhaps that would have been an improvement.

The dwarf-king glanced at his cook.

"Wine instead for the child," he said mildly.

Léirsinn didn't argue with either the term or the drink. She was happy to have something that might help her rid herself of the memory of the ale she'd forced down. Unfortunately, it did nothing to alleviate the discomfort she was feeling—and not just from the two liquids that had set up a sort of war in her belly. She made a valiant effort to avoid meeting the king's gaze, she who had never once shied away from facing the fiercest of horses. The kitchen was full of interesting things to look at, thankfully, which gave her a moment or two to gather her reins and assess her situation.

She was out of her depth. It was less painful to admit than she feared. She was an ordinary woman with a good eye for horseflesh and a steady hand to use in training them. Her encounters with powerful men had been limited to the peers of her uncle, which likely said most everything needful about the character of those souls. The king of Durial would have sent her uncle into a faint simply by scowling at him.

But she would make a better showing, if possible, so she ventured a glance at the king. He seemed to be sizing her up as if she were a wall he thought he might like to chip away at and see what lay behind it. She supposed things could have been much worse, so she left him to it.

What was worse, however, was noticing the way that the magic frolicking in her veins called to the spell of death in her pocket. It also seemed to wrap itself around the charm lying against her breastbone in a way that made her wonder if the damned thing might burst into flames before long. Her only comfort was supposing that it would consume her as well and she might at least have some peace as a result.

But until that happy time came, perhaps there were things she could do to improve her situation.

"Your Majesty," she began, "I would like to offer my apologies."

"As well you should, mistress," the king said, "for both my hall and my stables."

"I apologize, especially for the stables."

He smoothed his hand over his beard protectively. "Knowing you were aiming for me shouldn't lessen the sting of that, but I find it does. Apology accepted, though I blame that wee bastard for in-spiring you to do things you shouldn't have."

She was too far beyond changing course there, so she had no choice but to simply press on.

"He is what he is," she allowed, "but I still need him alive."

The king made a noise that sounded a bit like rocks tumbling down a well. "So says everyone I encounter of late, to my surprise. No doubt Fionne's runt is picking at things he should leave alone, though if Hearn is willing to trade me a pony for the lad's life, per-haps there are things only he can see to."

He looked at her expectantly. She realized she was facing the same sort of dilemma she had been with Acair's mother when the witchwoman of Fàs had waited with an ear bent for pertinent de-tails. She suspected Mistress Fionne was quite a bit fonder of Acair than the local monarch was, but at the moment she couldn't think of any reason not to divulge at least the main purpose of their travels. It might be what kept them both alive for a bit longer. She took a deep breath.

"He is on a quest."

"Is that what he's calling having another go at stealing the world's supplies of magic?" the king asked politely.

"This time he's off to *save* the world."

The king choked on his drink. If she'd known that sort of an-nouncement would have unnerved him so, she would have used that long before she'd used a spell.

The king dragged his sleeve across his mouth and looked at her in disbelief. "And you've put your life at risk for that whopping falsehood?"

She looked around to find the kitchen servants keeping a dis-creet distance, but she leaned closer to him just the same.

"He is on a quest to find the creator of a certain type of shadow," she said quietly. She sat back, then paused. "I don't suppose you know anything about shadows."

The king pursed his lips. "More than I'll own, to be sure. Tell me more whilst I down several cups of my very fine ale until I'm equal to believing that Fionne of Fàs' youngest brat might be about anything good."

Well, while the king of the dwarves might not have had fond feelings for her traveling companion, she imagined he did for the world in general. That and he hadn't tossed her in a dungeon when she'd set his beard on fire. Perhaps a bit of truth might even improve things.

"I'm not exactly sure where to begin," she admitted.

"Begin at the beginning," the king suggested. "Where did you first encounter him? Was he being pursued by mages trying to slay him?"

"Actually, I met him in my uncle's barn where he'd been sent to spend a year without magic, shoveling manure."

The king smiled pleasantly. "I like where this is going so far. How was he at it?"

"About as you'd expect," she said. "He wasn't allowed to reveal his identity, so I thought him nothing more than a pampered lord's son down on his luck. In the end, he invited me to come along while he looked for someone to take away that spell of death that stalks him."

"Invited," the king said with a snort. "I hope that's true, though I suspect you're leaving out details that are none of my affair. Very well, so you agreed to go along with him because he doesn't lack a gilded tongue under the right circumstances, and then what?"

"Somehow word got out that he couldn't use his magic and we've been on the run ever since."

"Who made that spell of death that hounds him?"

"He doesn't know. It almost killed him the day before we crossed your border. Prince Soilléir came when I called him—something I wouldn't have known to do if Acair hadn't been complaining about it under his breath on our journey from his mother's house—and he saved Acair's life."

"And gave you magic."

She looked at him seriously. "I asked for it."

The king fussed with his mug of ale for a moment or two, then looked at her. "I can't say that I blame you, gel, though there is a steep price to be paid for any essence changing. I assume you asked for it to protect that wee bastard?"

"I didn't know what else to do," she said quietly. "He is on a quest to find the maker of a particular sort of shadow that steals souls and he can't do that if he's dead. There is no one else to watch his back."

"I'm finding that I agree with you there," he said grimly. "I'm guessing Hearn has some inkling of what he's about, which is why he wants him still alive."

"I haven't discussed the particulars of that with him," Léirsinn admitted, "though you might be right. Do you have those sorts of shadows here, Your Majesty?"

He shook his head. "I've never seen one, but perhaps the maker of them can't find a spot on my soil to accept his foul creations."

"He might be afraid of you."

"He would have good reason to be."

She thought that might be true. "I understand Acair agreed to his year without—well, you know—because he wasn't enthusiastic about coming here."

The king smiled. "I never said the boy was stupid, just evil." He rested his elbows on the table and rubbed his hands together. "Nay, he's clever enough to know who to avoid most of the time, though I'm not sure you understand who he is. He has gone places and done things that should alarm anyone with sense, though that doesn't redeem him."

"And if he were trying to turn over a new leaf?"

"Well," the king said slowly, "I'm not one to hold a man's past against him unnecessarily, but with that lad, it would have to be several very large leaves." He looked past her, then shrugged. "Perhaps 'tis time to see if I can frighten him for a change and restore balance to the world."

"Shall I go groom your pony for you again, Your Majesty?"

The king laughed shortly. "I won't land on your bad side again, child, for fear of my front gates getting singed this time. And I won't slay your lover, if that worries you. Perhaps the world needs him alive for a bit longer."

"Then you'll just chat a bit?"

"Hearn said to leave him alive," the king said, "but there is a very wide gap between *alive* and *barely breathing*. I might see how wide that gap is." He paused. "I might make use of him for a different thing or two after all—besides distracting my kitchen maids, those poor innocent gels."

Léirsinn could hear the lassies swooning from where she sat and looked over her shoulder to find the source of the commotion. Acair was easy on the eye while covered in muck and lingering in a dwarvish dungeon, but cleaned up and exercising his considerable charm on every soul within earshot?

The king made a sound of disgust. "He's devoid of all morals."

She would have disagreed, but it was Acair after all. "I think it's a bit more complicated than that."

The king grunted, then looked up at Acair. "Sit and don't speak."

Acair pulled out the chair next to Léirsinn and sat. Food was laid out without delay, but she feared she wouldn't manage to do more than toy with it. There was no conversation going on between Acair and the king, but perhaps there was nothing useful to be said. The king spent his time sending Acair looks that bespoke dire intentions and Acair was applying himself to his supper with the single-mindedness of a man who hadn't eaten anything decent in at least a week. He also tossed back a mug of the king's ale with only a sigh of satisfaction.

"Delicious, as always."

The king was obviously unmoved. "Did you read the book I sent you?"

"I fear I didn't have time to indulge in more than a cursory glance, Your Majesty," Acair said. "I'm sure, however, that I will find it fascinating—"

"It was meant to be instructive, you fool." He shook his head. "You mages delve too deeply into things you shouldn't. Look where it gets you."

"I would have to agree," Acair said slowly. "On the other hand, I suspect you're never surprised by what your digging uncovers."

"I am not, which should terrify you more than it does." He finished his ale, set his mug down with enthusiasm, then pushed his chair back. "Come with me and I'll show you why you aren't wrong."

Léirsinn looked at Acair, but he only shrugged and rose. He held her chair for her, then took her hand and walked with her behind the king out into the passageway. She put her hand in her pocket to make certain Acair's spell was still there, but that didn't ease her any. For all she knew, the king would put them both in the dungeon and their last hope would be to use that spell and run.

She sincerely hoped it wouldn't come to that, but with Uachdaran of Léige, she just didn't know.

Five

A cair walked through passageways he'd previously skulked along with little thought for anything besides how to most efficiently help himself to a few of Uachdaran of Léige's best spells. He was going to need a proper rumination on all the things he had—and hadn't—managed to abscond with, but perhaps that could be put off a bit longer. At the moment, he was too busy trying to remember if the twists and turns they were making led to the king's dungeon or somewhere worse.

He felt Léirsinn squeeze his hand. Either she was trying to bolster his courage or she was preparing to give him a bit of comfort before he met his doom. He didn't ask her for the particulars. He had enough of his own dark thoughts to keep him occupied for the moment.

The king seemed to know where he was going in spite of the unrelenting gloom. Unsurprising. The old bastard was likely far more familiar with the dark paths lying beneath his hall than he cared to admit. Whether he only found gems there, not spells, only he would know.

Acair had his suspicions.

He'd had a quick look in the king's private books to try to verify the same, of course, but that had been decades ago when he'd been a bit more cavalier about someone else's ability to do him in. He'd only once managed to nip in and out of the king's private solar—an evening full of memories he absolutely didn't want to relive if possible—and he'd lingered in the king's library for a pair of hours. He'd made the proverbial beeline for the nastiest and most perilous pieces of the king's collection and hadn't been disappointed in what he'd found there.

Dwarves had strong stomachs for shadows, to be sure.

He preferred even his most evil of spells to come with a bit of elegance, but that didn't seem to be the case in Durial. Rough-edged, efficient, brutal things were apparently their preferred way of doing business, which he supposed he understood. No wonder Ceannairceach of Durial had wanted to escape, though he wasn't entirely certain living a life of exile was any better, particularly when that life was being lived with that absurd Baoth of Tòrr Dòrainn.

But, to each his own, he supposed. The king's daughter would spend her life with an elf who couldn't keep away from the nearest polished looking glass, and he would, with any luck, spend his in front of a hot fire, drinking exquisite wine and admiring the equally beautiful Léirsinn of Sàraichte.

Truly, he was a simple man with simple needs.

The king came to an abrupt halt. Acair nodded knowingly to himself over that. No conversation, no putting guests at ease with social niceties, just a sudden stop in front of a rough-hewn wall where death no doubt lingered on the other side. Whether it would come by sword or spell, he didn't know. Given that what lay on the other side of that wall might well be worse, he thought he might prefer to remain out in the passageway.

Uachdaran looked at him coolly. "Come inside."

"I'd rather not—"

"I don't give a damn what you want!"

That was certainly a sentiment he'd heard far too often over the past several months, but there seemed to be no escape from it quite yet. He steeled himself for entering what he wasn't entirely certain wouldn't be some sort of torture chamber and nodded his head with as much grace as he could muster.

The king made use of a rather ordinary and—thankfully—unmagical latch and pushed the heavy wooden door open. He walked in first, which Acair appreciated, then beckoned for them to follow, which Acair wasn't entirely sure he was going to enjoy. He followed, though, because he supposed it might at least buy him a bit of time to determine the best way to continue to avoid the gallows.

Or perhaps that would be unnecessary.

The chamber sprang to life with lights that were more otherworldly than anything he had seen during a lifetime of gazing at impossibly beautiful things. The walls glowed with a light that whilst retaining every color imaginable—and some he couldn't put a name to but would definitely investigate if given the chance—seemed to focus their efforts in a pale yellowish sort of business that looked a bit like mid-morning. Light fell from the ceiling as well, more sparkling and beautiful than anything ever produced by the finest of chandeliers created by the glass-smiths of Obair-ghloinne. The floor remained discreetly unlit, which he appreciated given that he might have hesitated to walk over it otherwise.

Léirsinn was gaping at the chamber with what Acair assumed was a mirror of his own expression. She looked at him and simply shook her head in wonder. He nodded slightly in agreement, then turned to the king.

"A spectacular hall, Your Majesty," he said sincerely.

"My lists," the king said. "I suggest a bit of exercise here."

Acair wondered how he might manage to extricate himself from the like without losing his head in the process. Whilst he wasn't at all opposed to a morning of lively sparring with both spell and sword, the thought of facing the intimidating dwarf-king of Durial whilst bumbling about as a mere mortal gave him pause.

"Alas," he said, putting as much regret into his tone as possible,

"I have no sword. I would, of course, be positively thrilled to admire even the least of what might come from your spectacular forge."

"Spells," the king said succinctly. "We'll bring our best to the fray and see who survives."

Acair was terribly torn. The chance to look over what he was certain would be a veritable feast of the king's finest, encouraging the king to blurt out each one and memorizing them as they left the hoary-headed monarch's bearded lips? The thought was enough to leave any mage worth his pointy hat a bit breathless. He had certainly learned more that way than from even the most thorough rummage through the private hosiery cabinets of king and mage alike. Unfortunately, he knew where giving voice to even the simplest spell would leave him, which made demurring a very bitter business indeed.

"I am simply crushed," Acair managed, "to decline your very generous offer." He pointed to the death-dispensing spell half-draped over his shoulder. "This lad here keeps me on my best, non-magical behavior."

The king didn't spare the beast even the briefest glance. "Do you honestly believe I cannot contain that wee thing there? How do you think the ceilings stay up in my mines?"

Acair had honestly never considered that anything magical might be involved in that, though he certainly hoped it was more than spells keeping everything from caving in on itself.

"I wouldn't want to put you to any trouble," he said slowly.

"No trouble at all," the king replied. "It would be a pleasure to see just how much pain you can endure without weeping."

Acair suspected that point had been found several days ago when he'd thought Léirsinn would never wake again. As an uncomfortable counterpoint to that, he decided it was useless to inquire how close to dead the king wanted him. If he emerged from his current scrape with any of his bones still intact, he would be fortunate indeed.

But the thought of using even a fraction of his own magic was intoxicating. He flexed his fingers before he could stop himself, though hard on the heels of that thought came another, less palatable one. He could trot out his best spells, true, but that sort of display would reveal more of what he could do than anyone watching might want to see. That would be doubly true, he feared, given whom he would be fending off.

"She'll have to know what you are eventually," Uachdaran said mildly.

Acair met the king's gaze. "I would prefer to put that off for as long as possible, if it's all the same to you."

The king looked as if he might have liked to offer a bit of comfort, but 'twas obviously neither the time nor place.

"She can stay and watch if she likes, though I wouldn't recommend it. I might miss with a spell and leave your innards decorating one of my walls."

"I thought you wanted that pony," Acair said before he thought better of it.

The king smiled. "Hearn said to leave you alive. He didn't say I couldn't rough you up a bit, now did he?"

That was unfortunately all too true. That happy thought kept him company as he watched the king order his wispy purveyor of death to go take a seat on a slab of stone jutting out of one wall. Perhaps that served as a gallery for spectators, though why a body would want to see what the king was truly able to do was anyone's guess.

Well, he would have been that body in a Diarmailtian minute, but he would have preferred to have been well-rested and taking notes, not standing unprotected in the king's sights.

A far different sort of spell dropped down in front of his keeper, leaving it spinning itself about and hissing furiously. Despite its nefarious designs, though, that shadowy creature was no fool. It cast the king an uneasy look, then helped itself to a seat on that benchlike rock where it commenced gnawing on its fingers.

Léirsinn was invited to sit with quite a bit more consideration, then a sturdy spell of protection was cast up in front of her.

Acair made note of both spells that had been used, then inquired after Léirsinn's comfort—gentleman first, mage second, when one's beloved was in the vicinity—but before he could get himself fully turned around and offer a few pre-duel niceties, he came face-to-face with the reality that on the list of Uachdaran of Léige's virtues, Nerochian ideals of fair play did not make an appearance.

He realized that, of course, only after he'd found himself flung back against a wall that he wasn't entirely certain hadn't given him a bit of a shove away from itself to leave him crumpled on the polished stone floor in front of it.

He imagined he wouldn't have been any more winded if the king had simply dropped a chunk of rock on him. Stars spun about his head, his chest screamed for more sweet, breathable air, and his tum took several violent turns arse over teakettle until it settled back into its proper place. He closed his eyes until he was certain he wasn't dead, then opened them and looked up.

The king was leaning over him, peering down at him with an expression of disappointment. "You're still breathing."

"Barely," Acair gasped.

"I imagine you don't find yourself in this position very often."

"I wouldn't admit it if I had."

"Then get up, you fool, and show me something more than your poorest efforts."

Well, that was offensive. Fortunately, Acair had endured far worse taunts than that. He crawled unsteadily back to his feet and moved a goodly distance away from that unforgiving wall behind him, giving himself time to find his footing. It was galling to realize he was hesitating, but too many months of being polite had apparently undermined his very foundations. He looked at the king.

"In truth, King Uachdaran, I hesitate to use what I could."

The king rolled his eyes. "Do you honestly think, *boy*, that you can best me?"

"I do know spells—"

"You know childrens' charms."

Acair was fairly certain he'd said the same thing to Mansourah of Neroche and could see why the prince had looked so annoyed at the time.

"You cannot harm me with your puny spells," the king continued with a shrug, "though you can certainly try."

"I have my father's spell of Diminishing," Acair bluffed. He decided that adding *mostly* would likely not improve his situation any, so perhaps that was something he could keep to himself.

"Bah," the king said, waving his hand dismissively. "Useless."

"There are many who would disagree with you, Your Majesty," Acair said. "Those missing all their magic thanks to my father's poorest efforts might find themselves atop that list."

"Your father, wean, is a pompous ass who didn't have the wit to manage what he unleashed."

"He is," Acair agreed, "but I am not my father."

"I suppose we'll see, won't we?"

There was that. Acair decided he'd done all he could to err on the side of politeness, then found himself far too busy trying to fend off the spells the king was suddenly hurling his way to do much of anything besides keep himself alive.

As he'd noted before, Uachdaran of Léige wasn't afraid of the dark.

He found himself immediately caught between the need to use magic to keep the king from slaying him and the reality that *using* any magic which would cause the spell of death he'd been cursed with to fall upon him and snuff out his life. Added to that were the additional problems of not wanting to offend even unruly, unsettling monarchs by using rather nasty spells himself, as well as not wishing to use said nasty spells lest that woman fifty paces from him lose her last illusions about any finer character traits he might or might not have possessed.

Fortunately—or perhaps not, given the circumstances—the

choice was made for him. He watched something vile coming his way and cast up the first spell of defense that came to mind—a rather quotidian piece of Wexham—half expecting the result to be finding himself ceasing to breathe not thanks to the king, but rather that damned spell sitting next to his lady.

He glanced in that direction rather unwillingly, then frowned in surprise. The king hadn't been lying about his ability to contain things, that was obvious. His minder spell was making noises of disgust and looked to be experimenting with a rude gesture or two, but it was obviously quite firmly attached to its perch.

What was the world coming to when a spindly fingered spell of death couldn't be bothered to hop to its feet and be about its business? It was insulting—

And that, he supposed, was going to be the last useless thought he was going to be thinking for quite some time.

Regardless of whatever else he might have been, Uachdaran of Léige was a first-rate mage. Acair wished desperately for the ability to divide himself in two so that one of him might engage in a friendly duel with the king whilst the other could take copious notes of every spell used. There was hardly time to admire the king's offerings and memorize them properly before he was forced to answer back with spells of his own.

The king's hoard was a veritable symphony of sharp things: painful, relentless, unforgiving. One spell was hardly sent off to do its worst before half a dozen others took shape, each seeking out the perfect spot guaranteed to inflict the most damage. Acair found himself stretching for things he didn't normally use merely to keep the king at bay. Some prissy elven princeling couldn't have fared better, surely.

Even with as exhausted as he still was, the pleasure of having his magic once again within reach was greater than he'd thought it would be. What was even better was the opportunity to, as his mother would have said, get his hands dirty.

Spells were exchanged, insults were hurled, and threats

breathed out with enthusiasm. He was fairly certain the king might
have smiled once, but it had been a feral thing that would have sent
shivers down his spine if he'd had the energy for it. He thought he
personally might have laughed at least twice.

It was also possible, he supposed, that he might have lost his
temper at one point and sent a spell slithering the king's way that
was rather beyond the pale. Even the king lifted an eyebrow over
it before he ground it under his heel. Acair glanced to his right and
made his greatest mistake of the evening.

Léirsinn was watching him, her face white.

He dropped his rather vulgar if not perfectly impenetrable spell
of protection in embarrassment and almost died as a result.

The king hurled a piece of magic at him that slammed into him
so hard, he thought his soul might have been knocked out of his
admittedly weary form. He went flying, landed flat on his back, then
slid across a floor that wasn't nearly as smooth as he would have
expected it to be given whose floor it was. He came to a stop with
his head against the toes of Léirsinn's boots, looked up at her, and
wondered if the present moment—the one where he was likely not
going to draw in all that many more breaths—might be the proper
one for a maudlin sentiment.

"I love you," he said, because it was the best he could do on
short notice and, truthfully, he thought he might not have another
opportunity to lay bare his tender heart.

Her mouth fell open. "You're daft."

"The king is going to kill me," he said. "I'm sure of it, horse or
no horse. I thought you should know how I feel before he kicks me
like a piece of refuse off toward the East."

She gestured quickly toward the middle of the chamber. "He's
coming to perhaps do just that."

Acair lifted his head to find the king standing at his feet, holding
out his hand. He wasn't entirely sure the man wasn't hiding a clutch
of nettles up his sleeve for use at just such an advantageous moment,

but clasped the king's hand just the same. He was hauled to his feet without much care.

"Ah, look who has come to watch," Uachdaran said. "Perhaps you know my grandson."

Acair uncrossed his eyes long enough to find none other than Aonarach of Durial standing just inside the door looking terribly unconcerned about the possibility of being slain by a spell gone astray. He knew the lad, of course, and had seen him loitering uselessly in various locales, looking discontented and dangerous. There were rumors linking him to dark deeds, but who had time to keep up with the ins and outs of dwarvish palace intrigue?

Well, he did when it suited him, though his reward for having indulged in the same during a previous visit to Durial had been a princess-wielded chair against the side of his head.

"Aonarach, see what you can do to him," the king said with an off-handed wave. "Just short of slaying him, of course."

"If you like, Grandfather."

Acair would have pointed out that no one had asked his opinion on anything, but he imagined that would have been a waste of breath. He also would have liked a quiet moment with Léirsinn to at least apologize for what she'd seen, but perhaps there was no point there either. He was who he was. No number of apologies would change that.

And at the moment, his main concern was keeping himself alive. Aonarach had obviously learned his manners from his grandfather. Acair supposed the only reason he hadn't been again flung against an unyielding wall was because he had been prepared for just that. He put his focus where it needed to be and contented himself with the thought of taking a bit of exercise with someone who didn't have the power to order his death for hurt feelings.

He suspected that in hindsight, he would count that as the moment when his stay in Léige truly went south.

After that initial bit of bad form on Aonarach's part, the duel carried on in the normal way. Acair hadn't expected anything terribly exciting from one of Uachdaran's lesser progeny and he wasn't disappointed.

What he hadn't anticipated, however, was a long-fingered bit of magic that reached out toward him, freezing him in place, stretching into the very essence of him —

"Where in blazes did you find that?" the king demanded.

The spell simply vanished as if it hadn't been there. Acair leaned over with his hands on his knees and fought not to lose his supper right there. He sucked in desperately needed breaths for a moment or two, then heaved himself upright, fully expecting to find the king striding out to chastise his grandson. But Uachdaran wasn't watching Aonarach, nor was he wearing an expression of fury.

Acair found that the king was watching him without any expression at all.

"That spell, Grandfather?" Aonarach asked mildly. "I can't remember exactly. I overheard someone using it recently, but I seem to have missed the final few words."

"Daft child, have you learned nothing from watching this bastard's father?" Uachdaran asked.

"Aye, what not to do if one wants the ultimate prize."

Acair folded his arms very deliberately over his chest and looked at the king's grandson as if he'd been a butler who had just spilled a bit of wine on his best shirt. What he wanted to do was gape at the fool and demand to know where he had found a spell that was uncomfortably similar to the one Cruihniche of Fàs had written in Léirsinn's book.

Where in the hell had the lad come by *that*?

"This is an outrage," the king said. "But outrages are best left for daytime, I always say. We'll discuss this tomorrow after breakfast."

Acair felt as if he'd been suddenly dropped into a dinner party where he knew no one and the usual rules of decorum were completely changed. Uachdaran of Léige had a reputation for dealing out immediate justice, not putting it off until after the next meal.

He stopped just short of scratching his head over what seemed so profoundly odd about the situation—and not odd in a way that left him wanting to indulge in a sardonic smile over someone else's having been maneuvered into place for nefarious purposes. It seemed, oddly enough, that Uachdaran had been wanting to rifle through his grandson's pockets—magically speaking—to see what sorts of foul things the lad was keeping there and had been waiting for just the right mage to come along—

He felt his mouth fall open in what he was certain was a terribly unattractive manner. He had just been used like an everyday hand-kerchief—not even a monogrammed sort—with intention of being subsequently tossed aside without care.

That was offensive.

Not that he hadn't done that kind of thing to others more than once in the past, but he'd had good reason and the mage—perhaps mages and a handful of crown-wearing lads, his memory occasion-ally failed him on those kinds of details—had deserved what he'd gotten. But surely King Uachdaran followed some sort of monar-chial standard when it came to making use of his guests in such a callous fashion.

More to the point, why was the king allowing his grandson to show off his wares, as it were, when those wares were so perilous?

"Sleep for what's left of the night," Uachdaran ordered brusque-ly. "Or, in your case, Master Acair, don't. I still owe you for a very large number of sleepless nights."

Acair cleared his throat and tried not to choke on his next words. "I apologize, Your Majesty. I've been a bit busy—"

"You'll unbusy yourself and be grateful if I leave you alive enough to do so. Go put those rivers back where they belong and stop using the others that run under my hall."

Acair nodded. He'd caused the king sleepless nights over more than one thing and he was definitely at the man's mercy.

"As you say, Your Majesty, I'll need to still be breathing to huff out the odd spell or two."

"I said I'd leave you alive and so I shall. But that will change abruptly if I find you in my solar, horse or no horse."

"I wouldn't dream of intruding there," Acair said.

The king actually rolled his eyes. "Your ability to lie is only eclipsed by your cache of truly disgusting spells."

Acair would have relished the compliment, but his need to correct the record took precedence.

"I never lie," he said. "'Tis my greatest failing."

The king grunted. "I'm certain that's what you tell yourself. Mistress Léirsinn, bring your lad back here tomorrow and have him teach you how to manage your fire-making. He has skill enough for that, I'll warrant. Aonarach, come along."

Acair didn't spare the breath to protest, mostly because the king had already walked away, his grandson in tow. He also didn't argue when Léirsinn caught him before he went down to his knees, though that was a near thing. He put his arms around her, leaned his forehead against hers, and shook right along with her.

"Forgive me," he said, giving voice to those accursed words as easily as if he'd been doing the like since the very moment he could speak. "In truth, I wish you hadn't seen any of that."

She pushed away far enough to draw his arm around her shoulders, then put her other arm around his waist.

"You talk too much," she said.

He thought he might have to do more than just talk to keep her safe in the future. He didn't anticipate another encounter with the king in his chamber of horrors, but should it occur, he would absolutely keep her out of the damned spot.

It occurred to him a short time later as he faced the guardsmen standing in front of her door, that locking her in that bedchamber might suit. With any luck at all, he might be able to enlist the aid of those lads there, one of whom he had most definitely encountered before.

"My apologies," he said without thinking, then shook his head. Three in one night. The world was truly going to split in two soon.

The dwarvish guardsmen didn't look to be in a forgiving mood, especially the one who looked as if he might be suffering from a colossal headache. The Nerochian coins Acair slipped out of his sleeve and handed over seemed to at least soothe the worst of the ruffled feathers. He walked into Léirsinn's chamber with her, then didn't protest when she pushed him over onto a sofa that looked a far sight cleaner than how he'd left it. Magic had its uses, to be sure.

She brought wine and poured herself a glass with a very unsteady hand. If she downed the entire goblet without pause, he was too much the gentleman to make any untoward remarks about it. It helped, he supposed, that he was also dispensing with good manners to simply drink from the bottle with rather rustic and uncouth gulps.

"Why did the king do that?" she asked.

"Beyond giving me a chance to preen and display for you?" he asked wearily. "I haven't a clue."

That wasn't the truth, of course, and he was appalled that the lie had tripped so easily off his tongue. He would be damned, however, before he voiced his thoughts.

"I thought he was going to kill you."

"He doesn't dare," Acair said seriously. "He wants that horse very badly."

She was silent for quite a while. "Those were very vile things going on below," she said finally.

"I am a very vile mage."

Her only response was to yawn, which he supposed was rather benign all things considered.

"I think you're quite a lovely man with terrible spells," she said sleepily. "You take the bed. I'll guard your granny's notes."

"They're under your pillow," he said, "and I am a gentleman. I'll take the floor."

She leaned over and put her head on his shoulder. "Acair, I don't think I can move."

And if she continued to say his name that way, without curses and hastily spat charms of ward attached, he wasn't sure what he was going to do.

She fished about in her pocket, then handed him his spell of death. "You might want that."

What he wanted was a moment to properly contemplate the woman's ability to encounter so many awful things without flinching, but he thought sleep might serve him better. He shoved his rune of death down the front of his boot, then caught Léirsinn before she simply tipped over off the sofa. He put her to bed, took off her slippers, then covered her up with a blanket.

He stretched out on the floor in front of the fire. Guardsmen were lurking outside the door, Léirsinn was obviously too weary to work any magic that might go awry, and his spellish shadow was sitting on a stool at his feet, watching him with those soulless eyes.

"Not to worry," he told it, "He bested me as well."

The spell drew its feet up onto the stool with it, wrapped its arms around its knees, and looked almost as unsettled as he felt.

He looked up at the ceiling and suspected sleep wouldn't come easily, despite how weary he was. It had been years, decades really, since he'd had so few reserves that using magic had left him that exhausted. Then again, fighting off the king's assault had left him digging deeper than he had in almost that long.

Then there had been that spell of Aonarach's . . .

He closed his eyes. One more day. One more day for Léirsinn to recover and for him to slip in and out of Uachdaran's solar to see if a piece of his soul might have been left there.

Then they would leave Léige one way or another.

Six

❧

Léirsinn tossed another forkful of hay into the empty stall where the king's prized bribe was wont to spend his days, then paused to rest. 'Twas possible she should have remained in bed for another day, but she hadn't been able to. Not just the habit of tending horses every day without fail, but the chance for a distraction from the chaos in her head had driven her outside at dawn.

She set aside the pitchfork and ushered the stallion back into his stall. She shut the door, but lingered there, pretending to fuss with the latch. That left her looking very busy, something she hoped would discourage anyone—namely King Uachdaran—from reminding her that he'd wanted her to go below with Acair and learn to use her magic. With any luck, she might be able to put that off for quite a while.

Besides, it wasn't as though she didn't know any mighty mages capable of doing anything she might need done. She turned and leaned back against the stall door where she could look at one of those across the aisle snoozing peacefully atop a bale of hay. She folded her arms over her chest and studied him dispassionately.

Acair of Ceangail made a very pleasant sight in spite of his apparent ability to pull terrible spells out of his pockets. She supposed the king of Durial had no room to criticize there, for his magic had been just as full of shadows. Watching the two of them go at each other the night before had been more than a little unsettling.

Then there had been that strange business with the king's grandson, something she would have rushed out to stop if the king hadn't caught her by the arm and shaken his head slightly. Watching that spell stretch across the chamber and reach toward Acair's soul had been horrifying. She'd waited for the king to stop the madness, but he had only watched it all as if he'd planned the whole thing.

Whatever she thought she might be able to do with the magic she couldn't control was nothing compared to what she'd seen, which left her wondering what in the hell she'd been thinking to ask for any of it in the first place. If Aonarach of Durial had come at her with that piece of nastiness, she would have simply fainted from terror.

In all honesty, it had been that last spell to send her out to the barn before dawn that morning. Busying herself with ordinary work that she knew how to do had seemed like a good way to forget what she'd seen.

She'd groomed three horses before she'd realized she had acquired a keeper in the person of that painfully handsome man over there. He had started the morning sitting on that bale of hay, but as time had worn on, he'd listed further and further to his right until he'd simply fallen over, asleep. At the moment that was fairly handy because it gave her a chance to watch him for a change.

Very well, so she'd known *of* what he could do because everyone he met seemed determined to remind him of all his bad deeds. But those had, in the end, been nothing but words.

Seeing it for herself the night before had been terrifying.

It wasn't that she hadn't encountered frightening things before. A handful of stallions that could have stomped her to death, surely. That shapechanging monster she'd lunged in Hearn of Angesand's yard, definitely. But in an arena, she knew how to tell her fear to take a seat and wait until she'd done what she needed to do.

But magic and that man there who had so much of it? That was something else entirely. She could hardly believe she'd insulted him so freely without having any idea of what he was truly capable of. Very well, so she had seen, *seen*, what warred within his soul in the king's garden in Tor Neroche, but she hadn't understood just what the dark contained. She half wondered if he knew.

It left her wondering what the other half of his soul might be holding within itself.

She knew what buckets held, though, and the one that had been set precariously on the saddle tree near him was about to lose what it contained right onto his head.

She had hardly begun to leap forward to grab it before she heard words be blurted out next to her, words that left the grain stopping in its tracks.

The stable lad she hadn't noticed standing nearby was obviously as quick with his hands as he was with a spell. He caught the bucket before it landed on Acair, scooping the grain back into it as he did so, while she stood in the aisle with her hands outstretched. She realized how foolish she looked and brushed off the front of her clothes in yet another attempt to look busy at anything unmagical.

"Good day to ye, mistress," the lad said breathlessly, setting the bucket on the ground. "Wouldn't want to wake such a one as this one here, aye?"

"Probably not," she agreed. She watched the boy hurry off, then walked over and felt her way down onto Acair's roost.

Things were occurring to her that hadn't before.

If an innocent stable hand could use a spell such as that with such success, well . . . why couldn't she? It wasn't a mighty magic, obviously, but she was never going to be a powerful mage.

She might manage something simple, though, and that simple thing might be enough.

Besides, that was the sort of business that would serve her well in many situations. She could watch a bag of oats burst, then mumble a few words and save herself looking for a broom. She could

keep the contents of buckets where they belonged. If she took a notion to experiment with something darker, she could corral flies and
do them in all at once, saving any number of horses endless torment.

For all she knew, she might be able to keep a certain spell of
death sitting on its hands while a man she thought she might just
love did what he needed to do.

She reached over absently to settle Acair's cloak over him more
thoroughly. He murmured something that sounded like *thank you*,
then drifted off again. She watched him for a moment or two, not
begrudging him his slumber. Every time she'd woken the night before, she'd found him standing at the window staring out into the
darkness, no doubt contemplating things she hadn't wanted to know
about. She imagined no one would be looking for him in a barn, so
perhaps he was safe enough on his own for a bit.

She looked about herself casually for a particular stable boy. It
didn't take long to spot him, mostly because he was the one lad there
who looked as if he'd just narrowly missed sending a black mage
into a towering temper.

Not knowing exactly how one went about the pilfering of a
spell, she supposed the best she could do was simply ask. The lad
in question didn't bolt at her approach, which was promising. She
stopped and leaned back against the wall next to him.

"What was that spell?" she asked casually.

He gulped. "Spell?"

She gave him the look she normally reserved for lads lying
about having done their chores and hoped it would be enough.

"I learnt it at my ma's knee," he said. "Child's magic. Useful for
keeping hens where they's meant to stay, aye?"

"Very useful," she agreed. "Can you teach it to me?"

"Oh, mistress," he protested, "'tis below the likes of you."

"I'm always on the hunt for new spells," she said, hoping she
sounded more confident than she felt. "If they're less than five
words, so much the better."

"If you say so," he said doubtfully.

"Do I have to wave any wands or make shooing motions at the victim—er, at the hens, or oats, or whatever is being, um . . . "

He looked as if his doubt might soon blossom into outright panic. "Nay," he said faintly, "just the charm."

She patted herself, but found she had nothing to use as a bribe. Her satchel was back in her bedchamber and she suspected Acair had not only her notebook but his spell of death secreted somewhere on his person. She was starting to see why he tended to acquire the odd item for use in the current sort of business. The best she could do was a roll she had begged from the kitchens earlier and put in her pocket just in case. She retrieved it and held it out.

The boy shook his head. "I'll give it ye freely, as 'twas given me."

Léirsinn put the roll back in her pocket for later use, then braced herself for some unintelligible bit of gibberish. To her surprise what the lad said made perfect sense to her. It was as if all that was required was to choke out a handful of words that wove themselves together like a net and caught whatever was trying to escape. Very useful in a barn, to be sure. Perhaps just as useful outside it, under the right circumstances.

She thanked the boy for his gift, then considered where she might test the spell without destroying everything around her. She repeated the words silently as she wandered out of the barn into the courtyard. The air was very cold and the sky full of heavy clouds, which she supposed was a good thing as it seemed to have driven most sensible souls indoors.

It was a perfect day to be about foul deeds.

She looked about herself for a likely victim, ignoring the fact that she felt like Acair of Ceangail on a less-murderous errand, then noticed a rather innocent but sturdy horse trough not twenty paces from where she stood. It had been recently filled, obviously, and the ripples from that filling were leaving water sloshing up against the sides.

Well, there was no time like the present to make an utter fool of herself. Besides, if a simple stable lad could do what she contemplated, why couldn't she? At least she was working with water, not fire.

She found a bucket lying tipped over next to a wall, an untidiness she never would have allowed in her barn, and tossed it into the trough. As the water was splashing over the sides of the stone, she quickly said the appropriate words.

She was slightly surprised to find most of the water was then contained inside the edges of the trough where it belonged. The bucket, however, was flung up into the air with far more force than she'd used tossing it into the water thanks to a geyser of water pushing it there.

Unfortunately, other streams started to tear randomly through her . . . ah . . . well, she supposed she could term it *her spell*, but even just the words sent a shudder through her that left her feeling decidedly not herself.

What she could say with certainty was that in the end, her spell hadn't done a very good job of containing anything.

She soon found herself surrounded by stable hands gaping just as she was at what was going on there with the water. She was starting to understand why Gair had had so much trouble with that damned well. Magic was more capricious than she'd suspected.

A single word was spoken from next to her. She watched, unable to move, as the water retreated back to where it had come from and the bucket fell down toward her upturned face. A hand reached out and caught it before it likely would have broken her nose. She took a deep breath, then looked to her right, fully expecting to find Acair there.

It was Aonarach, the king's grandson.

He handed her the bucket. "Might want to work on that," he said mildly.

She clutched it and watched him walk off toward the palace where he would no doubt enjoy a hot fire, cold ale, and vats of magic he could likely control without any thought. If she'd been one prone to envy, she might have indulged.

"You've been busy, I see."

She found that the king himself was standing next to her. She would have apologized for plying her dastardly trade on his courtyard, but he shook his head before she could even begin.

"Water was a good choice," he said approvingly. "And not entirely bad work there, missy. Striking out on your own, are you?"

She realized she'd given him the look she usually gave to cheeky stable hands only because he huffed out a brief laugh.

"I deserved that, I daresay," he said, rubbing his hands together. "I think, though, that you've avoided proper lessons long enough this morning. 'Twould be a pity to use that spell of containment on good Master Acair's wee companion and have it fail."

"It would, indeed," said a voice behind her.

Léirsinn caught the look of disgust the king directed toward the man apparently standing behind her and supposed Acair had definitely endured worse. She wondered, though, how long he'd been there and how much he'd seen.

"Luncheon," the king announced, "then a bit of work for you Mistress Léirsinn. Not that I care overly for the condition of your would-be lover there, but I do have strong feelings about the state of the world as a whole. Come along, lass, and we'll leave that mage there to follow us."

Léirsinn would have protested, but she couldn't come up with a decent excuse why she shouldn't agree to both so she simply fell in alongside the king as he tromped back through the puddles she'd left in his courtyard. Perhaps he considered those an improvement over smoldering ruins.

He paused on the steps leading up to his hall doorway, then looked at her thoughtfully. "I don't suppose Prince Soilléir told you what it was he put in your veins."

"I didn't ask," she said. "I didn't know there was a difference in, ah, you know—"

"There is," the king said. "I imagine your lad behind us could discover the truth of it given how he's forever turning over rocks he should leave alone simply to see what's under them." He snorted. "What I would like a peek at is what's running through *his* veins."

"Mine, Your Majesty?" Acair asked politely.

The king swore at him. "I wasn't talking to you."

Léirsinn didn't want to ask, but the question was out of her mouth before she could stop it. "It is elven magic?"

"To Ehrne of Ainneamh's everlasting disgust, aye no doubt, but that is the least of it." He sent Acair a calculating look over his shoulder, then looked back at her. "What comes from the land of Fàs is terrifying and shrouded in secrecy, which I'll admit is just how Cruihniche likes it. If that lad there had any idea what he could claim from his mother's side rather than Gair's, none of us would be sleeping well at night."

"Perhaps it's best he doesn't know then," she offered.

"Perhaps," the king agreed, "though I daresay he'll find out sooner than any of us is comfortable with. But until that terrible day, it seems as though the task of keeping him alive falls to you. Best to put a saddle on your magic and take it out for a trot this morning."

"While I appreciate the thought, Your Majesty," she said, making one last effort to spare herself, "I don't think—"

"Exactly," Uachdaran said, not unkindly. "That's half the trick of it, gel. If you think, the moment will pass and your lover there will be dead. Not that I would suffer any pangs of regret over that, of course, but you might."

"I feel a bit of a fever," she protested. "Perhaps even upset in my innards."

The king lifted an eyebrow. "No magic is wrought without a price, Mistress Léirsinn. There are times that price is very dear, indeed."

"You don't, if I might be so bold, look to pay any price," she said, because the idea that not only having magic but using it might be what finished her off had never occurred to her.

Uachdaran shrugged. "I've been doing it for so many years I don't notice weariness. I am also master here and Durial is an endless source of unyielding strength. You have only yourself to use, so be prepared for a bit of weariness."

She took a deep breath, but that did nothing to settle both the unease she felt and the unusual lethargy even using that simple spell had left her with.

"Food," the king suggested, "then take that bastard downstairs and see what you can learn. I'll do him the very great favor of keeping his spell busy for a bit. For your sake and the world's." He reached out and patted her on the arm. "You'll have to master at least the rudiments of it, my gel. Magic can be beautiful, brutal, and damned terrifying, but it *is* useful. Think of all that grain you won't have to sweep."

"I have stable hands for that," she said weakly.

The king only smiled and nodded toward the door.

An hour later as she stood in the king's cavernous exercise chamber, she wished she'd kicked up more of a fuss. She was standing shoulder-to-shoulder with Acair, looking at a pile of wood twenty paces in front of her and wondering if it might be too late to simply bolt for the door.

"I can outrun you."

She glared at him. "I doubt that, and stop peering into my head."

"You're not very good at hiding your thoughts," he said. "And for the record, I won't force you to do this. I would have advised against—" He blew out his breath. "Never mind."

She viciously suppressed the urge to wrap her arms around herself. "I don't understand how any of this works."

He put his arm around her shoulders and smiled. "Despite what most workers of the stuff would have you believe, there isn't much to it. You repeat the words of a spell, they'll rummage about in your veins for a bit of power to take to themselves, and there you have it."

"Rubbish," she said.

"It certainly seems like it at times," he agreed, "but as the king said: useful. I suppose before we get to the work of the afternoon, I should see if the king is as good as his word." He stepped away, then spoke a handful of words and opened his hand.

A ball of light appeared there as if by . . .

She blew out her breath as Acair closed his hand and the light disappeared. He turned and faced the door grimly, looking as if he fully expected a spell to come tearing through the wood and slay him. After a moment or two, he turned to her and shrugged.

"Still breathing."

"Thankfully."

He smiled and stepped back to stand next to her. "Let's carry on, then." He gestured toward the pile of kindling. "There's your intended."

She looked up at him. "I'm not sure that's the lad for me."

"Well, if you want my opinion on the matter," he said slowly, "the spell that gives you the most trouble is always a good place to start."

"Or I could try to work up to it with other things," she said. "Like a small pony before a feisty stallion."

"True, but these aren't horses."

She reached for something else reasonable to say, then realized with a start that perhaps there was nothing simpler than the spell he'd given her.

She turned and walked away because she thought better when she was moving, not because she wanted to escape. It took her one entire turn about the bloody chamber before she could force herself to stop next to a man who had likely made fire before he'd been able to walk. She wanted to glare at him, but all she could do was look at him and hope her expression wasn't as bleak as she felt.

"This *is* the simplest thing, isn't it?" she asked reluctantly.

He started to speak, then sighed. "It is the first thing I learned from my mother."

"How old were you?"

"Old enough to have a pressing need to set my eldest brother's trousers afire."

She wasn't accustomed to bursting into tears, but she was closer to it than she thought she might have been since that first night in her uncle's barn when she'd realized at the tender age of eleven what the rest of her life would look like.

He closed his eyes briefly, then carefully reached out and gathered her to him.

"I'm not going to stab you," she said, her words muffled against his shoulder.

"What I'm afraid of is that you'll set me on fire, if you want the truth of it," he said, sounding not in the slightest bit concerned. *"Fiery hair, fiery temper* is what I always say."

"You say nothing of the sort."

He hugged her tightly, then pulled back and took her face in his hands. She wasn't sure what she expected, but having him kiss the end of her nose and walk away was not it.

He fetched a pair of stools from near the king's gallery, then brought them over and set them down one behind the other. He sat, then patted the stool in front of him.

"I don't feel weak," she said crossly.

"I know. I thought that I would, lecher that I am, indulge in a fond embrace whilst you were distracted by other things." He paused. "'Tis possible that you'll also be less likely to bolt if I'm holding onto you."

He had a point, though she wasn't going to admit it. She sat down, cursing and feeling entirely out of sorts. Acair wrapped his arms around her and took her hands in his. She wasn't entirely certain he hadn't kissed her hair briefly, no doubt to inspire either courage or outrage.

"You don't have to do this, you know," he said very quietly.

She dug her wrist into one of her eyes because she had an itch, not because she was trying to avoid any untoward displays of emotion. "That horse is already out of the barn, don't you think?"

"I didn't want to say as much," he said quietly, "but aye, you're right about that." He took a deep breath. "Very well, let's attempt this together and see what it gets us."

There was something about a mage of terrible power and awful spells being willing to help her with things he had, regardless of what he'd said, likely been able to do the minute he could string words together that left her wanting to indulge in either weeping or howling. That he was being kind about it almost made it worse.

But she was no coward, so she took hold of her good sense and nodded. "What do I do?"

"The first thing to do is clear your mind."

"It was empty before," she said miserably.

"What a terrible falsehood," he said, sounding as if he might be smiling. "'Tis impossible with yours truly right here, no doubt inspiring thoughts of lust and riotous living. Just do your best. As for your business here, we won't be making any fire today, we'll be calling it."

She felt rather ill. "Is there a difference?"

"There is, but I guarantee you won't care what it is. Just trust that there is fire out in the great, wide world that is chomping at the bit to come do your bidding. I'll give it a little whistle first so you can see how 'tis properly done, then you try."

"You're insufferable," she said, knowing she sounded as if she were choking but unable to do anything about it.

"Yet still so damned charming," he said. "Prepare to be astonished."

She listened to him use the same spell he'd given her while she'd been sitting outside his dungeon cell not a handful of days earlier, the one that in her hands had set the king's hall—and his beard—alight. Now, she not only heard the words but felt the air shudder as fire came from nowhere and gathered itself onto that tidy pile of wood on the floor in front of her.

She took a deep breath. "You know I think this is ridiculous."

"Even now?"

"You're just engaging in theatrics."

"Well," he admitted, "it *is* what I do."

"It doesn't look all that evil, you know."

His breath caught on a bit of a laugh. "Thank you, I think." He took her hands and turned them palm up. "I'll save that for later. For now, you try that not-evil rubbish. Be ginger this time."

"No *oomph* behind it, is that what you mean?"

"You've been listening to my mother."

"She's the only witch I know."

"So far, and you're stalling."

She was and she didn't want to admit how comfortable she was doing just that.

He put his hands under hers and rubbed his thumbs over her palms several times. She imagined that was to soothe her, though she wasn't sure anything would at the moment. She took a deep breath, then breathed most of it back out before she said the five words that had given her so much trouble before.

A modest but perfectly suitable fire spluttered to life atop that same tidy pile of wood.

She gaped at it.

Then she gasped out a hearty curse.

The fire erupted into a bonfire-sized business that Acair smothered with a spell she didn't bother to listen to. He put his arms around her and laughed.

"Better," he said, resting his chin on her shoulder. "You should try again, perhaps without the *oomph*."

She rubbed the heels of her hands over her eyes and got hold of herself.

"Perhaps 'tis only that," she said. "My being so overwrought with worry about you, I mean."

"You wouldn't be the first lass to work herself into a state over my delightful self, but perhaps those are details you don't need at the moment."

She sighed deeply, then turned around on her stool so she could look at him. "You aren't at all what they say you are, are you?"

He caught his breath and looked as if a horse had just run him over. Having seen the results of that sort of thing more than once, she thought she might be qualified to judge the same.

"What a terrible thing to say," he managed. "After what you saw last night?"

She shrugged with a casualness she most definitely didn't feel. "We all have our flaws."

"My ability to wield a nasty spell is hardly a flaw."

She smiled because she suspected he was not quite as awful as he wanted everyone else to believe. "Even the worst horse can be reined in with the right master, you know."

"Your lack of respect for my mighty power is appalling."

She felt her smile fade. "I'm not afraid of you."

He looked as if he were still trying to catch his breath that had run off to points unknown. "I'm torn between assuring you that you should be and being flattened that you have me so tamed."

"Let me know when you decide." She started to face her charred pile of wood, then something occurred to her. She looked at him. "I could just light evil mages on fire, I suppose."

He looked genuinely shocked. "What a horrible idea."

"What would you do?"

"Humiliate them with a well-chosen spell or two, then leave them on their knees in front of me, begging me for their lives," he said with a shrug. "I would then look over their pitiful magic and walk away only after having pointed out to them that it wasn't worth the effort of pilfering."

"How is that any different?"

"Because I don't think you could burn someone to cinders," he said carefully.

"Could you?"

"Please don't ask."

She supposed she shouldn't. "Then I'd best work on the other so you can do what you must."

"That might be best," he agreed.

She turned back to face what was left of the pile of wood in front of her, then decided perhaps she would take the king at his word and just believe. She felt ridiculous, but she repeated the words faithfully and with as much detachment as possible.

Fire appeared atop the wood as surely as if she'd brought it to life there by normal means. More to the point, it stayed where she'd put it.

Briefly.

She was certain she hadn't added anything to it, but it suddenly burst into an inferno that she supposed would have singed them both if Acair hadn't doused it immediately.

"Well, I daresay 'tis as we thought: your foul temper causes your spells to run away with you," he said. "You might want to learn to control that."

She made a rude gesture at him, one she wasn't entirely sure she hadn't learned from his spell of death. He only breathed out a bit of a laugh, but she imagined he'd seen far worse.

She looked at her hands in his and supposed he was too much the gentleman to notice any stray tears of frustration she might have wept. She waited until she thought she could speak without her voice catching, then spat out what she'd been thinking for the past several days but hadn't been able to say.

"What if I can't do this?"

"I'm not sure we need to discuss what I'm willing to do to see that you don't have to," he said quietly. He squeezed her hands gently, then stood up, pulling her with him. "Let's take a healthful walk about the chamber and examine your victim from all sides. I find it's very useful to make a list of possible failings to point out during the appropriate moment."

She nodded, but didn't look at him. If he walked with her for more than a single turn about the king's chamber, he didn't make note of it.

She stopped by the door, set aside the very tempting idea of making use of it, then looked at him.

"I'm ready."

He leaned forward, kissed her on the cheek, then took her hand. "Again, then."

She nodded and walked with him back to their stools. She wasn't sure she would ever manage to control what her forays into a magical arena produced, but perhaps in the end it wouldn't matter. For all she knew, Acair would find a way to be able to use his magic and all she would need to do was stand by and, as he might have said, be astonished by his magnificence.

Surely she wouldn't be responsible for anything more than that.

Surely.

Seven

Acair finished yet another restless circle of Uachdaran of Léige's library and came to a stop in front of a surprisingly large window set in unsurprisingly thick walls where he had a full view of the darkness outside. The moon was but a sliver, but that didn't trouble him. That ability to see well in the gloom was perhaps, as he tended to remind himself as he prowled about darkened solars without knocking over decanters of rare port, the only decent thing he'd inherited from his sire.

He hoped Gair of Ainneamh, Camanaë, Ceangail, and half a dozen other places the man had claimed as home over the centuries had a perfect view of his shatteringly boring surroundings down there in that barren country of Shettlestoune, no matter the time of day.

He let out his breath slowly and pushed aside those thoughts. In truth, he tended not to think on his sire overmuch, mostly because it was a perfect waste of energy that could be better used being about his usual business of making the world a better place.

Which, as it happened, he was in the process of doing at that very moment. Léirsinn was safely ensconced in her chamber with Master Ollamh watching over her whilst the usual trio of the king's guardsmen was standing post. The king was no doubt looking over his mounds of gems and heaps of vile spells and deciding which pile to count first. He himself had put on his best manners and most trustworthy expression to secure an hour of liberty in the king's library, admittedly accompanied by the stern injunction not to let anything stray into his pockets.

That last bit he found rather insulting. As with most everything else in Léige, the king's books were too large and heavy to be stuffed in any pocket he possessed.

He supposed he might have put the king's mind at ease by assuring him that what he wanted to think about was not things that might topple thrones and ruin the peace of various Heroes, but rather the endless parade of horrors he'd seen in the king's lists the night before—though he supposed those things weren't mutually exclusive.

He was beginning to understand why Uachdaran of Léige was rarely invited to gatherings put on by workers of more fastidious magic.

He leaned against the window casement and thought back over the king's spells. He'd memorized everything flung his way, of course, with an exactness that might have even impressed his admittedly impossible-to-impress sire. Cataloging the offerings presently was a bit more difficult.

It wasn't that he wasn't familiar in a general sense with Durialian magic. He had nicked a pair of the dwarf-king's finest over the years, intriguing spells of forcing things to reveal what they didn't want to and making light where light shouldn't have been possible. After what he'd seen the night before, however, he was beginning to suspect that those spells had been deliberately left out in the open for any sticky-fingered guests whilst the true business of the kingdom had remained hidden.

The other truth he'd accepted, midway through fending off yet another volley of things that seemed to want to turn him into solid rock only after having smothered him by degrees, was that he'd been far too casual during his previous forays into Uachdaran of Léige's solar. If the king had been brandishing the goods without his usual hesitation the night before, who knew what else might be found with a bit of digging?

As he had noted to himself more than once, dwarvish magic didn't include any niceties or polite how-do-you-dos before smashing through defenses and dispensing whatever was necessary to do their business. Whilst he himself preferred a bit of finesse and refinement in his engagements, there were certainly times when it might be easier to simply come to the point of things right off. The king had shown him many tempting morsels. Spells of illumination, spells of containment, spells of stripping away all the dross to leave the true prize? Dazzling, truly. It might be time to have another look and see what the king had stuffed under his own sofa cushions.

The last thing that almost had him scratching his head was where that moody swain, Aonarach of Léige, had come by that spell of . . . he hardly knew what to call it. Not magic thievery, surely. He was very familiar with the peerless example of the same that his sire had created. It had been, if he dared venture into the darkness farther than even he might be comfortable going, a damned sight too close to what his grandmother had scribbled in Léirsinn's book. Not essence changing in the traditional sense, as he'd decided earlier, but definitely essence meddling.

A terribly intoxicating if not perilous bit of business, to be sure.

If Aonarach had dug that up in Durial, though, heaven only knew what else was lying about the kingdom just waiting for the right mage to come along and have a wee rummage about the old campfire and see what was lingering there in the ashes—

"There's something out there."

He stopped himself before he pitched into the heavy glass window. That was something that was going to change right off, that business of being caught off guard. He looked to his left to find the thoroughly unlikable product of dwarvish royalty and elvish princess standing there, looking at him from half-lidded eyes.

"But I don't imagine you need me to tell you that," Aonarach added, resting his shoulder against the opposite side of the window and apparently settling in for a proper chat. "I'm curious about what you've seen."

Acair would have told the lad tartly to mind his own affairs, but he simply couldn't bring to mind an appropriately nasty way to do so. The truth was, the man standing next to him made him uncomfortable. That was saying something because there were just so few disreputable sorts that he didn't care to rub shoulders with.

The why, however, was what caused him a rather significant amount of discomfort. It wasn't the man's arrogance, which he appreciated, or his stinging wit, which was admirable, or even his command of truly disgusting spells, which even Cruihniche of Fàs might have found worthy of a second look. It was that gaping hole he could see—metaphorically speaking, of course—lingering over Aonarach's heart. It was all he could do at present not to reach out and give the lad a brusque embrace whilst assuring him everything would no doubt turn out for the best.

Appalling.

He pulled back from that abyss of do-gooding before he slipped over the edge yet again and turned his attention to a more pressing need which was to find out where the lad had been nosing about for tricks of the old trade.

"Let's discuss spells instead," he suggested. "Where did you come by the one you used last night?"

The king's grandson lifted one of his shoulders in something of a shrug. "I have no idea what you're talking about."

Well, there was a word for that sort of horsing about and Acair used it without hesitation.

Aonarach smiled. "Language, my lord Acair. You'll offend my delicate sensibilities and then where will we be?"

"Outside your grandfather's gates where you'll find me in a far less forgiving mood than you find me at present," Acair said evenly.

"You can't have what you want from me if I'm too dead to give it to you."

Acair was fairly certain he'd had the same sort of thing spat his way more than once in the past, but that wasn't enough to put him off the scent at present.

"You might be surprised," Acair assured him.

Aonarach only shook his head, continuing to smile. "No need for threats. The truth is that I was scouting along our western border and eavesdropped on my grandfather and your grandmother having a chat."

"Hurling spells at each other, you mean."

"Exactly that. I didn't catch all of it, which is a damned shame. I nipped back home before I was caught being where I shouldn't have been—you'll understand that, I'm sure. The spell nagged at me though. Not essence changing, of course, because who in Durial has that kind of spell?"

"Who, indeed?" Acair agreed. He'd often wondered about dwarvish magic, though he'd always supposed Uachdaran of Léige was satisfied with his ability to coax sparkling things from rock all on his own. Where would be the sport in simply changing rock to gem?

"I tried to find the source here, but had to leave my search unfinished. Not sure where I'd be if I hadn't known about the side door. Grandfather doesn't like having his library investigated, but you understand that, don't you?"

Acair ignored the barb, mostly because it was all too true, then found himself willing to give the lad a second look. "Side door, did you say? I don't suppose you would feel inclined to point out where such a thing might be located."

"I might, for the price of a future introduction to your lady's sister."

"She has no sis—" Acair stopped and frowned, remembering an extremely brief conversation about the same somewhere in Sàraichte. "She *had* a sister, rather, but I believe her sister died as a child."

watching the front gates. I don't think you have a bloody clue who you're dealing with or what he truly wants."

"Am I to assume that you do?"

"Must I say it?"

"I think you would feel better about it if you did."

There, more friendly words instead of unfriendly fingers wrapped around the throat. Good deed accomplished.

Aonarach reached out and clapped a hand on his shoulder. "Sometimes, friend, we are far less important in the grander scheme of things than we believe. And I believe that is my cue to, as you would say, make an elegant exit stage left."

Acair was torn between feeling flattered that his words had made such an impression on the lad and being overcome with frustration that he hadn't beaten out of that self-same lad the details he'd needed. He leaned back against the stone because it seemed wiser to do that than stagger artistically into the nearest leather chair. He watched his recent tormentor leave the library, pulling the main door shut behind him, then considered what he'd just heard.

Less important than he believed?

That was offensive. There was a very long line of people who wanted him dead, beginning with that wee fiend's grandfather. Of course he knew he wasn't *always* topping everyone's list of mages to slay before luncheon, but that could have definitely gone without being said.

He walked over to a sideboard placed just close enough to the fire for the distance between a fine glass of whisky and a comfortable place to settle in to be not unmanageable, poured himself something from the decanter there, then tossed it back without bothering to sit. It hardly began to properly address the insults to his pride, but as tempting as another few fingers of what he suspected was Gairnish brew might have been, he would do better to be in possession of most of his wits. For all he knew, he might run across someone who *didn't* want him dead—apparently there were more of those lads making lists than he suspected—and he would want to scold them

Aonarach looked genuinely surprised. "Are you that stupid? He shook his head, possibly rolling his eyes as well. "Never mind She has something I want, so I'll just find her myself. As for the oth er, the second exit is over there in the corner, behind the bookcase and accessed by the usual lever of a cleverly concealed book. I'll let you decide which one."

Acair imagined that was as far as he was going to get with that, so he opted for another direction. "Anything else you'd care to share?"

Aonarach looked at him in silence for so long that Acair found himself almost nervous, he who made others uneasy with that sort of look. He was beginning to see why it was so effective.

"Grandfather had a book on his night stand for a fortnight or two recently," he said slowly. "Something about bad mages coming to worse ends. Rather tedious stuff, that, but I assume he had good reason to be amusing himself with the contents."

Acair imagined that had been the case, but wished to heaven the old bastard had left it as a place to rest his ale. The fact that he himself had brought along that very tome and tucked it under the cushion of the chair nearest the fire for a bit of light reading later was perhaps something he could conveniently forget to mention.

"I wonder why?" Acair mused.

"The kingdom is full of deep shadows," Aonarach said, "but he's heard rumors of shadows in other places. I don't suppose I need to point that out to you."

Acair hadn't intended to comment on the shadows he suspected Aonarach had explored, but that lad had definitely gifted him the opening he'd been waiting for. There was no sense in not taking it.

"I don't suppose you do," Acair agreed, "but why don't you tell me about the ones *you've* no doubt examined here in your Grand-pappy's environs?"

Aonarach looked at him without a trace of emotion on his face. "I imagine you'll discover everything you need to know about them without my aid, more particularly the ones created by that mage for their lack of good taste whilst having a full complement of slurs at his disposal.

He accompanied himself to a chair with a few bitter curses and retrieved the pair of books he'd brought with him from under the seat cushion there. He'd been fighting a gnawing feeling that his grandmother's map held secrets he would want to know sooner rather than later, but he forced himself to set it aside for when the whisky had taken full effect.

The second book was the one the king had foisted off onto him, that poorly chosen collection of lesser mages going about decidedly lesser deeds. If only the king had dog-eared a page or two that had intrigued him, the evening's task would have been more easily accomplished. But things were as they were, which left him doing all the dirty work, as usual.

There was unfortunately no bookmark loitering between any of those mediocre pages, never mind any hint that he could see of anything magical having been left behind. Unsurprised but determined, he began from the beginning, giving it the proper study he hadn't been at liberty to previously. He recognized many of the names, of course, but . . .

He held onto the page he had almost turned and wondered why it was that at the very moment one found something one hadn't been expecting, the world seemed to pause and hold its breath. Usually that came about thanks to some piece of mischief he was preparing to perpetrate, which left him thinking that the book he held in his hands might just be of more worth than he'd suspected.

One can hardly fully explore the underbelly of the fouler pieces of magick-making in the Nine Kingdoms without a brief examination of those who slither in and out of tales with astonishing cleverness and an undeniably theatrical flair.

Well, that made his non-appearance on the roster even more painful, but he made a note of the author's name to pass along to his mother just the same. Perhaps he would find himself sitting across the table from that man at some future supper where he could offer a gentle rebuke about omissions that had surely been nothing more than simple oversights.

Included on our list of mages who paired arrogance with foul deeds like another might pair a fine red wine with perfectly cooked beef is a man named Sladaiche —

"Is there anything you require, my lord Acair?"

Acair caught the book he had thrown upwards in surprise, rather thankful it had been a book and not one of the king's very fine crystal whisky glasses. Damnation, he had had enough of slinking about like a mere mortal. Things in his life had to change.

He looked at the trembling bard standing just inside the library door. "Nay, Master Eachdraidh," he said, wishing he sounded less hoarse and more annoyed. "I am well. Very kind of you to ask."

Master Eachdraidh bobbed his head and retreated, looking positively thrilled to be escaping. Acair found his place again in the king's book and had another look at the words that seemed to be glowing with a bit of their own importance.

Naturally, there was little patience for the petitions of Sladaiche, but such was the nature of the king of —

Acair blinked, then swore. Why, that was a damned smudge right there in the bloody book, just where it didn't need to be! He scanned the pages on either side of that salacious tidbit and found that there wasn't a single reference to the country in which that worker of perilous magic had been found. If he hadn't known better, he would have suspected that the whole bloody world was marshaling its forces for the sole purpose of causing him grief.

He reread the pages before and after the one with the smudge — put there, no doubt, by Uachdaran himself — but still found nothing of substance. As usual, he would have to poke his nose into places it shouldn't go and find out what he needed without help. He indulged in a hearty curse or two, then forced himself to turn another page.

Rumor has it he mistreated his horses, which earned him no affection from the stablemaster.

Horses. Of course. He should have known it would wind round to them in the end.

He considered things he hadn't had time for earlier. First, it wasn't possible that Uachdaran didn't realize what he'd ordered delivered. Acair suspected there wasn't a damned sliver of the worst quality quartz lingering in the most distant wall in his worst mine that Uachdaran didn't hear calling his name and asking permission to be carried off in some dwarvish pouch or other.

Nay, the king knew. Why he'd thought Acair needed to have it was perhaps a much more interesting question.

Second was the strange coincidence, something he rarely believed in, that he should be keeping company with a horse miss when the apparent maker of substantial mischief had run afoul of those noble beasts . . .

He closed the book, then stared at the fire for a bit, allowing his thoughts to gallop about without attempting to rein them in.

He had started out on the final leg of his penance tour expecting to face nothing more taxing than blisters on his hands from shoveling too much horse manure. Instead, he had found himself saddled, if he could use that term without any irony at all, with a quest to save the world from a man with plans to stockpile souls for his own nefarious purposes. He'd been gifted a collection of grandmotherly scribblings fit to undo the peace and quiet of innumerable mages of all stripes, then been handed another list of things to do that included a quest to find a missing page from a particular book of spells.

It was a formidable selection of things to see to whilst at his best, but he'd been given no choice but to attempt everything whilst oper-ating under vastly reduced circumstances.

He set aside the king's book, then opened up the little notebook his mother had gifted Léirsinn and his grandmother had filled with appalling things. He found the map she'd made and wondered if that aggressively drawn X resting right over his house might be something more than a pointed reminder that he hadn't yet invited her to supper.

Whilst 'twas true his house was spectacular, it was also rather too close to the border of Bruadair for comfort and he honestly couldn't think of a damned reason why he would want to travel so far north in the middle of winter. As a brisk, non-descript wind, the journey was nothing. In his present state, with at least one angry mage on his heels, the very thought made him want to reach for an-other glass of the king's finest, then go straight to bed.

Perhaps he was getting old before his time. All the excitement was giving him a tummy upset that he suspected would only be cured by completing his quest, donning a dressing gown, and retir-ing to a comfortable spot in front of the fire for the spring. Hot soup would be involved, he was certain.

Well, he might not see morning if those shouts he could hear coming suddenly from outside the door boded ill. Politely inquiring about the cause of the kerfuffle wouldn't serve him if the result was his being shown the way back to his dungeon abode. He knew he was likely being overly suspicious, but experience had taught him to be cautious.

Also, he just might manage a wee visit to places he shouldn't go whilst the king's relentless gaze was fixed elsewhere, so there was no sense in not making his own elegant exit offstage.

He heaved himself to his feet, shoving both books into the belt of his trousers, and walked briskly over to the wall where Aonarach had indicated the second egress from his current locale was located. He chose a shelf at random and ran his finger over the books until that finger came to rest on a heavy leather volume emblazoned in

gold with the title, *Famous Durialian Swords and Their Makers*. A likely
suspect, to be sure. He blew out his breath, then pulled on the book.

He wasn't past admitting surprise when necessary, so he freely
gaped at the bookcase as it creaked toward him. He didn't think,
he simply consigned himself to nowhere good, leapt behind it,
and pulled the case closed. The click that echoed was altogether
unwholesome sounding, but what else could he have done? There
was pompous trumpeting going on in the king's library accompanied
by the particular sorts of shouts guardsmen on the hunt tended to
make. Uachdaran might have been getting in a final dig whilst he
could, but there was no reason to be involved in it. Obviously it was
time to gather up his companion, saddle his horse, and ride off into
the arms of his Noble Quest.

Normally, his sense of direction was very good, but he had to
admit after a quarter hour that he was thoroughly lost. The floor
was perhaps a bit smoother than he would have expected, which
served him well considering he didn't dare fashion so much as a
marble-sized ball of werelight. In time, he came to a fork in the passageway. He didn't stop to consider, he simply took the right-hand
path and within ten paces had encountered a latch just hanging
there, attached to the wall.

He tugged and a door opened. He wasn't a fatalist, truly, but
there was a part of him that fully expected to find himself missing
his head as he poked that head out into what he immediately realized was a main passageway. There were no guards roaming about,
so he made a quiet exit from his former safe haven then jumped a
little when the door simply shut behind him without his aid. He was
somehow unsurprised to find there was absolutely no indication that
the door existed.

He considered, then decided that whilst he was at liberty to
open and close doors, there was no reason not to pop by His Majesty's solar and see if a bit of his soul might be lingering there. He
wanted to dismiss his mother's injunction that he needed to collect
pieces of himself for use down the road, but the more he thought

about the maker of those shadows and what he wanted, the better the idea began to sound.

He walked down the passageway as if he had every right to and realized soon enough where he was. A quick turn or two and ducking into a doorway to avoid a clutch of dwarves on their way to supper was enough to allow him to soon put himself in front of the king's solar. If he'd accidentally put out the nearest torch by dropping it and grinding out the flame with his boot, perhaps he could apologize for it later.

Burgling was best done as simply and unobtrusively as possible, which had been his guiding principle over decades of the same sort of activity. He preferred picking locks with a bit of complexity, but perhaps that would come back to haunt him at some point in the future. At the moment, what was haunting him was his own stupidity at having left his gear for his current activity in Léirsinn's bedchamber.

He sighed as silently as possible. Whilst it was tempting to just step back and give the door a good kick, he suspected that would not gain him entrance. He patted himself for anything useful to use in besting the door in front of him, then realized that was going to be unnecessary.

A key glinted in the semi-dark.

He wondered when his luck was simply going to run out, but apparently it wasn't going to be that day. "Thank—"

He closed his mouth around the end of that offering because he realized who was holding that key. He supposed the man—or dwarf-king, as it happened—could just as easily have been holding onto the key to the dungeons below except he knew those cells had no doors. Anything else would have prevented those jailors from enjoying the sufferings of those incarcerated there.

"Your Majesty," he managed.

Uachdaran barked out a word and werelight sprang to life above his head. His expression was not welcoming, and he made a production of pocketing his key.

"I told you to stay out of my solar."

Acair blurted out the first thing that came to mind and wasn't all surprised by what he heard.

"I apologize," he said, giving himself up for lost on that score. "If you'll have the truth, my mother suggested I go round and gather up lost bits of my soul. I think there might a piece in your solar. She fears that without a full complement, I will die if I attempt to face my enemy."

Uachdaran looked as if he'd heard worse ideas, but apparently the present moment was not the time to discuss them.

"I had the palace scoured for vermin after the last time you crawled through it," the king said tartly. "You'll find nothing of yours inside."

And that, Acair supposed, was going to be the best he was going to have from the monarch standing in front of him.

The king lifted his arm and pointed back down the passageway. "You'll want to be on your way immediately, for reasons I'll explain after my temper has cooled. I'll help you find the front door. Wouldn't want you getting lost and landing in my dungeon."

Acair supposed things could have been much worse, so he nodded and followed the king through the palace, thoroughly grateful that there were indeed no unexpected detours toward lower levels. He walked out onto the front stoop.

Léirsinn was standing there, swathed in lovely traveling clothes with both their packs sitting at her feet. He looked at her quickly, but she only nodded slightly. He had the appropriate books and the spell of death he'd fetched from under the king's chair on his person, but there were other things he'd collected on their journey that he hadn't wanted to give up quite yet. His pack looked robust, so he felt confident that Léirsinn had gathered up everything they both still owned. He took the cloak she held out toward him, then turned and made the king a low bow.

"Thank you. This is more —"

"It is," the king interrupted. "You may thank me by fixing those bloody rivers of yours."

"Of course, Your Majesty."

"If you fail I will hunt you down, slay you slowly, then hang your rotting corpse on my front gates for all to admire."

Acair didn't doubt that for a moment. "Of course."

"Your Granny is making mischief on my western border which gives you the perfect opportunity to scamper out the gates while watchers are distracted. I assume you're clever enough to know what I'm getting at."

Acair nodded carefully. "Thank you, Your Majesty."

"Just so you know, the lad you're running from hasn't attempted to lay any shadows on my land."

"Your spells of ward are indeed formidable."

"There is that," the king agreed, "though I suspect the truth is that he's too stupid to know what finds itself within my borders which, it galls me to admit, you are not. But that's your mystery to solve, not mine." The king nodded toward the courtyard. "There's your mount being brought, may he throw you off at his first chance. I'll do your lady the courtesy of a spell of un-noticing, though."

"Thank you, Your Majesty," Acair said. "I don't suppose you'd want to use it aloud, just so she'll hear how 'tis properly done."

The king rolled his eyes and brushed past him. Acair listened to the dwarf inquire politely after Léirsinn's comfort, then offer her a suggestion or two about places where she might push magelike companions off the back of her horse so she might ride freely into her future.

He picked up their gear and secured it to Sianach's saddle, climbed up behind Léirsinn, then listened to the king's very useful and surprisingly simple spell of un-noticing. Uachdaran shot him a look.

"I'll know if you use that in the future."

"With permission, then?"

The king swore at him and walked off to gather his men for that piece of mischief he seemed to be looking forward to on his western flank. Acair put his arms around Léirsinn and happily turned the reins over to her. At least that way, he might manage to avoid being bitten by his horse right off.

She stopped Sianach when they were just outside the gates, sitting in such darkness that Acair wondered if that spell of the king's would be necessary.

"Where to now?"

He took a deep breath and hoped he wouldn't come to regret their destination.

"Home."

Eight

❖

Léirsinn followed Acair through the woods and wondered if his brothers had ever managed to outrun him. Not only was he perfectly silent, he was relentlessly swift. She had perfected the art of being silent and unmarked, but she thought she might have met her match in haste.

She suspected he wasn't keen on the idea of being out in the wilds east of Durial without protection, which she appreciated. They had been covered by the king's spell of un-noticing as Sianach had bolted across the sky wearing only the faintest suggestion of dragonshape, though it had vanished once they'd put foot to ground again. Acair had remarked with only the lightest of sighs that the king certainly wouldn't want them unseen by the nymphs who controlled the rivers.

Sianach had disappeared, no doubt off to hunt for a late supper, and she had been perfectly happy to follow in Acair's footsteps. It hadn't taken long before she realized that what she was hearing hadn't been thunder, it was the rushing of mighty waters.

No wonder the king couldn't sleep.

Acair stopped so suddenly that she almost ran him over. He caught her by the arm to keep her from going sprawling, then held her until she was steady on her feet. She nodded her thanks, then looked out into a clearing that was large enough to have grazed one horse quite comfortably for a pair of hours. Beyond that seemed to lay the source of all the noise. She supposed there was at least one mighty river coming from the mountains and rushing over falls, though perhaps several met for a moment, then went their various ways.

She first thought that the gloom was less in that glade because of the mist reflecting even just the starlight, but she realized quite suddenly that it had everything to do with the man standing there.

Nay, not man, but an elf—and a king, by the look of the crown atop his snowy head.

The king caught sight of Acair and gasped. Léirsinn would have glanced at Acair, but she realized moving was going to be very unwise. The glint of a sword not a hand's breadth in front of her face was proof enough of that. Obviously there was a previous relationship between the monarch in front of her and the man beside her, though she didn't dare speculate on what it might entail. She watched the king doff his crown and clutch it with both hands which she supposed rendered that speculation unnecessary.

"You," he snarled.

"I'm beginning to wonder if anyone ever remembers my name," Acair muttered, then he stepped in front of her and started to make the crown-clutching monarch a bow. A different sword flashed silver in front of him before he could.

"Dionadair, leave it," the king said. "I'm perfectly capable of seeing to this disgusting worker of vile magic myself."

Léirsinn stepped in front of Acair out of habit. To his credit, he took her gently by the arm, pulled her back to stand behind him, then made the king a very small, very careful bow.

"King Sìle," he said politely, "my most abject and heartfelt apologies."

"For what?" the king snapped. "You've wreaked so much havoc

across the whole of the world, I doubt you can remember what mischief you made within my borders!"

Léirsinn thought the king might have a point there. She eased forward to stand next to Acair, then felt his ever-present shadow wedge itself between them, its arms around their shoulders. She didn't blame Acair for dealing it a firm elbow in its non-existent gut, but it remained unfazed.

"I will provide you with a list of offenses at my earliest opportunity," Acair said, "and apologize for each in turn. Until that time, if I might present my companion, Léirsinn of Sàraichte. Léirsinn, His Majesty, King Sìle of Tòrr Dòrainn."

She started to make him her best curtsey, then she actually heard the name Acair had said.

"Oh," she said, feeling her mouth then drop open. Only good sense stopped her from blurting out that she remembered that Acair's father had wed the youngest of a certain King Sìle's five daughters. She imagined the king in front of her could finish that tale well enough.

"And his lovely guard captain," Acair continued, "Dionadair of Tòrr Dòrainn. Also various and sundry other elven warriors of unimpeachable bravery, courage, and beauty—"

"Oh, shut up," the king grumbled. "Why are you here?"

"I am—"

"About some mischief, no doubt," the king interrupted. He paused, then frowned a bit more. "Why do you have that magic, mistress? And why are you keeping company with that bastard there?"

Léirsinn realized the king was speaking to her. It then occurred to her that he was asking about the business in her veins that seemed to have perked up as if it had sensed some other sort of magic that it recognized. She supposed she wasn't surprised for even she could see what was sparkling in the air around the elven king.

"Ah," she said, trying to invent something on the spot that would save them from another trip to a different dungeon, "the tale is long and very interesting, but the shortened telling of it amounts to the fact that my lord Acair is off to do heroic deeds and put a stop to a vile and pervasive evil. I have come along to help him as I may."

There. That sounded reasonable as well as a bit like something Acair would have said. She was starting to understand why he spewed out so many compliments and apologies when meeting those who might want to put a sword through him first and ask about his intentions later.

"And if I might now offer that apol—" Acair put in, then he shut his mouth.

Léirsinn caught the tail-end of the look the king had sent him and supposed he was wise to not offer anything but silence at the moment. The king turned an only slightly less skeptical look on her.

"Where did you encounter him?" he asked.

"He was shoveling manure in my uncle's barn," she said.

"Was he?" the king said, looking slightly more interested. "Tell me that went on for quite some time."

"Not as long as she would have liked," Acair put in, "and if I might encourage perhaps a less-visible presence here?" He lowered his voice. "I'm being hunted."

"Well, of course you're being hunted," the king said with a snort. "Anyone with any sense wants you dead. Dionadair, take the lads and have a look around to see who we might want to reward for their good intentions. I can contain Fionne's runt for a bit myself."

Léirsinn didn't flinch as the king came to stand directly in front of them only because she'd spent a lifetime not giving any indication of her unease. She had to admit to being overwhelmed, though, by the sheer beauty of the monarch in front of her.

"'Tis his glamour," Acair murmured. "Powerful stuff, that."

The king leaned closer. "As is my magic, whelp, so you'd best not be reaching for any of your nasty little spells. Oh, and what do we have here?"

Léirsinn felt Acair's spell shiver a bit before it slipped between them and made the king a low, shadowy bow. If it shared some sort of silent dialogue with the old elf, she wouldn't have been surprised. What did surprise her was how it deserted them both and went to hover at King Sìle's elbow.

"Yet something else that wants to do you in," the king said pleasantly. "I approve. Now, Mistress Léirsinn of An Caol, what is your role in this quest?"

Léirsinn realized at that moment that she was past surprise when it came to what those of a magical bent might know about her, though the place where she'd been born was certainly nothing she had ever shared with anyone.

She paused. She had told Acair's mother, true, but she suspected Fionne of Fàs didn't visit all that often with the monarch standing in front of her.

"I'm just the stable hand," she said.

Sìle studied her in silence for a moment or two, then nodded thoughtfully. "I think I might be wise to leave this alone, but I also believe that my aid will be required. I will do what I can."

"Very gracious, Your Majesty," Acair said, sounding very surprised.

"I wasn't talking to you," the king growled, "though I understand you're carrying one of my spells in your black heart." He huffed a bit. "Don't want it getting pilfered by some lesser mage before I can pull it from your chest myself."

"You've been talking to your grandson," Acair said.

"I have, and you may cease with those hushing motions you're making—eh, what, Dionadair?"

Léirsinn noticed only then that the king's guardsman had returned. He stepped up to the king's side and leaned in to have a quiet word with his liege. King Sìle frowned.

"I believe you would be wise to attend to your affairs here quickly and be on your way. I'll remain long enough to keep your lady company whilst you do what you must."

"'Tis beyond what I could ask, Your Majesty," Acair said, "but perhaps you might want to reconsider a safer locale—"

"Spare me your concern," the king said shortly. "There is little left in this world that leaves me pacing the floor at night, though I understand from my good friend Uachdaran that such is not the case for him. I also understand you're responsible for that, so I won't stand in your way of fixing it. Dionadair, Rùnach told me this little fiend cannot use his magic, so go with him and aid him with what he needs."

"As you will, my liege."

Léirsinn watched Acair walk off with the king's captain and reminded herself, as the silence grew uncomfortably long, that she wasn't unaccustomed to important lords and their ilk. Then again, the lords her uncle entertained weren't all that important and they definitely didn't simply drop their crowns into a place of invisibility, then mutter threats under their breaths in languages that sounded like running water.

"That is an interesting charm you wear."

Léirsinn looked at the king in surprise, then put her hand over the dragon charm Mistress Cailleach had given her. It occurred to her then that it was lying atop her cloak, visible, even though she usually kept it tucked away against her skin. Perhaps it, like her magic, had recognized someone it had an affinity with.

"I know the man who forged it," the king continued. "I believe he tinkers with such trifles whilst waiting for his horseshoes to cool."

"Does he?" she asked, beginning to understand why Acair's mother was forever reaching for a notebook. She suspected she might come close to filling one with just the appalling things she'd heard over the past few weeks. "Is he a farrier, then?"

"A very fine one," the king said, nodding. "Should you and I meet again in the future, I'll arrange an introduction. I believe you two would have much to discuss."

"Thank you, Your Majesty," she said, feeling a bit unbalanced by his generosity. "A happy coincidence to meet when I have this and you know its maker."

"Ah, coincidence," the king said. "I'm not much of a believer in it, gel." He folded his arms over his chest and nodded. "Take the man who made your charm, for instance. A very famous blacksmith in his day, but with a love for horses that saw him venturing to other places outside his own forge to shoe kingly steeds. Who's to say that one night whilst fashioning that, he envisioned an equally horse-mad lass who might need a bit of fiery courage to put up with her truly disreputable companion?"

Normally she would have said it sounded like absolute rubbish, but she'd seen so many unbelievable things over the past several weeks that even that didn't sound unreasonable.

"Miraculous," she agreed.

"Also miraculous is the fact that the fiendish bastard you're keeping company with is pursuing a different sort of path at the moment," the king said with a snort, "unlike his previous one which is littered with monarchs and their ilk knocking their knees together in fear."

"I'm assuming Your Majesty doesn't find himself amongst that group," she said with a smile.

"Absolutely not," Sìle said. "That isn't to say that I'm not well aware of your questionable friend's having tip-toed through my garden at least once. He's fortunate I didn't catch him at it."

She clasped her hands in front of her and decided that when it came to Acair of Ceangail's illicit activities, silence was her best choice.

The king shot her a look. "Discreet, are you? He'll appreciate that, I'm sure." He shook his head. "I don't want to credit him with more than he deserves, but he is at least attempting to undo what he did to vex the king of Durial. As for anything else, who knows?"

"He saved my life," she offered.

The king tilted his head. "Did he, now. How?"

"He helped me escape my uncle who wanted to slay me," she said. "He also rescued a horse I loved from that Droch person in Beinn òrainn."

The king frowned. "These acts of goodness are unsettling coming from him, I'll admit."

She nodded, though she didn't agree. Then again, given the king's relationship with Acair's sire, she decided that trying to convince him that Acair might not be as terrible as his father could likely go safely unattempted.

"I've been visiting my grandson and his bride in the north," the king said suddenly, as if they'd been talking about nothing else, "admiring the tapestry of the world and the players involved, then paused here to stretch my legs. There's a matter of chance for you."

"How long have you been waiting, if I might ask?"

He shot her a disgruntled look. "Long enough to think I need to have a chat with your mount about the virtues of haste." He shook his head. "I don't like to involve myself in the matters of the world, to the surprise of many no doubt, but I was told someone was hunting you and that you might require aid. I'll keep that mage occupied long enough for you and Fionne's wretched offspring to find somewhere safe to hide. If such a place exists for him, that is."

She wished she'd had posh manners to put on, but the best she could do was her most polite smile. "Thank you, Your Majesty. I didn't realize there were so many good people in the world."

"I think you might be surprised, gel, though even the good ones aren't going to be too fond of your lad who is now coming our way." He frowned at Acair. "Finished?"

"Thank you, Your Majesty," Acair said gravely. "You have allowed me to see to a task I don't think I could have managed otherwise."

The king grunted. "I'm under no illusions about your ability to make trouble, but you're welcome just the same. Off you go, the both of you, and save the world. I'll see to him who vexes you if he strolls by."

Acair looked at him seriously. "Do you know who it is?"

The king drew himself up. "Do you honestly believe that I

would bother myself over some self-important, unimpressive worker of lesser magic?"

"Then you do know him."

The king shook his head. "Vermin are all the same," he said. "Not worth the trouble to turn over the rock to see what's underneath. I'll simply keep an eye out for whatever crawls after you. I'll also provide you with half an hour's head start. 'Tis the least I can do for this poor girl who I hear gave so much to keep your sorry self alive."

Acair took a deep breath, then made the king a low bow. "My gratitude, Your Majesty."

"I did it for her, whelp."

"I know, Your Majesty."

Léirsinn found herself shaking hands with the king in a friendly fashion, then forced herself not to be thoroughly distracted by the handful of elvish guardsmen she hadn't seen clearly before. They were without a doubt the most beautiful creatures she had ever seen.

"I have elven blood too, you know," Acair murmured in her ear.

She would have given him a bit of a shove, but that would have taken time away from looking at the king's guards. She managed to stumble off and skirt the edge of the clearing, but that was perhaps only because Acair had taken her by the hand and tugged. She could hear Sianach trotting along behind them, wearing some sort of four-footed shape she didn't bother to identify. At least they wouldn't be making the rest of their journey on foot.

Acair paused on the edge of an outcropping of rock overlooking a large waterfall. There was a bridge there, gleaming dully in the gloom, but she didn't think attempting the path down to it was anything she wanted to do in the dark.

"Did you do what you needed to?" she asked.

He shot her a quick smile. "For the most part."

She tried to dredge up a stern look but feared she had failed. "You are absolutely incorrigible."

"And I paid a steep price to the nymph who guards that bridge.

Tonight cost me a necklace of my grandmother's that seemed to be clamoring for an adventure when I found it in her solar several months ago."

"I'm not at all curious whether or not it was given to you fairly."

"Fairly fairly," he said. "It fair leapt into my pocket as I passed through her solar, but if it eases you, she's the one who shoved it there. I'm guessing she trusted I would find someone else appropriate to annoy with it."

"How so?"

"I understand at certain times of the year, it sings an off-key Durialian drinking song. I would suspect the gem was hewn out of Uachdaran's mines without his permission and he enspelled it as it was being helped across the border in some granny's purse."

She shook her head. "I'm beginning to understand where you get your bad habits."

"My grandmother is always up for the odd, ribald jest at others' expense," he agreed. "The larger the crown—or the arrogance of the lad or lass wearing that crown—the better. In this case, that necklace was very useful. I thought it best the guardian of the waters be too distracted to notice I hadn't kicked all five rocks back into their previous spots."

"Three, then?"

"I'm offended."

"Four, because you're on your best behavior."

He smiled and whistled softly for his horse.

❊ ❊ ❊

She couldn't say she would ever travel comfortably on the back of a flying beast of any sort, but she couldn't argue with the view.

Acair patted her hands, snugly encased as they were in the gloves that King Uachdaran had so kindly gifted her, then pointed over to the right. She looked over Sianach's scaly dragon wing, expecting to see . . . well, she wasn't sure what she'd expected. Not what she was looking at, surely.

An entire day had passed and the sun had long since begun its descent through the western sky, but there was more than enough light for her to see clearly what was below them. Acair's horse-turned-dragon skimmed over a faint breeze coming ashore which gave her the chance to view the coast in all its glory.

Directly beneath them was a crescent-shaped bay complete with perfect sand and crystal bluish-green water. Sianach swooped toward it, then turned abruptly, giving her full view of the rugged coast that lay to the north. Past a certain distance up that coastline, she could see nothing but open sea.

Sianach dove down toward the earth with an unseemly haste that should have left her worried that they'd finally been caught, but she suspected he was simply in a hurry to go off and look for supper. He landed a decent tromp away from the beach but only twenty paces away from a house. She slid off his back, waited a moment or two until her legs had recovered from hours in the saddle, then turned to gape at the building there.

The entire front of it was made of nothing but glass. She had the feeling that being inside would only be different from standing outside on the shore because of the protection from the elements. Sturdy wooden beams separated the enormous sheets of glass from each other and held up a heavy, beamed roof. She suspected the entirety of her uncle's barn might fit inside what she could see from where she stood.

Fuadain of Sàraichte would have ground his teeth to powder with jealousy over it.

She looked at Acair to find him watching her with perhaps the most guarded expression she had ever seen him wear.

"Is this yours?" she asked.

He nodded. "Like it?"

"I've never seen anything so beautiful in my life," she said honestly.

He smiled slightly, then walked around Sianach's smoking nostrils to put his arms around her.

"Now, don't fall to pieces on me and burn the damned place down with one of your maudlin displays," he warned.

"You are an ass."

"I hear that more often than you might imagine." He sighed deeply. "'Tis just a pile of wood and stone, but rather handsome just the same, I suppose."

She turned her head and rested her cheek against his shoulder so she could better look at what he'd created. She wasn't surprised, actually. It was Acair after all and he could certainly trot out very fine manners when they were called for. That his home should be so lovely was perhaps nothing unexpected.

"I never bring anyone here," he said quietly.

"I can understand why," she said. "It would utterly ruin your reputation for murder, mischief and what is the third?"

"Mayhem," he said dryly. "You haven't seen the condition of the kitchens, so don't speak too soon. I'm very rarely home, so the provisions might be a bit sparse."

She pulled away and looked at him. "Why?"

He looked profoundly uncomfortable. "I'm not sure," he hedged. "A poorly stocked wine cellar, probably."

"Too much peace and quiet, more than likely. Who knows where that might lead."

"Ye gads, woman," he said faintly, "have a care for my poor self. I refuse to admit to anything, though the thought of depriving the world of my sparkling wit and flawless manners does leave me feeling slightly hollow inside. So many fine suppers, so little time to attend them all."

She shook her head in disgust, then waited. He seemed to be in no hurry to go inside, which she found less comforting than alarming.

"What is it?" she asked uneasily. "Lose your key to the front door?"

"Well, that's the thing," he said slowly. "There's a spell."

She wondered why she hadn't realized what that faint shimmer of something over his home had been. It could have been mistaken for a fine evening mist, but once she realized what she was looking at, she could see that it was anything but.

"It lets me sleep at night," he said. "Protection, avoiding death, that sort of thing."

And, was almost out of her mouth before she realized what he was getting at.

"And you can't undo it now—wait, nay," she said, holding up her hand. "Knowing you, the spell will allow you through with only yourself as the key, but no one else. Is that it?"

"Aren't you like a duck to water with all matters magical," he said.

She took a deep breath. "That's fine. You go and I'll find somewhere to hide."

He looked at her in surprise. "Of course you won't. Either we both go, or neither does. I think you can use your spell of containment to terrific reviews. Let's try it on our wee friend here and see how it goes."

"And if I fail—"

"You won't. Take your spell out, wrap it around that lad there, and I'll get us through whilst it's busy trying to free itself."

"Sianach, as well."

He blew his hair out of his eyes. "Aye, damn him. I'll pull all three of us through, then we'll go see if there are any apples left in the bin."

She knew she should have been flexing her fingers and preparing to trot out the second of the two spells she knew, but all she could do was stand there like a terrified colt and shake. Acair closed his eyes briefly and pulled her back into his arms.

"You are unnerved," he said, "and you have reason for it. The first time I had to remove that damned Falaire from his stall, I felt the same way."

"This isn't the same thing at all."

"You have no idea how unnerved I was. No magic and that enormous maw reaching for my arse? Terrifying. Now, go ahead and do your worst. I'll see to our other business here."

She nodded, though the icy cold running through her was even less pleasant than the usual fever her magic seemed to carry with it. She put her shoulders back and looked at Acair's surly companion.

"You're going to stay here," she said sternly. "I don't care what someone has instructed you to do."

The spell glared at her belligerently, but she expected nothing less.

She looked up at Acair. "Please don't die."

He looked as if she'd just kneed him in the gut. "Stop that," he said hoarsely. "Any more of those maudlin sentiments and you'll destroy not only my house but my poor self with your magical stylings."

She couldn't argue with that, but trying to remain calm was more difficult than she wanted to admit. She imagined they would have perhaps the space of a single heartbeat to leap to safety before that spell of death fell on him and slew him, never mind how well her own attempt at containing it might work. She stood where Acair advised her to, assuming it would be but a single step through to safety, then she looked at his spell.

She resisted the urge to cross her fingers, then simply repeated the words the stable lad had given her. At the same moment, she heard Acair say something that she assumed was the key to opening the shield over his house.

She realized abruptly that no matter how well her spell of containment worked on grain, it didn't have quite the same effect on that dreadful spell there. The beast lunged for Acair, its shadowy hands stretching out toward him—

She stepped in front of him and heard something snap. Someone made a noise of pain. She didn't realize until she found herself on the ground, half sprawled over a black mage who was still breathing, thankfully, that the person crying out had been her.

She sat up and looked down.

Her forearm was bent in a way it shouldn't have been.

"Don't move."

Acair's voice sounded very far away. She had some sympathy for Mansourah of Neroche and his broken arm. How he'd managed to ride all the way to Acair's mother's house to have her heal it for him, she surely didn't know. She felt something cold start at the base of her spine and work its way up toward her head.

She watched Acair take off his cloak, shredded as it had been into nothing but tatters, and make a sling out of it. He looked at her.

"You could faint, if you liked."

"You could knock me out, if you liked."

"I would never strike a woman. Here, hold on. We'll go inside, then see to fixing this."

She didn't want to ask him how. The pain in her arm was blinding, though she realized she was starting not to feel anything else. She looked at his spell of death and thought it might have looked slightly apologetic. She imagined she might want to have words with it later about perhaps selecting other victims.

Acair bent, lifted her carefully in his arms, then walked to the front door.

"Are we safe?" she managed, starting to feel herself slipping into darkness.

"Perfectly. Trust me."

She wondered if he would be gratified to know she did.

Nine

Acair had had many women swoon artfully into his arms, but never in his life had one done so thanks to a terribly broken arm she'd earned whilst about the business of saving his sorry arse. Truly, things had to change before he was fit company only for that collection of banished elves Ehrne of Ainneamh left weeping at his front gates.

"I can walk," Léirsinn said through gritted teeth.

"I'm certain you can," he said, "but allow me the pleasure of carrying you just this once."

He nudged the door open with his knee, almost going sprawling thanks to that damned Sianach bolting into the house in feline form, then carried Léirsinn inside. He shut the door behind them with his foot and strode toward the kitchen, not stopping to light any lamps. He knew his way around well enough in spite of how seldom he found himself there.

He was beginning to think that needed to change.

"And you're certain we're safe," she said faintly.

"Perfectly," he said, refraining from pointing out that she'd already asked. He honestly couldn't blame her for being worried, but he knew what sort of spell covered his home. "No one will enter. In fact, I'm not sure anyone but Soilléir knows I live here."

"No long lines of beautiful women waiting outside to beg for your attentions?"

"Not here," he said cheerfully. "You have the honor of being the first lass I've lured into my sumptuous web."

"I think I'm flattered," she said faintly.

He was floored, actually, but that had nothing to do with her and everything to do with the usual sort of company he kept. That he was more comfortable keeping that company far away from his own four walls than allowing them anywhere near them was telling.

He walked into the kitchen, pulled out a chair with his foot, then set Léirsinn down on it as gingerly as possible. If he almost lost her to senselessness when he helped her rest her arm on the table, he wasn't surprised. He'd seen several terrible things, but the angle at which her forearm was abruptly pointing left him feeling rather faint himself. Worse still was that he had no skill to set it on his own.

He quickly built a fire in the hearth, then sat down in the chair next to her and put his hand on her back, partly to soothe her but mostly to make certain she didn't pitch forward out of that chair and onto the floor. He was handy enough with his own bumps and bruises, but he couldn't remember the last time he'd used a spell of healing beyond slapping one on someone else so he could torment them a bit more.

The only thing that gave him any comfort at the moment was knowing exactly how impervious the spell laid over his house—

He froze. His spell was designed to keep out everything and everyone who wasn't him, unless he had specifically allowed them inside it.

What might that mean for that damned spell of death?

"I'm going to go fetch you something to drink," he said, which he would just as soon as he'd engaged in a little experiment that might or might not leave him dead. "Don't scamper off quite yet."

She only groaned and cursed him. He left her to it and made

for his front door at something close to a run. He wrenched it open, then was somewhat relieved to find there was nothing waiting for him there save that spell of death caught up in the web of protection that lay over his house like a clear dome.

He didn't think; he simply held out his hand and made a ball of werelight—from Fadaire, as it happened, in honor of Rùnach. He would have permanently changed it into a ball of quartz and set it aside to be later tossed with enthusiasm at Soilléir of Cothromaiche's head, but alas, one made do with less when one's catalog of enchantments was missing a few critical entries.

That terrible spell of death shrieked as if it had been stabbed with a thousand daggers.

Yet it remained trapped.

"Shut up!" he exclaimed. "Ye gads, man, my *father* can hear you in Shettlestoune!"

The spell fell silent. The look of malevolence it sent his way would have alarmed him had he been made of less stern stuff, but he was who he was and he had definitely seen worse. He waited, but still drew breath. That he was surprised by that said more than he liked about the state of his life at present.

Being able to use his magic however, even just inside his own home, was an unexpected turn of events.

He stepped back inside the house, slammed the door shut behind him, then lit the hallway lamps in a thoroughly magical fashion as he passed them. He rummaged about in his study for the most potent bottle of whisky he could find, then walked swiftly back to the kitchens.

Sianach was giving his feline self a wash in front of the fire, and Léirsinn was still sitting where he'd left her, her arm resting on the table at that unwholesome angle. He found a glass, poured her a generous amount of what he was sure would do her a world of good, then sat down next to her. She opened her eyes and took the glass he handed her, then stared at it as if she had no idea what to do with it.

"Drink," he suggested.

She nodded, then downed most of what he'd given her. He was half surprised it didn't come right back up, but the gel was no weak-kneed miss. She sat still for a moment, then looked at him.

"What now?" she said hoarsely.

"Well," he said, removing the remains of his cloak from around her arm with a silent spell, then cutting her sleeve away with the dagger shoved down his boot that he sharpened with an equally silent but different spell as he drew it, "let's have a look and see where we are."

She looked at him blearily. "You're using magic."

"To my surprise," he said, "aye, I am."

"And you're not dead."

"Not yet, darling," he said. "Apparently my ability to craft a spell of protection is as formidable as I always thought it to be, which is a fortuitous turn of events given my limits as a proper physick."

She shifted, then winced. "Can you set this?"

"Better than that," he assured her. "Whilst I should probably lay out all the possible magics we could use and let you choose the one you fancy the most, I think the ferocious growling of your tum and the fact that you just knocked back a substantial amount of my favorite libation might leave you a bit more short-tempered than usual. Let's settle for Fadaire."

She leaned her head back against the chair and closed her eyes. "I thought you never used prissy elven rot," she murmured.

"Clever you for reminding me of my own standards," he said, "but I have to admit it is a rather pretty magic. I'm quite sure King Sìle would approve of having it used on your fetching self, though I'm guessing he would be less thrilled about my being the one to use it. Let's see if we can't hear him roaring all the way from Uachdaran's most comfortable guest chamber."

"You talk a great deal," she whispered.

He shot her a quick smile he was certain she hadn't seen, then bent to his work. He did indeed know several spells of healing, though it probably said more about him than he wanted it to that he didn't use them all that often. He also knew more Fadaire than Sìle of Tòrr Dòrainn would have been happy with, but he would offer an apology for that later.

Or not, more than likely. He suspected he might have used up a millennia's worth of fawning words of regret in just the past half year alone.

He began the spell carefully, partly because he wasn't entirely sure how much of the pain the spell would take away whilst doing its goodly work, and partly because the magic was beautiful and brought an undeniable peace along with it. He had used it before for a thing or two and found it coming reluctantly to his call. Perhaps that had something to do with his bloodright to Ehrne of Ainneamh's magic, but he'd never cared to investigate that overmuch.

At the moment, however, Fadaire seemed to feel that having a few of its relatives lingering in the vicinity of his own black heart was reason enough to do his bidding. He spoke the final words and watched them fall softly onto Léirsinn's arm. He could hear the faint echo of her bones knitting together, then watched as that elvish business worked its way out through her flesh and up not only her arm, but his. He sighed in spite of himself. Whatever King Sìle's faults might have been, he was at least the guardian of a truly lovely magic.

He looked at Léirsinn to find her watching him with tears streaming down her face. He cleared his throat to cover his own emotion, only surprised that he didn't cough out a handful of Fadairian sparkles as a result. Never mind any of his previously complimentary thoughts, the damned stuff was going to be the death of him some day.

Léirsinn moved her fingers, then pulled her arm from under his hand and held it up. She looked at him in astonishment.

"That's healed," she said faintly.

"You stepped between me and death," he said easily. "Again, I wish you wouldn't."

"It has become a bad habit," she agreed. "And look at what it got you. Your shirt is in shreds as well."

"I'll go find something else." He rose. "Make as at home, of course."

He decided to ignore the expression she was wearing, as if the words simply didn't have any meaning for her.

Her uncle had many things to answer for.

He fetched something from the armoire in his bedchamber, then returned to the kitchens to find them empty. He ruthlessly ignored the panic that flashed through him and decided that the sooner he had food and a decent night's sleep, the better.

He found Léirsinn by his front door. She hadn't opened it; she was simply standing there, staring at it as if she couldn't decide whether she should stay or go. He moved to lean against the wall opposite her.

"Thinking of bolting?" he asked mildly.

She looked at him in surprise. "I wasn't, actually. I was just wondering why you had no lock. Then it occurred to me that you aren't afraid someone will come in because you have . . . you know."

"Magic?" he asked. "Aye. But it is what I do, isn't it?"

She didn't look particularly comforted. "What about the spell over your house?"

He considered what he might say to reassure her, but supposed none of it would matter. He knew what the spell was capable of because he'd made it so he might have one place in the wide, terrible world where he could sleep in peace. He also suspected that hearing about the inner workings of the magic involved would interest her as much as knowing the precise ingredients in Sianach's supper might interest him.

"Oh," he said with a shrug, "'tis just a little mixture of this and that. The frame is a spell I found lying about in, as irony would have it, Uachdaran of Léige's forge, but the rest is just pedestrian stuff I'm not sure I could bring to mind."

She only watched him, silently.

He suppressed the urge to shift uncomfortably. In the interest of continuing his slide into that warmish pile of virtue entitled Honesty, he had to admit he knew exactly what he'd put into the damned thing and could likely point out where each layer began and ended. What covered his house was elegant, direct, and fatal to anyone who thought to try to best it. It had occurred to him, no doubt during that same bit of thinking about how useful it would be to leave pieces of his power under various thrones and sofa cushions, that he might someday find himself with a need for a refuge. He'd constructed his spell with the caveat being that he would always be allowed through it with only his sweet self as the key.

Léirsinn's having managed to contain that mysterious spell of death long enough for him to pull her through his arguably best piece of work was something he was going to have to think through a bit more. That said piece of foul magic now found itself trapped in the web of his own spell was something he would face after he'd poured himself something very strong to drink.

"Let's just say it will hold," he said finally.

"Not even Soilléir could breach it?"

"Well, now isn't that an interesting question," he said, reaching for her hand, "and one for which the answer is far more entertaining than you might expect. I'll tell you all about it over supper."

"A lock first?"

He realized quite suddenly that she was afraid. Hard on the heels of that came a terrible suspicion that she might be afraid of *him*. Perhaps what she'd seen in Uachdaran's cavernous chamber had . . . well, he should have insisted that she leave.

He hadn't, though, and there was nothing to be done but press on. He stood there for a moment or two, finding himself with a new appreciation for her ability to approach any horse no matter how skittish and leave it not bolting the other way. He carefully took a step closer to her and held out his hand toward her.

"Fadaire can be a bit of a bother sometimes," he said casually. "My half-brother Rùnach healed me with a piece of it, as you know, and I vow I've been given to all sorts of uncharacteristic displays ever since. Tears, maudlin sentiments, the overwhelming desire to write Nerochian questing poetry and bore everyone in the vicinity with my droning readings of the same."

She put her hand in his, which he supposed was promising.

"I suppress it all, stellar soul that I am," he continued, "simply because my overarching purpose in life is, as you know, to make the world a better place. Now, let me go fetch our gear, then we'll find something hopefully edible and sleep in peace. If I use any magic, I'll do it aloud so you might be properly dazzled by my mighty skill."

She stopped him. "Must you go outside?"

He decided at that moment that perhaps she was less afraid of him than she was *for* him.

That was almost worse, actually.

"I promise you that I will return," he said seriously. "Here, stand at the door and watch."

She looked none-too-happy about the idea, but she released him and nodded just the same.

He stepped outside and walked down the path to collect their packs. He ignored the death-dispensing spell suspended in his very useful and businesslike piece of protective magic, then scanned the path to the shore, looking for mages who wanted him dead. He saw nothing, but that was somehow not all that reassuring.

He walked back inside his house, shut the door firmly, then wove a simple spell of imperviousness over it. He left a delicate tassel hanging from the doorknob, then looked at Léirsinn.

"If you feel the need for fresh air, just give that a tug and off you go. Perhaps you heard your name mentioned amongst those fine words which means that you'll be able to come back inside, no pulley needed."

"And no one else can?" she asked, looking rather less comfortable than he would have hoped. "Come inside, that is."

He slung their packs over his shoulder, then reached for her hand. "No one," he assured her. "Well, save a master of epicurial delights who comes to stay from time to time, but even he would need to knock thanks to that new lock."

"You have a cook," she said in disbelief.

"Occasionally," he said. "You might be interested to know that offering him a position with my vast and impressive entourage almost started a war, but to pacify the short-tempered monarch I stole him from I've arranged a sort of share-and-share-alike bargain. Sadly, I've been off groveling so often over the past few months that I felt it only fair to release the man to appease the monarchial palate until called for again."

"Good of you."

"I thought so," he agreed. "He does keep up with the larder just the same, so there might be bits of dried fruits and cured meats with perhaps even a hastily scrawled recipe or two lurking there. If he's been particularly diligent, we might find things still resting comfortably in the garden."

He continued talking about things he was fairly certain might even have caused the current monarch of Gairn, a man notorious for his complicated culinary stylings, to indulge in a yawn, dropped their gear just inside his study, then carried on with her to the kitchen. He saw her settled near the fire and made his way out the back door to the garden.

He looked at the lovely, orderly collection of rows and boxes and hedges and acknowledged that even though he visited on occasion, he had never once pulled anything out of that ground to eat.

Carrots and potatoes were what he needed, though, so he used a quick spell of revealing to encourage his garden to cough up the same. Veg leapt out of the soil and arranged itself in a tidy heap. He collected everything, then looked over his shoulder to find Léirsinn standing on the landing there. He would have asked her if anything else sounded appealing, but realized that she wasn't watching him.

She was looking beyond him to the shadows under the trees.

He knew what she was seeing without having to look himself. *Bloody hell.* He hadn't expected anything less, which should have left him insisting that Léirsinn remain inside. More the fool was he that he hadn't taken his own inklings to heart. He took a quick tour of the spell laid over his house and the surrounding environs, but found it undisturbed.

He strode back up the pair of steps leading to his house, ushered Léirsinn inside, then shut the back kitchen door. If he dropped a spell over it that would have taken a score of dwarvish miners a year with both axe and spell to chip through, he didn't imagine anyone would blame him.

He subsequently cleaned, chopped, and boiled his findings in the usual fashion, shooing Léirsinn back to the fire after she dropped his knife and almost impaled his foot with it. He rummaged through the larder and found cheese, apples, and a very nice bottle of wine. That, he supposed, was going to be the best he could manage.

He suspected his companion wouldn't taste any of it.

He cleared off the table after supper, then decided there was nothing to do that couldn't wait until the morning. He banked his fire in the normal way, gathered Léirsinn up with her gear, then showed her to his very best guestchamber.

"Oh," she said, "this is much too . . . " She stared at the chamber for a moment or two, then nodded and looked at him. "Thank you."

"Of course," he said, ignoring the crack in her voice. "I'm only a pair of doors down the way if you need me."

She nodded.

He refrained from begging her not to run off during the night because self-control was, as King Uachdaran had so wisely pointed out recently, one of his most desirable virtues.

He made sure she knew the way to a different guest chamber for all the necessary ablutions, then waited until she'd shut the door in his face before he walked off to his private study.

It was a lovely, snug spot connected to the library by means of a graceful set of heavy wooden doors which he currently closed because there were times he preferred to sit in a smaller room to be alone with his thoughts. If those thoughts had previously concerned, as his mother would have said, merely general naughtiness with only the occasional venturing to heights of true mischief, perhaps 'twas best he just keep that to himself.

He built a fire with his own two hands for the sport of it, then decided nothing was going to make his head pound any worse than it was already so there was no reason not to pour himself a hearty glass of brandy. He did, then sat down with a deep sigh.

He waited for deep thoughts to come, but found he was only equal to sitting and staring into the fire. The world still turned and shadows were still being made, though apparently not everywhere, and he would need to determine why. A mage that spoke in shards of metal was standing outside his house, watching silently, for reasons that could certainly have been explained by the usual reasons mages watched him, but somehow that answer seemed a bit too convenient.

Finally, his grandmother had handed him a mysterious map that seemingly led right to where he was sitting, which he suspected was not an accident.

He sat with those thoughts until thinking them any longer undid any relief his drink had offered him. He rose, saw to putting the house to bed for the night, then went to the front door and opened it. Seeing that nothing had changed with that blasted spell of death was reassuring, though he caught himself on the verge of something that felt a bit more like concern and a great deal less like fury over its existence.

He drew back inside his house, shut the door, then resealed the lock before he completely lost any sense of himself.

He unapologetically exchanged the hallway's werelight for something a bit paler and dreamier made from Fadaire. If Léirsinn awoke, assuming she managed to fall asleep at all, she might be soothed by it. At the very least, she wouldn't run into anything.

He retired, but found that in spite of the exquisite surroundings and the peace in which to enjoy them, he was uncomfortable. Obviously his guest was suffering from the same thing. He might not have heard her pass by his bedchamber if he hadn't been expecting the same. Credit where it was due, though: the woman could walk almost silently. He didn't want to think about why she'd mastered that skill, though perhaps ponies were lighter sleepers than he supposed.

He was grateful for an armoire full of comfortable gentlemen's nighttime attire. He rolled out of bed, gathered up a thing or two that a shivering stable lass might find to her liking, then made his way soundlessly to his study.

Léirsinn was sitting huddled on the floor in front of the hearth where she had added only a single, rather inadequate piece of wood. Acair draped a luxurious silk robe about her shoulders, set the rest of his burdens down on a chair, and brought the fire back to life in a perfectly pedestrian fashion. He then went to fetch a pallet and more blankets. Perhaps all she needed to feel safe was a bit of undemanding company.

He walked back into his study to find that whilst she had shifted to one side of the hearth, she was still sitting on the floor and looking profoundly uncomfortable. He ignored how the sight of that gave him pains in the vicinity of his slightly broken heart and decided deeds not words were what was required.

He made a rough bed out of admittedly very fine materials, stretched out, then looked at her.

"Join me?"

"Lecher."

He smiled. "Not tonight, I fear. You'll have to hold out hope for better things in the future."

She rolled her eyes, but she abandoned her post next to the fire and lay down next to him. He didn't argue with her when she turned away to face the fire. He waited until she was settled before he put his arm around her and laced his fingers with hers. Icy still, which led him to suspect her trembles were less from the chill than they were from other things.

"Did you conjure all this up?" she asked, finally.

"Fetched it from a closet, rather. Utterly unmagical geese gave their all, I'm sure."

She was silent for so long, he thought she'd finally fallen asleep.

"I will protect you," she said very quietly. "I just need to catch my breath first."

He found absolutely nothing in his vast repertoire of off-hand remarks that was equal to responding to that. His eyes burned terribly, but perhaps he couldn't be blamed for it. He leaned up on his elbow and kissed her cheek, trying not to think about how many times in his very long life he had gone to sleep next to a woman he had wept over not once but twice. The number he would likely eventually have to give his mother for her history was zero.

"You're a bit of a weeper, aren't you?"

He smiled. "What an outrageously insulting thing to say."

"I'm going to wake up with a cold thanks to you."

He laid back down, put his arm around her again, and thought she might be right.

"Acair?"

"Hmmm?"

"What about your spell?" She paused. "You said only Soilléir could get through it?"

"Ah, I did promise you that tale, didn't I?" Perhaps he might bore her to sleep. Given the identity of the essence-changing protagonist in the promised escapade, that was entirely possible.

"You did."

He propped himself up on his elbow and tucked her hair behind her ear. "Well, as you might imagine, I am very fond of a decent night's repose followed by drinkable coffee that bears no resemblance to the sludge my mother makes."

She looked over her shoulder and smiled faintly. "It was terrible."

"I think she does it on purpose to discourage lengthy stays by her houseguests, but that's just my theory. As for *my* hospitality, let's just say that I'm extremely choosey about who comes inside my front gates. Not even my sire could break that spell."

She looked as if she very much hoped that might be true. "But Prince Soilléir?"

"Not even he could, though I imagine he wouldn't bother to try." He paused. "Let me rephrase that. Whilst he absolutely could not breach my spell in its current state, he could change it into something else entirely using one of those damned spells he's so stingy with and definitely walk right through it. The thing is, making that change to my spell would take a mighty piece of magic on his part. He would have to hope he had the strength left afterward to fight off what I would do to him for his cheek."

"All magic comes at a price," she said slowly.

"As you know," he agreed.

"Do you pay anything?"

"The better question is, would I admit it if I did? But because you've asked, I'll give you the easy answer which is that it depends. Little magics? Nay. I've been using them for so long that they don't trouble me. Too much Fadaire—and I know, I said I rarely used it which I'm finding is less accurate than I would like—tends to give me a headache in the same way too much desert might."

"I can only imagine," she said.

"I'm certain you can. As for other things?" He shrugged as best he could. "Large pieces of magic leave me flattened for a few days, but nothing worse than that. So to answer your original question, aye, there is a price to be paid and not even I manage to escape it. As far as the other goes, I'm guessing Soilléir can do any number of things without needing even the briefest of naps. That comes from the power that is his bloodright, though I would assume that there are things that would tax even the limits of that."

"Has he ever had a go at your spell?"

"Now, *this* is a very amusing little tale," he said. "Why don't you come a bit closer and I'll do it justice."

She pursed her lips. "I'm close enough, thank you just the same, and I refuse to be distracted."

He wished he could say the same thing, poor hopelessly lost fool that he was. He decided it was nothing short of exceptional discretion that kept him from commenting that she had no doubt turned over so she could admire him more easily. He rested his head on his fist and put his hand over hers. If he made a point of not inquiring about whether or not her trembles were from his charming self instead of fear, well, he was a gentleman. Her fingers that she intertwined with his were still very cold, which he supposed was answer enough.

"So, to continue," he said, pulling himself away from things he couldn't solve at the moment, "I was off one day investigating things that intrigued me when Prince Soilléir caught me lifting up the corner of his grandfather's ermine-trimmed robe — magically speaking — just to see what sorts of things might tempt an enterprising lad such as myself. He did me the great courtesy of accompanying me back to my humble abode where I nipped inside my own border and then offered a pointed remark or two about either his grooming or his dress — the details escape me."

"I imagine they don't," she said dryly.

He smiled briefly. "Perhaps not. Suffice it to say, he indulged in a little performance of what he can do, because he's an impossible braggart when he thinks no one important is watching. Properly cowed, I promised never to darken his grandfather's back stoop again. He very kindly repaired the hole he'd put in my spell, then planted in front of it a very nasty patch of nettles which I'm quite sure will outlive me by several centuries. I'll show you the spot in the daytime, if you like. But if it eases you any, there isn't another soul walking the Nine Kingdoms with his power. I suppose we should all be grateful he's a decent soul, all his catastrophically boring ruminations about virtuous living aside, or we would be doomed."

"I can see why you want his spells."

"You might also understand why he won't give them to me."

"To be honest," she said quietly, "I'm not sure I do."

He found that all he could do was stare at her, mute.

She leaned up and kissed his cheek. "Thank you for the story."

"I don't know how else to help you," he said before he thought better of it.

"That you're trying is breaking my heart a little."

"I'm having a bit of heartburn over the notion myself," he said, finding the lie tripping off his tongue like a Diarmailtian school lad who'd been let off early for his summer holiday. "Cad that I am, of course. Give me a moment to dig deeper for some spellish nastiness. That might suit you better."

She smiled, then rolled over. "Tomorrow."

He wasn't sure whether to laugh or weep. He was so damned turned around in so many ways that he honestly had no idea where to begin in recapturing the vile, ruthless mage he'd been not a month earlier.

He put his head down and decided that if he survived the night in any fashion, it would be a bloody miracle. There were, of course, several people he could blame for his current straits.

First on the list was his own mother who had given him a name and a suggestion to raid her mother's private books which had led to his grandmother's having given him a map that had led him to his own home. Uachdaran of Léige had furthered the misery by dropping a grandson with a terrible spell in his path, likely not simply to entertain him. And then there was the most egregious meddler of all, Soilléir of Cothromaiche, who had practically handed him the key to his grandfather's library and invited him to come in and nose about in the man's books.

If he'd been on his own, his extensive repertoire of terrible spells at his fingertips and no pressing supper plans on his calendar, he would have been skipping merrily off to wreak a bit of well-executed havoc.

Instead, he was, at least outside his own gates, as defenseless as a prince of Neroche in a gilded ballroom, he was continually being reduced to tears by the courage of a spectacular horsewoman, and he was endlessly being hounded by a mage who seemed to think that lurking in the shadows and attempting to look intimidating was going to convince the rest of the world he possessed any power at all.

"You think too loudly," Léirsinn murmured.

"Do I?"

"You do," she said. "Go to sleep, darling."

He smiled, closed his eyes, and gave himself up for lost.

Ten

Léirsinn stood on the threshold of an unrepentant black mage's lair and felt as if she'd wandered into a dream.

She had seen the sea before, of course, having lived within a decent walk's distance of it, but she had never seen such a perfect stretch of it. The pale-hued sand gave way to a glorious blue-green water that she had to admit looked a bit like Acair of Ceangail's equally lovely eyes. She could hardly believe he possessed a place so beautiful yet so rarely stayed there.

He was a mystery, that lad.

She pulled the shawl he had given her earlier more closely around herself, leaned against the doorframe, and simply breathed in the healing breeze. It was so perfectly normal, she never would have guessed in whose doorway she stood. She'd woken that morning to find him bringing the fire back to life through ordinary means. She'd told him that he hadn't needed to, but he'd shrugged and admitted that he rarely used magic on those even rarer occasions when he was home. He hadn't volunteered a reason for that and she hadn't asked him.

Perhaps he too needed moments where he was simply a man going about his daily affairs without being overwhelmed by the impossible things that made up the rest of his life.

Those impossible things seemed to have become a part of her world as well, though, whether she wanted them to or not. Kings, elves, magic, mages chasing after Acair to slay him. She would have said she felt completely out of her depth, but standing there in the doorway of a house that overlooked the sea, she realized that wasn't what she was feeling at all.

She felt . . . safe.

She couldn't remember a time during the past score of years when she'd felt anything like it.

She suspected it might not last as long as she would like, but she was going to enjoy it while it did. Who knew that perhaps she wouldn't find herself a spot like what she'd seen up the coast from the vantage point of Sianach's back the day before. A few more coins, a bit of luck, and perhaps a man who had too much land and needed a buyer for some of it.

She wondered where she might find one of those.

She continued to stand there until even her luxurious wrap became no match for the chill. She stepped back inside, then closed the door and wondered what she was meant to do with the tassel hanging there. She had pulled on it to release the spell and open the door, but she hadn't gone far enough outside for it to close behind her. She finally stepped away from it only to hear a spell click as surely as if it had been a proper lock.

She gave the damned thing another tug, and the spell unlocked itself just as it had before.

Perhaps Acair was right and magic did have its uses. She suppressed a shiver just the same, then turned and walked slowly back through his house.

She stopped on the threshold of his library. The doors had been pushed open and lights set all about the room at exactly the right height. A fire burned in the hearth with two inviting chairs set to either side. The walls were lined with bookshelves containing more books than she'd ever seen in the whole of her life. A table was set in front of windows on one wall, placed in just the proper spot for making use of sunshine or starlight. There were other things as well: sideboards, other chairs for reading, the odd stool standing ready to provide that extra height to reach things just beyond one's fingertips.

It was a place created by a man who loved better things than counting his piles of gold.

The man who obviously loved books and comfort, however, looked as if he might not care about either at the moment. He was standing with his hands on his table, swearing, and looking as if he'd spent a good part of the morning dragging his hands through his hair.

She wondered if she should clear her throat to announce her presence and avoid being impaled by the pencil he was holding as if he intended to slay someone with it. He glanced at her, then straightened.

"Forgive me," he said. "I didn't see you."

She smiled. "All that apologizing is going to ruin you for polite company."

"I fear you might be right." He tossed his pencil onto the table, looked at her, then froze. "What's wrong?"

She walked into the middle of that beautiful room full of comfortable things and stopped, mostly because she had no idea where to start in describing where her thoughts were leading her. She could have said that she worried her grandfather would be slain before they could get to him. She also could have said that she'd spent the night dreaming about the mage who stood just behind the edges of Acair's spell, waiting for them, and she feared there was no way to best him.

Or she could have admitted the worst thing of all which was that no matter how long she looked at the sea, she couldn't stop wondering how she was going to spend the rest of her life with magic she had most certainly asked for but wasn't sure she could live with running through her veins.

She rubbed her arms suddenly. "When will your fire heat up?"

"Almost immediately after you drink that brandy I've set on the mantel to warm for you."

"I'm not sure I can," she said with a shudder. "I'm not sure how *you* drink it."

"So says the gel who tossed back all that whisky last evening with the enthusiasm of a Meithian princess trying to forget her last encounter with a prince of Neroche." He walked over to the hearth, fetched her the glass that was indeed sitting on his mantel, then brought it back and handed it to her. "You'll be warmer, at least."

She had a sip of something she wished she'd left alone, then gave him the rest. "Disgusting," she said hoarsely.

"Not nearly as awful as what King Uachdaran brews," he said, draining her glass and returning it to the sideboard. "Come and sit, darling. I'll put more wood on the fire for you."

She nodded, realizing then how accustomed to his very lovely manners she'd become. She sighed deeply, then went to perch on the edge of a chair drawn up to his library table. She looked at the papers spread out everywhere and noticed that atop them all was a map she hadn't seen before. She imagined he'd drawn it himself given that there were marks where she could remember having seen those terrible shadows. There were also Xs where she knew they'd encountered the mage following them, including the spot where she'd asked Soilléir to give her what currently ran through her veins like a fever.

She looked up to find Acair sitting around the corner from her, watching her with those pale, sea-green eyes of his that saw more than she wanted him to.

"I don't want to talk about it," she said, holding up her hand to hold him off.

He smiled briefly. "So many possibilities there."

She gestured toward the spot on his map where she'd lit half the forest alight, then realized that location was rife with possibilities as well. She cast about for anything else to discuss.

"I wonder if Mansourah is . . . ah—" Damnation, but that was no easier than anything else.

"Alive?" He sighed deeply. "As much as I love to mock him for his failings, I have to concede the lad is canny. For all we know, our common enemy was either too distracted or too stupid to hunt him down and finish him. I'm not looking forward to facing my sister if that isn't the case."

"She's very fond of you."

"Her husband will be much less so if I've lost his brother," he said grimly. "We'll go look for him once we've attended to this business—and that other thing you don't want to discuss."

She supposed that since she had seen him at his worst, he might as well see her at hers. She clasped her hands together and took a deep breath.

"I'm terrified," she admitted.

"There's no shame in that, love," he said quietly.

"But you aren't, are you?"

"Do you think I would admit it if I were?" He looked at her seriously. "He can undo it, you know. Soilléir, I mean."

She knew who he meant, but couldn't bring herself to say as much. "I thought you said the change back was never perfect."

"That's what he claims, but I think he lies more than he's willing to admit. He will undo what's been done, not only because he'll want you to be at peace but because he knows what I'll do to him otherwise."

She felt herself relax almost to the point she'd reached standing at his front door, looking at the sea. "Planning on engaging in that essence meddling of yours?"

"I will meddle until he begs me to stop," he muttered. He leaned forward and propped his elbows on the table. "The truth is, I would rather you not have to use anything. You have no idea how much it galls me to see you in this position because of me."

"It was my idea," she said, beginning to wish she'd continued on with her avoidance of the whole subject. She gestured to his map.

"What did you discover about your grandmother's map besides that list of places you wouldn't want to go?"

He rubbed his hands over his face, then shook his head. "Nothing interesting save perhaps wondering why my house figured so prominently on it. I finally decided that she covets my stash of port and doesn't want me to drink it all before she can lay her greedy hands on it."

She ran her fingers over places on his map that she recognized. The only thing that did for her was to put her forearm in front of her where it reminded her that she'd broken it terribly. She wasn't sure she would ever forget the sight of it bending where it hadn't been meant to.

Now, though, 'twas difficult not to simply stare at it. Though her flesh hadn't been torn by her bones, there was still a spot where it looked as if the magic might be lingering on her skin in one of the most beautiful rashes she had ever seen.

"Fadaire is a beautiful magic."

She looked up. "How do you know any of it?"

He gave her the same very small, mischievous smile she'd watched him attempt with his grandmother. Unlike Cruihniche of Fàs, however, she was anything but immune. She was rather thankful, all things considered, that she was sitting down.

"The better question is," he said, "did the king catch me pinching any of his spells? The answer is, nay, he did not, though I'll admit I ruthlessly took advantage of his having temporarily handed off his kingly topper to his eldest son for a bit whilst about the genteel work of recovering from some mighty piece of magic or other. That son, Prince Làidir, is loyal, conscientious, and never saw me hopping over his father's proverbial garden fence to rummage about in the old rutabaga patch."

She could just imagine. "Did you know his daughter?"

"Princess Sarait?" he asked. "Only well enough to say that she was far too good for my sire. I'm not sure why she wed him, though I suppose he can be charming when he needs to be. More than one mage has succumbed to his chumminess over supper only to regret it before sunrise as he was sent on his way without either his pocket money or his magic."

She wished she could have dismissed it all, but unfortunately she knew better. "So, your father stole magic, and the mage you're looking for steals souls, but is it the same thing?"

He looked up from what he'd been absently sketching in the margins of his map. "What a thought," he said faintly. He looked off into nothing for a moment, then shook his head. "I wouldn't put one's power and one's soul into the same pot, so to speak, though in theory I suppose the end result is somewhat the same. I suppose the most we can be grateful for is that whilst my sire's spell is perfected, this mage's is not. Otherwise, as we've discussed before, we'd all be nothing but soulless husks."

She watched him continue to draw mythical beasts along the edge of his map and wondered how many of them came from his imagination and how many he'd actually seen. She wasn't sure she wanted to know.

"Your spell of death seems to have rounded up a few pieces of you." she offered. "Funny that your mother suggested the same thing, isn't it?"

"I'm not sure that's the word I would use, but aye, the whole thing is unnerving. I understand why she suggested it, but why is that damned thing trapped in the spell over my house when I'm able to walk through that same spell as if it weren't there?"

"Not enough of your soul in its possession?"

"Does that sound as daft to you as it does to me?"

"I might not be the best person to ask about anything to do with magic," she said honestly. "It all sounds daft to me."

He set his pencil aside and rubbed his hands together. "Answer me this, then: Why are we seeing so many spots in so many locales and none in others?"

"Because there's something there that he wants?"

"Agreed, but what? I've been looking at this damned map all morning and can't find a single pattern that isn't utter rubbish."

She decided that he reminded her of a feisty, frustrated stallion who had spent too many days locked in a stall. What he needed, she suspected, was to get out and run, though she supposed he wouldn't manage that. A distraction, though, wasn't unthinkable.

"Let's speak of something else," she suggested. "Tell me the difference between essence changing and your grandmother's spell. And remember that I think 'tis all foolishness."

He rubbed the spot between his eyes, looking as if it pained him. "The changing of an essence is permanent whilst her spells are more like a flirtation with a change. Not permanent, though for a time the results are eerily similar."

"Why have such a thing?" she asked.

"So you might pin a mage down and rifle through his pockets whilst he can only remain there, mute and furious?"

She laughed a little in spite of herself. "You're an awful man. Do you never work for your gold?"

"I'm offended," he said, sounding anything but. "I'll have you know that the funds for the glorious hovel you're sitting in came from a series of days full of honest labor. You might be surprised how much gold desperate monarchs are willing to pay for a finely crafted spell."

"Is that true?" she asked skeptically.

"I never lie, as you know. The spells I created for my royal clients were, if I might say so, absolutely spectacular, even if they may or may not have come with an expiry date."

She rolled her eyes and tried not to smile. "You're vile."

"But charming, which you have to admit. There were no complaints and several offers of more commerce should I decide to take up the pitchfork down the road, if you know what I'm getting at. 'Tis tempting, given the location of this luxurious perch, to add a bit to my empire."

"Where are we exactly?" she asked.

"The land was part of Wychweald, though I'm not sure that's where it originated," he said with a shrug. "There is a ruined shell of a hall up the way, so perhaps this belonged to that kingdom in times past. As to how I came by it, I went to King Stefan and bought it from him for an eye-watering price."

"In spells or gold?"

He looked at her knowingly. "Both, and clever you for considering that. I was perhaps more fastidious than I needed to be about this place, but the gold was earned fairly and from less unsavory things than I might have otherwise created."

She watched him as he spoke and saw him again how he'd appeared in the king of Neroche's garden, standing perfectly balanced between light and darkness. Perhaps he was not so much a mystery as a man full of profound contradictions.

The sunlight that filtered in from the window was pale from its winter's arc, but it suited him perfectly, that dark-haired, sea-green eyed man who no doubt had women fighting each other to land in his path the moment he walked into any ballroom. She understood. He'd been shoveling manure—badly—and swearing when she'd first seen him and she'd been tempted to put the back of her hand to her forehead and swoon artfully onto the closest bale of hay.

"Who are you?" she wondered.

"A vile black mage taking a breather from the usual business of wreaking havoc," he said wearily. "I will return to it with renewed vigor, purpose, and commitment the first chance I have."

"Where does saving my grandfather fit into all that?"

"Not yourself?"

She shrugged as casually as she could manage. "I can see to myself. I worry about him."

"I'll see to him as I promised," he said, "then the world had best brace for the onslaught of my wrath."

"As you will, Acair."

He didn't move. "That doesn't terrify you?"

"I'm not afraid of you."

He let out his breath slowly. "Not even after what you saw in Uachdaran's cellar?"

She wasn't sure what she could possibly say that would make any difference. He was who he was, as was she. What she thought she might possess was less a tolerance for difficult things and more an acceptance of things as they were, but perhaps that could remain unsaid.

She considered his map and looked at the coastline he'd drawn. The ruined castle was there, but also that little stretch of land that looked just big enough for what she hardly dared hope for. She reached out and traced her finger along it, finding herself unable to look at him.

She wondered, in a place where she almost couldn't allow herself to go, if there might be a small piece of unwanted land there where she might build a house with a barn. Nothing like the grand house she sat in presently, of course, but a modest abode with a pair of bedchambers for her and her grandfather. She had the money Mistress Cailleach was keeping for her, after all. Who was to say that in time she might not have enough to purchase it?

She couldn't look at him, but she rested her finger on that part of his map that indicated a spot north of his house.

"Will you let me buy a bit of this and build a barn there?" she asked carefully.

"That wasn't an answer."

"You already know the answer, I imagine." She looked at him, then. "So, will you?"

"Nay."

She had to simply wait for a bit until she thought she could speak. "I see."

"I will build you a barn, though," he said quietly. "You may fill it with as many ponies as you like."

"Of course," she said, hoping she sounded as if she weren't cursing herself for being disappointed that she might be nothing more than a stable hand to him. "You would need someone to manage the horses."

"I thought Doghail might be better suited to that, if you think he would be interested. I have other things in mind for you."

"Do you?" she asked, wishing she'd kept her bloody mouth shut to begin with. "I can't imagine what."

He looked at her steadily. "I told you in Uachdaran's lists how I feel."

"Oh," she said, though she was fairly certain there had been no sound behind the word. "I thought that was the last gasp of a man who thought he wasn't going to see dawn."

He shrugged. "The truth comes out at odd times."

If there was color creeping up her cheeks, she thought she might manage to blame it on the brandy. She watched him reach over and cover her hands with his. She looked at her arm that he had healed with a magic so beautiful she was still a bit blinded by it, then at his hands that had wielded that same magic.

"So," she said slowly, "you don't want me as a stable hand?"

He pulled away. She thought she might have said too much, then she realized he had gotten to his feet and come around the corner of the table. She found herself pulled to her feet and into his arms. He smiled briefly, then bent his head and kissed her.

Well, she would have been the first to admit she was not the best judge of the same, but in her opinion he was very good at several things, the business of romance included. She wasn't quite sure if she should feel faint or indulge in completely inappropriate laughter, but what she did know was that she was definitely out of her depth at present.

She managed to catch her breath eventually, though she wasn't unhappy to have help staying on her feet.

"Was that a proposal?" she managed. "Or just a substitute for a maudlin sentiment?"

"Perhaps a bit of both," he said.

She leaned up and kissed his cheek. "I'll leave you to decide and go make supper."

"Must you?"

She pulled away and glared at him, but her heart wasn't in it. "I am not so terrible a cook."

"Darling, you . . . " He shook his head. "You look over maps and *I'll* go forage for something edible." He started to walk away, then turned back around and caught her hand. He hesitated, then leaned forward and kissed her softly. "Don't bolt on me."

She shook her head. "I won't."

He looked at her for a moment or two, then nodded and walked out of the library.

She took a deep breath, then looked for a distraction before she found herself thinking about . . . things.

Doghail would have looked at her, laughed, then walked off, shaking his head. She thought she might rather have a bit of a lie-down, but if Acair caught her in a faint over a simple kiss, he would likely never let her forget it. Better to busy herself doing something more productive than swooning over a man.

Never mind that she thought she just might love that man in truth —

She forced herself to put one foot in front of the other and wander through his library. She wasn't sure if she wanted to know where he had come by all the books there — he was who he was, as he said. She was somehow not at all surprised to find things shelved in an organized fashion.

She stopped at one point and put her hands on a shelf, then decided that perhaps resting her forehead there might be an even better idea. She closed her eyes and let the silence of Acair's fire soothe her. Given that the flames in his mother's house had sung a song that had nagged at her almost unpleasantly for days, she appreciated the fact that Acair's fire was simply that. Perhaps he had built it that way to give her some peace.

She wouldn't have been surprised.

She opened her eyes and straightened, then had to look a second time at the books sitting on the shelf in front of her face. Her memories of her childhood were distressingly few and unfortunately faint, but there was something about the book in front of her nose that seemed familiar. The color of the spine perhaps. She imagined Acair wouldn't care if she had a look at it, so she reached up—

"Léirsinn, supper!"

She hesitated, her curiosity warring with her belly. She supposed books weren't going anywhere and supper might be, so she left the book where it was—half pulled out from its fellows—and imagined it would be there when she returned.

She wandered back to the kitchens, ridiculously comfortable slippers on her feet, and found Acair busily stirring something in a stew pot. He was frowning at it thoughtfully.

"Won't be long now," he said. "I hope we can choke it down."

It smelled better than anything she'd ever cooked, so she imagined she wouldn't be complaining. She collected things she thought might be useful, then arranged them on the table. She thought it looked complete, though admittedly her experience was limited to rare glimpses of her uncle's fancy dining chamber set for guests and even rarer trips to the pub.

Supper was, she found, very good indeed, though the company would have been worth much worse fare. She finished, then simply rested her chin on her fists and watched Acair sit back and swirl his wine in a beautifully cut glass goblet. The firelight sparkled against the facets in a way that reminded her she was definitely not having supper in a barn.

What was familiar, however, was the collection on the table that looked as if it had come from some pocket or other. She hadn't known a stable lad who hadn't continually maintained a collection of useful bits and bobs, so perhaps Acair wasn't all that different in that respect. She pushed aside her bowl and gathered his pile toward her. It sparkled right along with his wine glass, though she supposed that was the rune sporting his spell of death to reflect the firelight most beautifully. She reached out and began to idly sort everything.

"If you tell me you're deciding between nicked and earned, I will shout at you."

She smiled. "Of course you won't. I just find it interesting what lads consider valuable."

"You never know when a bit of string will turn the tide," he agreed.

She doubted that. His bounty consisted of several loose gems, a folded doily—

She looked at him in astonishment.

He shrugged. "There was one under a crock of butter in Uachdaran's kitchen. I flattered the most susceptible-looking kitchen maid for it."

"You're absolutely incorrigible."

"And my grandmother is absolutely terrifying. Facing Uachdaran's fury seemed a much more pleasant prospect than showing up to tea at her table without something to appease her."

She shook her head and turned back to the pile. The remaining items consisted of that golden wafer slathered with a self-casting spell of death and a stub of a pencil. He was his mother's son, certainly. She nudged the gems into piles by color, ignoring the fact that she'd done the same thing on the floor in front of his mother's fire very late one evening. If she hadn't, if he hadn't grumbled over the fact that Soilléir of Cothromaiche's aid seemed to be limited to doling out runes, she wouldn't have known to use that same rune to call for Soilléir's aid, and they certainly wouldn't be enjoying a hot fire and full stomachs at the moment.

"You're not afraid anyone will rob you?" she asked, looking at him.

"Me? Never. That said, I only carry a few things I value and tuck others in select spots." He paused, then shook his head. "I think I might regret having asked Odhran to keep that rune for me, though he wasn't without his own store of magic."

She sat back and looked at him. "Who slew him in truth, do you think? That mage in the glade?"

"I've wondered," he said slowly, "though I can't imagine why unless 'twas simply for spite. Though he certainly has the power to do so, his spells aren't terribly impressive."

"Didn't he force Mansourah back into his own shape?" She listened to the words come out of her mouth and didn't bother to marvel over them any longer. The descent into madness was complete.

"That isn't difficult," Acair said. "I've done it scores of times. Now, dear old Gran could do the same and keep a lad in a shape he didn't care for quite a bit longer than he liked, but, again, that's essence meddling for you." He nodded knowingly. "Makes you wonder whose pockets she's rifled through, doesn't it?"

She smiled in spite of herself, but couldn't bring herself to speculate. She picked up the golden disk and watched the way the firelight glinted off it, giving no indication of what terrible spell it contained.

"How many stalls for your ponies?"

She put his rune on the table and slid it across to him, then gathered her courage. "I couldn't let you build me a barn," she said, though those words cost her quite a bit. "I have a little money saved with Mistress Cailleach, though."

"I see," he said slowly. He twisted his rune of death over his knuckles, one by one, for a moment or two, then looked at her seriously. "I understand the need to be independent."

"I could learn to play cards."

"Haven't we had this conversation before?"

"That was before I saw the ocean a hundred paces from your front door, then looked back and saw that you came along with it."

He blinked, then bowed his head and laughed. "You are going to be the ruination of me." He shook his head and smiled. "What if I gave you the land, I build you stables to go on it, and you use your powers of persuasion with the good lord of Angesand to convince him to sell us a few steeds? You can breed them and sell them thereafter for eye-watering prices whilst I keep my hands in my own pockets, not in your clients'. Best behavior and all."

She rose, gathered up bowls, then leaned over and kissed him on the cheek. "*That* is an interesting proposal."

"I'm thinking about more than horses," he protested.

She could hardly believe he might be, but as she'd reminded herself earlier, she was completely out of her depth. That place was less uncomfortable than it had been before, though.

She put things in the sink, then felt her hand be taken by a man with terrible spells who had come to stand next to her. She looked at him gravely.

"I have a little money—"

"Nay," he said.

"Shall I offer you maudlin sentiments instead?"

"And have you burn not only my house but my sweet self to cinders?"

She shook her head. "Perhaps just your heart."

He closed his eyes briefly, then pulled her closer and wrapped his arms around her tightly.

"Damn you," he said, sounding as if he were suffering from a bout of emotion himself. "You must cease with these vicious attacks on my good sense. There won't be anything left of me to see to this questing business if you don't leave me be."

"I have the feeling you'll survive," she said wryly.

He released her only far enough to put his arm around her. He kissed her hair briefly. "I'll keep you safe," he murmured.

She looked up at him quickly, but he only smiled.

"Maps and whisky. 'Tis our only hope."

She thought he might just be right about that.

Eleven

Acair suspected that if too many more mornings passed when he was up before dawn without a nefarious reason as inducement, he might as well resign himself to never having a decent morning's lie-in again.

He came to himself to realize he was sitting at the table, pencil in hand, and a notebook was open in front of him. Worse still, a list had been made of all the things that vexed him, yet he had no memory of having made it.

Ye gads, he had become his mother.

He pushed the tools of her trade away from himself, rose, and began to pace. He walked along the walls, running his fingers occasionally over books that he had been collecting over decades of—mostly—lawful activities. No carefully made lists of evil mages flew off the shelves from their spots inside dust jackets. No tomes full of vile spells spewed out their contents so he had no choice but to catch hold of them. No massive volumes of Important Nerochian Virtues fell off shelves to clunk him on the head on their way to perhaps land on a toe and cause him pain.

He leaned against a shelf and wondered briefly what would happen if he chucked the whole business into the closest imaginary rubbish bin, gathered up his delightful horse miss, and decamped for some lovely piece of shoreline in the south where they might luxuriate in the sunshine and make inroads into many bottles of the local drink of choice.

After the previous night's foray into matters of the heart, he suspected a better idea had never occurred to him.

Unfortunately, behind altruism and honesty, his next most prominent virtue was industry. He couldn't leave the world to the whims of a lesser mage when there were stones he could be nudging aside. He blew out his breath, pulled himself up by his bootstraps, and walked back over to his table where the fray awaited.

The first thing he encountered was that damned map his grandmother had made him, which left him mentally back at her front gates, wondering what the hell she was up to. Cruihniche of Fàs never did anything without good reason, especially if she thought it might stick a staff in the proverbial spokes of someone's heavily laden cart. He was beginning to fear that the spell she had given him had been less a gift than a means of sending him turning in circles, questioning every piece of magic he'd made over the course of his very long life.

That wasn't to say that he hadn't early on in his career as black mage extraordinaire taken a look at his grandmother and sized her up as a potential possessor of magical goods. It was a testament to his youth and arrogance that he'd noticed nothing past the rather ordinary business a pair of her daughters used to make lace and keep bees.

In his defense, he'd had no reason to expect anything more. His mother had power, of course, but she generally used it to torment houseguests and her various progeny. He couldn't think of a single spell guarding her house that hadn't come from someone else's collection. Familiarity bred contempt, or so the saying went, and he'd launched himself out his mother's front door without a backward glance, his sights set on the magic of the high and mighty of other lands. It had honestly never occurred to him that Fàs might have its own version of the same.

He was beginning to think that oversight on his part had been a grave mistake.

He set aside the map with its unsettling X drawn with many flourishes over his own damned house, tossed into the same pile a random sheaf of paper that had a series of rather rude doodles drawn alongside a decent representation of a fierce dragon spewing out lethal flames toward a certain essence-changing prince, and decided that perhaps a different approach might be called for.

He sat, pulled out a fresh sheet of paper, and started a list of people, not events. The cast of players in the drama that had become his life was haphazard, to say the least. It ranged from those he could name—Aonarach of Léige, his own grandmother, Soilléir, Léirsinn—to others he had no name for—the mage following them so relentlessly, a portly orchardist from his past, and a mage who had seemingly made the stealing of souls his life's work.

He set aside the easier things first. Aonarach of Léige, that unruly royal spawn, had obviously spent too much time in his grandfather's mines and the lack of air had led him to imagining things that couldn't possibly be true. The boy's spell had been unsettling only because it was so close to his own grandmother's. The request for an introduction to Léirsinn's sister had been nothing short of daft. Perhaps a carefully penned note suggesting the virtues of taking healthful air in the palace gardens would be the kindest thing he could offer.

His grandmother had more than enough incentive to want to keep him busy and out of her linen closet, which likely explained why she wanted him wandering in remote paths. He couldn't think of any reason past that why she would find herself embroiled in his current quest, so he tucked her comfortably back in her solar where she couldn't trouble him further.

He'd already consigned Soilléir to a fiery fate, if only on paper, which was no less than he deserved. At least the man wasn't knocking on the front door, delivering more quests.

Léirsinn was last on that short list, but certainly not last in his thoughts. He was tempted to go check on her simply to have an excuse to look at her, but she was likely catching up on some very well-deserved rest. He would leave her in peace until he'd found at least one answer.

He turned to the collection of souls he couldn't put a name to and considered each in no particular order.

First was the orchardist he had bumped off his ladder all those many years ago. His most vivid memory of the spell he'd tossed into the fire was his disappointment over its lack of desirability. Soilléir had insisted that it was the same spell that someone — presumably the orchardist — had cut from one of the books in his grandfather's library, but Acair could hardly believe that.

For one thing, he couldn't imagine anyone having bothered to steal what he remembered as a paltry spell of thievery. Second, if the spell had done what it had been intended to do, why hadn't the orchardist used it long before now?

There were only two answers that made any sense: either the spell continued to be as pedestrian as he'd found it to be all those many years ago or it simply didn't work at all.

But if the latter were the case, why wrap it up and use it to lure a bastard son of the black mage down the road into his house to steal it?

Acair had no illusions left about his father's character, so whilst altruism would never have found itself on any list that applied to him, pride certainly would have. If someone had taken something of his — children, spells, his favorite dinnerware — Gair would have retaliated immediately and with a devastating fury. Only a fool would have provoked him thus.

Nay, either Soilléir was mistaken, something else had been stolen, or, as he feared, there was another, more unpleasant quest in the offing. Something about the whole thing didn't smell quite right, but he couldn't bring himself to start sniffing in that direction quite yet.

He looked at the second entry on that particular list, namely the mage who wanted the power of souls so badly. If that man was actually Sladaiche, as his mother had intimated, then tracking him down would take time, but it wouldn't be impossible. After all, discovering secrets that didn't want to be revealed was one of the things he did best. That, he suspected, might actually entail a lengthy troll through Seannair's library. Heaven only knew what sorts of things that man had hiding amongst extensive studies on the art of taxidermy and the cultivation of root vegetables. Acair decided that could be penciled in near the top of his next to-do list for that reason alone.

Last on the list but perhaps the most pressing item there was the mage who stood outside his house, that uninspired worker of pedestrian magic who spoke in shards and seemed to be waiting for something. He hadn't robbed anyone recently, nor had he rifled through any chests of spells. The only thing that made any sense at all was that he had crossed paths with the fool at some point in the past, done him dirty—and given the quality of the man's spells, he had likely done him a great favor there—and now the mage so slighted had decided the time was ripe for a bit of revenge.

Unpleasant, but not life-threatening. If he had to keep a step ahead of the man for the next year until he had his magic under his hands again, so be it. He was capable of biding his time as well.

There was a blank space on that large page and he watched his hand as it wrote down what he realized he had been avoiding thinking about seriously. It was perhaps the least of the things that should have vexed him, but he found it was the one that left him with the most discomfort in the vicinity of his heart.

Who had slain Odhran of Eòlas and had that same man then stolen the spell he himself had hidden in his tailor's workroom?

He sat back and looked up at the ceiling. He considered himself fairly discreet, but he was the first to admit that boasting of his mighty magic had been a failing he'd engaged in more than once.

Had some enterprising soul overheard him trumpeting his own magnificence at supper in Eòlas, then made inquiries about the establishments he frequented or where he bestowed his coveted commerce? And if the latter had intrigued anyone, would there have been any trouble discovering Master Odhran at the top of his list of sartorial destinations?

He shook his head at his own stupidity. There he'd been, not a trio of weeks earlier, heedlessly sending a message to that self-same tailor, advising him to expect a visit at some point during his stay. He had then made that promised visit only to find his tailor dead.

He took a deep breath and forced himself to look again at that evening with detachment. His tailor had borne no marks from a commonplace weapon, so the likelihood of a spell having been what finished him was very high. The goods in his workroom hadn't been tossed about, which suggested that it hadn't been a random burglary. That his own spell of distraction had been stolen suggested that someone had either known beforehand it was there or suspected it might be there and forced Odhran to reveal its location.

He supposed a third possibility was that finding that spell could have been simply good fortune, though it would have taken a mage with decent abilities to have recognized it for what it was.

Then there was that damned note Léirsinn had found that had announced, *I'm watching you, but you knew that.* Unoriginal and uninspired, but he was, sadly, accustomed to lesser offerings.

He supposed those words could have been dashed off by any noblewoman within a hundred-league radius of the city, but the uncomfortable truth was that they were almost identical to the missive he'd received whilst he and Léirsinn had been taking refuge in Tor Neroche. There had been no doubt in his mind that *those* words had been penned by a man with magic.

Nay, the author had been the same, which likely meant that they had been written by the mage who had stolen his spell.

Why was the question he simply couldn't answer.

He rubbed his hands over his face, aching for the freedom of flight in a way that left him almost unable to draw breath.

"Acair?"

A soft knock startled him, but he managed not to fling anything in the air or knock over any of what he could see had become a rather alarmingly large collection of cups and glasses.

"Come in," he called.

Léirsinn leaned in past the door. "Supper?"

He blinked and turned toward her. "Is it that late already?"

"I'd call it a very late lunch," she conceded. "I'm just not sure you've eaten anything today. And if you make any untoward remarks about my cooking, I will throw something heavy at you."

He heaved himself up out of his chair, gathered up half a dozen cups and glasses, and crossed over to her. "I'm still unsure where it was I went wrong with you. No one dares speak to me so carelessly."

She only smiled and went to fetch the rest of the evidence of how long he'd been at his current slog. He staved off the impulse to ask her to carry him as well and followed her to his kitchen where she had set up a very respectable collection of edible things.

He ate without tasting anything and had no idea if he'd made decent conversation or not. His head was full of impossible questions and his eyes were full of mountain ranges and coastlines and the courses that rivers took through plains and valleys.

What he needed was a better vantage point.

He came to himself to find he was holding a knife in his hand and staring at nothing. He blinked and focused on Léirsinn sitting around the table from him. She was simply sitting back in her chair, watching him thoughtfully.

"Forgive me," he said, the words feeling, unsurprisingly, as familiar as a pair of well-worn slippers. "My mind is elsewhere."

"I'm sorry you can't, you know." She made flapping motions with her hands.

"As am I," he agreed. "I would very much like—"

He stopped speaking because the possibility that occurred to him suddenly was almost enough to still even the continual stream of terrible thoughts that ran through his mind like a mighty Durialian river.

He *could* shapechange.

"Acair, you worry me."

He pushed back his chair. "Let me help you with these dishes, then I believe I'll go stretch my legs."

She nodded and rose as well, but she was watching him far more closely than he was comfortable with.

His inability to make idle chatter was coming back to haunt him at the moment, for he had no means with which to distract her. Hardly had he dried the last plate and stacked it again before he realized that she had placed herself between him and the doorway that led to the rest of the house. She was wearing a look he imagined had inspired countless stable hands to blurt out their plans for mischief before she had even asked.

"I'm going to have a little look up the coast," he admitted, finding himself, metaphorically speaking, standing there in dung-covered boots and holding onto a pitchfork.

"Are you mad?" she asked incredulously. "You know what's out there!"

"I'll slip out the back. He'll never know."

"And what will I do if you don't come back?"

"Well," he said, wondering what sort of list might be best. "You'll tell Sianach to take a winged shape, then you'll walk out of my spell and fly to somewhere that appeals. Cothromaiche, if you like. Seannair is daft as a duck, but still a decent fellow. The schools of wizardry—nay, Tor Neroche. Better still, Angesand. Hearn will give you a choice refuge with all the horses you can stand to ride."

"Nay," she said, "what will I do without you?"

It took him a moment to realize what she was getting at. He looked at her then, that glorious red-haired woman who had been ripped from the life she knew, thrown into a life she'd never asked for, and sacrificed what would no doubt be the peace she might have looked forward to in order to keep him safe, and he wondered if he'd heard her wrong.

But nay, she was simply looking at him as if she might have been concerned that he would nip out the back and be slain.

He caught his jaw before it made an abrupt trip south — something he was having to do with unsettling regularity. And damn those bloody magics in his chest, Fadaire and that rot Soilléir had crammed inside him, if they didn't tangle themselves together in a fond embrace and give his heart a mighty squeeze. He could hardly catch his breath. Worse still, he felt torn between weeping and . . . well, weeping. He cleared his throat roughly.

"I didn't realize you'd burned supper," he said, grasping manfully for something that sounded reasonable. "Smoke is still lingering terribly, you know. Best open the back door next time."

She walked over to him, leaned up, kissed him, then put her arms around his neck.

"You are a terrible man," she said quietly.

"Such sickly sweet sentiments," he said, clutching her to him so tightly he wasn't entirely certain he hadn't heard her squeak. "Awful wench that you are."

"But you're very fond of me."

"I am. And I'm quite sure you return the feeling, though driving me to such displays is a very poor way of expressing it."

She whispered something in his ear. He wasn't sure if it had been an expression of mild affection or a salty *you're a complete ass*, but he decided perhaps the exact words didn't matter. He understood the sentiment.

He pulled away. "I'll return soon."

"I can't stop you," she said slowly.

"You can't."

She looked at him seriously. "I wouldn't actually try, if you're curious. But if you aren't back by morning, Sianach and I will find you, then I will give him leave to stomp the life from you."

He brought her hand to his mouth and kissed it with as much gallantry as he possessed. "You do love me."

"I might tell you when you return," she said, "so you'd best be careful, hadn't you?"

He thought that might be another fact for his mother to make a note of: the number of times in the course of his very long, perilous existence anyone had pointed him toward the door with those words.

The number was still zero.

He made Léirsinn a low bow, then slipped past her and out the back door as a chilly winter breeze.

H e flew along the coast, covered in a vile spell of un-noticing—Lugham, it had to be said—because it would definitely discourage anyone from having a closer look at him bolting across the sky.

If he turned east and took more time than necessary to fling himself out across the expanse of water that separated his land from Bruadair, who would know? That dreamspinning bride of Rùnach's might, but surely no one else.

He would have wept if he'd been the sort of lad to indulge. Never again would he ever take his magic for granted. The thought was so profound, he suspected he might have to pen a restrained thank-you to both Rùnach and Soilléir for that realization. He also might have to take them to supper and drop something in their stews just nasty enough to leave them indisposed for a day or two, then remain helpfully nearby and do nothing but watch them retch until they wept, but he could do nothing less. Altruism was, as usual, his watchword.

He looked behind him, but found no one there. That was another thing he might not have appreciated as thoroughly had he not spent the past several weeks being hunted. He couldn't say he enjoyed that sensation very often—he tended to be the one on the prowl, as it happened—but perhaps that also needed change in the future.

There was also something useful about being near the sea and having brisk sea air blowing the cobwebs from one's mind. His mother claimed too much time in his study had driven the illustrious and admittedly unreasonable Gair of Ceangail mad. Whilst he suspected his father's madness had come from other sources, he couldn't deny that he tended to become a bit testy when cooped up for too long.

So in honor of the absolute perfection of flying without worrying about his steed taking a bite out of him, he set aside thoughts of things that troubled him. He would enjoy the last of the day's light by making a lazy journey back over to his side of the bay of Sealladh, having a little look at the ruin up the way that he'd never had the chance to investigate properly, then swooping up a bit higher to make note of the lay of the land for use in correcting his grandmother's map. He was certain she would be gratified to know where she'd drawn amiss.

He might have to drop that note off at the front gates and be back over the border before her minion reached her solar door, but that was something to be considered later.

He didn't hurry, even though there was a storm brewing and the winds were growing fierce. He also didn't bother to fight the current as it drove him toward the shore.

He did pause in the air above that ruined keep. It left him wondering why he'd never bothered to take a closer look at it previously. Well, perhaps that was less true than he would have liked. There was nothing there, certainly no well-laid table or comfortable salon. Why would he have donned rough boots and tromped about a perfectly savage collection of stones?

He rose with a goodly on-shore breeze and checked the identifiable landmarks against his memory of the same. Bruadair lay across the bay to the east, cloaked in its usual shadows of things that dis-

couraged a closer look. Over to the west lay his home, a handful of
mountain ranges of various sizes, and many lakes and rivers.

He held himself in the same place for a bit, realizing then what
struck him as odd. He hadn't noticed what a short distance it was
around the bay from his house to that ruin, or that there seemed to
be a hint of a trail winding its way through the forest hugging the
northern feet of the Sgùrrach mountains. He supposed that worn
track would eventually become completely overcome by the trees,
but he wondered just how many years ago that had been the thor-
oughfare linking the keep to his land.

He supposed the next time he found a place to build a house, he
might do a better job of looking about to see what sort of neighbors
he stood to inherit. He'd been so concerned about those damned
nightmare creators to the east that he hadn't thought to have a
proper look to the north. Lesson learned, indeed.

He set that thought aside for contemplation with a stiff drink at
his elbow and decided to simply accept that his house was down-
wind from a fascinating ruin. It was a haunting place, to be sure,
especially with the sun heading toward the west and casting the
ruined tower into deep shadows—

Shadows. Why did it always come back to that?

He would have shaken his head if he'd had a proper head to
shake, but things were happily what they were. He turned toward
home and let his thoughts wander right along with the evening
breeze.

The one thing his father had taught him, perhaps the only useful
thing, was that an enemy who was unnamed could not be bested.
Knowing his father, weaving a mage's name into his mighty spell of
Diminishing had been not only vicious, but necessary. For himself,
he simply wanted to put a name to the mage wanting an endless supply of souls so he might know where to go digging to determine just
how the man was creating all those pools of shadow.

He swirled down just inside the edge of his spell, resumed his
proper shape, then continued to wear his spell of un-noticing as he

walked away from his house down to the shore. For some reason, he felt as though the places his thoughts were taking him required some sort of grounding.

Perhaps he couldn't name that maker of shadows, but it occurred to him with a flash of something he might have called insight if he hadn't been so damned tired, that he might be able to at least take the mage following him off his list.

He had to admit it hinged on the fact that that shard-spewing mage had made no move to assault him, not even in that glade on the other side of Durial. He would have considered that odd, but he himself had stalked several souls over the years, waiting for just the right time for the proper bit of revenge. His brothers and sundry relations might be able to speak to that with a fair bit of enthusiasm.

Perhaps he had run afoul of the man at some point in the past, the time had come for retribution, and a finely honed sense of vengeance demanded that he exact the final piece of it only after a lengthy stalking of his victim.

He paused in mid-step. What if the truth had been right there in front of him the entire time and he'd simply been too distracted to notice it?

What if the shard-spewing mage was indeed that orchardist whose spell he'd tossed in the fire all those years ago?

The idea wasn't entirely farfetched. The man had, after all, been robbed and humiliated. What if he'd bided his time, nurturing his grievance until the chance came to get back a little of his own? Perhaps a hearty bit of terrorizing had been the only possible way to mollify the dignity of one who had been knocked off his ladder and left flailing on the ground in a flurry of cloak, half-rotten peaches, and rather unimpressive curses.

The timing was odd, to be sure, though it wasn't as if the man could possibly have known that one day he himself would be placed under an injunction not to use his magic. Soilléir was a colossal bore at parties, but he was notorious for his ability to keep his mouth shut. Rùnach was even more tight-lipped, if possible.

Besides, they wanted him alive. Where would be the sport for them if he popped off before they'd had their full year of humiliation?

Odder still was how it had all come about. First he'd been chased by that cloud of mage, only for the herd to find itself thinned and the shard-spewing mage to be the last one left standing. Patience was one thing, but that sort of holding back from the fray was almost impolite.

He walked back up to his house, through his spell of protection, then paused to look up the way toward where he could see the faintest outline of the keep there. It was full dark and there was no moon, but the stars were bright enough, he supposed. That they were out and so clearly was a bit startling. He had been gone longer than he'd thought.

He frowned thoughtfully as he walked around to the back of his house, lost in thought. He paused at the back door, then looked off into the forest.

He was somehow unsurprised to find his enemy keeping watch.

Considering how rarely he came home and how few people—if any—knew where it was, how did that mage there come to find it?

There were very odd things afoot in the Nine Kingdoms, to be sure.

He let himself into his house, slightly gratified to find the door hadn't been bolted against him. The fire in the kitchen was low, but still burning. He realized that the makings of tea were there, plus a bit of soup left to warm. He stood there and looked at them for a moment or two, bemused, then made himself a very late, hasty supper.

He walked quietly through his house and found Léirsinn asleep in front of the fire in his study. He wasn't sure she would ever use that luxurious chamber he'd offered her, but perhaps she felt more secure where she was. He leaned against the doorway and watched her for a moment or two, that flame-haired, flame-tempered, impossibly courageous gel—

"You should come to bed."

He blinked and realized she wasn't as asleep as he'd thought.

Those were certainly words he'd never expected to hear from Léirsinn of Sàraichte, but the hand waving she did immediately following uttering them was somehow rather reassuring.

"I don't mean that. You should come sleep. I can hear you cursing from here and I don't think it's helping you."

He left his shoes by the wall and padded over to the hearth in bare feet. He sat down on a stool and sighed.

"I'm too restless to sleep."

"Something to drink?"

"Why not a game of cards instead? I'll owe you a kiss for every hand you win."

She sat up, her glorious red hair cascading over her shoulders, her stunning self looking so fetching in the nightclothes he'd loaned her that he thought he might cheat just to lose.

"You are thinking lewd thoughts."

"Of course," he said lightly. "You know me. Predictable, as always."

She patted the spot next to her on the very unmagical, not entirely uncomfortable pallet he'd made for them the night before.

"Why don't I read you a tale instead? Do you have any faery stories?"

"None that would inspire pleasant dreams," he said grimly. He pulled a deck of cards out of thin air. "This is less perilous."

She studied him. "Will you cheat?"

"To lose? Absolutely."

She smiled. "All right. How was the sea?"

"Glorious."

"You look more at peace, all things considered."

He made himself comfortable on the floor across from her and wished he could agree. Unfortunately, the truth was that he had more questions than answers and no amount of scrawls on parchment seemed enough to shift the balance of that. The list of people who might want revenge against him was, he suspected, commensurate with the number of black mages in the world who wanted the same. He supposed there were those without magic who also might want to see him eating a few just desserts, but those lads and lassies didn't speak in shards.

He just didn't understand why now.

"I'll go find something to drink."

Be careful was almost out of his mouth before he came back to himself and heard what she'd said. He watched her walk across his study to look for things he was quite certain she wouldn't want to imbibe.

He rubbed his fingers over his eyes, shook his head to bring back a decent bit of good sense, then started shuffling. Léirsinn was in his house and they both were safe.

That might be enough for what was left of the night.

Twelve

Léirsinn stood inside Acair's library and wondered if he didn't have just too many books.

She was half tempted to go back to what she'd spent most of the morning doing, namely standing at the front door, looking out at the ocean. 'Twas true that she'd also peered out of every door and window, admiring the mountains behind the house and the deep forests on either side, but somehow she'd always found herself back watching that glorious stretch of beach in front of her. It had taken a great amount of self-control to shut the front door a few moments ago and be about something useful.

She was finally starting to feel a bit more like her old self, though she suspected she would never feel entirely the same again. That wasn't anything she particularly wanted to dwell on, so she faced the staggering number of books in front of her and made her best guess as to where to start looking for a name to put to that mage that watched them from under the trees.

She walked along the walls of shelves, stopping to touch books that looked interesting, but she didn't pull any of them out from their places. Though she thoroughly enjoyed reading, she hadn't had the luxury of time for it very often. Mistress Cailleach had loaned her various things over the years: books on healing things with herbs, romantic tales of yore—obviously wept over more than once—and at least one very small tome on winning wars against trolls and their ilk.

Conspicuously missing, however, had been anything to do with mages, witches, or spells. Given whose great-aunt Mistress Cailleach was, Léirsinn now thought that had shown great restraint on the woman's part.

Acair's library, however, was very different. She found everything from histories of countries she hadn't known existed to beautifully illustrated treatises on varying species of animals to detailed drawings of various castles and buildings. She raised her eyebrows over the dozen heavy, obviously well-loved books making up that last group. She suspected he'd used them more than once to aid him in less-than-legal activities.

But in addition to all those lovely but fairly ordinary offerings was a very robust collection of all things magical including a grimoire that gave her chills just looking at it. She suspected that if Mistress Cailleach ever came to visit, she and Acair might be engaging in a bit of a tussle for possession of that thing.

She continued to simply wander, ignoring the lights that brightened at the first sign of squinting on her part—perhaps keeping company with a mage had its advantages after all—and found herself back where she'd been earlier that morning: at a loss for where to start.

It was no wonder Acair was so frustrated.

She stopped and put her hands on a shelf to give herself something to hold onto while she took a moment to remember all the reasons she had asked for the magic that had at least taken a bit of a rest from tormenting her. The only one that came to mind had to do with a man who had gone off to look for answers in the garden earlier, so perhaps she could be forgiven if she simply credited her request as fondness for him and let it go.

She bowed her head and breathed for a bit until the blood rush-

ing through her veins didn't sound so loud in her own ears and the
magic Acair had used to heal her arm had stopped sparkling at her.

She opened her eyes and lifted her head, then blinked. She realized she was standing in front of that book she hadn't quite pushed
back into its place the night before.

A Child's Book of Heroic Tales

She closed her eyes briefly again, then opened them, hoping she
would see something different there in front of her.

She didn't.

She clutched the edge of the bookshelf and felt the very air
around her become still in a way she'd never before experienced.

'Twas ridiculous, of course. She was doing nothing more interesting than looking at a child's collection of tales. It was something
that could have been found in any number of places, surely.

The world was full of libraries that were full of that sort of thing.
The university in Eòlas was one such place that she'd seen for herself. Even there they no doubt had the odd copy of something fit for
a child lingering on some shelf or other.

Acair's library was less extensive, true, but still jammed full of
the written word. She should have expected to find numerous examples of all sorts of books written about all sorts of subjects sorted
lovingly into their proper order.

She had just never expected to find something she had seen so
often in her parents' hands sitting on someone else's shelf.

She trailed her finger along the spine. Her parents hadn't owned
very many things that she could bring to mind, though what did a
child remember? Hers had been a home full of laughter, enough to
eat, horses to ride, and tales read before the fire every night.

Tales from books exactly like the one she was looking at.

Actually, there had been three books. Each had had its own
particular color on the cover: blue, green, and brown. Those covers, from what she remembered, had been engraved with mythical
creatures. That trio of books had been stored in a prominent place

on a shelf, a comfortable distance from the fire but well within reach of anyone who might want to take them down and linger in their pages.

She remembered it had been her brother to first deface one of them. She'd found him leaning over the final empty page, drawing a knight brandishing a sword and preparing to go off on his warhorse to do noble deeds.

She had gasped at his audacity, but he'd been unrepentant. *A lad with questing in his future*, she remembered him saying, *needed to get an early start*. Why he thought scribbling in the back of a book was the appropriate way to set off on that sort of path she couldn't have said. He'd written his name in bold letters under the knight, so perhaps he'd had a point.

Because of their unbreakable code of camaraderie, she had stood should-to-shoulder with him to face their parents' wrath. Their younger sister had followed their examples and taken his other side.

Her parents' punishment had consisted of a serious lecture on the precious nature of books in general and extra barn chores for the three of them for at least a month. She had overheard them later discussing with affection what a fine thing it was to have children so loyal to each other, so perhaps they hadn't been all that angry. She had loved horses, so more time with them hadn't seemed like anything but a relief from the other studies her mother and father had thought appropriate for their children.

Her parents had also decided at that point that each of them might claim one of the books if their early artistic works were confined to the last page. Endpapers, her father had called them. Hers had been blue, the color of the sky and, from what she'd been told as a child, the color of the sea under the right conditions. Her brother's volume had been brown.

She looked at the green spine of the book in front of her and forced herself not to leap a conclusion that might not be true.

Printers made copies of books, surely. Children's books likely provided them with a decent income, so why not press numerous copies of each?

And of course the cover would be the same. After all, why not create an engraving plate that would stamp the same image in relief on scores of the same book, much like blacksmiths created forms for the making of horseshoes and nails and all the other useful items they produced? No sense in having to reinvent something every time one wanted to make a copy of it.

Surely.

She could see her mother running her finger over the raised image of the pegasus there on the cover. She could hear her father laughing over the notion of a faery leading that same pony and a witch trailing after them wanting her mount back. *Brooms, Muire, don't allow for a decent saddle, as you surely know by now.*

Her mother would have failed miserably at sending him a stern look, her father would have laughed and leaned over the book to kiss her, and she would have been watching them and wondering how it was that she had been so fortunate to have such parents as those.

She closed her eyes briefly, gathered the last vestiges of her good sense, and pulled the book from its spot on the shelf. What she was certain of was that she wouldn't find her sister's addition to the final page.

She opened the book and started from the very first story, a tale of an elven princess who left her home, looking for an elusive stranger who had once passed through her father's land and stolen her heart. After that followed tales of faeries, kings, evil sorcerers, and workers of magics of all sorts.

All the things her sister had loved.

She had to admit that she read more slowly than she needed to, but she came to the end far sooner than she wanted to. She stood there for far longer than she should have with her fingers gingerly holding the last page.

She finally gathered her courage and turned the page before she could think about it any longer.

A child's drawing was there of a horse, a girl, and a boy.

She closed the book with a snap and almost shoved it back on the shelf, but found that all she could do was hold it and try to catch her breath.

Why did that book find itself in Acair of Ceangail's private library? It wasn't possible that he'd had anything to do . . .

Anything at all . . .

Surely, not.

She stood on the edge of something that terrified her and couldn't find the courage to look at what lay there. Books found their ways into the hands of those who loved them through strange and unusual paths, no doubt. That her sister's sole possession should find itself so many leagues away from where her sister had once held it meant nothing.

But if it did—

She gathered the tatters of her courage, then stepped up to the edge of that abyss and looked into its depths. Admittedly she had seen things that had called into question everything she believed. It was also true that Acair of Ceangail had likely done things she wouldn't want to know about.

But she had seen him in the king's garden in Tor Neroche, standing there perfectly balanced between good and evil and she knew what was in his soul.

She took a step backward from that terrible place and that great pit faded to nothing. There were things she could believe of many people, but believing that of a man who had wept over her, who knew that her parents had been slain when she was a child, who in spite of perhaps several other things he would rather have been doing, had promised to try to heal her grandfather?

She could believe many things of him, but not that.

She dragged her sleeve across her eyes and was momentarily blinded by a few Fadairian sparkles that seemed to have worked their way through the fabric of her sleeve. She took a deep, steadying breath and wondered what she was to do now.

"Léirsinn?"

She looked at the doorway to the library and wondered how long Acair had been standing there.

"Are you unwell?"

"I'm fine," she croaked.

He walked across the beautifully patterned rug comfortingly free of shadows and came to stand in front of her. He frowned.

"You don't look well."

"I was reading."

"Tales of horror and woe?"

She shook her head and held the book out. "I found this."

He peered at it, then shot her a dry look. "Faery stories?"

She found that all her protestations aside, all she wanted to do was stand there and weep. She felt as if she were holding onto a hinge-pin that trapped her between her past and her present and was making a horrendously loud noise as it turned.

"Do you remember where you got it?" Her hand was trembling, but she hoped he wouldn't notice. "I'm just curious."

He took the book, studied it, then smiled wryly. "I do, as it happens, for it cost me a ridiculous amount of my own coin." He looked at her again, then frowned. "You're very pale. Let's find somewhere to sit—"

"I'm fine," she said, perhaps more sharply than she intended. She attempted a smile. "Sorry. I'm just restless."

"Well, I understand that." He ran his finger over the cover, tracing the shape of the pegasus there.

Léirsinn suddenly wished she'd agreed to the idea of a chair.

"You know, this is a strange little book. I was skulking about somewhere I shouldn't have been—in Bruadair, if memory serves—and a peddler almost ran me over on the sidewalk with his cart of treasures. I gave his wares a look, because you never know what you'll find in a dusty corner, and he insisted that I needed this."

"Oh," was the absolute limit of what she could manage.

He shrugged a bit sheepishly. "Foolish, I know, but 'tis a lovely thing, isn't it? But I'm always a bit dazzled by a tooled leather cover, truth be told."

"Beautiful," she agreed.

He looked at her and smiled. "If you tell me you had one as a child, I will refrain from pointing out how jaded you've become in spite of it."

She took the book as he handed it to her. "Something very like it," she lied. "You can blame my parents for filling my head full of this sort of rubbish."

His smile faded. "I'm sorry," he said carefully. "The memory must be difficult."

She shook her head. "Actually, it isn't," she said, finding it was true. She took a step back. "I'll keep looking."

"I'll read to you tonight, if you like."

"From this or from that book King Uachdaran gave you about terrible mages?"

"Your choice. The content will be about the same, I'm guessing." He nodded toward the door. "There's stew, if you're hungry. Coming?"

"I'll be there in a minute," she said. "I'll put this back."

He nodded, looked at her with another faint frown, then walked toward the door. Léirsinn turned to the bookcase, but found she couldn't place the book back where she'd found it. There was something about it that wrenched at her heart in a way she couldn't begin to describe.

Acair had bought it from a peddler. Her relief over hearing those words was as terrible as the abyss she'd almost stepped into at the thought that he might have gotten it another way.

"Léirsinn?"

She couldn't turn around. "Aye?"

She heard him come to stand next to her but she couldn't look at him.

"Is that your book?" he asked quietly.

She had to take a deep breath. "My sister's."

His breath caught.

She looked up at him then. He looked as surprised as she'd ever seen him, but his eyes were full of the terrible thoughts she'd already entertained.

"How do you know?" he asked, looking as if he wished they were speaking of anything else.

She held the book out. "Look in the back."

He took the book with a hand that was no steadier than hers, then held it with both hands for a moment or two, as if he hardly dared open it. She watched him take a deep breath, let it out carefully, then flip the book over and simply open the back cover.

Marching into the middle of the fray instead of lingering on the edges. How like him.

He studied the childish drawing there, then looked at her. "Not much of an artist, was she?"

Léirsinn supposed she might have made a noise that sounded a bit like a sob, but she couldn't be sure.

"She was only nine," she managed.

He lifted his eyebrows briefly. "Then I'm being overly critical." He looked at her thoughtfully. "Did she look like you?"

"I think so," she admitted. "I don't remember any longer. My brother didn't have red hair, if that lets you sleep better at night."

"Got it from your mother, did you?"

"To my father's horror, no doubt."

He closed his eyes briefly, then handed her the book. "Did you think I'd murdered them for it?"

"Oh, Acair," she said, and damn her traitorous eyes if they didn't start up that ridiculous burning again. "Not in truth."

He looked a little shattered. "Are you certain of it?"

"Would I be here if I wasn't?"

He walked away. She watched him go rest his hand on the mantel over the elegant stone hearth and wondered if he planned to toss himself into the fire there, or toss *her* in instead. In the end, he simply stood there with his head bowed for longer than she would have thought possible, but the man was patient, she supposed.

She also supposed he would stand there all day if she didn't make the first move. After all, she was the one who had suspected him of murder. She took a deep breath, stuck her sister's book on a shelf, then walked over to stand next to him. She put her hand on his back as he had done to her so many times and thought she might understand why he did it. He smiled briefly at her, then looked back into the fire.

"I have done things I regret," he said quietly, "and other things I'm not sorry for in the least. But I have never harmed a woman or a child."

"And that, my lord, is why I'm still here."

He looked at her then. "Of course that's not the reason. You're here because you're mad for me and the thought of life without my sparkling self in it is just too tedious to contemplate."

"That might be true," she agreed. "Thank you for keeping her book safe."

"We'll read it to our children."

"Aren't you a presumptuous ass."

He only looked at her as if he wasn't sure what, if anything, he should do. She supposed that if he could march into the fray without edging up to the battle, so could she. She ducked under his elbow, then straightened and put her arms around him. If it took a moment for him to return the embrace, well, she supposed she couldn't blame him.

"I am a vile man," he said finally.

"Of course," she said easily. She laid her head on his shoulder and sighed. "What is the worst thing you've done? Go ahead and confess. You'll feel better if you do."

"In what sense of the term *worst*?"

She shrugged helplessly. "I don't know. What would I consider

horrifying? Or put yourself in Prince Soilléir's shoes. What would
he want to know?"

"Nothing, given that he knows it all already," Acair muttered.
"Which list would you like me to make first?"

"Start with the worst things," she said, closing her eyes. "We'll
leave the noble items for after supper."

He sighed deeply. "Very well. I've wreaked havoc and made
people miserable all over the Nine Kingdoms. I've left kings weeping over their favorite treasures that I nicked without so much as a
twinge of conscience. I've vexed my brothers and several of Sarait's
children until I was almost satisfied they would lose their wits."

She hadn't met his brothers, but she imagined they might have
deserved at least a little trouble.

"What else?"

"I brought an entire mountainside down on my half-brother
Rùnach and his bride. Does that count?"

She pulled back and looked at him them. "Did they live?"

"Aye, but no thanks to me."

"Well, that might qualify as something rather terrible," she said.
"Anything else?"

He sighed and pulled away, but she realized he had only gone as
far as the chair set near the fire. He held open his arms and looked
at her expectantly. She supposed she might have more answers than
not if she kept him pinned in a chair, so she went to sit on his lap.

"Well?"

He looked more hesitant than she'd ever seen him. She considered fetching him a large glass of whisky, but she supposed that
what he had to tell her might be too serious for even that.

"There was once a mage in Tosan," he began slowly.

"Sladaiche?"

He shook his head. "Not him. Not a man without power, either,
and one who favored my father's magic."

"Were you defending your father's honor?" she asked.

"Hardly," he said with a snort. "We were simply insulting each other with words and spells, as mages do absent anything else useful with which to amuse themselves, and I didn't care for the way he treated his wife."

"You?"

He smiled wearily. "Aye, me, the one always in the running for the mage everyone wants to slay."

"Very near the top, I daresay."

"Thank you."

She smiled. "Go on."

"I drove him mad until he lost all sense and ran off the edge of a cliff into the sea."

"I see," she said slowly. "And what did you do to his widow?"

"For," he corrected. He considered, then shrugged lightly. "It doesn't merit a mention."

She only watched him silently.

He blew his hair out of his eyes. "Very well, I gave her a purse that endlessly spilled out Nerochian gold sovereigns. The spell was constructed to outlast her until the youngest of her ten children had breathed his last."

"You," she said seriously, "are shockingly bad at black magery."

"Do not spread that about, woman. I will deny it to my dying breath." He dragged both his hands through his hair. "I either need to fly or kiss you until we've both forgotten this recent conversation."

"Why not both?"

He looked at her in surprise. "Now, there's a thought. Would you like to fly with me? I could change your shape for you."

"Could you?" she squeaked.

Damnation, tears and sounding like a ten-year-old gel. She wondered what else the day might lay upon her that would be worse.

"Darling, you might be surprised what I can do."

"I imagine I might not be."

He didn't move. "Do you trust me that far?"

The gods help her, she actually did. She took a deep breath and nodded.

"Then let's go." He helped her off his lap, then took her hand and pulled her toward the library door. "What do you fancy?" He slid her a look. "In shapes, of course. We can discuss the other later, after we've returned."

That, she decided abruptly, was what leaping straight into the fray got a woman. Commitments to activities that merely thinking about left her almost speechless with terror.

"Perhaps I should wait by the fire."

"Oh, nay," he said, continuing to tug. "This is why one should be careful when negotiating with a ruthless worker of evil."

"Acair," she said miserably.

He stopped and turned to her, pulling her into his arms. "A poor jest, darling. I won't force you to do anything you don't care for. I braved horse work, of course, but if this is too much for you . . . "

She pulled back and tried to find something in her not-so-limited collection of slurs to call him that wouldn't hurt his feelings but might put him in his place. Unfortunately, all she could do was stare at him, torn between terror and a rather unsettling twinge of something she might have termed curiosity if she hadn't known where that sort of thing led.

He looked at her seriously. "You do love me."

"At the moment, I can't remember why," she said, finding her mouth appallingly dry. She searched frantically for a reason why she couldn't do what she'd agreed to do, then hit upon her salvation. "How will we come back through your spell?"

He blinked a time or two, then swore. "Damnation, but that's inconvenient."

"My heart breaks over it, but there it is," she agreed.

"I suppose you're then left with my stew."

She could have been left with much worse than that, she supposed.

She walked with him from the library to go in search of supper and reminded herself that if anything held true in Acair of Ceangail's world, it was that he didn't lie.

Not that she would have needed to have heard him confess anything. She had seen what lay in his soul.

It was enough.

A pair of hours and a decent bowl of stew later, she sat with him on the floor in front of his fire in the study. He was stretched out next to her, his cheek propped on his fist, watching the fire. She reached out and brushed a lock of hair out of his eyes.

"I am sorry," she said quietly. "About before."

"Would you like to know what the worst part of it was?" he asked, still watching the flames. "Well, aside from the fact that you think me capable of murder."

"You boast about it endlessly."

He shot her a disgruntled look. "You needn't take me that seriously."

She wrapped her arms around her bent knees. "What is the worst part?"

"That it hurt," he said with a sigh. "Me, the lad with no feelings to wound."

"Does it still hurt?"

He looked at her. "Thinking to make it better somehow?"

"Are you always this unrepentant a flirt?"

"'Tis wooing, Léirsinn. A different dance entirely."

"And how many times have you danced that dance, my lord Acair?"

He pursed his lips. "This is my first turn on that particular ballroom floor, which is likely why I seem to be doing it so poorly."

"I don't think you're doing it poorly."

He sat up and thanked her properly for her trouble, she would give him that. She also tried to give him a bit of a nudge to put another piece of wood on the fire, then ended up doing it herself. She sat back down and found he was watching her in what seemed to be one of his favorite positions, cheek on fist.

"Would you care to hear the very worst?"

"Must I?" she asked, pained.

He shook his head. "I'm not poking at you about that and you needn't have apologized. You had good reason, and I'm sorry for that. Nay, the worst of this is that I'm afraid I might never manage to go back to what I was before."

"Unrepentant flirt or terrible black mage?"

"Oh, the first is definitely in my past. The second, though, is what worries me. If word gets out, how will I ever enter another chamber of nobles and be satisfied with simple greetings instead of wails of terror?"

"Poor you," she said dryly.

"I will hold you responsible."

"I'm sure you will."

"My *mother* will hold you responsible."

She blinked. "Now, that's a terrifying thought."

"If that doesn't give you terrible dreams, I don't know what will."

"Odious man."

He shot her a small smile. "But you adore me."

"'Tis hard not to."

He put his hand on her back. "If you go fetch that book, love, I'll read to you. Or you can read to me, if you'd rather. I'm interested to find out what your parents put into your wee heads."

She pushed herself to her feet, retrieved her sister's book off his shelf, and resumed her place in front of the fire. She looked at the pegasus on the cover, then shook her head. She never would have imagined that such a thing existed, never mind that she might one day ride one. She looked at Acair to find him watching her gravely.

"Why did the peddler think you should have this?" she asked.

"I have no idea, though I'm not one for coincidence."

"You and King Sìle share that opinion."

"Don't tell him. He'll never sleep well again." He sat up and held out his hand. "Make yourself comfortable and I'll take up reading duties for tonight."

She stretched out on the floor next to where he sat crosslegged with his back against a chair and sighed.

"Thank you."

He reached out and put his hand briefly on her head. "My pleasure, darling." He paused. "Perhaps that peddler had a feeling that this might someday find itself back in the proper hands."

"Do you believe that?"

"At the moment, Léirsinn, I hardly know what to think. My mind is full of things that feel like broken pieces of a polished glass that need to go back together but seemingly have no way to do the same."

She tapped the cover of the book. "Faeries and heroes. You'll feel better after you indulge."

"I seriously doubt that, but I'll humor you." He opened the book and started to read.

She thought she just might love him in truth, unrepentant worker of terrible spells and possessor of a tender heart that he was.

He was so thoroughly not what she'd expected to find anywhere along that road that had begun at her own family's hearth with that same book, but she wondered how she could have expected anything else.

Thirteen

A cair dragged his sleeve across his forehead and sneezed. He wasn't one for tidying with his own hands when magic could do it for him, but his current project of digging about in a trunk he'd found stashed behind a winerack in his cellar seemed to suggest that was the proper way to go about it. The whole damned thing reeked of something foul.

Dust, definitely. Magic, possibly.

He'd thought it best to proceed gingerly.

Or so he had when he'd first found the trunk, which for a change hadn't been just after dawn. He'd managed to sleep well past sunrise, thankfully, but he'd woken with a pounding headache for his trouble. A finger or two of whisky hadn't done anything but make him short tempered.

Léirsinn had promised him she wouldn't apologize again for thinking him capable of slaying her family, which he'd begged her through his haze of pain and irritation not to do, then given him a wide berth.

Left to himself and firmly caught between regret for his reputa-tion and fury that the thought of attempting to recapture the vileness of the same going forward left him feeling slightly uncomfortable, he'd donned the proverbial hairshirt and decided he would do things he didn't particularly feel like doing.

Digging through the garden shed was one and that had gone about as he'd suspected it would, leaving him muddy and cross.

Rummaging about in the cellar had been but another slide down into a pit of misery and frustration. He could remember with unfortunate clarity the precise conversation he'd had with his very mortal master craftsmen whilst they had been about the noble labor of building his home.

What of this trunk, my lord?

Leave it, I'll attend to it later.

So said every cavalier lad who hoped *later* meant *several hundred years in the future when the bloody thing will have disintegrated.*

He straightened, groaned at the ache in his lower back, and wished that he hadn't started in the other end of his very large house. If he'd come straight to the cellar—yet another in a long series of lessons learned—he would have found the trunk before he'd wasted half the day looking for things he'd imagined he wouldn't want to see. And what had he found at the very end of his tedious morning?

Horseshoes.

He knew he shouldn't have been surprised. Those damned nags were going to be the death of him.

The trunk was full of all sorts of other things he supposed might have been useful in a barn. A record book listing the incomings and outgoings of necessities, several useful pieces of tack, and, as he'd already noted to himself, half a dozen horseshoes that he suspected not even Léirsinn would want.

He retrieved one just the same, slammed the trunk shut, then kept himself warm and happy with a few choice words as he climbed back up the stairs to the kitchen. He dropped the horseshoe on the table, glared at his horse-turned-useless-puss who was currently snoozing comfortably on the hearth rug, then took himself off to rid his clothes and person of dust and cobwebs.

Half an hour and a few more sneezes and curses later, he walked into his study with the sole purpose of finding something very strong to drink. He didn't usually indulge before sunset, but it had truly been that sort of day so far. He almost plowed Léirsinn over before he realized she was coming out where he intended to go in. He caught her by the arms, looked at her, and cursed those bloody magics in his chest that were making absolute ruination of his poor heart.

He pulled her into his arms and held her perhaps for a bit longer than was polite, but she wasn't elbowing him in the gut so perhaps she didn't mind.

"Acair, I—"

"Don't."

"I wasn't going to apologize," she said, her words muffled against his neck. "I was going to show you something interesting."

He didn't move. "Will I enjoy it?"

"It has to do with magic."

He sighed and loosened his grip on her, but found that he couldn't let her go. "I'm not sure I want to see it. Let's go find something else to do. I have some ideas that involve you, me, and copious displays of affection."

She laughed a little as she pushed away from him. "You're impossible, and you're still going to want to see this."

"Might I have more whisky first?"

"Nay, you may not. Do you know what's interesting?"

"My fetching, manly form?"

She rolled her eyes, then paused. "Well," she conceded, "that too, but look at this." She held out her arm.

"Beautiful," he said, fighting the urge to simply side-step her and head straight for the only thing he thought might save him.

"Nay, look more closely."

He conceded the battle. There were few others in the world, he was certain, who possessed his unwholesome ability to concentrate on the task at hand until that task surrendered with a wail of defeat, but he thought he might be facing one of them in the person of that glorious red-haired gel there.

He looked at her arm, then at her face. "It pains me to admit as much, but I have no idea what you're trying to show me except your lovely self which is leading to more thoughts of doing anything but the difficult work that lies before us."

"I'm flattered," she said, holding her arm up closer to his face. "Look again at the spot you healed."

He did, then shrugged, finding himself truly at a loss. "I'm torn between apologizing and telling you that you're welcome."

She took him by the hand and pulled him over to the window. A fine mist had already rolled in from the sea, but the soft light that remained was ample to see by.

"Watch what happens," she said. She pressed on the little pool of Fadaire that lingered there on her skin. "See how it scatters, then pulls back together?"

He put his hand over his chest protectively. "I'm afraid to look in a polished glass now."

"Nay," she said impatiently. "Remember how Falaire shattered those shadows, then they drew back together?"

He frowned. "In Sgath and Eulasaid's barn?"

"Aye. Isn't that strange? And look at how this does the same thing, only this comes back together in a lovely way. That pool of shadow in your grandparents' barn was far different." She looked at him. "Why does evil have all those pointy edges?"

He felt his mouth go dry. "Like shards."

She nodded slowly. "Odd, isn't it?"

He felt as if his entire being had become one of those ridiculous pools of shadow that Falaire had stomped to oblivion. The pieces came at him from all directions, then clicked back into a perfectly miserable whole.

Shards, shadows, his spell in Diarmailt that cast shadows, a mage who created shadows that stole souls . . .

He would have felt his way down into a chair, but he was no

fainting miss. He staggered artistically over to his sideboard and poured himself a large glass of whisky. He tossed it back without so much as a gasp and came back up with his throat on fire but his head absolutely clear. He could hardly believe he hadn't seen it before.

That shard-spewing mage was the one making those pools of shadow.

He leaned his hands on the sideboard, grateful he wasn't shaking badly enough to leave bottles rattling, and let that thought simply stand there in front of him it in all its simplicity where it might possibly be joined by other useful thoughts.

If that same mage was creating those shadows and the purpose of those shadows was to steal souls, then that mage's intention was to steal souls.

But if that were the case, why now?

He bowed his head and blew out his breath, then forced himself to start from the beginning and walk again down the path he'd been on, searching for things he might have overlooked.

He'd first noticed the lads following him when they'd left Aherin. He'd been so damned distracted at the time by his fury over Soilléir's leaving him helpless that he couldn't have said if the mage outside had been in that pack of jackals or not. The first sense he'd truly had of a single mage with mischief on his mind had been when Miach had handed him that bloody, overdone missive.

He'd realized soon after leaving Tor Neroche that the cloud of mage had turned into a single hunter, but he'd assumed that lone mage had been someone he'd done dirty in the past who had decided the time had come for revenge. Coming face to face with the man and watching spells come out of his mouth in impossibly sharp spears of darkness hadn't changed his opinion.

I'm the one with all the spells.

Well, that was a ridiculous boast, but if one had a spell to steal souls, perhaps all the other spells in the world simply didn't matter.

He straightened and rubbed his hands over his face, wishing

he'd questioned Soilléir a bit more thoroughly in that glade. He remembered with unfortunate clarity the man rambling on about spells and souls and missing one of the former, but the conversation had been distressingly empty of particulars.

The one thing he thought he could allow to stand as fact was that the mage following him had stolen his spell in Eòlas, which meant he had also likely slain Odhran, and left behind that childish note. If he was also the one making those shadows, then it was obvious that while he claimed to have mighty spells, he was missing at least one piece of the spell he likely wanted the most.

His hands twitched before he could stop them. What he wanted was to put them comfortably around a certain essence-changing prince's throat, but perhaps that wasn't a useful thought to be entertaining at the moment. He rubbed his hands together to keep them busy, then continued on the path that seemed to be unfortunately laid out in front of him.

Soilléir's had said that the spell stolen from his grandfather's library was the same spell—a copy, no doubt—that Acair had tossed into the fire all those decades ago. That was a spell for stealing souls, however, not creating shadows.

But if—*if*—the mage outside was the same one who had stolen Seannair's spell—whatever its true purpose was—then that made that man standing under the trees of his forest the orchardist that he himself had insulted all those many years ago.

Ninety years was a very long time to wait for revenge.

It wasn't as if there hadn't been ample opportunity for the man to see to it long before the present moment. He himself had spent decades going about in the open, walking along dusty roads with no one guarding his back, gliding across ballrooms with naught but a woman's gown to hide behind.

So many opportunities to execute a deft piece of payback, so why not before now?

Unless that mage outside didn't want revenge.

He would have said that he couldn't understand that, but unfortunately he did, all too well. If he hadn't, he wouldn't have had to look much further than his own family tree to find Gair of Ceangail perching there as the absolute embodiment of patience whilst about the vile work of herding his prey along an ever-straitening course that led to the end of the maze where there was no escape. There were others, to be sure, but he thought he might need to take a seat before he began scrutinizing that list.

Nay, he was missing something and he scarce had the stomach to wonder what.

What he needed to do was get above it. He was in the midst of the maze and there were simply too many possible pathways to see the pattern whilst looking at them from eye level.

He came to himself to find that he was standing in the middle of his library, staring at nothing. Léirsinn was watching from the doorway, hovering there as if she suspected she might need to make a hasty escape sooner rather than later.

He sighed. "Forgive me. Lost in thought."

"What can I do?" she asked.

"Distract him so I can fly?"

She smiled gravely. "Of course."

T he pleasure of flight was undiminished, he found as he hurtled out to sea as a chilly winter wind. If he ever managed to be free of that damned thing that dogged his steps, he would never take it for granted again. He left his thoughts behind and turned north, out toward the open ocean where there was nothing but sea and sky.

He flew until the sun began to sink in the west and the shadows started forming over the coastline.

An unsettling sight if ever there were one.

He slowed his flight as the winds near the shore buffeted him, bringing some sense back into his poor overworked mind. What he needed, he decided as he kept himself from being dashed against the rocky shoreline to the north of his home, was a holiday. No wonder

Soilléir seemed to take them with such regularity. Very restorative, no doubt.

He wandered over the same landscape he'd looked at the previous day, only things occurred to him that hadn't before.

The track that lay to the south of that ruined keep, the keep that most definitely could have been merely the start of a rather substantial settlement, was less faint than he'd thought before. In fact, if the forest hadn't taken it over, it could still have been considered an easy way to go from that ruin to his house. Perhaps there had been something important on that piece of land where his house currently stood.

He wondered if he should go have another rummage through that trunk in his cellar.

He decided that he would do just that before his thoughts carried him off to places where he was quite certain he wouldn't want them to go.

It took less time than he was comfortable with to gain his own home. He slipped through his spell of protection and resumed his proper form, though when he moved to dissolve his spell of unnoticing, he hesitated. That might have been courtesy of the sight of his enemy standing a hundred paces away in a spot between his house and the shore.

That was something he simply couldn't get past. Admittedly, he and Léirsinn hadn't been wearing any sort of spell of un-noticing on their way to his house, but Sìle had given them a decent head's start and he hadn't seen anything behind them the entire time they'd flown home. In fact, the first he'd seen of that mage there had been when Léirsinn had noticed him standing in the shadows beyond the garden. How was it possible for him to have found them without having had any idea where they were going?

Unless he'd known the lay of the land himself.

That thought was startling enough all on its own, but still the question remained: why hadn't he come before?

Acair studied the hooded figure standing close enough that a half-decent spell of death would have felled him instantly. It was definitely the mage from the glade. Acair could see shards wrapped around the man's neck like a scarf.

Other things, though, struck him now that he was at his leisure to mark them. The man certainly knew how to be still, though perhaps that had been to his detriment. He himself had never been one to mock another for the measurement of their waistline, but that man there had obviously spent too much time sitting and thinking and not enough time rushing about from one bad deed to the next.

And that was, he had to admit with surprising reluctance, the same man who he'd knocked off his ladder all those many years ago.

The orchardist had been sporting a close-trimmed beard, if memory served, but not one of a handsome fashion. Too much scruff down the neck and not enough left on the chin, certainly. Even at the tender age of eight, Acair had possessed opinions on the same thanks to his sire. Gair, for all his faults, had at least possessed the commitment to cutting an acceptable figure.

I'm watching you . . .

Watching, not acting? What sort of half-arsed business was that? Watching and waiting for what?

It wasn't pleasant to think about, but how many times could that mage there have simply slain him in his sleep? More particularly after he'd been gang-pressed into servitude by those giggling gels who had left him no choice but to comply with their ridiculous and quite perilous demands?

I'm watching you . . .

Not a surprise, he supposed, given what he now realized. The only question was, how long had that man there been watching him, waiting for the perfect moment for revenge?

He turned and walked into his house, kicking off his spell of unnoticing like a pair of muddy boots just outside the door. He shut the front door behind him, leaned back against it, then sighed deeply. Well, there was one question answered, he supposed.

Naming the man, however, might be a bit . . . more . . .

Time slowed to a crawl before it simply stopped.

He felt as green as a village lad on his first journey to a city containing more than one pub. He also supposed that if he didn't stop having to shake his head over his own stupidity, he was going to be forever lost for anything useful.

He walked through his house and into his kitchen. He continued on until he was standing by the table where he had honestly eaten only a handful of meals and most of those had been with that beautiful red-haired lass who was so fond of horses.

A horseshoe lay there, in the place where he'd left it, the single trophy he'd liberated from that bloody trunk languishing in his cellar. He looked at it and several things he hadn't considered before clicked into place, in exactly the same way that pool of shadow Falaire had destroyed had come back together.

Was the mage standing outside his house Sladaiche?

He found it surprisingly difficult to breathe for all the questions that then came at him with the unrelenting ferocity of Durialian dark magic.

Was *that* why his grandmother had scrawled that damnable X over his house? Had she known? Had his mother known?

Had *Soilléir* known? Was *that* why he had intimated that Acair needed to go where he himself could not walk?

Because the answer was in the cellar of his own bloody house?

He heard Léirsinn come into the kitchens and groped for some sort of pleasant expression to put on his face.

"How was the sea?" she asked with a smile as she passed him.

"Glorious," he said hoarsely. "Not to be missed. You'll have to come with me sometime."

"A thrilling prospect, truly."

"You *have* been too long in my company," he managed. "Listen to you being sardonic with so little effort."

"'Tis contagious," she agreed. She nodded at the table. "Starting a collection for your barn or is that something Sianach dragged in?"

He put his hand on the horseshoe because he suddenly felt a

bit as if he weren't precisely where he was, an alarming sensation if ever there were one. He supposed that might be as close as he would want to come to fainting from surprise.

"Um, aye," he said, scrambling for something to say that sounded reasonable. "Found it in the cellar."

She looked at him in surprise. "Was there a barn here originally? I looked at your grandmother's map while you were gone and wondered. If that's the case, I'm guessing there might have been an arena once where your garden is now."

Of course. He knew he shouldn't have been surprised.

He didn't argue when Léirsinn pulled out a chair and gave him a bit of a push down into it. She was, after all, rather strong for a wench.

He drank what she handed him which he found was water, not anything more useful. At the moment, he suspected anything that left him looking as if he were merely sitting in his kitchen for a decent chat before supper couldn't be a bad thing. He sipped, nodded when he thought her conversation merited it, and tried not to look as blind-sided as he felt.

I'm watching you.

He almost snorted. Apparently that was the case and it left him wondering just how long that had been going on.

I'm watching her . . .

Acair heard something shatter. He realized as he looked down that it was his glass that was lying there in shards at his feet.

Shards. Ye gads, would the word never cease to torment him?

He thought he might understand how it felt to be kicked by a stallion. He couldn't have lost his breath any more thoroughly or abruptly if he *had* been. He would have staggered, crediting the same to a little foray into his cook's hidden bottle of sherry, but his recent encounter with fierce ocean winds had left him perfectly sober.

Frighteningly sober and apparently lacking in the good sense that grounded a black mage to his higher purpose of making life a misery for everyone he came into contact with.

What if that mage hadn't been chasing him?

What if that mage had been after *Léirsinn* all along?

"Don't move."

He wasn't sure he could. He sat there and watched stupidly as Léirsinn started to clean up the glass. He came back to himself as she reached for a particularly large, jagged piece, then sent the lot into oblivion with a quick and dirty spell. She blinked, sat back on her heels and looked up at him.

"Aren't you handy," she said slowly.

He could only look at her, mute. He rose, pulled her to her feet, then pasted on a smile.

"Would you do me a favor?"

"Of course."

"Ah," he said, casting about for something to say, "could you find me a bottle of wine? From the cellar?"

She looked at him as if he'd lost his wits. He understood. If he could have caught enough breath to agree with her, he would have.

"Anything special?" she asked.

"Whatever suits," he said. "I left my boots at the front door. I need to go fetch them."

He turned and walked away before he had to say anything else inane, realizing as he opened his front door a handful of moments later that he was already wearing his boots because he'd never taken them off to begin with.

He didn't think, he simply walked down the pathway and through his spell.

He supposed he might later have the presence of mind to be relieved that his ever-present spell of death had detached itself from the spell protecting his home and come to stand next to him. That would no doubt be tempered by the knowledge that it was only standing so close because 'twas a bit easier to slay something if one had that something within arm's reach.

The mage facing him, that rotund little man with the terrible power but so little imagination, merely stood there, a hundred paces away, doing nothing.

Saying nothing.

Simply watching.

"Acair?"

The mage turned his head sharply and looked in the direction of that voice.

Acair continued on with his newfound habit of not thinking. He merely stepped back inside his spell, ignoring the shrieking of his deathly shadow as it couldn't follow him, and walked up to the front door. How he managed a smile he hoped was confident and unassuming, he wasn't sure. Years of practice at theatrics, no doubt.

"Darling, 'tis cold outside," he said, shooing Léirsinn inside and shutting the door behind them. If he locked it with a resounding click, so much the better.

"What were you—"

"Lost my spell there for a moment," he said, lying with an abandon that might have almost rivaled his recent realizations for sheer awfulness. "A drink, love, don't you think? Chilly out."

She looked at him as if she'd never seen him before. He understood. He hardly recognized himself, either.

He found himself enormously grateful for a spell that covered his house with an imperviousness that even Sìle of Tòrr Dòrainn, an elf famous for his own spell covering his realm, might have given a brisk nod of approval to.

At least he hoped it was impervious.

He shook his head sharply. Of course it was. He had poured quite a bit of his own . . .

He indulged in an impolite epitaph or two and wondered when it was that he would stop encountering realizations that made him want to go have a little lie-down. He had poured a rather decent amount of his *soul* into his spell of protection because it had seemed like a reasonable use of what he had to hand. It also made it rather convenient, as he had so recently noted to himself, when it came time to pop in or out of his own dwelling. Just a bit of shorthand to keep himself from being crushed to death.

He found that he couldn't speak and Léirsinn was kind enough not to force him to. She was also kind enough to hand him a glass of whisky when he collapsed into the chair in front of the fire in his study.

He couldn't believe he hadn't considered it before. A testament to his own arrogance, to be sure. Even Aonarach of Léige had needed to point out to him how unimportant he was in the grander scheme of things. He was tempted to wonder about that lad's part in the whole damned play, but he dismissed that immediately. Aonarach was a youth and apparently fixated on the sister he thought Léirsinn might still have, not other, more unsettling matters.

"Did you find anything?"

Acair looked at the glorious woman he had considered naught but a simple stable lass and wondered what part *she* had to play in the madness.

Not that he couldn't think of several decent reasons why someone would want her, but he was also hopelessly fond of her for reasons that had nothing to do with magic or shadows or draining the world of anything beautiful.

Why would a mage who made shadows with the express purpose of stealing souls want that lass there?

"I think you need something to eat."

He nodded, though a turn about the old place to make sure all the corners of his spell were tucked in tightly was definitely going to be called for first.

He followed her to the kitchen, furiously reassessing his strategy for keeping himself—and Léirsinn—safe and whole.

If he couldn't protect her, he would have to arm her as best he could. He suspected she wasn't going to like that at all, but he had no choice.

It might be the only way to keep her alive.

Fourteen

L éirsinn wondered if taking the heaviest thing within reach and beaning a black mage with it would be counted as murder or a service to mankind.

"Again," that black mage said briskly.

She looked at him and wondered where the rather charming, conflicted man she'd fallen asleep next to on the floor of his study the night before had gone.

In his place was an impossible — and impossibly annoying — bastard son of the worst black mage in recent memory who was living up to every nasty thing she'd ever heard about him. If he had been tracking her with evil intentions at the ready, she would have found the first mage-king available and hidden behind his skirts for as long as necessary.

She would have looked around for Sianach to invite him to do some damage to his master, but even Acair's horse had deserted her. She was simply left with a man who had perhaps lost all his wits during the night.

She should have insisted that he go sleep in his comfortable bed while she stayed in front of the fire. That glorious goose-feather pallet was so much more luxurious than anything she'd slept on in her uncle's barn, it was as if she were sleeping in one of the palace guest chambers she had recently visited. Acair, however, was no doubt accustomed to much finer trappings.

Then again, perhaps that wouldn't have mattered. He'd been silent during supper the night before, then seemingly consumed with rereading his grandmother's notes and his own after that. He'd spent more time than not simply staring off into nothing, only occasionally shaking his head as if he couldn't quite believe something.

She'd been afraid to ask what that something might have been.

She'd woken several times during the night to find him either sitting in the chair at her feet, staring into the fire, or gone. If she hadn't seen the faint light coming from under his library door, she would have thought he'd decided to take a star-lit flight to the ruin up the way.

Dawn had provided her with a taskmaster who hadn't let her have more than a crust of bread before he'd hustled her out to the back garden. The sun had been up, but had scarce managed to melt away any of the patches of frost. Acair had provided her with a very warm cloak and fine gloves, but that had been the extent of it.

He had then cast up a shield of sorts under his spell of protection. She'd hardly had time to admire it, much less ask why he thought it to be necessary, before he'd been hounding her to take her magic out of the stall and put it to work.

She'd complied because she'd been able to see the wisdom in it. She had practiced calling fire until, to her great surprise, she'd been able to do so without setting the entire garden alight.

But had that been enough? Nay, it had not. Without so much as a nod of approval, that damned mage there had demanded spells of containment.

She'd used the one Uachdaran's stable lad had given her, which had been sufficient for grain but not entirely enough for that spell of death still trapped out front. It had, however, worked well enough against fire. Finally succeeding at it after countless attempts had earned her only a faint lessening of her spellmaster's perpetual scowl before he'd turned to other things.

She was starting to have sympathy for those horses she'd worked without pause until they'd been forced to acknowledge she was master.

"I'm tired," she said, because that was understating it badly. She was so exhausted, she could hardly see the garden in front of her.

"Try calling fire again," he said mercilessly.

She shoved aside thoughts of murder and mayhem, firmly refusing to acknowledge how delightful they sounded at the moment, and looked at the pile of wood there before her. She knew the spell of fire-calling so well that she thought she might even be able to write it down and teach it to someone else. Five words, that was all, that caused the air to shudder around her, the magic in her veins to leap up and dance a merry jig across her soul, and flames to burst to life atop those poor charred bits of felled tree.

She took a deep breath, stilled her mind and her heart, and summoned fire. She was almost too weary to be satisfied that it had come as commanded.

"Contain it."

She would have cursed Acair as her fire began to spill off the wood—his doing, obviously—but she was afraid it might find its way to her and burn her very lovely boots that the admittedly impossible man next to her had also given her that morning.

She used her lone spell of containment. The fire stopped in its tracks and sighed.

Then it burst into towering flames, something she most definitely hadn't given it permission to do.

Acair cursed, smothered it again, then looked at her.

"Again."

She called on every smidgen of self-control she possessed to keep herself from reaching out and bloodying his nose.

"I've done it well already this morning," she said tartly. She decided that adding *mostly* was not going to help the situation any. "Shall I drop it on your sorry head?"

"You might try," he said rather coolly.

She wondered absently if he could possibly be as merciless to those whose magic he wanted as he was presently being to her. Deciding that it was likely nothing she wanted to investigate further, she took a step back, away from things she couldn't face any longer.

"I'm finished."

He wasn't having any of it. "One more time."

"Nay."

"*One more time.*"

She looked at him, then did the most sensible thing she'd done all morning.

She turned and walked away.

"I didn't say you could go."

She froze, then turned around slowly and looked at him. Admittedly, she could hardly see him for the pain that burned like a bonfire behind her forehead, but he didn't need to know that.

"Do not," she said crisply, "tell me what to do."

"Fine," he said, throwing up his hands. "Go, then."

"I will, thank you very much."

She supposed he was swearing at her. She wasn't sure, only because she couldn't hear him over the curses she was throwing over her shoulder at him. She walked inside his house, slammed the door shut behind her, and looked for something to drink. Water, because she was already ill from spells and anger and no small bit of confusion and dismay.

What in the hell was he doing?

He didn't follow her, which didn't surprise her. He hadn't been particularly polite, but he hadn't been nearly as rude to her as she had been to him. Perhaps all those years of having to bite her tongue had finally added up to one time too many and he had borne the brunt of all that pent-up fury.

She stood in front of the kitchen fire and fought to simply stay on her feet. Magic did not come without a price to be paid, as she'd already known, but the exhaustion she felt at present was terrible. At least she'd managed to use the two spells she knew without completely destroying Acair's house.

He had tried to teach her a spell of un-noticing, but that had been just too complicated. Not even having him write it down had helped, though she had to admit he hadn't said a single insulting word about her having needed such a concession.

That man was, as she'd noted before, a mystery.

She was tempted to shuffle over to the back door and have a little look outside to make certain he was still there, but decided that perhaps she needed a bit of distance from the scene of her earlier triumph and he needed a bit of distance from her own surly self. That didn't mean, though, that she couldn't at least keep him company from a different part of his garden.

She finished her cup of water she wasn't entirely certain hadn't come from an enspelled well, filched his cloak he'd left draped over the back of a kitchen chair, and went to look for a different exit to the outside.

She walked into a room at the back of his house that overlooked the garden. It was, as seemed to be a common thing for him, full of enormous glass windows. She'd used it previously to gawk at the mountains behind his home, though she could see how it might be a lovely place to sit and look at things when the weather was foul.

She opened the door that led out to the garden, quietly eased outside, then came to a skidding halt. She felt her way down onto the closest bench, not caring in the slightest if it might be covered with snow or dew or bird droppings.

Acair was standing on the edge of his vegetable patch. That wasn't noteworthy. That he was using magic that made her ill just to watch certainly was.

She looked up at the sky. Mid-day light was harsh anyway, but at the moment there was no lovely curtain of un-noticing for the sunlight to filter through. His spell of protection was still covering the house and gardens, but there was nothing there to warm that cold, pale winter sunlight. There was also no delicate veil to shield him from prying eyes.

Eyes belonging to that mage she could see standing on the edge of the forest behind the garden.

She imagined she didn't need to point that out to Acair. She also realized very quickly that what she'd seen in Uachdaran's lists had been Acair being polite.

He wasn't being polite presently.

Perhaps that black mage there had spent too much time doing good and felt the need to return to his roots. Perhaps he thought a little display might encourage his enemy to hike up his robes and dash off to less dangerous locales.

All she knew was that if she'd first met Acair of Ceangail in his present mood, she would have turned tail and fled and felt perfectly justified in doing so.

What he was doing was spectacularly horrifying. Spell after spell, terrible magic after terrible magic, things built, things torn down. His rage took shape into things that he subsequently destroyed so thoroughly that nothing was left, not even a shadow of what had been there before.

She should have gone back inside, but she found she couldn't move. She was exhausted from what she'd already done in the garden that morning, true, but what kept her firmly planted on that bench was something different.

If Acair could use that magic, she could watch him do it.

If he thought to intimidate his enemy, she couldn't think of a better way to do it. She was frightened almost to the point of senselessness and she was fairly certain he had a few warm feelings for her. What he was showing that mage out there should have left the man fainting in truth from fear over the possibility that any of it might be used on him.

It turned into a very long day, indeed.

The sun was well into its afternoon trail toward the west before

Acair finished. He snapped the spell shielding them back together as if it had been a crisp, invisible velvet drape, then turned and saw her.

She hoped he wouldn't mind if she simply turned and used one of his tidy hedges as a place to lose that crust of bread she'd ingested earlier, which she did. She didn't expect him to help her, and he didn't. She finally stopped heaving, dragged her sleeve across her face, then straightened and looked at him.

He was standing a handful of paces away watching her, terrible, beautiful, conflicted man that he was.

She could feel the power pouring off him in waves and that more than anything she'd seen in so many days of encountering impossible things convinced her that she had completely underestimated him.

He was not a horse who could eventually be controlled. He wasn't a stable lad who could be reasoned with. He wasn't one of her uncle's noblemen who could be ignored, or even her uncle himself who could be deferred to. He was a mage of staggering power and ruthless determination.

It was no wonder other mages wept and scattered when they saw him coming.

She took a careful breath. "What," she asked, "was that?"

He only shook his head sharply.

"Acair—"

He stepped back. "If you touch me," he said flatly, "I will shatter."

She believed him. "I won't."

"I'm going to go wash off all this evil."

"You do that," she managed.

He walked past her, giving her a wide berth.

She didn't watch him go.

S he paced through the parts of his house that weren't near his bedchamber, partly to give him privacy but mostly to give herself time to come to terms with what she'd seen.

She wondered if King Uachdaran had known how much restraint Acair had been showing down in his underground arena.
Likely so only because she suspected the king was surprised by very
little. The business with Aonarach had been strange, but perhaps
there was some unwritten code amongst mages that said one didn't
slay the relatives of one's host. She had the feeling if Aonarach had
been sitting next to her an hour ago, he might think twice about pro-
voking Acair again in the future.

Why Acair had felt the need for that sort of display that morning was curious. She understood the necessity of releasing a bit
of pent-up energy. She had shooed countless ponies into turnouts
where they could run until they had run themselves out.

But, as she'd noted before, Acair was not a horse and that business out there hadn't been a mage simply taking his spells out for a
canter around the arena.

She walked into his study without thinking and found him
standing in front of the fire, his hands on the mantel, leaning against
it as if he were simply too weary to stand. His hair was still damp
and he looked fresh-scrubbed, but he was definitely not at peace.

She would have turned around and left him to himself if she'd
been a different sort of woman, but she was accustomed to facing
feisty stallions head on. She reminded herself of that as she walked
across the room, sat down, and looked up at him. He didn't look as
if he intended to speak any time soon, so she opened the conversational stall door herself.

"What are you doing?" she asked.

"Remembering who I am," he said hoarsely. "Darkness is my
birthright and use it I shall until the world ceases to turn."

She had no doubt he would. She leaned her head back against
the very fine leather of that chair and studied him.

"Why did you do all that?"

He shot her a look that she was certain was exactly the sort of
thing she slid stable lads who asked questions they already had the
answers for.

She nodded. "To discourage him from coming after you."

He took a deep breath, but said nothing. She would have assured him that no one with any of their wits still in their possession would have approached him after the display he'd put on, but she supposed he knew that already. If his intention had been to show the mage lurking in the shadows what he was capable of, he had definitely accomplished that. She wasn't sure why that morning had seemed like a good time for it, but it wasn't as if he'd been able to use his magic freely before then.

What she couldn't understand was why he'd been so hard on her.

The truth was, he hadn't until that morning pushed her to do anything but dabble in magic. In fact, if she were to be entirely honest, aside from a very easy morning of not much at all in Léige, he hadn't pushed her to learn anything. She had no idea why he'd changed his mind . . .

She felt her thoughts come to ungainly halt.

There was no reason for him to indulge in that sort of flourishy display for himself. Surely the mage outside his spell knew who he was and what he was capable of.

There was even less reason for him to push her to learn any sort of spell beyond simply containing that spell of death so he could use his own magic.

Unless he didn't fear for himself.

She found herself on her feet. Easier to run that way, perhaps, though she wasn't sure where she thought she would go. She simply stood there, shaking, as things occurred to her that hadn't before.

There was only one reason why Acair would want her to have more spells than a simple one to keep that spell of death bound so it wouldn't slay him.

She felt her heart almost stop.

"He doesn't want you," she managed.

Acair only looked at her, silent and grave.

She felt a horror descend that was far worse than what had

caught her by the throat when she'd realized her uncle was plotting her murder.

"Me?" she asked, but the word came out as barely a whisper.

He only shook his head slowly. "I don't know."

She was torn between weeping and howling, so she chose the most sensible reaction which was to do neither.

"But I'm nobody—"

He reached over and pulled her into his arms. She would have pointed out that he was robbing her of her ability to breathe, but she realized fairly quickly that he was the only thing holding her inside herself.

Her world was suddenly ripped from her as if by claws. She was beyond weeping, beyond fleeing, in a place so far beyond fear that she wasn't sure she would ever feel anything else.

And the only thing keeping her from shattering was a man who was capable of creating and destroying horrors that she had never seen even in her worst nightmares.

"That's why you made me do all that," she said, finally, her words muffled against his shoulder.

"Aye."

"And why you used all that . . . "

"I want him to know exactly what I'm capable of," he said harshly. "And what I will do to him if he harms you."

She laughed a little, wondering if it sounded as unhinged to him as it did to her. "A hero from Neroche could not have been more chivalrous."

She wasn't sure what to call the noise he made, but it was a decent mirror of the anguish she felt.

He held her for so long, she wondered if the rest of the afternoon had passed and night had fallen. She closed her eyes, pressed her face against his neck, and simply shook.

She realized he was smoothing his hand over her hair, as if he sought to soothe her. She took a deep breath, then let it out slowly.

"Thank you."

He pulled back, kissed her quickly, then stepped away.

"Strong drink," he said firmly.

She looked at him. "I can't believe this, you know."

He hesitated, then shook his head wearily. "He doesn't want me, Léirsinn."

"How do you know?"

"Because last night I stepped outside my spell, faced him, and he only yawned. He heard your voice and things changed." He took a deep breath and let it out slowly. "He doesn't want me."

She caught his hand before he passed her. "I can't do this," she said, then she paused. "How do I do this?"

"How like you," he said quietly. "Testing the ground, then rushing out to stomp the bloody hell from it."

"Why does everyone want me dead?"

He smiled without humor. "I honestly don't know, love. You haven't done anything to merit it."

She sighed. "I apologize. I said that unthinkingly."

"Oh, I've earned the ire of those who would like to see me breathe my last," he admitted. "You, on the other hand, haven't. Perhaps your uncle hired that man out there because he thought you would one day rise up to challenge him for his hall."

"Fuadain has sons of his own."

"Sons can be poisoned."

She gaped at him, but he only shrugged.

"It has been done before. I'm guessing your uncle wouldn't be above it. I've found that men who suspect terrible things of others generally entertain those same thoughts themselves in the dead of night."

She wished she could fly, though at the moment leaving the safety of his spell sounded like the worst idea she'd had in years.

"I think you're wrong," she said. "I'm sure of it."

He nodded slightly. "As you say."

"Agree with me, damn you!"

He only stopped and looked at her, his face full of pity. No fear, though, and that surprised her.

"You're not afraid."

"I am never afraid for myself," he said slowly.

"And for me?"

"I'll find a way to keep you safe."

"That wasn't an answer."

"I refuse to give you an answer for that."

She went into his arms. If her knees gave way, well, he was a gentleman after all and knew when to keep his mouth shut.

He also carried her with a fair amount of gallantry the entire three steps it took to reach one of the chairs in front of his fire. She thought sharing chairs with him might be becoming something of a bad habit, though she couldn't remember when it had started— well, she supposed that wasn't true. She had a vague and unpleasant memory of almost fainting in his arms after she'd shot bolts into two mages hovering over him, preparing to slay him. She thought they might have briefly shared a stool while those mages had simply vanished into thin air.

There were several things, she decided, that she might not want to think about again.

"I can move," she said.

"Why?"

"So your legs don't lose all feeling?"

"I'll wiggle my toes occasionally."

"Good of you."

He sighed. "Altruism, I'm beginning to find, gets me into all sorts of trouble."

She gave in and made herself comfortable, then leaned her head against the winged side of the chair back where she could watch him. His expression was grave, but there was no fear lurking in his eyes. Then again, he was accustomed to people wanting him dead.

"Would you prefer to have the lamps brighter?" he asked quietly.

She shook her head. "You're very beautiful by firelight."

"I was just going to say the same thing about you." He put his arms more securely around her and sighed deeply. "I'm sorry about this morning—and no comments about all this apologizing being the ruination of my code of conduct, if you please. I'm keenly aware of how far down the path toward syrupy sweetness I've strayed."

"If it eases your conscience any, I've been harder on horses that I loved," she offered. "And I apologize for being rude to you."

"Aren't we just the picture of polite, almost connubial bliss."

"More treacle from you, my lord?"

He smiled that small smile she imagined got him more things he wanted than awful spells ever had, but he apparently found no need for any for comment. He simply combed his fingers through her hair with one hand and kept his other arm around her. It was, she had to admit, surprisingly comforting.

She only wished it were enough.

"What will I do?" she asked, finally.

"You can make fire—"

"Call fire, you mean."

He nodded. "An important distinction. You can call fire and contain things. Very useful skills, those."

"Do you have other short spells?"

He smiled gravely. "A few."

"How many?"

"I'm too weary to count them all, but I'll make you a list in the morning."

"We could go collect more of your soul," she said, knowing it was a last-ditch effort to keep herself from having to use what she'd asked for. "Then you would have what you needed, aye?"

He looked at her seriously. "I'm not sure we have the time, if you want my thoughts on it."

"Then what will we do?" she asked miserably.

"Well, I've been thinking," he said slowly. "We have a spell of death that requires nothing from either of us." He shrugged. "It might be worth making a handful of others for use in a pinch."

"Won't that cost you bits of your soul?"

"There isn't all that much left to take. I'll make a few, sleep like the dead for a day or two, then we'll be off and doing."

"And what am I to do while you're doing that?" she asked, pushing aside her unease over the thought of being alone inside with that mage lurking in the forest outside.

"Refrain from burning the house down?"

"What about a spell of werelight?" she asked. "Could I do that?"

He smiled. "I imagine you could."

"Let's go, then." She pushed off his lap only to have him catch her and pull her back. "What?"

"You don't need to go outside to practice that," he said. "I think we should stay right here by the fire where it's warm."

She imagined he was less concerned about staying warm than he was staying out of sight, but she suspected she didn't need to acknowledge that.

"I can only manage five words," she warned.

"Fadaire will do it for you in three."

"Oh?" she asked in surprise. "What will King Sìle think?"

"He'll never know."

"I'm beginning to suspect that might not be as true as you would like."

"I'll take responsibility for you. But let's try it later. I think I might need a nap soon." He paused, then looked at her seriously. "About this morning—"

She shook her head. "I know what you're capable of."

"Nay, about pushing you so hard." He sighed. "Listen to me apologizing as easily as if I've done nothing else for the whole of my life." He reached out and touched her cheek. "Please don't tell anyone. And, you know, forgive me."

"You were trying to keep me safe, I imagine."

He only nodded, closed his eyes, then gathered her more closely to him.

S he lost him to hopefully peaceful dreams shortly after supper, so perhaps all that magick-making was more draining than he wanted to admit. She had no idea what the hour was, but it was full dark outside and a faint new moon had already risen.

She found she didn't care for being alone. That was odd considering how alone she had been up until she'd met a black mage who taught her elven magic so she could hopefully not set his house ablaze.

She jumped a little at the shadow that appeared at her elbow, then realized it was simply Sianach having assumed the form of a great, hulking hound. He put his snout on her knee and looked at her pointedly.

She scratched him behind the ears. "Don't bare your teeth at me," she warned.

He lifted his head and displayed longer canine teeth than any hound should have had.

"Sianach," she said in disapproval. "That isn't reassuring."

He licked her hand, then lay down and put his head on Acair's foot. She supposed that if anyone came inside, he could snarl at them to discourage anything untoward. Short of that, she had no idea what she would do to protect any of them. Elvish werelight likely wasn't going to be much use, so perhaps Acair had the right idea about other spells that would work all on their own.

She got up after a bit because she couldn't sit still any longer. She wandered through his library, looking for anything that didn't lay out spells or relate tales of mythical beasts and men. She was tempted by a treatise that discussed the trade routes through Tosan, but settled for a history of Fearranian lacemaking.

She tucked the book under her arm and walked through the house a final time, an enormous hound suddenly walking next to her with his head under her hand. There was nothing stirring, but she supposed she shouldn't have been surprised. Acair's spell was reputedly impenetrable. If she took a little detour to the kitchen and fetched the largest knife she could find, well, she suspected he would understand.

She went back to his study, shut the main door and the door leading to the library, then set the kitchen knife on the mantel, back so far that it wouldn't fall off accidently yet be within reach if necessary.

She turned to her reading for the evening, a sleeping mage and terrifying hound at her feet, and hoped she could distract herself from the reality of her life until she was too weary to even dream about it.

That mage out there wanted her.

She couldn't imagine why.

Fifteen

Acair walked through his house with a fair bit of unease,
understanding in that moment what Hearn of Angesand
might feel if he woke to find one of his barn doors open.

Whilst he suspected such a thing likely never happened to that
good horse lord, he feared he might not be so lucky. He also suspected Hearn never waited until the morning sun was streaming
through his great hall before being about his business. Perhaps there
was a lesson there for him about the hours kept by horse people,
more particularly a gel who hadn't been sleeping peacefully next to
him when he'd woken not a quarter hour earlier.

He paced through his house not because he feared Léirsinn had
run away during the night but because it was a fine distraction from
other lessons he might or might not have learned recently.

For instance, who would have thought that his arrogance—
something he had never considered a flaw before—would have
blinded him to the fact that perhaps he was not the one being pursued across the whole of the Nine Kingdoms? The idea that someone would see him and not want to kill him was something he wasn't
sure he cared for. One tended to reach a certain status in life and
learned to appreciate the opportunities that came with that position.

Being able to sneer at all those who wanted him dead was a simple pleasure, but one he'd come to enjoy.

But how was he who had never once considered the safety of another going to keep a magick-making horse miss safe?

He'd planned for it, of course, but—also something he had to admit with a fair bit of shame—as a corollary to his own neck-saving. That Léirsinn should be the primary target of a mage with the sort of vicious nature the lad in the woods seemed to possess was something he had completely missed.

He could hardly bear to think about all the other things he might have missed.

At the very least, he thought he might have a name for their enemy. He also supposed he could credit the man, *Sladaiche*, with having stolen his spell of shadow making from Odhran of Eòlas, for all the good it would do him. It had been meant as a distraction, not a means of stealing souls, though it did artistically scatter rats and snakes and other things he didn't particularly care for in all directions when used. Perhaps he would suggest that Sladaiche hold onto it given that he would never have the imagination to create anything like it himself.

He might also suggest that Sladaiche accept that it would be the very last thing he saw before he was repaid for the slaying of a certain tailor of their acquaintance.

He turned away from thoughts of revenge and pressed on to things he had definitely missed in the past. According to Soilléir, whose busybody's ways would certainly make him an authority on it, Sladaiche had lived next to Ceangail at least long enough for Acair to have knocked him off his ladder after having found his spell to be worthless, the same spell that Sladaiche had apparently stolen from Seannair of Cothromaiche's library decades earlier, a theft that Soilléir couldn't seem to solve himself.

Did no one make copies of anything any longer? He despaired for the world, truly he did. Even his mother duplicated her endless notes. He was fairly certain she had a copy or two of Diminishing

hidden in her house, which was likely why the place was crawling
with spells even Acair had made a point of avoiding.

The last thing that troubled him more than he wanted it to
was why he was still so damned out of sorts over the thought that
when Léirsinn had seen books that her parents had owned, her
first thought had been to suspect him of stealing those tomes and
her second had been that he might have been the one to murder her
parents.

It was enough to make a black mage weep into his silk-lined
cape, oy.

Then again, what else was she to think? Wasn't he the one who
had told her that after his stint of do-gooding was done, he fully intended to return to his life of villainy?

He realized he was staring stupidly out the glass walls of his
front parlor into the blinding rays of a just-risen sun. He wondered
if that damned Ubhan of Bruadair was sending him nightmares to
be enjoyed during the daytime now. His house was just too close to
their border. Who knew what sorts of nasty things leached over the
same to vex and annoy?

Things had to change. He wouldn't survive the spring with the
way events were carrying on, dragging him along in their wake. The
bouts of self-reflection alone were about to do him in.

He made his way back through the house, looking in various
chambers with increasing amounts of unease, until he finally found
himself opening the kitchen door to the garden. If he didn't find
Léirsinn soon —

He ignored the wave of relief that almost brought him to his
knees, merciless, untouchable lad that he was.

Léirsinn was standing there, looking at the pile of wood they'd
left there the day before.

He staggered outside and sat down on the top step not because
he thought he might fall there if he didn't, but because he thought it
might make him look a bit more relaxed and carefree.

The garden was still full of shadows, of course. Again, horse people seemed to have an unwholesome relationship with dawn, something he had definitely discovered thanks to his experience of trying to keep up with a certain one of their number. He smoothed his hand, magically speaking, over the curtain of invisibility he'd set inside his own spell, then lit discreet lamps in the parts of the garden that needed them. Léirsinn startled, then visibly relaxed.

Poor gel.

He didn't move, though, because he'd slept with her in his arms for the whole of the night without even the most chaste of kisses and he was, after all, only full of so much self-restraint. If he wrapped her in a fond embrace at the moment, he feared he might not be able to release her.

She turned and walked over to him, then knelt on the step below his and put her hands over his arms, crossed as they were atop his knees.

"I'm not sure I believe this," she said, looking terribly hopeful. "What could he want with me? And why now? I've been in a barn, unprotected, for years."

He slipped one of his arms from beneath her hands, then reached out and tucked a lock of flaming hair behind her ear. He leaned forward and kissed her for good measure, but not nearly as thoroughly as he would have liked. Self-control was, as at least one monarch had pointed out recently, one of his most desirable virtues.

"I don't know the answers to any of those questions," he said carefully, revisiting the idea of pulling her into his arms and keeping her there for several decades. At least that way she would be safe.

"Who is he, do you think?"

"Sladaiche."

She pulled back, looking as if she'd seen something very vile writhing in a pile before her feet. He understood that more fully than he wanted to admit. She took a few steadying breaths, then looked at him.

"Does he want me because I want you?"

He almost fell off his perch. "Damn you, Léirsinn, give a little hallo of warning before you say that kind of thing."

She smiled, but she looked rather ill, to be honest.

"You're charming when you're startled."

"Well, stop it," he said crossly. "I like to look fully in control of myself and everyone around me at all moments."

"Frustrating that you aren't, isn't it?"

"All part of my master plan, darling. Lull the rabble to sleep, then take over the world. Not," he added, "that I've had any success so far at controlling you. I haven't given up the fight yet."

"You'll never manage it."

"I'm coming to terms with that in my own way. Don't twist the knife."

Her smile faded. "I don't have anything anyone wants."

"I assume you're not lumping me in with that lot of uneducated cretins." He reached out and looped his arms loosely around her shoulders. "Obviously I have work yet to do in convincing the loveliest, most courageous, decent, and, dare I say it, most discerning woman in the whole of the Nine Kingdoms that she might have drawn the attention of someone besides my own sweet self."

"I am nothing more than a stable hand."

"And I'm nothing more than a bastard."

"Your mother is a witch and your father a prince's son."

"Your father is a lord's son and I didn't ask my mother to delve into your dam's genealogy yet. Who knows what we'll find?"

"I think you're wrong."

He nodded slightly. "I might be."

"What could he want from me?" she whispered.

"Come sit next to me and keep warm, then we'll noodle it around a bit and see what comes up."

She looked absolutely devastated. "How can you be so calm—never mind. This is what you face every day."

He pulled her up to sit next to him, then drew a warm cloak out of thin air and wrapped it around the both of them.

"Aye, well 'tis all too true," he said easily, "but the difference is, I deserve it. You don't." He put his arm around her shoulders. "We could go inside, if you prefer."

"I'm fine."

She was shivering, but perhaps she hadn't noticed. He had another look at the spell he'd cast up to shield them from prying eyes, then turned to the pile of wood there in front of them. He considered for a moment the sort of fire he could make that would be warming but beautiful. Léirsinn had seen enough from him that hadn't been so beautiful, to be sure.

"What are you thinking?"

He looked at her, her lovely visage so close to his that he found himself a little dazzled by the leafy greenness of her eyes.

"I'm having trouble holding a thought," he admitted.

She smiled and elbowed him gently. "I'm sure you aren't. Are you going to build me a fire?"

He supposed he could do a little experimenting with things that intrigued him. Since he was definitely going to be completely flattened by the end of the day anyway, no sense in not taking his Gran's spell out for a brief canter about the old place. He imagined weaving it aloud was a very bad idea indeed, so he settled for a few theatrical hand wavings and a silently recited spell of essence meddling.

Léirsinn gasped.

He had to admit, he did too.

"What is that?" she said faintly.

"I believe most people call it *fire.*"

She shot him a half-hearted glare. "I meant, what magic was that?"

"Can't remember," he said.

"You're a terrible liar and that is an exceptionally lovely bit of work there."

He leaned closer to her. "Granny's magic," he murmured in her ear. He straightened and put his arm back around her shoulders.

"I'm not sure why I'm surprised, but I am. I expected it to light *me* on fire."

"There are dragons in the flames."

"Are there? Hadn't noticed."

"Did you do that?" she said, watching the flames with an expression of wonder on her face.

"Might have."

She turned that look on him. "For me?"

"Well, I don't see any other red-haired lassies who breathe fire hereabouts."

She smiled. "Who are you?"

"Today, darling, I have absolutely no idea."

She leaned her head on his shoulder and sighed. He rested his cheek against her hair and watched the flames dance. He had to admit he was a bit surprised that his grandmother's magic hadn't first done what he'd asked, then suddenly turned on him and incinerated him, but perhaps she was fonder of him than he supposed.

Taking air that was simply air and not full of the seeds of fire waiting to be magically harvested, so to speak, then forcing it into fiery shapes where it lingered in a more permanent state than he was accustomed to finding it . . . now, that was something. He half expected Soilléir to come charging into the garden to protest someone using anything that came close to his own mighty magic.

"Did you call that fire or make it?"

"Neither."

She lifted her head and looked at him in astonishment. "Did you *meddle*?"

"I did," he said, feeling a bit awed by the same.

"Would your grandmother be proud or furious?"

"Well, she did give me the spell," he said. "I'm half afraid to look around lest using it has cracked the world in two in places I can't see."

"How long will it last?"

"That is the question, isn't it? I'm not certain I have the patience to wait it out, and I'm certainly not going to leave you out here to do the work for me."

"I'm not sure I want to stay out here without you," she said seriously. She watched the flames for a bit longer, then frowned. "There's something about it that seems familiar."

"Lingering indigestion from substances imbibed at my granny's tea-table, no doubt."

"No doubt," she agreed.

He sat with her in what turned out to be a lovely, companionable silence for perhaps longer than he should have, but the work that lay ahead of him was going to be heavy. He wasn't afraid of it, naturally, though he had to admit the thought of leaving Léirsinn on her own whilst he was senseless from the efforts gave him pause.

The fire burned out eventually, though it took a good hour before it even began to fade. He watched, his arm around a lovely, courageous woman who didn't seem to mind just sitting with him there and waiting until the flames disappeared as if they had never been there to start with.

He sighed. "Well, there's that. How about breakfast, then I'll be about my labors? I'll need to make a list of vile things that might be useful, which fortunately won't take all that long."

She caught his arm before he rose. "Look."

He stopped in mid crouch, then straightened as she stood up next to him. He realized what she was looking at, but imagined no one else needed to make any note of it. He nodded slightly, then walked with her back into the house, shut the door, then dropped a spell over it to lock it. He looked at her.

"I didn't imagine them?"

"Those dragon shapes burned into the wood?" she asked. "Not unless I'm dreaming with you."

"We're close enough to Bruadair where that might be possible," he admitted, "but in this case, I imagine not. I wonder what that means?"

"Are you going to investigate?"

He smiled. "You know I will. Later, though."

"I'll leave you to it—"

"Nay, stay," he said. He paused. "If you will. I wouldn't mind the company."

"If you like."

What he would have liked was an entire afternoon with nothing more to do but walk on the shore with her, but things were what they were and he had serious business to see to.

The sooner it was finished, the happier he would be.

An hour later, he sat at the kitchen table and considered what lay there in front of him. He'd decided on coins from Sàraichte only because Léirsinn was familiar with them. Not that she couldn't have learned another country's coinage, of course. He just knew that if she wound up needing to use one of them, she would be under a decent amount of duress. The less she had to think through things instead of simply reaching for a weapon and using it, the better.

He glanced at her, sitting next to him at that comfortable round table in front of the fire, and realized she was watching him, not what he'd laid out there. He blinked in surprise.

"What is it?"

"Just watching you think," she said.

He shook his head. "I forget to be discreet in your company."

"I'd rather know," she said simply. "You don't seem overly concerned."

Obviously she wasn't able to hear the blood pounding in his ears and those damned spells intertwined in his chest setting up a frantic chorus of something that might have resembled cries of warning if he'd been susceptible to that sort of thing. He decided to credit it to questionable porridge a pair of hours ago and move on.

"We should think about what you'll need," he said, deciding it might be best to simply side-step the question.

"But you'll be there."

He paused and considered what he might say that would be true but not disheartening. He reached out and covered her hands that were clasped together on that rather lovely wooden table.

"I plan to be," he said carefully.

"You won't like what I do to you if you aren't."

He leaned over and kissed her, partly because her hands were shaking even though the hearthfire felt uncomfortably warm to him, and partly because he was simply besotted. She wasn't what he'd expected and losing his heart to her was . . . well, at the moment he realized it had been inevitable.

"I'm properly cowed," he said, pulling away. "No wonder those ponies in your barn never misbehave."

She didn't look particularly comforted, but she nodded just the same.

"You'll be there," she said firmly.

"I will, but should I be momentarily distracted by the odd mug of drinkable ale or sparkling spell, I want you to have a full complement of things at the ready."

He was coming very close to lying, which he imagined she knew, but he wasn't about to say aloud that if he were dead, he wanted her to be able to escape to a land that contained someone powerful enough to protect her from the mage loitering outside.

Those safe havens were going to be, he feared, fewer than either of them would have wanted.

He considered, then decided perhaps 'twas best to have the uncomfortable conversations over with before he began his work.

"If something happens to me —"

"You'd best make sure it doesn't," she said fiercely.

"I will reward you properly for that when I have a lengthy moment," he said with a smile, "but whilst we're both not in the middle of peril, I'm going to give you a list."

"But," she began, then she stopped. "Very well."

"You don't have my enemies," he said, having a fairly good idea of where she'd been going with that. "You do, however, have a very powerful one out there, so you need to find someone who can protect you. You know I will never willingly give up that spot next to you that I so richly deserve by virtue simply of my massive amounts of charm and—dare I say it?—very fine kisses."

She blushed. He was fairly certain of it.

"You talk too much," she said weakly.

"My worst failing, right behind having too many vile spells," he agreed. "But let's discuss the very unlikely possibility that you might need help from someone besides me. Soilléir will be your best choice, as much as it galls me to admit as much. I'm guessing he'll be at the schools of wizardry, though I imagine he'll have a fair idea of where we are just the same."

"I don't want to run into that Droch person," she said with a shiver.

"Not after our having stolen—"

"*You* stole him."

"Not after *my* having stolen a horse he wanted," Acair said. "We might consider Inntrig, instead. Seannair would be able to keep you safe and send for Soilléir. If you're on the other side of the mountains, go to Hearn or my father's parents."

"Your grandparents."

He had to take a bit of a breath over that. "Aye, my grandparents. Miach and Mhorghain would also be able to keep you safe. I might even pause before going up against that lad, young and green as he is."

"This list sounds a little familiar," she said slowly.

"It is," he agreed, "but there's a reason for that. Whilst there might be others who could give you a safe harbor, those are the souls I would actually trust."

"But it isn't going to be a concern because you're going to do what you do with those," she said, waving at the coins with a hand she'd pulled out from under his, "and that's going to be enough."

If her hand wasn't steady, he thought it only polite not to make any note of it.

"It will be. Now, let's see what we have already."

She slid what he'd retrieved from Uachdaran's throne over to their right. "Death."

"Very useful, but fairly permanent. We have five coins here, so I'll make you five spells. We'll use more powerful spells on higher value coins, does that suit?"

She nodded, though she looked rather ill. He shared the feeling, actually. If something happened to him and he left her —

He pushed aside the thought and concentrated on what was before him. He set the sovereign aside for use with something he was fairly sure she wasn't going to like, then looked at the remaining four. He thought for a moment, then looked at her.

"You can make fire and contain things."

"I also did make werelight last night."

And so she had. Sìle, he suspected, might not even slay him if he ever had the pleasure of watching Léirsinn work a spell that didn't immediately explode into something quite different. Fadaire was very circumspect when it came to that kind of thing, or perhaps it drew some restraint from the spell that occasionally sparkled on Léirsinn's arm.

"You did," he agreed, "and you were brilliant at it. As for these, let's make un-noticing, fettering, some sort of shield, and distraction."

"Distraction?"

He realized he was making a copy of what Sladaiche already had of his, but perhaps if used together, they would cancel each other out and leave Léirsinn happily making a successful escape in a different direction.

He looked at her carefully. "It will create shadows all around whomever you fling it at, causing him a great deal of frustration and a decent reason to start screaming. I suggest you fling and turn away."

"I've seen what you can do," she said quietly. "I'll take that advice. What's the last one for?"

He picked it up and fingered it for a moment or two, then looked at her. "Shapechanging."

She gaped at him. "Me?"

He nodded. "You'll decide on a shape, then clap your hands together with it between your palms. I suggest wind, but that's just me. You'll be invisible and able to flee."

"But," she said faintly, "how will I—well, I won't need to use it, so never mind."

"I don't think you will," he said carefully, "but should that change, you'll use this, then make a leisurely journey to one of those souls we've discussed. They'll help you return to your proper form. I'll make that so even Soilléir won't have to work too hard to remove the spell."

She attempted a smile. "Will you two ever share a companionable mug of ale?"

"Doubtful," he said, "but I do trust him with this much."

He didn't add that trusting the whoreson hadn't worked out all that well for him so far, but he thought in this the man might be able to confine himself to simply removing a spell, not making any untoward additions.

"Do you want me to leave you to this?" she asked.

He hesitated. "I might go into my study, if you wouldn't be offended. The work on the first four isn't difficult, but the last one will be."

"I'll make some soup, then." She looked at him quickly. "We have everything needful inside."

He rose, pulled her up into his arms, and held her until he supposed if he didn't let her go, he wouldn't manage to.

"An hour," he said, "no more."

H e supposed, an hour later, that he should have patted himself on the back for being so businesslike about slathering parts of his soul on Sàraitchian bits and bobs, but the truth was, the only thing he could think about was how delighted his great aunt would have been to have been tossed a pair of his best efforts in payment for a day-old fish. He left his work on the mantel, then stumbled to the kitchen, feeling thoroughly wrung out.

If he made it through supper, 'twould be a miracle.

Léirsinn looked up from her soup pot when he walked in, then set her spoon down and walked over to him. "You should go to bed."

"I'll sleep in the study with you," he said. "Wouldn't want to deprive you of the view, of course."

She pushed him down in a chair and put a bowl of something that smelled rather delightful in front of him. He looked up at her blearily.

"I'm impressed."

"Don't be," she said, sitting down next to him. "I found your cook's cache of herbs and recipes. Do you never come in this room?"

"Not when I can help it," he said. "I'm going to be even less likely after tasting your wares here. Well done, you."

He made manful efforts to stay awake, but even attaching simple spells to inanimate objects was exhausting. Putting that spell of shapechanging on that sovereign had almost done him in.

He realized Léirsinn had rescued his soup before he'd nodded off into it, then felt her take his hand and pull him up. She pulled his arm over her shoulders.

"Walk."

He'd heard worse ideas, so he trusted she would put him to bed somewhere reasonable. He soon found himself stretched out in front of the fire in his study, Léirsinn sitting next to him. He reached up and touched her cheek before he lost all his strength.

"Don't go outside," he said wearily.

"You're sure that's Sladaiche?"

He nodded, fighting a mighty yawn.

"And he's also the orchardist?"

"I daresay."

"Why did he leave you that spell all those years ago, do you think?"

"Perhaps he thought my father might know how to finish it," Acair said, turning toward the fire and noticing only then that she had taken off his boots.

"Would he have?"

"I'm not certain he would have bothered."

"But if you trade pieces of your soul for black magic, wouldn't that be useful?"

"I never said my father was particularly smart," he murmured, "just power hungry."

"Why would he want me?"

He pried his eyes open and looked at her. "You have something he wants."

She looked at him blankly. "I am no one."

"Must we do this again?" he asked, ignoring the crack in his heart that he was quite certain was reflected in his voice.

"I'm serious. You might want me, but you're obviously blinded by my formidable ability to set things on fire."

"It is impressive," he agreed, feeling his eyes close relentlessly. He was honestly past fighting the weariness any longer. "And your red hair," he murmured. "Don't forget your red hair."

"You've met red-haired women before, I'm certain."

"None that I remember speaking to," he protested, though he supposed that wasn't entirely accurate.

Then again, the only one he could think of was Ruithneadh's wife, Sarah. She was one of those dastardly dreamweavers, though, and capable of all manner of terrifying things. She and Léirsinn should never meet over tea. They would likely burn the whole damned world to cinders.

Well, and that gel who had helped him escape the gates of Eòlas after he'd sent Léirsinn and Mansourah off on his horse. She'd had red hair . . .

"I wonder if he was in Briàghde when those mages wanted you dead. That mage said you knew too much."

He pushed aside things he simply didn't have the strength to contemplate and struggled to focus on what she was saying.

"Those lads—oh, those mages," he said, realizing he was slurring his words but unable to help himself. "Braggarts. Know the type."

He was the type, but he imagined she already knew that. He groped for her hand and felt her brush his hair out of his eyes. It was perhaps one of the most profoundly intimate gestures he'd ever experienced, but, he had to admit, he had been accustomed in the past to tiara-wearing princesses wielding fans and perhaps one too many witches and magick-possessing noblewomen wielding spells.

What a lovely change.

He squeezed her hand and felt himself slide into darkness.

Sixteen

Two days later, Léirsinn sat in the same place, watched the man lying on the pallet in front of the fire, and wondered if he would ever again wake.

After the events of the morning, she was wishing quite desperately that he would.

Perhaps *events* was overstating things. She'd had a single event that had completely changed her opinion of those coins sitting on the mantel and left her counting them over and over again in her head, reminding herself of what they would do if she needed to use them.

Sianach lifted his head suddenly and that motion alone almost left her jumping out of her skin. He looked at her as if she'd lost her good sense, which she feared she might have. She put her hand over her chest to keep her heart where it was meant to stay, then reached out and patted Acair's pony on the head.

He licked his chops—she didn't want to know what he'd hunted out in the garden—and put his muzzle atop her bare foot. Comforting, if she could ignore the teeth that were still a bit too large for his mouth and weren't exactly pleasant against her flesh.

What was less pleasant was thinking about what had happened to her earlier that morning.

She shouldn't have gone out to the garden. She was fairly certain Acair had roused long enough the day before to remind her that she should stay inside. She was absolutely certain that she'd suggested tartly that he mind his own affairs and leave her to do as she pleased, but by then he'd fallen back asleep and likely hadn't heard her.

When it came to mages and magic, she thought she might want to take his suggestions more seriously the next time around.

An innocent walk out in the garden, though. What could possibly have gone amiss there? She'd had confidence in Acair's spell, so her most pressing concern had been finding a cloak to use in warding off the chill.

The mage had been waiting just outside the garden gate. How he'd known she was outside she didn't know given that Acair's spell of concealment had still been hanging there, doing what he'd created it to do.

Perhaps Sladaiche had heard the back door open. Perhaps Sianach's barking had alerted him to someone in the garden. Perhaps he had simply taken a stab in the dark and crossed his fingers that someone had come outside. She wondered if he'd actually believed that she would be foolish enough to simply walk through the gate and give herself up for lost.

She hadn't expected him to fling a shard of magic toward the house that she'd been convinced was going to go directly through what lay over the garden and slay her.

Acair's perfectly impenetrable spell had fluttered just the slightest bit, once, then gone on about its glorious task of keeping her safe.

She'd turned and walked calmly back the way she'd come. If she'd only managed that for a total of four paces before she'd bolted up the stairs and into the house, slammed the door shut, then fetched a chair to wedge under the latch, she supposed she was the only one who would know. Sianach had barked at the door immediately after, which had almost sent her into a dead faint.

She'd been tempted to leave him outside to fend for himself, but she wasn't that cowardly. She'd brought him in, replaced the chair, then run through the house to perch on the edge of her current roost and indulge in a prayer or two that Acair would wake. She'd made a fire, but that had burned to embers an hour ago and she hadn't dared go outside for more wood.

The fire leapt to life suddenly and she shrieked.

"Just me," Acair said hoarsely.

She realized he was awake and watching her. She dropped to her knees next to him and suppressed the urge to fling herself at him. He reached for her hand.

"How long?"

"Almost two days."

He put his free hand over his eyes, then groaned. "My apologies."

"Right out of the gate with one, I see."

"Terrifying, isn't it?"

She thought that was quite a bit less terrifying than what she'd experienced earlier, but perhaps that was a tale better saved for later. She was happy to simply sit there and not be alone. Well, she supposed she was happy that her companion was alive and awake, but perhaps she didn't need to admit that at the moment.

She realized he was stroking the back of her hand with his thumb.

"You're safe, darling."

She took a deep breath. "I know."

"Anything interesting happen?" he asked.

"I didn't use all of your tokens," she managed. "There's one left."

He looked at her in surprise, then his eyes narrowed. "A very poor jest, that one."

"Just a bit of good-natured sport," she said, her mouth dry. She imagined she didn't need to say how close she'd come to rummaging around in his purse for his spell of death just in case.

She was starting to see why mages used them.

"Stop holding up that polished glass so I might see all my flaws," he muttered. He sat up, then apparently regretted it. He lay back down with a groan. "Any change?"

"He tried to break through your spell."

Acair put his arm over his eyes, then let go of her hand and held open his other arm. "Come keep me in one piece for a moment, love."

She stretched out next to him and tried not to wail, though she supposed if there were a place to fall apart, 'twas there. If he noticed how badly she was shaking, he made no mention of it. He simply put both his arms around her and held her close.

She didn't want to admit it, she who had taken care of herself for so long with only the aid of her sharp tongue and a riding crop, but there was something profoundly comforting about being held by a man who had stepped between her and harm's way more than once.

"You're thinking lovely thoughts about me," he whispered. "I can tell."

"I might be."

"You should unburden yourself and tell me all," he said, "but let me hear this other bit first. Veg before dessert, as my scrupulous dam always taught me."

"Did she?"

He grunted. "You don't want to know what she taught me. She also has sweets for breakfast, so that might tell you more than you want to know. What happened?"

"I went outside for a walk," she said unwillingly.

"I'm certain you did. Was my spell of un-noticing still intact?"

"It seemed to be," she said slowly.

"Did he know you were there?"

She nodded. "He tried to break through your spell. I didn't pro-voke—"

"Léirsinn, of course you didn't," he interrupted. "You haven't done anything to him. If anything, he should be coming after me for leaving him falling off his ladder in a tangle of flailing limbs and hu-miliation. He's simply a marginally powerful fool with hurt feelings. We'll find out what he wants, then I'll see to him."

"How do you bear any of this?" she whispered.

He sighed deeply. "Decades of bluster and terrible spells."

She tilted her head back where she could look at his face. "Are you truly never afraid?"

He glanced at her, then looked up at the ceiling. "Do you hon-estly believe I'll answer that?"

"You might," she said. "If you think it will help me."

"Ye gads, woman," he said faintly. "The things you say."

She only waited. He glanced at her, frowned, then looked back up at the ceiling. He was silent for so long, she wondered if he wouldn't answer her after all. In the end, though, that lad there was never afraid, not even of prying questions. He'd said so on more than one occasion.

"I was afraid once," he said slowly. "And if you repeat this, I'll deny it."

"I never would."

"Which is why I'll be honest with you." He let out his breath slowly. "I was, as it happened, nosing about in a place where I shouldn't have been."

She leaned up on her elbow and looked at him. "You?"

"I know," he said dryly. "So out of character."

"I'm guessing you were rummaging through someone's solar, looking for things they might not want to share?"

He put his hand on her back, perhaps to keep her from flee-ing, though she suspected he was patting her in an effort to soothe himself. *That* was definitely something she wasn't about to point out to him.

"Exactly that," he said. "The mage in question lives in a tatty little keep just over the border from Tor Neroche. I had reason to believe he might be hiding a spell very like Diminishing under the blotter on his desk, so I walked right in his front door, bold as brass, and ran up the stairs to his solar. Surprisingly enough, he caught me at it."

"You must have been very young," she said in surprise.

He lifted his eyebrows briefly. "You would think so, but let's just say the memory is rather too fresh for my taste. I'll admit that I was very surprised to find that his solar was completely impervious to any of my escape attempts. The only place akin to it that I've ever seen is Uachdaran's dungeon. Lothar of Riamh, though—" He paused. "Without giving you details that will leave you with nightmares, I'll just say that to save my own sweet self, I actually uttered the word *please*."

She could hardly believe her ears. "You didn't."

He smiled. "How flattering that you find it as preposterous as I do. I did nip out a window after he'd opened it to air the place out thanks to a particularly fragrant manuscript I lit on fire in a final effort to irritate him."

"Is that true?"

"Mostly," he said. "I also may have clunked him over the head with a candlestick as he was turned the other way, raging over his papers that I'd mussed whilst about the goodly work of trying to find his spell of magic thievery."

"But surely you weren't afraid."

"I was beyond afraid," he said, "but again, I'll never admit as much. The only place I've been more afraid was Léige when I thought I might never see you again."

"Honestly?" she asked, ignoring the way her heart broke a little at his words.

He put his hand behind her head, then leaned up and kissed her briefly. "Honestly," he said.

"What of saving the world from that mage outside?" she managed.

"That has always been substantially farther down the list of things that keep me up at night." He lay back down, then reached for her hand to put it palm-down on his chest. He covered it with his own, then sighed. "Sladaiche isn't without power, but I'm not afraid of him. I'm furious that Soilléir has left me unable to see to him properly, something for which I will definitely repay him when I'm able."

"I imagine he knows that."

"I remind him of it every time we meet." He paused, then looked at her. "I think we should leave today, if you're not opposed to it. Inntrig is close enough that we'll reach it by sunset without hurrying if we go now. I'll be able to cover us in spells to get us there safely, though I can't guarantee they'll be pleasant."

She wondered if they might be making any journey at all with how weary he looked. "Are you certain?"

He rubbed his hand over his face, then shook his head and sat up, pulling her with him. "The exhilaration of being in a library where I'm not supposed to be will perk me right up, I'm sure. Why don't you fetch your gear and I'll meet you in the kitchen? We'll slip out the back and be on our way. We might even manage to elude that damned spell of death out front if we're particularly canny."

She suspected not, but stranger things had happened.

She crawled to her feet and pulled him up to his. She would have told him that he wasn't fit to go anywhere except back to bed, but she supposed he'd been worse off.

She fetched her pack and satchel, left them by the door that led out to the garden, then decided her time would be better used following Acair to make certain he didn't fall asleep on his feet than hovering by the back door and fretting.

She found him simply standing and staring at the map on the table in his library.

"Acair?"

He glanced at her and smiled, then held out his hand. She walked over and took it, which she supposed was becoming something of a bad habit. Then again, so was becoming far too accustomed to feeling ridiculously safe in the embrace of a terrible black mage.

Who wasn't all that terrible, it seemed to her.

"Have all your answers?" she asked.

"As many as I can stomach for the moment," he said. "Perhaps the rest are in Seannair's library. I have the feeling there's something there that Soilléir wants me to see, damn him to hell for refusing to simply hand it to me."

"Does he usually have reasons for that sort of thing?"

"Unfortunately," he said sourly. "What they are is anyone's guess." He kissed her hair, then stepped away. "I'll put the house to bed and we'll go. We might manage a meal in Inntrig if we're fortunate." He paused. "You could take your sister's book, if you like."

"You keep it for me," she said. "It would be safer here, I think."

"The first of many tomes on fantastical creatures we'll read to our brood of half a dozen children."

She looked at him and damn the man if he didn't wink at her.

"Three handsome lads like yours truly," he said pleasantly, "and a trio of red-haired, feisty little lassies who will lead everyone around them on a merry chase, just like their mother. I will, of course, be greeting all suitors at the door with my most terrible spells lined up out front in a tidy row, just so there's no confusion about how I'll allow those gels to be courted."

"I still haven't heard a decent proposal in any of that," she managed. She hardly knew whether he was serious or not and thought she might not want to break her heart over the thought.

"Actually, I thought I'd ask your grandfather for your hand first," he said casually. "Before I asked you."

She looked at him quickly and found that he wasn't looking particularly unconcerned. If she hadn't known better, she might have thought he looked just the slightest bit unsure.

"You . . . " She found she couldn't say any of the things she was thinking without feeling foolish, so she simply looked at him.

"Rendered speechless by my mere presence," he said solemnly. "You might be surprised how often it happens."

"Or I might not be."

"You might not be," he agreed with a smile. "I'll close up the rest of the house if you want to go and gather up your coins."

"Why don't I just come with you?"

"Of course, love," he said quietly.

She imagined he realized that was less about his flawless face and more about not wanting to be alone, but the man was perceptive.

It took far less time than she liked before she was standing at the back door with him, his damned horse sitting at his feet, drooling, and thought she might lose what little breakfast she'd managed to choke down a quarter hour before.

"How will we do this?" she croaked.

He looked at her in surprise, then closed his eyes briefly before he gathered her into his arms.

"I won't tell you not to be afraid," he said quietly. "Fear isn't necessarily a bad thing from time to time. Keeps a wise lad from doing something stupid whilst the rest of the fools rush in and perish, as my mother would say. There also might be something in there about that rushing being what rids the world of mindless yobs, but you know her."

She almost smiled. "Your mother is a wonder."

"She's terrifying and for good reason. As for the other, you're wise to be cautious, but you have many weapons to hand. You still have your coins?"

"Aye."

"You remember how to keep grain from tipping out of buckets whilst simultaneously setting fire to annoying lords' trousers?"

"I'm insulted," she managed, "and you should be afraid I'll set fire to *yours* for that ridiculous question."

He patted her back. "I'm properly cowed, believe me. I've watched you at your work."

"I think I like it better when you can use your magic."

He laughed a little. "Now, *that* is something I never thought to ever hear you say."

She pulled back far enough to look at him under the lovely werelight he'd hung over their heads. "I'm not sure how we'll do this."

He considered, then pulled away and reached for her hand. He led her over to the kitchen table, lit a fire in the hearth with a spell she didn't hear, then pulled out a chair for her. He waited until she was seated, gentleman that he was, then sat down facing her.

"We'll give my horse a moment to have a proper nap there by the fire," he said, "and discuss our strategy for a moment or two. Wine?"

"I'm not sure anything would help at this point."

"Then I won't offer you anything stronger," he said with a smile. He leaned forward and took her hands. "I don't know how it is with horses, but with mages there is a fine line to walk between killing them outright and allowing them to do themselves in, so to speak."

"Would you slay him?" she asked faintly.

"If it came to a choice between your life and his? Without a second thought. But if I slay him, we will likely never know what spell he's using presently, never mind what spell he's still looking for. Leaving something like that out in the world—and believe me, I can hardly believe these words are coming out of my mouth—for some enterprising mage to simply pick up and tuck in a pocket would be rather disastrous."

"You'd best be careful," she said seriously.

He looked a little startled. "Why?"

"People are going to find out the truth about you and the quests will never stop."

"Take that back," he said, looking genuinely appalled. "Every last word of it."

She smiled. "I won't. So, where does that leave us?"

"It leaves me unnerved at what you've wished on me, but I'll hide when any messengers show up at the front door and leave you to attend to them. As for our current business, I think we should see what Seannair's library holds, then accept the inevitable."

She supposed she didn't need to be a mage to understand where he was going with that.

"You'll have to face him," she said quietly.

"And you'll have to contain that bloody spell of death outside so I can," he agreed. "Unless I can determine in the meantime how to destroy it."

"But it has parts of your soul you've collected."

He pursed his lips. "I'm not entirely sure my mother didn't invent that on the spot just to annoy me, but I can't deny what I've seen. I'm not sure what good those bits of myself will do me, but in the end it might not matter. Even if you can only hold off that spell long enough for me to do what needs to be done, it will be enough."

She closed her eyes briefly. "And if I can't?"

"I have a very useful spell of death in my pocket."

"But you'd rather have answers."

"I would," he agreed. "Not only might he have other spells waiting to be nicked and used, he also likely knows how to reverse what those pools of shadow have taken, if that sort of thing is even possible. I owe Hearn at least an attempt to find that answer. Your grandfather as well, possibly."

"And if he slays you?" she asked, forcing herself to speak calmly when what she wanted to do was weep. "I'm not thinking only of myself, though I am because I'm not sure what I would do without . . . well . . . "

"You want to protect yourself so you might spend the rest of your life leaving me forgetting to drink my tea before it grows cold because I've been too busy being mesmerized by the color of your hair." He shrugged lightly, though he didn't look particularly casual. "A little self-serving, that, but I understand."

"You're trying to distract me."

"Turn about and all that." He held out his rune with the spell of death attached. "Take this."

She didn't want to, but he didn't give her any choice. He took her hand, put it on her palm, and closed her fingers around it.

"If something happens to me, you'll throw that at him in the confusion, without mercy and without hesitation. The world will survive. Then you'll shapechange as we've discussed and head for the closest bolt hole." He bent his head, kissed her fingers, then stood up. "But it won't come to that."

She couldn't begin to entertain thoughts of what her life would look like if that weren't the case and, surprisingly enough, that had mostly to do with that man there.

She rose, put her chair back where it was meant to go, then watched Acair as he went to fetch her satchel from the back door. He brought it over, created a pocket under the lid with magic she didn't recognize, then tucked the spell of death inside it. He put the strap over her head, settled it on her shoulder, then kissed her quickly.

"You won't need that," he said quietly, "but there's no sense in not having a fall-back plan."

She nodded, then tried not to shiver as the fire extinguished itself. The werelight was very faint by comparison, but she didn't ask him to make it brighter. She imagined he would douse it entirely before he opened the back door.

"Your house is beautiful," she croaked.

He pulled her into his arms and held her tightly. "We will return, darling. I promise."

She would have attempted a nod, but it was beyond her. "What now?"

"I'm going to create a little something with my grandmother's magic and send it off northward whilst we nip off to the east and a bit south. We'll be at Seannair's gates by sunset if Sianach behaves himself." He pulled back, kissed her on both cheeks, then looked at her. "You'll do what's needful and so will I. This is just one more step forward."

She didn't want to say that she'd grown too accustomed to the peace and safety of his house to want to step away from it at all, but she imagined she didn't need to.

He picked up their packs before he took a deep breath and led her outside.

S he decided many hours later that he had known how long it took to reach the palace of Inntrig because he'd been there before on one of his forays into places where he shouldn't have gone. There was something comforting about knowing that with Acair of Ceangail, some things never changed.

Twilight had fallen, which she might have found pleasing at another time. Presently, standing a hundred paces from gates she wasn't sure they would manage to enter, she found the dark unnerving. She stood with her hand on Sianach's withers and waited for her legs to stop shaking.

She distracted herself by examining the rather inadequate defenses that kept the king of Cothromaiche from being overrun by the rest of the world, then looked over her shoulder before she could stop herself.

There was no one behind them, but she wasn't reassured. Sladaiche was just as likely as they were to be wearing a spell of un-noticing. What was even less reassuring was realizing that she was starting to find magic as normal as barn work.

"Léirsinn?"

She looked at Acair standing next to her, cloaked and hooded as he was, and shook her head. "I'm appalled by my own thoughts."

"Shameless vixen."

She couldn't even dredge up the glare he deserved, so she settled for a deep breath. "I wasn't thinking lecherous thoughts about you, I was contemplating magic."

"That might be worse," he said. "But whilst you're thinking those sorts of thoughts, let's speak again of how we'll proceed from here. You'll need to remove our spell of un-noticing, but make a production of tugging on that thread I showed you before. I'm going to be doing everything I can to remain unobtrusive." He paused. "And just so you're not surprised, my welcome here, should it come to that, might not be warm."

She started to agree, then it occurred to her that there might be things she needed to know. "What haven't you told me?"

"Whatever can you possibly mean?"

She shot him a look, but he only smiled and shrugged.

"You know me," he said easily. "Off doing things I shouldn't more often than I should."

"Are you going to be specific so I know why the king wants you dead?"

"If you must know," he admitted, "I laid a spell on the king's hunting gear that caused arrows and whatnot to sprout flowers and vile smells—I know the two aren't usually connected, but I was feeling particularly clever—when pointed in the direction of whatever hapless thing he was stalking at the time." He paused. "I may or may not have also snuck into his bedchamber and written, *I cannot find my arse with both hands* on his nightcap in letters only others could see."

Considering all the things he could have done, that didn't sound all that terrible.

"Why do I have the feeling that isn't all?" she asked.

He sighed deeply. "Very well, I also pinched his crown and tried to seduce one of his granddaughters, but in my defense I had no idea who she was—well, that isn't true at all—but I was much younger and perhaps a bit stupid."

She could only stand there and gape at him. "How old were you?"

He shifted. "Old enough to know better. She was also boasting of being betrothed to my half-brother Rùnach. I couldn't not stir up a bit of trouble. Trust me, he had a narrow escape there and so did

I. She was also dark-haired and substantially older than she looked. Lesson learned."

She retrieved her jaw from where it had fallen. "Is that so."

"I've set my sights on younger women, if you want the truth."

She would have mocked him for being far too old for the likes of her, but it occurred to her quite suddenly and rather unpleasantly that she would likely not see the far side of four score while he most certainly would, and then some. Even if she did live longer than that, he wouldn't look a day older than he did at present.

But *she* most certainly would.

He stepped closer, slipped his hand under her hair, then kissed her. She would have reminded him that they were in a bit of a hurry to get inside to relative safety, but perhaps the gate guards could wait. She also didn't protest when he wrapped his arms around her and held her close.

"You know," he said very quietly, "we might, if you're interested, rely on my ability to weasel impossible spells out of almost anyone I meet and see if a long and happy life might be granted to us together."

"Is that possible?" she said, ignoring the anguish she could hear even in her own voice.

He nodded. "If you're interested in a long and happy life with one such as I, that is."

"Are you going to change your crown-nicking ways?"

"Quite possibly not."

She leaned up on her toes and kissed him quickly. "Just don't hide them under the bed."

"If you insist," he said, but he didn't move. He looked over her head for a bit, then met her gaze. "Are you interested?"

"Is that a proposal?"

"Almost."

She took his hand because that seemed more sensible than throwing herself at him, on the off chance the gate guards could see through his spell. "Then, aye," she said simply. "Almost."

He cleared his throat roughly. "I'll see what I can do." He took a step back and winced at Sianach's nose snuffling his hair. "Please, get us inside so I can put this uncontrollable nag in a stall and we can be about our business. I'd like to be in and out before dawn."

She thought that sounded like a bit more of a visit than she wanted to make, but 'twas too late to change course at present.

Acair reached out and rapped smartly on the gates. "Look down your nose a bit more, darling."

She nodded, put her shoulders back, and hoped that would be enough.

She could hardly bear to think about what might happen to them inside such a place if not.

Seventeen

Acair walked behind Léirsinn, holding on to the reins of his horse who had, for a change, decided the time was not right for a bit of a nibble, and started a new list of things for which he would need to repay a certain Cothromaichian prince.

Masquerading as a servant to that glorious woman dressed in the finest traveling clothes he'd been able to provide for her was not one. He would have trailed behind her carrying her gear for as long as allowed.

That he thought he might be sleeping in the barn instead of with her in his arms, on the other hand, certainly might be. Hoping that no one would notice that he'd come brazenly through the front gates was definitely another.

Asking Léirsinn to put herself in peril to slip out of what he was sure would be a very fine guest chamber and let him in the back door was going to go at the top of that list.

The time for that happy bit of retribution would surely come, but he had other things to see to first. It was tempting to breathe a little sigh of relief at how well things had gone so far, but he knew that could change very quickly.

So far, so good, though. They had survived the gauntlet at the outer gates of Seannair of Cothromaiche's palace, such as it was, without incident. Being assigned an escort to lead them up the way to the palace proper had been expected as well. Léirsinn didn't give herself enough credit for fine manners. The guard captain—a man Acair should have remembered, but didn't—had fallen all over himself to assure her that she would be immediately settled in the best guestchamber available.

Acair understood. She was glorious in her incarnation as highly skilled horsewoman. She was nothing short of stunning whilst wearing the persona of high-born noblewoman.

He wondered sometimes just who she was.

On the other hand, he had absolutely no doubts about who he was and what he could do. Unfortunately, he had the feeling King Seannair didn't either, and he might not be as enthusiastic about those skills as someone else. If he could simply slip in and out without seeing the king, his granddaughter Annastashia, or any number of other relatives who might want to stick a knife between his ribs and give it a friendly twist, he would count the visit a success.

He paused a deferential number of paces behind his lady as she was greeted by one of the palace butlers. Acair did recognize that man and thought he might be wise to keep his head down lest memories of a filched bottle of particularly fine port come to mind and trouble the man overmuch.

"My uncle is Fuadain of Briàghde. My servant and I need shelter for the night, if it wouldn't be too much trouble."

Acair admired her posh vowels and crisp consonants for a moment before he remembered who he was supposed to be. He nodded to her before she was led into a palace so rustic that it made Léige look like Chagailt by comparison and hoped it wouldn't be the last time he saw her.

He followed a stable lad along paths and to what turned out to be a rather decent set of stables. That he'd never noticed them before said much about his previous modes of transportation, he had to admit. He paid the stablemaster for Sianach's keep, oversaw the stabling of his horse as though he actually knew what was supposed to happen, then happily left the more pedestrian work of shoveling and feeding to those whose business it was.

"You might beg a meal from the kitchen," the stablemaster said, tossing the suggestion over his shoulder as he strode off to see to his equine business.

As tempting as that was, Acair thought he might be better served to skulk about in the back garden and wait for a light to come on in the vicinity of where he knew the guest chambers were located. At least he would know where Léirsinn would be sleeping. Getting inside the palace would be a different task entirely, but he'd certainly done that before. He found a shadowy spot under some trees, ignoring what the inclination for that suggested in relation to his quest, and waited.

Inntrig was a very odd place. Too quiet for his taste, and not just in the sense of having so little society to enjoy. The whole damned place was just so *ordinary*. Trees were merely trees, flowers bloomed without any extra spells brightening up their blossoms, and benches simply sat there in the faint light of a waxing moon without offering any invitations to rest before he went off to look for a few spells to stick in his pockets.

Perhaps that said more about the spells likely tucked away in places no one wanted to talk about than he'd considered before. When a country produced magic of that sort, perhaps a little peace and quiet was the very least the rocks and rills could offer. He didn't care for that sort of silence overmuch, but perhaps the locals enjoyed it.

He saw a light go on and had to remain where he was for a bit until his relief over the sight had passed. A chamber on the ground floor, no less. Perhaps that charmed life he'd enjoyed for so many decades was coming back for another go.

He looked around himself to make certain the garden was comfortably empty, then started for the palace. He kept to the darkest parts of the garden, though, until he found the window that had been opened. He indulged in a brief curse or two on principle alone. It wasn't that he wasn't grateful for the ease of slipping into a particular woman's bedchamber, it was that he was appalled Seannair didn't have better spells of ward guarding the same.

Or at least he hoped Seannair didn't have spells of ward that he couldn't see.

He stood under the window, suppressed the urge to offer up a romantic sentiment or two, and instead tossed Léirsinn his pack. He supposed it would be safer in her chambers than out in the barn, not that there was anything in it he particularly needed. He jumped to catch the edge of the windowsill, then helped himself up thanks to a few judiciously placed toes in the cracks of stone that definitely should have been attended to sooner.

That was exactly the reason he'd been very specific about the construction of his own abode. Admittedly, his house was all one level, but it was impervious to assault. He would definitely be patting himself on the back for that bit of foresight the first chance he had.

He swung his legs over the windowsill and hopped into Léirsinn's chamber. He looked around and nodded approvingly.

"Lovely," he said. "I think you should secure all our accommodations from here on out."

She was staring at him in a way that made him suddenly—and surprisingly—nervous. He suppressed the urge to toss off a flowery comment about wallpaper and carpets and instead simply waited to see what she was about. Perhaps she had decided that a different life might—

"How old is the king's granddaughter?"

Well, that was the last thing he'd expected. "I beg your pardon?" he hedged.

She only looked at him steadily.

"No idea," he said without hesitation. "The gods only know what they do in this place to look so young, but I'm guessing 'tis untoward. She might be two score, she might be two hundred. I didn't want to ask for fear of what she would do to me. Why?"

"No particular reason."

If there were anything he'd learned about Léirsinn of Sàraichte, it was that she never did anything without a reason. He stood there and studied her for a moment or two, then it dawned on him what she was thinking. He walked over to her and stopped just short of putting his arms around her. He did reach out and take one of her hands.

"You know," he said quietly, "absent extorting a spell from an essence-changing prince or elven king in order to live out very lengthy lives in bliss, which we discussed earlier, 'tis entirely possible that we might fall off a dragon one of these days and perish together."

She looked at him and smiled faintly. "Is that meant to make me feel better?"

"Me, rather," he said honestly, "because I'm finding the thought of a life without you in it to be rather intolerable."

"Would it be rude to say I'm surprised to find I'm feeling the same way?"

He smiled. "Very, and 'tis a great whopping lie. I have a very vivid memory of the first time you laid eyes on my fine, strapping self. Admit it. You were lost in an instant."

She released his hand and put her arms around his waist. "Terrible man."

He wrapped his arms around her and rested his cheek against her hair. He supposed if time had stopped at that moment, it would have been enough. He'd never thought to be so appallingly content, but there it was. Comfortable slippers, a glass of Gairn's finest, and a good book —

"Ye gads," he said faintly. "I've become domesticated."

"Have you?"

"Well," he said, "perhaps only now and again, when I need a rest from the general havoc-wreaking and spell-poaching I enjoy so much." He sighed deeply. "Léirsinn, my love, we'll either hope for that fiery end together, or I will indeed find a way to bargain something for a substantial amount of time together."

"Can that be done?"

"If my gilded tongue won't save the day, I'll trade bits of my soul for the same."

"And you would do that for me," she said, sounding very surprised.

"I would."

"You're not offering any flowery sentiments," she said slowly.

"You render me speechless more often than not—"

A knock sounded at the door, almost sending him pitching backward out the window. He caught the satchel Léirsinn tossed him, then looked for a handy place to hide. It wasn't that he wasn't accustomed to taking a little dive over the back of any sofa that presented itself for use in such an activity, but Inntrig was what it was. Léirsinn's chamber contained nothing but a pair of very rustic chairs, a bed with no room underneath, and a wardrobe that a child wouldn't fit in. The whole damned place wasn't meant for anything but austere living.

There was only one solution and he settled for it with a light sigh. He tiptoed over to the doorway with Léirsinn, then flattened himself back against the wall out of sight and hoped for the best.

Léirsinn looked at him. "I love you."

"Ye gads, woman," he wheezed, "again, a little warning next time."

She only smiled, then opened the door.

"Forgive the lateness of the hour," a warm, honey-toned voice said smoothly. "I am Astar, grandson of the king. Welcome to Inntrig."

Acair rolled his eyes. He could think of several things to call the man standing out in the passageway—*bloviating windbag* came first to mind—but perhaps that could remain unsaid. He supposed he might also have kept up a running mental commentary about the man's dress, his table manners, and his habit of driving every sensible miss from the room with his inability to count to four and caper about to the simplest dance pattern, but that was likely something better left for another time. He would have to settle for a bit of eavesdropping.

"Traveling alone is dangerous, but I understand you have a servant at least."

Acair scowled. Aye, and one *with* the ability to memorize not only dance patterns but nasty spells.

He listened to Léirsinn deflect and demur and was torn between admiring her skill at the same and ruminating over why it was he disliked the king's grandson so thoroughly. He had encountered Astar several times in various locales, but he'd been even less likely to socialize with that one than he had been with, say, Mansourah of Neroche.

As he'd said before: Cothromaiche as a whole was just so damned *ordinary*.

But their spells weren't.

"Oh, that isn't necessary," Léirsinn said, "but thank you just the same."

Acair dragged himself back to the present and wondered what he'd missed.

"Then allow me to have something sent up," Astar said. "Surely you must be hungry."

"The chambermaid brought refreshments," Léirsinn protested. "It was very kind."

"I insist. I'll return in a quarter hour."

Léirsinn ended the conversation far more politely than he would have, then shut the door. She looked at him.

"Soilléir's cousin?"

"Aye, and Annastashia's brother," he said sourly.

"The granddaughter you tried to seduce?"

"As always, *tried* is the word you should concentrate on," he said with a shiver. "If the world tallied up the reprehensible things I'd only *tried* to do, I daresay my reputation would be as sterling as

Mochriadhemiach of Neroche's. Well, perhaps not his, and why are we having this conversation?"

"Because you're charming when you're startled and even more charming when you're flustered."

He pulled her into his arms and hugged her so she wouldn't see him indulging in a discreet blush. "I am not flustered. I'm appalled by your lack of proper respect for all the terrible things I've actually *succeeded* in doing, but we'll discuss that later after we've survived that fool likely wanting to come inside with your tray and hover over you whilst you try to choke down what Seannair's cook can produce. I can guarantee you it will involve wild game and inedible veg. I'll need to find somewhere to sit that out."

"There is an armoire over there."

"Aye, fit for a child, which I am not, but I suppose there's no other choice. Tuck me in, darling, and I'll wait out supper. Don't save me anything. I'll just lift a pair of those dry, unappetizing biscuits and try not to crunch in my closet."

She only laughed at him, which he thought was slightly unkind given the straitness of where he was going to be trapped during what he hoped would not be a long meal. She did do him the favor of rearranging the items provided in that armoire for a guest's comfort. If those were limited to frilly, feminine things that left him swathed in colors he wouldn't have worn if death had loomed, well, at least he was providing some amusement for her.

He decided that until the doors were closed, he would have another look at his gran's notes to once again see if there was anything he'd missed. If he found himself joined by a gel who perched uncomfortably atop several pairs of silk slippers to keep him company, he wasn't going to complain.

He read until he realized she wasn't reading with him, she was watching him. He used his finger as a bookmark, closed the notebook, then leaned over and kissed her. It was becoming a very bad habit, that business there.

"I'm going to look mussed," she said.

"All part of the plan, darling."

She pulled away and smiled at him. "You are absolutely incorrigible. I'm assuming you've run afoul of that man threatening to feed me?"

"Unfortunately," he agreed. "He has terrible manners, but I'll allow that he's quite a bit cannier than he looks. He also has a cache of spells I wouldn't mind rifling through, but I've never managed to find him napping, if you know what I mean."

"I do," she said. "Essence changing?"

"They would never trust him with those," Acair said with a snort, "but he's unearthed some other darkly interesting things. I'm guessing he found those whilst nosing about in the corners of the cellar where his cousin is too fastidious to go."

He supposed he didn't need to add that Soilléir had likely gone places he himself might hesitate to consider, but he wasn't in the mood to credit that overly wholesome worker of spells he desperately wanted with anything good.

"Why did your granny draw those bees?"

He looked at the pair of fuzzy fiends lingering on the edge of the map, then shrugged. "She hopes I'll kick over a large hive of the same? One of my mother's sisters, Fiunne, I believe, claims Fearann as her home. I imagine that in addition to keeping bees and making lace, she spends copious amounts of time trying to pretend that her land isn't simply an island in the larger sea of Fàs as a whole."

"Is it on your list of places not to go?"

"Absolutely, mostly because of the catastrophically boring nature of what they do there. If they use any essence meddling, I'm sure 'tis only to keep the bees immobile whilst they go about the dastardly work of stealing their honey. At this point, nothing would surprise me when it comes to my grandmother. And there, poor gel, is your supper at the door."

She pushed herself out of the closet. "I'll make this brief."

"Your tum will thank you."

"Oh, don't worry," she said, leaning over and kissing his cheek. "I'll save you some."

He supposed he made some remark that sounded more like a plea for mercy than anything saucier, but the closet door had already been shut. He tried not to give into despair. If the smell of supper didn't fell him, having to listen to Astar make small talk likely would.

'Twas obvious, though, that Léirsinn had had a great deal of practice in politely hurrying along lords who might have wanted to linger. Acair found himself with hardly a cramp in his thighs thanks to having his knees drawn up to his chin before Léirsinn was opening the door and freeing him from his prison. He paused, then sniffed.

"I've smelled worse," he allowed.

"So have I," she agreed. "Help yourself."

He supposed he might not mind if he did, so he finished what she had left, downed a mug of an undemanding and rather watery ale, then nodded. "Let's be off."

"Now?" she squeaked.

He smiled. "The sooner, the better. We'll find what we need, I'll nip back out your window, and we'll be on our way before dawn."

"Do you have a destination in mind?" she asked.

"*Not here* was my first thought, but we'll see what presents itself after we've seen what we were meant to find."

He had thoughts about gingerly asking Léirsinn if she would be willing to retrace her steps back to her childhood home, but he wasn't quite ready to bring that up. There was enough that lay in front of them already without adding anything more distressing to the evening.

He handed her back her satchel, watched her put his grandmother's notes inside it, then made certain the window was closed. No sense in letting any riff-raff in whilst they were away.

He very studiously avoided putting himself in that class of rabble-rousers and continued on.

He paused by the door, then looked at her. "Would you mind taking a peek into the passageway, just in case?"

"Of course," she said. She took a deep breath, then opened the door and looked out.

He decided he wouldn't say anything about how carefully she did the same or where she might have learned the skill. Her uncle had many things to answer for. A wee nip in and out of Briàghde was definitely going on his list of things to see to later.

"Empty," she whispered. "What now?"

"Library."

She nodded and stepped back. He eased past her and slipped out into the passageway first, then waited for her to follow him and close the door softly behind them. He took a moment to get his bearings, then decided that he definitely should have insisted that Soilléir draw him some sort of map. He considered the lay of the land from the garden's perspective and decided to go left, away from the kitchens. It would likely take them closer to Seannair's throne room — such as it was — than they would enjoy, but there was nothing to be done about that.

He nodded, then turned and ran directly into a body that hadn't been there a moment before.

A body belonging to none other than Astar of Inntrig, busybody extraordinaire. He supposed it could have been worse. He could have run into Annastashia.

"Give me one reason not to slay you where you stand," Astar said in a low voice, "or, rather, turn my sister loose on you. I'm not sure which would be worse."

"I think you know," Acair said before he thought better of it.

"One reason," Astar repeated evenly.

"Your cousin sent me."

Astar uttered an epitaph better suited for a barn, which Acair thought best not to comment on. The lads in Inntrig could have used a bit more time in polite society, something he also decided might be better left unsaid.

"He's telling the truth."

Acair would have begged Léirsinn to leave him to his fate and save herself, but perhaps 'twas too late for that. She had already moved to stand shoulder-to-shoulder with him. He supposed the trio was completed by that damned spell of death standing there with a bit of a slouch on her far side.

"Why don't we go back inside and discuss this like civilized folk?" Léirsinn said calmly. "There might be wine left."

Acair had definitely heard worse ideas. He also supposed that with a decent bit of luck, he might manage to render his foe unconscious, stuff *him* in that damned armoire, then be about his business and away before he came to.

He wasn't surprised when Léirsinn opened the door and Astar waited for him to follow her in. Perhaps the man had had the same idea when it came to his location for the rest of the night. He entered ahead of one of Seannair's many progeny, then was somehow unsurprised when Astar simply stood there in the middle of the chamber instead of looking for a seat. There were many things that could have perhaps been said about that prince, but that he was casual about guarding his grandfather's property was not one.

Astar looked at Léirsinn. "Who are you?"

"Fuadain of Sàraichte's niece," she said, "as I said."

Acair cleared his throat. "And I am —"

"I know who you are!" Astar shot him a look of loathing, then turned back to Léirsinn. "Did he abscond with you?"

"Of course not," Léirsinn said without hesitation.

Astar frowned. "I hesitate to believe ill of a woman so beautiful, but I wonder that you're keeping company with this bastard here. As Lord Fuadain's niece, you should be looking in better places for a companion."

Léirsinn only inclined her head. Acair thought he might want to compliment her on that the next chance he had. He felt decidedly, if not politely, put in his place and that look hadn't been directed at him.

The next one, from Soilléir's cousin, *was* directed at him and it had been a very unfriendly look, indeed.

"I don't believe Léir would send you anywhere but to Hell."

"Trust me," Acair said, "I think that would be his preferred destination for me, but things are what they are. I'm off doing his dirty work, if you want as much truth as I can give you."

"Hmmm," Astar said, looking no less unfriendly but slightly less murderous. "Somehow, that doesn't surprise me. What is that spell there that dogs your steps?"

"Something designed to slay me if I use any magic," Acair said. He suspected he was one wrong word away from a very swift trip to Seannair's most uncomfortable cellar, no doubt to be put into a cask next to the one that held the king's crown, so perhaps a bit of honesty couldn't go wrong. "I had thought 'twas your cousin to fashion that spell, but he claims not."

Astar looked at him in surprise. "You don't recognize the magic?"

"Do you?" Acair countered.

"Well, dolt, of course I do." He looked at Léirsinn. "As should you, given the magic in your veins. Who put *that* there?"

"Ah—"

"Perhaps the better question is, why?"

Acair wanted to point out that Astar had an annoying habit of interrupting. Most of the poor souls who found themselves trapped in conversation with him generally wanted to find themselves somewhere to sit and something strong to drink until he talked himself out. As usual, that was likely an observation better left for a different time.

He pulled himself back to the mystery at hand.

"This spell that haunts me," Acair said, "'tis not of Caocladh. I'm certain of that."

Astar looked at Acair in surprise. "I cannot believe that you of all people don't recognize it."

"That could mean so many things," Acair began.

"Don't count on me to enlighten you," Astar said with a snort. He looked at Léirsinn. "But still, *why* do you have that magic in your veins? Ah, never mind. I understand now."

Acair felt his ears perk up and was fairly certain Léirsinn elbowed him with excessive force, unerringly, in a very tender spot under his ribs. It would leave a bruise, of that he was certain.

"It was a gift," Léirsinn said easily. "From someone who knew I needed to offer aid in a particular quest."

"I imagine I know who that someone is. Why he chose that particular stuff is perhaps something you don't want to discuss." He took her hand and bent low over it. "You should rethink the company you're keeping."

"Thank you, Your Highness," she said politely. "I'm sure I'll take that to heart."

Acair found himself the recipient of a look from Astar that in any other circumstances he would have repaid with a half-hearted invitation to a duel, time to be determined when he might feel inclined to rouse himself out of bed to attend it. That he could at the moment only smile politely was yet another thing to add to the list of indignities he would most certainly be handing to a different Cothromaichian prince for his perusal before he helped that man meet his very timely, very painful end.

"You should be very far away before the sun rises," Astar suggested.

"I believe I've said the same thing to your cousin," Acair said before he could stop himself. "More than once."

"No doubt." Astar yawned behind his hand. "Lady Léirsinn, I believe I feel the need for a pleasant stroll through the passageways. I can only assume you might wish to join me. If I lose you at some point near the library, I'll assume you can find your way back to your chamber?"

"Thank you, Your Highness," she said. "Very kind."

Acair found himself with the prince leaning in a bit more closely than he was comfortable with.

"If you stray from the library," he said in a low voice, "I *will* hunt you down and slay you myself."

"That would be a far less painful death than what your sister would inflict, I imagine."

"No imagination needed, and you would consider my offer a mercy if you knew how true that was."

"I appreciate the concession."

"Don't make me regret this," Astar said, pulling back. "I'm doing it for that woman there who deserves far better than the likes of you."

"I'm trying to be worthy of her."

Astar's snort almost felled him where he stood, but, sadly, he was accustomed to worse.

What he wasn't accustomed to, however, was an escort to a place he wasn't supposed to be. He trailed after Léirsinn and her royal companion until they paused before a particular set of heavy doors. Astar shot him one last warning look, then simply continued on down the passageway as if he had places to go and things to do.

Acair wished he'd had the time to properly appreciate where he was, but he thought he might have to be satisfied with simply shaking his head as he opened the heavy wooden doors of Seannair of Cothromaiche's library. He slipped inside that inner sanctum with Léirsinn, then shut the doors quietly behind them.

He pulled her over away from the entrance on the off chance some offended monarch or other might come rushing inside and flatten the two of them, then wondered why he hadn't had the foresight to demand from a different princely grandson exact directions to books that were missing pages.

What he also hadn't considered asking was just what the hell Soilléir had put into Léirsinn's veins. Worse, it had never once occurred to him to ask Soilléir to identify the magic that had created that spell of death that haunted him.

"Any ideas?" Léirsinn whispered.

He had several and most of them had to do with what he would do when he had his fingers and Soilléir's neck close enough for a brief encounter, but perhaps those were thoughts he could enjoy later when he was at his leisure.

He looked at Léirsinn. "Not a one," he said helplessly. "Let's find ourselves a darkened corner and see what comes of it."

He caught her very weak glare even in the gloom and smiled, then took her hand.

"I mean books, darling. I realize it's difficult when you have me within reach, but try to focus on the task at hand."

"I'm going to push you off the back of the next dragon we ride, just so you know."

He suspected she just might.

He nodded toward the hearth to their right and supposed a bit of a pause there might give them at least some idea of the lay of the land, as it were.

He had the feeling Astar might rethink his generosity, so the sooner they had found what they'd come for, no doubt the better.

Eighteen

Léirsinn looked over King Seannair's seemingly endless collection of books and thought she might want to find somewhere to sit. The likelihood of finding what they needed without an extensive, lengthy search was probably very small.

"What are we looking for again?" she murmured.

"Something with a page or two missing," Acair said. "As giddy as I generally am over the sight of a well-stocked library, I'll admit this is rather daunting."

"I don't suppose they have a shelf marked *Things Acair of Ceangail Shouldn't Read*, do they?"

He smiled briefly. "If they don't, they likely should."

"This will take years," she said.

"We might have to try a spell to shorten our search." He turned to her. "You'll have to do it, so stop eyeing the exits."

"I'm not eyeing, I'm merely judging the distance between myself and the closest one."

He reached out and pulled her into his arms. "There, now there is no hope of escape for you. The inconsequential nature of the spell I'm going to give you should put you to sleep, but the exhilaration of being where we're not supposed to will counter that, I'm sure."

"How many words?" she asked reluctantly.

"Four," he said. "Or thereabouts."

"What does it do?" she asked, pulling back far enough to look at him. "And realize I don't really care."

"I know," he said. "This is another of those spells that would be terribly useful for all sorts of things, though. Revealing where you might have left your house key or your favorite pair of boots. You might even use it to track down a particularly fine pony who had escaped to look for better victuals."

"Did you steal it from King Uachdaran?"

"How easily that word trips off the tongue," he said. "And to refute the slander, nay, I most certainly did not steal it."

She pulled away from him and sat on the edge of one of the chairs in front of the hearth. Easier that way to ignore that her knees were unsteady beneath her. "Tell me the tale."

"You're stalling, but I'll humor you, as always." He leaned back against the mantel and clasped his hands behind his back. "It was given to me by the king's daughter."

"When you were stealing *her*," she pointed out.

"I wasn't stealing her, I was liberating her, and the wench is very persuasive. You might like her, should you ever meet. Her hair is more the color of vast amounts of dried blood, but there you have it. You gels from that corner of the palette seem to share a propensity to bend yours truly to your wills and pleasure."

"You said you didn't know any red-haired women."

"Her hair isn't red," he pointed out. "And to continue, the king has some substantial locks on his gates, but even the locks are hidden. She thought it best not to use any magic to undo those locks, which I agreed with, so she traded me a spell of revealing for my skill with exiting whilst using only my wits and two hands."

"So, what exactly does this spell do?"

"It uncovers things that don't want to be found. I'm guessing our good dwarf-king uses it to sniff out the best veins of silver and gold, but we'll use it to see if it will give any tome our enemy has touched a bit of nudge out from its fellows."

"I might bring the whole library down on us."

"You might," he agreed, "so be ginger. Don't give my spectacular visage and enviable form another thought until you've finished with your work. Then lust away."

She had to admit he was very handsome and had the right idea when it came to how that might be distracting. She took a deep breath and let him pull her to her feet.

"I'll try."

He retrieved a slip of parchment from a pocket. "Here's the spell."

She looked at him in surprise. "Did you plan this?"

"Not in any nefarious way," he said easily. "I had a wee think back in my study whilst I was making your coins and suspected this might come in handy. I'm unfamiliar with Seannair's safeguards, so I thought it best that I not even whisper the words of any spell lest even that identify me."

She supposed she didn't need to point out that Prince Astar might already have rushed off to find his grandfather and tattle, so perhaps all she could do was set aside her unease and do what needed to be done.

She followed him across the beginnings of the library shelves to a deep-set window. She took the paper he handed her and looked at what he'd written.

"Four words," he said. "Drop the appropriate name—you know which one—right in the middle, and there you have it."

She read them to herself and was absolutely appalled to realize they made perfect sense to her. She looked at Acair, open-mouthed.

He smiled. "You see."

"I do."

"Try it, then, and let's see what comes of it."

She took a deep breath, forced down a vague feeling of dread, then repeated the words, inserting Sladaiche's name where Acair had told her it should go.

She was certain the whole library would come down on top of them and bury them, but she only heard a handful of books drop in the distance and a trio right next to where they were standing. It definitely could have been worse.

She realized only then that she had actually used a spell that had done what she'd asked it to without any complaint. She felt a little ill, but she supposed that might have been from the magic, not from her surprise.

Acair bent and picked up a thick tome that she was rather glad hadn't fallen on her head, then frowned at her.

"Headache?"

"Stomachache, rather," she said, putting her hand over her belly.

"That's dwarvish magic for you," he noted. "Brutal stuff, even the most pedestrian of spells, which that one was not despite its length. Do you want to sit?"

She shook her head. "I'll be fine. Is that anything interesting?"

"Nerochian Axioms for Healthful Living. Heavy, of course, so it doubles as a means of rendering one senseless before the cover must be opened."

She smiled. "You aren't serious."

"I'm not." He squinted at the title, then handed it to her. "'Tis a lexicon, which I'm guessing will be just as dull as the other would have been. We'll have a look at it though. If you can fetch the other stragglers here, I'll go find what I heard fall in the distance."

She nodded, holding the book close to her.

He smiled and leaned closer to kiss her quickly. "That was very well done, darling."

She watched him walk away and could scarce believe she'd managed to do what she'd needed to. She was half tempted to make werelight, just for the sheer sport of it.

She refrained, though, because she feared she might just burn the place down in her enthusiasm.

She picked up the other two books lying there on the carpet, then made her way across to a shadowy spot near the fireplace to wait. It was unsettling to be touching something that Sladaiche of a place yet to be named had apparently touched at some point in the past, so she set them down on the floor and waited.

It was only moments later that Acair found her, his hands full of other books. He stopped next to her, then apparently caught sight of her expression.

"What is it?" he asked carefully.

"You were right," she said. "He was here."

"I'm as surprised as you are," he admitted. "I *knew* it. Damn that Soilléir. He could have done this himself."

"I don't think he had put that name to that mage, though. Remember his surprise in the glade?"

"I daresay I've forgotten most of that morning and that is on purpose. There's a corner over there near that library ladder that looks discreet enough. You can try your werelight and we'll see what we have here."

She happily settled in on the floor with him, as hidden as possible, and took a deep breath before she used the spell of Fadaire he'd pinched from Sìle of Tòrr Dòrainn. Perhaps it was the magic knit into her forearm that made it work so well, but she had no trouble with it and it didn't even give her a headache.

"You are a wonder."

She felt herself blush. "I'm trying not to think about it. I was half afraid I would burn the library down."

"I don't think Fadaire would do that to you," he said with a smile. "Well, we have seven books, an interesting number on even the most ordinary of days. Let's divide and conquer."

"I don't know what to look for," she protested.

"I'm not sure I do either, but why don't you keep those two and I'll look through these. I suppose we're simply looking for pages that aren't there."

She shivered. "How did he get in, do you think?"

"That is a very good question," he said. "An equally interesting question is *when*." He turned to her. "Soilléir didn't say exactly when the theft had occurred, did he?"

"I wasn't at my best," she said slowly, "but nay, not that I remember."

He sighed deeply. "I'm not sure knowing that would have changed things. I'm guessing once Soilléir discovered the threat, he encouraged his grandfather to put up some sort of safeguards." He looked at her in surprise. "You know, now that I think about it, that may very well be the case."

"What do you mean?"

He rubbed his hands over his face. "I'm an idiot. He put that spell over the entire country two decades ago. Before then, it was an open secret that Seannair hardly knew who came and went. He's famous for hiding his crown in a bloody bin of dried beans, which left his kitchens ransacked more than once."

"As well as this library?"

He shook his head. "Nay, it has always been a bit difficult to get into."

"You would know, of course."

"Of course," he said with a smile.

"But what about Prince Soilléir's spells?" she asked. "Were they just left lying about?"

"Definitely not. I'm guessing he was already working on them before he could toddle across his nursery and keeping them to himself as soon as he understood what they could do. I'm honestly not certain how many of his family members have the key to the chest full of them. I've always suspected he has them written down somewhere, but I couldn't begin to decide where that place might be. Those spells in the hands of someone truly evil . . . "

She didn't want to follow that thought to where it would lead. Those spots of shadow were awful enough.

"The spells of ward on the border are more recent." He frowned suddenly. "I would say within the last score of years, no longer. I told you about my having investigated the same to see how difficult it might be to simply saunter in and have a peep in the king's armoire."

"Or bean barrel."

"Exactly that," he agreed. He considered, then shook his head. "I built my house almost a score of years ago, but I'm not that undesirable a neighbor. Soilléir didn't set those spells simply to keep me out."

"Nor are you that close," she pointed out. "I left my parents' home almost a score of years ago. Nineteen, to be exact. Odd, isn't it?"

He looked slightly green. "I assure you, darling, that I would not have gone down on bended knee at the time, if you'll forgive my lack of enthusiasm over the idea. I would say, though, that we were engaging in far different activities at the same . . . ah—"

"Same time?" she finished for him, reaching out to steady him. "Why is that odd?"

He shook his head sharply. "I think too much. I would need to see what else was happening in the world at that time besides my paying exorbitant sums to have a house constructed whilst I wish I had been rescuing the youthful version of yourself to put you somewhere safe. And aye, I think it was about that time that Soilléir did something about his grandfather's appalling lack of concern over his safety."

"But someone could have gotten inside the library before then."

"Having hid their essence?" Acair asked. "Possibly. There are certainly spells that will take everything that makes you yourself and smother it until you might forget who you are."

"Have you ever done that?"

He shook his head. "Don't care for it, actually. I can't breathe. I have occasionally used something to still the magical waters, if that makes any sense. Saves burying your magic then having to dig it all back up again. There's a layer of un-noticing that goes with it." He lifted his eyebrows briefly. "'Tis a spell of my Gran's, if you want the truth of it."

"An interesting woman, your grandmother."

"Shrewd and calculating is closer to the mark perhaps," he said, "but aye, interesting nonetheless. It makes me wonder how many things I've simply walked right past without seeing them." He looked off into the library for a moment or two, then blew out his breath. "Best not to think about that. Let's see what we have here."

She nodded and looked at the books she held in her hands. The first turned out to be an herbal that she supposed would have been useful, but she wasn't one for medicines past horse liniment. She checked it for missing pages, then set it aside as complete. She held the second book up to the werelight she'd asked that beautiful elvish magic to make . . .

She wondered when she might stop seeing things that left her wanting to weep and howl at the same time.

The exact color of blue the cover had been dyed was difficult to discern in the faint light, but the dragon lying there with his head resting on his scaly tail certainly wasn't.

She shifted to sit closer to Acair.

"Are you unwell, darling?"

"Just chilled," she lied. She looked at the book in her hands and wondered if her soul would crack in two if she opened *that* one.

Dragons and Other Mythical Beasts

Of course. She hadn't thought about the title in years, but there it was in front of her. 'Twas entirely possible, as she'd thought in Acair's library, that printers made several copies of books to sell. There was no reason to suspect that the book she held in her hands was anything but a copy that had somehow found its way into a palace library.

What she *was* certain of was that she wouldn't find her own addition to the book on the final page. If memory served, she had drawn a picture of an ocean she'd never seen, a wizard standing on the edge of that ocean casting his spell for his true love to come find him, and a dragon snoozing peacefully at his feet.

She had been, she had to admit, very silly as a girl of ten summers.

She opened the book, then froze. There had been a tale there of a dragon, that much she remembered, but that story was gone. She flipped through the rest of the book until she came to the endpapers.

She found she simply couldn't turn the page.

"Léirsinn?"

She handed Acair the book. "The first tale is gone."

"How do you—oh, I see." He held the book up and looked at the front of the book where the pages had been cut out, then shut the cover and looked at the spine. He froze, then let out his breath slowly. "The second volume in the series, is it?"

She could only nod.

"Might there be an addition at the back?"

"Aye, but I don't have the courage to look." She met his gaze. "You do it."

He simply looked at her for a moment or two. "Yours?"

"I'm not sure." She hesitated. "It might be."

He flipped through the pages from the beginning, gently, as if he held a great treasure, then he paused as well before he turned the final sheaf. He finally turned the page.

A child's drawing was there of the sea, a dragon, and a man.

He ran his finger over it, then looked at her and smiled. "Breathing fire even all those years ago, were you?"

"Apparently," she said, ignoring the crack in her voice.

"Handsome lad there. One could argue that the coast there looks a bit like my bay."

"One could."

"I hesitate to say it, but your sister was a better artist."

She elbowed him in the ribs, perhaps harder than he deserved, but he only huffed out a bit of a laugh before he shifted and put his arm around her.

"I love you, even if you cannot draw."

"I was a prodigious dreamer, though," she said archly.

"I suspect you were." He hugged her briefly, then released her and handed her back her book. "I think you should keep this one. I'll repay Soilléir for it later by not slaying him whilst he's asleep. What was the first tale about?"

She opened her mouth to speak, then found she couldn't. She could scarce believe what she was thinking, but it was undeniable.

"Léirsinn?"

She turned a bit and put her mouth next to his ear. "It was a tale about a dragon who had lost his soul and all the things he had to do to recover it."

He bowed his head and made a noise that might charitably been termed a laugh had they been in different circumstances. He slid her a look.

"Did he find it?"

"I believe so."

He leaned his head back against the wall. "Do you remember any of it?"

"I remember the entire thing."

"Then come very close and whisper it in my ear. I think I need something else to think on for a moment besides what's in front of us."

She did, because the tale wasn't terribly long and because she'd heard it so many times — and read it herself perhaps more — that she thought she might never forget it.

"Lovely," he said, sighing. "And it gives me hope for my own black soul — or the pieces that are missing of it, rather."

"Why would someone want it, though?"

He looked at her. "No idea. And why not take the entire book, if one's fancies run to childrens' tales?" He shook his head. "Let me have a wee peek at what I have here, then we'll see what we need to do."

She nodded and kept hold of her book. She could see it in her parents' hands, hear their voices as they read from it, feel the heat from the fire at her back as she sat safe and comfortable with the day's work finished.

"We might manage to have those pages back at some point, perhaps."

She realized Acair was watching her. She considered, then shook her head.

"The memories are enough." She set the book aside and looked at what he held on his lap. "What do you have there?"

"A history of blacksmithing and some enormous tome on the proper training of horses. I imagine you wouldn't find anything new in either. There's a ledger here, but that's also staggeringly boring."

She took it from him and glanced through the first few pages. "This is a stable ledger. 'Tis sloppy, if you want my opinion. Not even my uncle would have allowed anything like it."

"Fascinating."

She tapped one of the pages. "Look at the dates. Are those actual numbers?"

He peered at the ledger, then shrugged. "I would say I can scarce believe anyone would care about the incomings and outgoings of a barn a hundred years ago, but you horse people are particular about your doings. I'm guessing this can't be the only ledger the stablemaster has kept."

"It wouldn't be," she agreed. "Odd that this was the one that our particular mage has touched, though, isn't it?"

He blinked, then shut his mouth. "Or perhaps less odd and more alarming. Let's keep it for the moment."

She took it and put it with her own blue-hued book of dragonlore. She didn't look at the cover, but she supposed she could be forgiven if she traced the shape there with her fingers just the same. She supposed other than that, she had never seen any of her other possessions from before.

It was profoundly strange to have something in her hands that had belonged to her in a different lifetime.

She leaned back against the wall and rested her head on Acair's shoulder. Magic, she was finding, was a bit more taxing than she would have thought. Not even a full day of riding horses was so draining.

"But we didn't find what Soilléir sent you here to find," she whispered.

"What he sent me to steal, rather," Acair said grimly. "I daresay it has already been stolen."

"Which doesn't make any sense either," she said. "If the spell were already stolen, what would there be left for you to take?"

"Perhaps he wanted me to make off with his grandfather's cache of after-supper treats and confused *sweets* with *souls*, then completely panicked when he saw how close I was to repaying him properly for what he'd done." He let out his breath slowly. "I'm not exactly sure what I expected, but you did a fine job finding us these."

"A pity we couldn't use a spell that didn't need a name."

"As in something that vomited out books that had been poorly shelved by unnamed but portly orchardists?"

She smiled. "Something like that." She looked at the barn ledger on her lap, then lifted her head and looked at him. "Didn't Soilléir say that mage we won't name had treated his ruler's horses poorly?"

Acair sighed. "Aye, but I'm guessing there are many who could answer to that charge." He lifted the ledger and glanced through it. "I'm guessing that if he had anything to do with horses, he didn't last long near them, but what do I know? Perhaps fine lords don't care."

"Even my uncle cares," she said seriously, "and he can't tell a good horse from a bad one. Then again, neither can Slaidear, which my uncle knows, I believe. Keeping him from ruining everything that came through his barn is probably why I was allowed to stay so long before my uncle decided my life needed to end."

"I wouldn't be . . . surprised . . . "

She listened to his voice fade and looked around her carefully, wondering if they'd been discovered.

Then she realized he had become very still. There was something about his stillness, though, that left her feeling something it took a moment or two to identify.

Fear.

That was it. Fear.

She shifted to look at him. "What is it?"

He looked at her slowly. "Are all stablemasters that inept?"

"I have no idea," she said, helplessly. "Slaidear doesn't ride willingly, but that might be because he doesn't ride well."

"He is a bit thick through the middle."

She nodded.

"So was the orchardist."

She scrambled to her feet, but he was there with her, holding her by the arm before she could bolt. She wasn't certain where she would have gone, but *away* seemed like a good destination.

"When did Slaidear come to the barn, Léirsinn?"

"I don't know," she whispered. "I can't remember."

He put on a pleasant expression. She knew, because she'd watched him do it with others. It was the same expression he wore when he was trying to put someone at ease, though she supposed he wasn't doing it with her because he was on the verge of attempting to intimidate her.

"Think back," he suggested gently. "Was he there when you arrived?"

"I think I might be ill."

"I think I might join you," he said frankly, "but later, when we've a nicely patterned settee before us and the king nowhere in sight. We'll puke together down the back of the cushions. I know these are difficult memories, if you can bring them to mind at all. I wouldn't blame you if you couldn't. Do you remember his being there when you arrived? Perhaps the day after your grandfather fell ill and your uncle sent you to the barn? Was he there then?"

She turned and walked away a pace or two, then looked out into the rich darkness of the king's library. She forced herself to revisit a time she hadn't thought of in years. Unfortunately, there was a decent reason they were uncomfortably clear.

She turned and returned back over the same two paces she'd used to escape what she could scarce face.

"There was a different stablemaster," she said slowly. "I went inside the barn to find him beating one of the lads, almost to death. Doghail pulled me behind him and hid me."

"Of course he did," Acair said quietly.

"He was gone a few days later. That first stablemaster, that is. Slaidear was there next. It could have been a fortnight, perhaps not that long." She considered, then shook her head. "I don't remember him doing anything useful, if you want the truth of it. He stopped pretending to train the horses and left them to me years ago. I even decided which ones to buy. I thought it was because he realized he had no eye for them."

"I imagine that's true as well."

She looked at him, feeling horror descend. "He isn't . . . "

"Try the spell again, Léirsinn, and use his name instead."

"I have to go to the window," she lied. "I can't remember the words."

He only nodded and picked up the books. He shoved five into a random shelf, kept the ledger and her blue-hued book of faery tales, then took her hand and walked with her to the window. He pulled the slip of parchment from his pocket and handed it to her, then smiled briefly.

"You'll be fine."

She would have protested that she most certainly wasn't going to be fine, but the dream she'd had in King Uachdaran's hall came back to her—rushed at her, actually—in a way that left her realizing that whatever was behind her was on fire and the only way out was to walk off a cliff into darkness.

"I would hold you," Acair said very quietly, "but I fear you might pull some of my power to you."

She shook her head. "I'll do this."

"Of course you can, love."

She stilled her mind, then whispered the words of the spell, using a different name, one she was convinced would do nothing at all.

A book leapt off the shelf in front of her and fell at her feet.

Acair picked it up "Damnation."

"What is it?"

He held out a book, then opened the cover.

All the pages were missing.

"Well," she said uncomfortably, "that's something, isn't it?"

"And not a damned thing on the cover to tell us what had been inside. I'm guessing the contents were removed several decades ago." He looked closely at the cover, then swore and shoved it in the shelf above his head. "Useless. Why this answered to Slaidear and not Sladaiche is something I believe we'll leave as a mystery for someone else. I think we might be finished here. Can you put these in your satchel for the moment? I'll carry them later."

She shot him a look, but supposed she didn't need to add that she was accustomed to carrying saddles and hay. He only smiled and handed her the books.

"Let's be away before we're caught. I think we have what we came for."

"Is there time to look for that finely patterned divan?"

He laughed softly. "We'll befoul it a different time and blame it on Soilléir. Off we go."

She wondered, a moment or two later, if they ever might manage to exit somewhere they weren't supposed to be without having the master or mistress of the house catch them before they could.

A faint light appeared next the hearth. A fire joined it, blazing to life tidily in that same hearth.

Acair sighed, then took her hand. "It could be worse," he murmured.

She decided to withhold judgment for the moment. A blond man sat there, dressed in well-made but not excessively fine clothing. His boots, however, were very nice, indeed.

Acair stopped in front of him and made him a low bow. "Your Highness."

"My lord Acair."

Léirsinn wondered if the day would come when she would stop being surprised by the people Acair knew—and those who knew him.

"If I might present to Your Royal Highness my beloved companion, Léirsinn of Sàraichte," Acair said formally. "Léirsinn, this is His Royal Highness, Coimheadair, the crown prince of Cothromaiche."

Léirsinn attempted a curtsey to go along with Acair's very posh accents, but it didn't go very well. That was definitely something she was going to have to work on when she had a bit of free time.

"Sàraichte," Prince Coimheadair said with a frown. "Don't you mean An Caol?"

"Your Highness?" Acair said.

Léirsinn realized the prince was looking at her, but she wasn't sure what she was supposed to say.

"Don't you know who you are, little one?"

Acair caught his breath, almost so quietly that she would have missed it if she hadn't been doing the same thing.

"Your Highness, why do you say that?" Acair asked.

"Well," the crown prince of Cothromaiche said with a shrug, "because I knew her mother, of course."

Nineteen

Acair spared a moment to wonder when he was going to manage to exit a solar without running afoul of its owner.

He shook his head wearily. Yet another thing to add to the list of things to avoid in the future. No more quests, no more flinging his possessions up in the air when taken by surprise, no more unexpected revelations about the people around him, and definitely no more lights springing to life thanks to the current landlord's hand.

He realized Léirsinn had been invited to sit. He hadn't, but he hadn't expected anything less. Prince Coimheadair, for all his slightly odd quirks, was in the end a king in waiting. Other men simply did not sit in his presence. Acair was perfectly happy to stand behind Léirsinn's chair and look deferential whilst he determined when and how they might escape with not only their lives, but the books they had filched still in their possession.

Slaidear.

He could scarce believe it. Why the hell hadn't he seen that coming his way?

He watched Léirsinn hand over the spoils and wondered if he should just give the quest up for lost right there or plead for another hour or so to mourn the saving of the world that might not happen.

He realized the prince was giving him a look that he had absolutely no trouble interpreting. His chances of avoiding death by some painful Cothromaichian method were very slim indeed.

The prince looked at the book of faery tales, then at Léirsinn.

"My child," he said slowly, "why this?"

She was sitting with her back ramrod straight, her hands demurely folded in her lap. Acair would have shifted slightly to put a reassuring hand on her shoulder, but he suspected she wouldn't need it.

She was a wonder, that lass.

"The book is mine," she said.

"How did it come to be in our library?"

"A very good question, Your Highness," she said politely. "I believe I would count it a fortunate rescue, nothing more."

Acair would have laughed, but he caught the tail-end of another cool look sent his way by his primary tormenter's father. What he wouldn't have given to have had Soilléir right there where he could have given the whoreson a wee shove into his papa's comforting arms, then caught his horse gel's hand and bolted from the library at a dead run.

The prince handed it back to her. "I will discover why it was unfortunately no longer in your possession and see that the miscreant is punished. Until that time, accept my apologies for the apparent theft."

"Oh," Léirsinn said, sitting back the slightest bit. "Very generous, Your Highness, but I'm sure it was nothing more than a happy accident that it found its way here. Please don't make a fuss on my account."

"My dear, I couldn't think to do less. Your mother was a frequent guest here before your brother was born and I bought many a horse from your father. I met him several years before they wed, of course."

Acair supposed no one would notice if he simply leaned a bit on

Léirsinn's chair to keep himself from pitching forward over the back
of it onto her lap.

Her mother? Her father?

"I'm surprised," Léirsinn said faintly.

Acair thought *gobsmacked* was perhaps a better word, but he
didn't imagine anyone would care what was running through his
head.

"Why is that, my dear?"

"Well," Léirsinn said slowly, "I didn't realize he had traveled so
far north of Briàghde before he wed my mother."

"Oh, I was speaking of your father," Coimheadair said with a
fluttering of the fingers of one hand, "not your step-father."

A book landed on the floor. Acair reached around to pick up
the faery tale book that had slid off Léirsinn's lap, then caught the
prince's eye and sent him a pointed look. The prince nodded for
Acair to sit, so he pulled over a fireplace stool—no sense in not keeping up the appearance of respect—and sat down next to Léirsinn.

"I believe I've stepped in it now," Prince Coimheadair said,
looking genuinely distressed. "Did you not know, child? Lord Acair,
what of you?"

"Hadn't the foggiest," Acair said, too rattled to pull out his best
courtly manners and give them a snap to rid them of any residual
wrinkles. "Would Your Highness permit me the familiarity of taking
my lady's hand?"

Coimheadair waved him on, then turned back to Léirsinn. "I
won't add to your discomfort, Mistress Léirsinn, for I can see these
tidings come as a surprise. I suppose they would, given how young
you were when your sire was slain. Oh, and there I go again, speaking out of turn."

Acair would have shaken his head, but that wouldn't have done.
A few things became clear to him, however, that hadn't before.
Seannair seemed to be clinging rather firmly to the crown he never
wore, which Acair had always credited to the stubbornness of a
crotchety old bastard who simply hadn't hunted enough pheasants

over the centuries and was determined to live long enough to fill his tally and then some.

Coimheadair of Cothromaiche had always been a rather quiet man, but Acair had assumed that came from standing so long in his father's shadow. Now, he began to wonder if perhaps the prince simply didn't have the temperament to rule the country.

No wonder Soilléir had gathered up all the spells of essence changing and hidden them away for safekeeping.

"Oh, please go on," Léirsinn said.

Acair dragged his attentions back to the conversation at hand and wished rather fervently for a notebook and a pencil. There was obviously no fighting it any longer: he had become his mother.

"Your father was Niall of Ionad-teàrmainn, the lone survivor of his particular line, I believe. I'm not certain of your mother's roots, which is a failure on my part. Tracing lines of that sort is one of my pastimes."

"Fascinating," Acair said sincerely. "You must turn up some interesting things."

Coimheadair huffed a little in pleasure. "I must admit that is the case more often than not. Ionad-teàrmainn is the land across the great bay of Sealladh from Bruadair, but I'm guessing Lord Acair, that you must know that already."

Acair was grateful he'd had the foresight to plant himself firmly on his stool. No more tipping backward with legs and arms waving frantically in the air. No wonder Sladaiche wanted revenge. He was likely still smarting from having endured the same.

"I just discovered it recently," Acair managed, wishing that *recently* meant a score of years earlier instead of *just now*. He wouldn't have chosen a different place to build a house, certainly, but he might have been more inclined to have kept watch for former neighbors with murderous intentions.

"I believe in their language, the name means *refuge*. Their history is full of wars and strife with Wychweald, of all places. Lord Acair, I heard tell you were considering settling there, though 'tis a bit close to Bruadair for comfort, if I'm not wrong?"

"You're not wrong," Acair agreed faintly. "And aye, I did build a house there."

"What did you call it?"

"Tèarmann," Acair said, ruthlessly suppressing the urge to shift uncomfortably. Naming a home was perhaps a foolish thing, but there was a part of him—perhaps a very large part—that had wished for something . . . well, something different.

"Sanctuary," Coimheadair said with a smile. "Apt, if I might be so bold, and very lovely. I didn't realize you knew any of their tongue, though I'm not surprised."

"I didn't," Acair managed. "I believe I might want to learn a bit." And by *a bit*, he meant more than just making a derivative of something he'd found carved into the ruins of a foundation stone he'd had tossed in the rubbish heap before his own foundations had been laid.

"We had a lexicon, rather heavy and substantial, though I'd have to look for it. Their language is almost forgotten, though dredging it up might be something you'd be interested in." The prince recrossed his legs. "Very fine horse people there, of course, which, Mistress Léirsinn, might appeal to you. Unfortunately, there was trouble several centuries ago. The exact dates escape me, but I could find them later, if you like."

"Brilliant idea," Acair put in, deciding he might have to retrieve that lexicon he'd reshelved so badly.

The prince frowned at him, no doubt on principle, then continued. "Tosdach of Briàghde was traveling through An Caol with his son—"

"Tosdach?" Léirsinn. "My grandfather? Er, I mean—"

"Your step-father's father? Yes, that is correct. His son, your step-father Saoradh, met your mother as he and his father were traveling hereabouts. Your mother was a delightful woman, my dear, and having three young children . . . " He smiled gently. "I believe, romantic that I am, that it was love at first sight. Saoradh didn't have your father's eye for horses, of course, but perhaps that didn't matter. There is a part of me that always believed that your mother was the keener horsewoman. Not to disparage your sire, of course."

"Was she from An Caol, then?" Acair asked. He might have thought the prince a very silly man, but His Royal Highness did have a way of sniffing out connections that even Fionne of Fàs might have admired.

"Fògarrach," Coimheadair said. "Near An Cèin, which I'm sure you know. An Caol was originally settled by the last few stragglers from Ionad-teàrmainn, which you might not know."

"I didn't," Acair said. "Your research is impressive, Your Highness."

The prince looked pleased. "Fògarrach's people aren't elvish, but there are the occasional star-crossed love matches. I believe Ceannairceach of Léige can attest to the lure of that."

Acair chuckled politely. "I believe she can and I paid a steep price for her happiness."

"So I hear. Léirsinn, my dear, a glass of sherry perhaps?"

"I'm fine—"

A bellowing in the distance that sounded far too much like the call of a hunting horn had the prince jumping to his feet. Acair was almost tempted to mention that His Highness looked a bit like a fox who knew his time was up, but alas, he had grown soft so he forbore. He was beginning to suspect he would never again be his old self, full of vim, vigor, and acerbic remarks.

"My father," Prince Coimheadair announced. "You should hide." He pointed to a tapestry to the right of the fireplace. "There's a closet behind that. My sire will never look."

Acair caught the books the prince tossed at him and leapt with Léirsinn toward safety. His Highness held the tapestry for them until Acair managed to find the latch and open the door, then he dropped it. They barely had time to stuff themselves inside and pull the door to before the braying reached the library itself.

"Pitiful," Acair whispered. "No copies and no decent sense of subterfuge. 'Tis a wonder the whole damned place hasn't been overrun before now!"

The words were scarce out of his mouth before he realized a rather unsettling fact.

They were not alone in their closet.

A faint ball of werelight appeared over their heads and he looked to his left to find none other than Soilléir of Cothromaiche, youngest son of the crown prince and possessor of a countenance that was just slightly green, standing there looking profoundly guilty.

"You!" he exclaimed, understanding at that moment why he was the recipient of that greeting so often.

"My lord Acair," Soilléir said, inclining his head politely. "Mistress Léirsinn. We might want to forgo pleasantries for another moment or two."

Acair clamped his lips shut simply to keep himself from wasting breath swearing. That was a welcome distraction, given the straitness of their quarters. He was himself not a small man. Soilléir, unfortunately, was not a slight fellow either. He supposed if either of them had tended to portliness like Sladaiche, the current arrangement might have been a bit more tolerable. At least that way they could have elbowed pudge instead of muscle.

The single thing that saved his annoying companion from death was the fact that he'd had the good sense to put Léirsinn on his right as they crowded into that bloody closet. If he'd had to contemplate that damned whoreson being closer to her than was polite . . .

"You're growling," Léirsinn breathed.

It could have been much worse, he supposed, but he decided that wasn't worth mentioning at the moment, either. For all he knew, any breathing out threats, no matter how richly they might have been deserved, would leave them all suffocating before Seannair managed to finish complaining about his latest hunt and trundle off to bed.

"Death," he mouthed at Soilléir.

Not so much as a snort in return. Perhaps the prince had heard that threat more than once.

Eventually, silence fell out in the library. Acair elbowed Soilléir with perhaps a bit more vigor than the moment called for.

"Go look."

"I'm not supposed to be here."

"You live here!"

"Sshh," Soilléir said, sounding more like a guilty youth than a man of mature years full of spells that gave the rest of the world nightmares.

"You cannot tell me you're afeared of your grandsire," Acair whispered furiously.

"He'll cut me from his will."

Acair heard Léirsinn laugh softly which was likely the only thing that saved the mage to his left from a proper throttling. He suspected Soilléir was vexing him on purpose, but there was no room to get his hands up and around the man's throat, so perhaps there was nothing to be done but keep a tally of abuses to be repaid later.

He concentrated on simply breathing lightly until the silence had gone on for what felt like hours. He glared at Soilléir.

"Do you need a wee glass to scry the scene to make certain they're gone or are your ears enough?"

Soilléir said nothing, but Acair flattered himself that if the were-light had been brighter, he would have been able to see a flicker of fear in the man's eyes.

He was a dreamer, but there it was.

Soilléir eased the door open, listened for a bit longer, then pushed opened the door fully.

"All safe," he said, stepping out and holding the tapestry away from the wall.

Acair invited Léirsinn to follow him as he made certain Soilléir's ears weren't failing him, then he saw her settled in her chair there by the fire. He set his burdens of the written word by her feet, then turned his attentions to the man who had caused him so much trouble. He folded his arms over his chest slowly, hoping to send the message that he was choosing not to commit murder right there on Seannair's library hearthrug.

Soilléir sat down in his father's recently vacated chair and smiled faintly. "I see you've made it this far."

"No thanks to you."

"You might be surprised."

"Did you know?" Acair demanded.

"Know what?"

"Who I was meant to be looking for," Acair snapped.

Soilléir lifted a shoulder in a half shrug. "I know many things."

Acair patted himself figuratively for something sharp to plunge into that damned essence-changer's chest but, as was his lot in life at present, managed nothing but a noise that came far too close to *mewling babe* for his taste.

"You *useless* whoreson," he said.

Soilléir only shrugged, something he seemed to do with frightening regularity. "I am a pragmatist."

"*I* am a pragmatist," Acair shouted, then remembered where he was and with what secrecy he was supposed to be there.

"Then perhaps we are more alike —"

"Do not even start with that," Acair growled. "If you tell me that you've sent me scampering over the whole of the damned world simply to bring me here where you could tell me what you could have told me anywhere else, I vow I will cast aside my better instincts and slay you where you sit."

"There were conclusions you needed to come to on your own," Soilléir said simply.

Acair shook his head in disbelief. He realized with annoyance that he had shaken his head so often over the past year that he had acquired a permanent crackle in his neck. He blamed Soilléir and Rùnach. He would also be damned if he would ask them to see to repairing the damage. Who knew what sort of sparkling rot they would leave rampaging about his fine form in the process?

"You could have told me and saved me all this trouble—"

He stopped speaking. It was becoming an alarming habit, that realizing that he was on the verge of saying things he shouldn't. Admittedly, he had a far better guard over his tongue than most of his family, but he had never shied away from flinging a well-conceived barb or a hastily slung-together insult and the consequences be damned.

Trouble, however, at his current juncture included a red-haired stable gel who had sacrificed not only her momentary peace of mind but likely her future peace as well simply to keep him alive. He didn't dare look at her lest he see her reaction to his heart sitting so prominently, as the saying went, upon his sleeve. He knew as he had seldom known anything in the past that Soilléir had known what he would find in that barn. He shook his head slowly.

"Impossible."

"Is it?"

"You didn't."

Soilléir smiled very faintly. "There is a rich history of that sort of activity in my family. I'm not sure you need worry, though. She might not be interested in you given that I don't see any sort of betrothal ring on her fingers."

Acair glanced at the woman in question's fingers and almost suggested a rude gesture she might make with at least one of them, but perhaps that was an insult better saved for later.

"I'm working on it," Acair said. "Why are you here?"

"Unforeseen circumstances," Soilléir said succinctly.

Acair realized he'd finally reached a point with the mage across from him where he was simply past surprise.

"I didn't intend to be," Soilléir added, looking the faintest bit unsettled. "Events—or uncontrollable players in those events, if you will—took a turn I didn't anticipate."

Acair felt one of his eyebrows go up and he heartily agreed. "A wench," he said in awe. "A wench has thrown you for the proverbial loop."

"What is it your mother says about your untoward deeds?"

"*If you can't name them, I won't claim them,*" he said. "Pithy, but a bit too much on the rhyming side. My mother, as you might imagine, doesn't care."

"She doesn't," Soilléir agreed, "and she's right about many things. Also, you two should go now." He paused. "Please."

Acair would have looked around himself in an exaggerated fashion, then made some cutting remark about the state of the world as a whole, but the truth was, he was just too damned unsettled to.

"You'll need to help us out the back gate."

"I wouldn't think to do otherwise," Soilléir said.

Acair suppressed the urge to swear at him. "Let me be more specific. You'll need to get us over the border, invisible, with a distraction to draw eyes off us—on the off chance your damned spell isn't enough."

"A distraction won't be a problem," Soilléir said, "and my spell will be enough."

"For more than one journey through the air."

"I'll give Léirsinn the key to use in removing it so you might use it as long as you like." He rose and held down his hand for Léirsinn. "A safe journey to you, my dear."

Acair was surprised she didn't clout him on the nose, but that gel had more restraint than he did. He refrained from muttering threats under his breath because they were, after all, trying to go about in secret.

He retrieved the lexicon on the off chance he might need to use it as a weapon in a pinch, dared Soilléir to make any comment about removing it from his grandfather's library—which he very wisely did not—and invited the man to join them in making a discreet exit out Léirsinn's window after they retrieved their gear from her chamber.

The one thing he could say—and he did so with only a slight

gritting of his teeth—was that whatever else his faults might have been, Soilléir of Cothromaiche was as good as his word. Within minutes they were safely in the air under cover of a spell that was so beautiful, he thought he might have to remove an item or two from the *Reasons to Slay a Certain Essence-changing Whoreson* column of Soilléir's ledger after having heard the man weave it over them.

He'd memorized it, of course, because that was what he did.

A charmed life and a terribly courageous woman with whom to enjoy it.

He thought things just might be looking up.

T he sun was setting as they walked through the village of An Caol, still cloaked in that spectacular spell. He'd studied it as they'd flown and realized at some point during that flight that it was the same spell Soilléir had used in that rustic little pub in Neroche. At the time he had found the magic odd, but he couldn't have said why. Now, he knew better.

It was the magic of Fàs.

He was definitely going to be having a wee visit to his grand-mother's solar, bribes in hand, to tattle on Soilléir. With any luck at all, there would be a battle of words and spells between the two of them that would be decent entertainment for the summer. He would, of course, be sitting by with notebook in hand. His posterity would thank him, no doubt.

He also wondered why he hadn't taken the trouble to make note of that magic earlier. He was beginning to suspect that the magic of Fàs, honed to perfection in that tiny duchy of Fearann, hid behind honey and cones of thread to throw inquisitive mages off the scent. He had no idea what the stuff was really used for, but he would defi-nitely be giving it a closer look when he was next at his leisure.

That might come after he'd unraveled what it was that Soilléir had so carefully placed in Léirsinn's veins and the reason why.

He realized she had stopped. Sianach, currently wearing his

drooling, hell-hound shape, had slipped his once equine head beneath her limp hand and given it a nudge. She patted him absently, but said nothing. She was simply looking at the very modest little house in front of her.

It had to have been her parents', that much was certain. Acair wasn't sure what the proper thing was to do at the moment, but didn't wince when she groped for his hand and held it a bit too firmly. She looked away from the open doorway and met his gaze. He expected to see agony in her eyes, but there was only a solemn sort of peace.

He hardly knew what to think. She was so . . . whole. He was perhaps a bit too accustomed to rubbing shoulders with people who wanted as much from him as he wanted from them. That woman there, though. That red-haired, lovely, courageous gel who had put the fate of the world before herself was unlike anyone he had ever met.

"I will," he said seriously, "beggar myself to buy you as many Angesand ponies as you can ride."

"You're daft," she said with an affectionate smile.

"And soon to be very poor from said beggaring, but I'll rob a few unwary monarchs so you have enough feed and hay."

"Altruistic to the last," she noted.

"That I am, love." He hesitated. "What can I do?"

"Come with me inside?"

He took a careful breath and nodded. There was nothing else to be said and he wasn't at all sure what he would find, but it had seemed as though their current footfalls were simply more steps on a journey that had been set out for the both of them long before they would have considered the same.

Soilléir saying *take her home* as he'd shut that damned border spell almost on his arse had been something to consider, of course.

What he hadn't expected, however, was to realize that he had walked through that village himself decades ago.

"Are you unwell?"

He looked at her quickly. "Rather I should be asking you the same."

"You've been here."

He wasn't entirely sure how to respond. "I believe so," he said slowly. "If you want the entire truth, I believe I may have met your father's father."

"My father, or my step-father?"

"Your father, Niall," he said carefully, "though he was a youth at the time. I'm sorry to say I can't remember his father's name, though I think we could find it easily enough. We'll put my mother on the trail when next we see her."

She took a deep breath. "I suppose my grandfather is no longer that, is he?"

"I think he would be heartbroken if you didn't claim him as yours." He thought she looked a bit ill, but he was afraid to ask her if that was from where she was standing or whom she was considering wedding. He decided abruptly that he didn't want to know, so he cleared his throat and settled for the easier concern. "I could go in—"

"I'll come."

Sterling, beautiful, fearless gel. He nodded, then shot Sianach a pointed look. His horse turned in a circle a time or two, found himself a spot by the front door, and sat back on his haunches. Bared teeth gleamed brightly in the gloom, which Acair supposed was the best they were going to do for any sort of alarm. He took Léirsinn's hand and walked inside her house.

It was as empty as he would have expected it to be given that the front door no longer hung there. He would have released her, but she didn't seem inclined to let go of his hand and he certainly wasn't going to argue. He supposed there would be nothing of interest to see—

"Look."

At any other time, that tone and that word would have had him doing a little caper of delight over the thought of unexpected spoils where they shouldn't have been, but at the moment they filled him with a particular sort of dread. He followed the direction in which Léirsinn was pointing and realized there was something on that rough-hewn mantel.

There was no reason not to look and innumerable reasons why he should.

He walked over to the hearth with Léirsinn next to him and looked at the missive sitting there. 'Twas so like that moment all those years ago when he'd found that spell sitting atop a different mantel, wrapped up and irresistible for a lad of eight summers, that he could hardly breathe.

Léirsinn looked at him, then reached out, but he caught her hand.

"In case there's a spell of harm attached," he said seriously.

She looked at him as if he'd lost his wits. "And 'tis better that you touch it than I?"

"I think so." He took the missive, popped open the seal, and pulled forth a handwritten note. He considered, then looked it over for spells. He saw none, which he supposed was an improvement over his last bout of mantel razing.

"Well?"

He held it out. "We've been invited to a house party."

"You mean *you* have been invited," she said slowly.

He shook his head. "The two of us. In Tosan."

"But it's a trap."

He would have called it a final meeting, but he was perhaps more cynical than she was. He nodded, then looked at her.

"Do you care to remain for a bit?"

She shook her head. "Perhaps another time."

He understood. He walked with her out of the house and paused just outside the doorway. He released her, tore the missive in half, then cast it on the ground. He was utterly unsurprised to watch it catch fire and smoke terribly before it burned itself out.

"Reply sent," he said with a shrug. He reached over and

scratched his horse behind his ears. "Sianach, we need to go. Back up and into something with wings, if you please."

"You're very calm."

He shrugged. "I am never, ever afraid. Well, I might be of horses, if you want the entire truth. And snakes. I don't care at all for snakes."

"Will we reach Tosan safely?"

He sighed deeply. "The final meeting won't happen if we're too dead to attend. We'll be safe enough."

Though what would happen once they walked through those mediocre palace doors was anyone's guess.

He waited for his hell-hound to have a proper stretch, then walk away from the house and take the shape of a terrifying black dragon with numerous red-tipped scales. He looked at his love.

"We'll be there by dawn, I imagine," he said quietly. "Why don't you ride before me and try to sleep some."

"I was going to say the same thing to you."

He smiled and pulled her cloak up around her chin. "You just want an excuse to hold me in your arms, you shameless vixen."

"Do I need to resort to that?" she asked archly.

He certainly hoped she didn't, but he imagined he didn't need to say as much. He put his arm around her and pulled her toward their mount. Perhaps they would divide the journey and take turns trying to rest.

Unfortunately, he feared that what awaited them, soulless black mage that he was and terribly courageous horse miss that she was, might require much more than sleep could furnish them.

Twenty

❧

Léirsinn wondered why it had never occurred to her that the palace at Tosan wouldn't have wood shavings on the floors and mattresses stuffed with hay.

Perhaps the luxury of her surroundings had something to do with arriving at the front door in the company of an elven prince's grandson. Acair wasn't at all shy about using his connections to his father's family, though perhaps just the thought of hosting a black mage of such terrible reputation but flawless manners had been enough to cause the lord and lady of Tosan to rouse themselves before dawn to greet him at the front door.

They had been escorted with all decorum and not a few guardsmen to a chamber that definitely hadn't seen any equine visitors recently. Water for washing, tea and a light repast, and a maid and manservant had been provided for Lord Acair and his affianced lady without delay. Léirsinn had done her best imitation of Acair in skirts, which she suspected had amused him almost to the point of wheezing, but what else could she do? She was so frantic with worry and concern, she was almost beside herself.

She was tempted to go look behind the sofa and under the bed for hapless stablemasters idly counting their evil spells, but she thought that might leave the servants wondering if she'd lost her wits.

"I believe my lady will simply require some rest," Acair said, shooing servants toward the door. "Breakfast would be lovely, however, and please send my thanks to His Grace for the hospitality."

Léirsinn turned as she heard the door shut and lock, then wondered if anyone would think her unreasonable to have left both her dignity and her shoes by the hearth as she bolted across the chamber and threw herself into Acair's arms.

"Well," he said, staggering a bit, "I hate to go to such extremes to have you right where I want you most, but if this is what it takes."

She couldn't find the words to make even a poor response to that, so she simply closed her eyes. He no doubt knew exactly what she feared, so there was no point in talking about it. She stood there and shook until he put his arm around her shoulders and pulled her over to the hearth. He sat down and pulled her onto his lap, then wrapped his arms around her.

That helped, but not much.

"This is very fine," she said, searching for something unremarkable to discuss. "Not a boot scraper in sight."

"Contrary to your previous opinion of it?"

She sighed. "What did I know? I thought Sàraichte was vast."

"I'm sure the local burgess would be flattered, but nay, Sàraichte is only a tiny spot within the larger country of Siochail."

"Never heard of it," she said, wishing that were still the case at present.

"There is absolutely nothing interesting there," he said. "The place is so large and full of hamlets and farms that it can't scrape together enough royalty to have a seat on the Council of Kings. Tosan is the capital and the current lord of Tosan styles himself Duke, but who granted his family that honor is anyone's guess. At least the accommodations are less terrible than I expected them to be."

She pulled away far enough to be able to look at him. "I think it helps to be the grandson of a prince," she offered.

"Bastard and horse gel or children of nobility," he said with a shrug. "I'll take the former for home, but I think we can happily use the latter for decent seats at table and chambers that look like this. It has been done before, believe me. And I believe that's breakfast knocking at the door, if you're interested."

She nodded and crawled to her feet, then went to stand with her back against the fire. The servants Acair let in were quick about their work of laying things out on the table near where she stood, and Acair was equally swift at inviting them to leave. She poured tea for them both, but managed only a sip or two before she found she couldn't choke down any more.

She sat, though, because she thought she might manage not to drop anything if she were closer to the table than standing would have put her. Acair made substantial inroads into finishing what was there. She had noticed him scrutinizing things for what she assumed were spells or poisons, but apparently he hadn't found either.

"Will he come inside here?" she asked, when she thought she couldn't hold onto the question any longer.

Acair shook his head. "He can't have what he wants if we're dead."

"You've said that before."

"Unfortunately, that's because 'tis true." He set aside his cup. "Do you have your coins?"

"I left them in my satchel, but that's just here by the hearth."

He fetched it, then removed the coins and his spell of death from the pocket there. He put the books on the floor, then considered for a moment before he laid the coins and rune on top of them. He sat down on the sofa and patted the spot next to him.

She joined him and was rather thankful to be sitting closest to the fire, though she suspected that had been deliberate on his part.

"Where do you usually keep your gear?" he asked.

"Hoof pick down the side of my boot," she said with a shrug. "I don't carry anything else."

"I think I should have found you a decent swordmaster from

Uachdaran's garrison," he said grimly. He settled back against the divan and sighed deeply. "That and a dagger from his forge. This is what I get for being so principled. Never again, I tell you."

She smiled in spite of herself, then wedged herself just behind him where she felt appallingly safe. She rested her head on his shoulder and sighed.

"Do you think he's still, well, Slaidear?"

"That is the question, isn't it?" He reached for one of her hands and held it in both his own. "If he is going about in his persona of stablemaster, he'll have trouble moving about freely here without a very good reason. I guessing at the very least he inspired someone to send Fuadain an invitation. I'm sure he will have found a way to come along."

"I'll be surprised if Fuadain manages to reach the table instead of finding himself face-down in a horse trough," she said. "Why Slaidear hasn't murdered my unc—well, you know who—long before now, I don't know."

"I would assume Fuadain is useful to him as a distraction, if nothing else."

"I still don't understand why he didn't slay me in the barn," she said. "Or you, for that matter."

He shifted a bit to look at her. "Do you think he was the one who sent those mages after me that night?"

"I honestly couldn't say for certain," she said. "I was so horrified by the idea that I didn't pay attention past wondering how to keep you alive."

"A life without yours truly was just too bleak to contemplate, I'm sure."

"You might be surprised how true that is."

She found herself the recipient of one of those charming little smiles he'd used on his grandmother and wondered, as she had then, how anyone told him nay.

"Stop that," she said weakly.

"I think I won't."

"I am unmoved."

He leaned over and kissed her softly. "You aren't, but I won't force you to admit it." He straightened with a sigh. "You horse people are as impossible to control as the ponies you love, I'm finding. As for the other, whilst I think Slaidear may be stupid, I think he's patient. You have something he wants. I would very much like to know what that is, but I won't put you in danger to find out."

"But I don't own anything past the coins Mistress Cailleach keeps for me, this dragon charm, and that crossbow and bolts we left behind, which he likely now has. What else could he possibly want?"

He considered her so closely for a moment or two that she thought she should perhaps be nervous. She might have been, if he hadn't been who he was, which was as unlikely a thought as she'd ever had.

"Might I look at that charm?"

"Of course." She pulled the necklace over her head and handed it to him. "King Sìle told me he knew the man who made it."

Acair looked at her in surprise. "Did he? When?"

"When you were off not kicking rocks back where they were meant to go."

He smiled. "Never close all the doors right off is my motto. And Sìle said he knew the man who made *this* particular charm?"

"Aye, though how he would know that I don't know. He also said the man who made this also makes horseshoes."

Acair choked. She would have patted him on the back, but he held up his hand before she could.

"I'm well," he managed. "Did he say where?"

"He didn't, just that he would arrange an introduction if I liked." She paused and looked at him. "An elven king, no less, arranging things for me."

"I think you underestimate your ability to make an impression," he said with a smile. He held the charm up and studied it for a moment or two. "Does it do anything odd?"

"It grows unusually warm from time to time."

"Well, there is magic folded into the silver, but damned if I know what it is from just a quick look." He shook his head. "Horseshoes and dragons. I think, darling, that your quiet life in a barn was perhaps an illusion." He handed it back to her. "Let's go sleep for a pair of hours, then we'll pore over those books and see if we can find what we're missing."

She imagined it might take more than a pair of hours to leave her equal to doing anything but pacing and fretting, but she was desperate enough to try almost anything to give herself a bit more strength.

She thought she might understand why a mage might want the same, though stealing that strength from someone else was something she couldn't fathom.

"Sleep," Acair said, standing and holding down his hand for her. "We both need it."

She let him pull her to her feet, but she found she couldn't move. "I'm afraid to close my eyes."

He winced slightly. "And me with no spells of ward. Let's do this. You sleep and I'll keep watch, then we'll trade. Here, we'll bring your coins with us. Just don't use them on me, aye?"

She nodded, gathered up the coins he'd made her, and hoped she wouldn't have to use them on anyone else quite yet.

She realized only after she'd woken that several hours had passed. If Acair had slept during any of that time, he didn't seem inclined to mention it and he made no complaints about having remained awake so she could sleep. He seemingly had no compunction about nodding off with her manning the defenses, though, so she suspected he hadn't even napped.

He was a very light sleeper, though, in spite of that. Brushing the table still laden with the remains of their breakfast with only the back of her hand had him sitting up, fully awake. She waved him back to his rest and took up a post in front of the hearth.

She wished desperately for a horse and an open field. The urge to flee was almost overpowering.

She gave herself a good shake and walked over to look at the books left spread out on the sofa. She sat down and picked up the first one she came to without any idea of what she was looking for. She did that with horses more often than not. After all the years she'd spent looking them over, she had become confident in her ability to spot a gem amongst lesser offerings.

What had served her best, though, was to simply get on their backs and allow them to show her what they could do. Perhaps that didn't work with books, but she was out of ideas on what might. Perhaps starting from the top of the pile and working her way down would reveal something she couldn't have foreseen.

She started with the barn ledger. She could hardly believe the dates there, but if Acair's sire had lived a thousand years already, perhaps a stablemaster who had been let go a hundred years previously wasn't unthinkable. She tucked a few details away for discussing with Acair later, then looked through the other things they'd brought with them. Interesting, but not particularly noteworthy.

She wound up finally with her own book in her hands. She sat back against the sofa and closed her eyes, holding it close. It was a very odd feeling to have something in her possession that she'd had as a child, then lost. She was tempted to wonder how it had found its way into King Seannair's library, but perhaps that could safely be left to Prince Coimheadair to investigate.

Stranger still was why that first story was missing. If Slaidear had indeed been the one to have taken it, the question was why would a grown man have removed a tale about a dragon from a children's book?

Admittedly, the dragon had lost his soul and gone looking for it in odd places, but both the dragon and his search had been nothing more than a product of someone's imagination. It wasn't as if the dragon had said . . .

She felt her entire being stop. Her heart, her breath, her swirling thoughts.

Full stop.

It wasn't as if the dragon had said anything, was what she'd been thinking.

But the beast had . . .

"Léirsinn?"

She was certain she'd jumped half a foot, right off the divan. She knew she'd thrown her book up into the air because a hand reached out and caught it. The rest of the books next to her tumbled to the floor at her feet.

Acair looked at her and held up his hands slowly.

"Friend, not foe."

"You're too quiet," she managed.

"Says the lass who has left me startled more often than not. You were lost in your reading, I think. I called you three times, if you're curious." He looked at her with a slight frown. "What is it?"

She leaned over and stacked the fallen books on top of each other, then took back her own when Acair handed it to her. She held it, then looked up at him. "I might need something to drink."

He didn't move. "You found something."

"I'm not sure."

He frowned thoughtfully, then poured things into glasses. He sat down next to her and handed one to her. "Water for you, darling, and whisky for me."

She took his glass out of his hand, had a sip of his brew, then deeply regretted it. She handed it back to him and settled for the water he'd poured for her.

"I think I might need to walk," she said, feeling a little light-headed.

"We'll take a turn about the chamber," he said slowly. "I don't think we dare go outside, but this is the very last time that is the case." He took their drinks and set them on the table, then pulled her up with him. "What did you find?"

She took the arm he offered, then walked with him around the edge of a chamber that she realized was far larger than she'd thought at first. Somehow, that didn't ease her all that much, but as he said, perhaps it would be the last time being in a confined space would be necessary.

"I looked over King Seannair's barn ledger," she began. "He bought a horse three hundred years ago."

"Let's acquire that particular pony, then," Acair said with a snort. "Just my ancient sort of nag. I imagine it will be far too tired to do any damage to my fine form."

"I suspect so. That was also only the first of many horses he bought over the course of those subsequent three hundred years."

"So, Seannair has purchased many ponies over the centuries," he said slowly. "Any ideas from where?"

"From *whom* is a more interesting question."

He looked at her. "Look at you peering into musty old corners. The next thing we know, you'll be wanting your own set of tools for the picking of locks."

"I'll leave that to the lad who already has them," she said uneasily. "As for the other, I don't think I would have noticed if the horses hadn't come through a particular line."

"Do not tell me they have their own equine family trees."

"You know they do," she said. "Three hundred years ago, Seannair bought a horse from Flann of Ionad-teàrmainn."

"I don't suppose there's a description of either the lad's flaming red hair, or perhaps the color of that pony, is there?"

"Does calling it a chestnut suffice?" she asked. "And aye, that's what they call it. So, the interesting thing is, King Seannair continued to buy horses from that particular line from that same family, though two hundred years ago—and believe me I can hardly choke this out—the horses continued to come from that line but the barn moved."

He stopped and looked at her in surprise. "You can tell that from a ledger?"

She nodded. "I could tell you what they were fed almost to the week, if you were interested."

"I am absolutely not," he said with a shudder.

She smiled briefly. "I didn't think you would be. But that line of horses continued to be sold to the king until twenty years ago."

He caught his breath. "Who was the last seller of that particular line?"

"Muireall of An Caol."

"Of course," he said quietly. "I'm assuming she was selling a pony descended from those lads who peopled a barn in Ionad-teàrmainn."

Léirsinn nodded. "If you can believe that. And here's something else. Remember the book you set aside about farrier techniques?"

"Boring stuff, that."

"It might have been less dull if we'd known it was written by the man who's been shoeing Seannair's horses for the past three hundred years."

"I wonder if he's the same lad who made your dragon charm?"

She shrugged. "King Sìle didn't tell me his name, but I wonder." She paused, then looked at him. "I've been thinking about something else."

He only waited. That he didn't make some insulting comment about that having been a challenge for her . . . well, she knew she should have been accustomed to that by then, but that didn't make it any less lovely.

"I was thinking about that fire you made from your grandmother's spell in your garden," she said, finally.

"With the dragons, in honor of you."

"Aye, that one." She hesitated, then cast caution to the wind. If he was going to think her a fool, he could. "Did you hear it? The song it sang?"

"Ah," he began slowly, "nay. What was this song the fire was singing?"

"This will sound daft—"

"Many important things do," he said. "Go on."

"I thought I was dreaming that song," she said. "I heard it in your mother's house."

"The mind boggles," he said with a shiver, "truly it does."

"I finally figured out where I'd heard it before." She took a deep breath. "It was a lullaby my father used to sing."

He closed his eyes briefly. "When you say your father, do you mean your step-father?"

"Nay, my father. I'm almost sure of it."

He looked at her in surprise. "Did your parents have any magic?"

She looked at him helplessly. "My mother? Nay. My father—or step-father, rather—I don't remember him ever using any. What my true father had, I have no idea."

He paced with her for several minutes in silence. "Prince Co-imheadair said your sire was the last of his particular line," he said thoughtfully, "so that leaves us without anyone to ask. But one wonders what went on in his homeland, aye?"

She nodded hesitantly, then decided there was no point in not speaking her mind. "I was wondering where you might hide a spell, if you had a spell to hide."

"Besides under sofa cushions and thrones?" he asked with a faint smile. "I suppose I tend to tuck things in books, but as we can see with those spells from Ionad-teàrmainn, that goes awry more often than not."

"But the spells you hid, the ones that work on their own. Why did you choose where to put them?"

He shrugged. "Because hiding things in plain sight, or as near to it as I can manage, tends to leave things undisturbed. Evil little mages are always on the hunt for things lurking in the shadows, not ordinary items sitting out in the open."

"Then what do you think about that book we found that had just the cover left? Do you think Slaidear is the one who took whatever was inside?"

"Spells of revealing don't lie," he said slowly. "Whatever it contained—and I'm guessing it was spells—was definitely removed and more than likely by him. Why?"

"Do you think he's also the one who cut the pages from my book of faery tales?"

He nodded. "Same answer there. And just so you know, my nose is starting to twitch with this direction you're taking. What are you getting at?"

She was rather glad he had put his hand over hers on his arm to keep her somewhat captive. If she'd been able to, she suspected she might have run right out the door and continued on until she could breathe properly again.

"We can sit, if you'd rather," he offered.

She shook her head. "That won't make it any easier." She took a deep breath, then stopped and looked at him. "If he is the one who took that story, it made me wonder why he would have wanted it."

He only waited.

"I started thinking about your runes that look like coins and things, but have your power and magic hidden in them. That led me to wondering if someone might not just hide a spell in a book, but hide a spell inside a tale inside a book."

His mouth fell open, but he seemed to be incapable of speech.

She nodded. "Everything comes back to dragons, doesn't it?"

"Ye gads," he said, looking stunned. "So you're saying that someone hid a spell in that tale from your book that is no longer there."

She shrugged helplessly. "I was just thinking that it was odd that the dragon said so little."

He frowned thoughtfully. "I can't say that's unusual. A taciturn lot, those scaly beasts. Hearn might have a different opinion, but . . . why do you ask?"

She pulled away from him and walked back over to the fire. She looked over her shoulder to make certain he was following her, though she supposed she needn't have. He was hard on her heels, wearing a gratifying look of concern.

She sat down on the sofa and dug out the notebook that contained his grandmother's map. She pulled a pencil from her satchel, turned to a fresh page, and wrote down the words the dragon had spoken. She knew they were exactly as they'd been written because they were burned into her memory.

She handed the notebook to him. "That's what the dragon says."

He read it, then dropped the notebook. She picked it up, then handed it back to him.

"I think this is from the same language my father spoke. I can't be certain, of course, but they have the same sort of cadence my father's lullaby had." She looked at him helplessly. "Like a horse's gaits, you know. They all might canter, but each horse will have his own individual way of doing that." She paused. "What do you think?"

He looked at her with an expression of awe. "I think you are a miracle."

"What is that magic, do you think? Perhaps whatever they used in Ionad-teàrmainn?"

He looked up at the ceiling and shook his head. "And there I've built a house atop the damned barn." He rubbed his hands over his face. "If your true sire's family came from there, and Slaidear was the one who was exiled for his activities —"

"Perhaps he thought someone in my family had the spell?"

He looked at her in astonishment. "I can't believe we didn't see this before." He read the words again, then frowned. "This isn't complete, though."

"How do you mean?"

"The spell."

"Oh," she said. "I suppose not."

"We'd all be husks otherwise. Though even just this much is

terrifying." He shivered. "I can hardly believe anyone would write even this much down, and you know I have a decent stomach for terrible spells—"

A discreet knock sounded against the door, interrupting him. He handed her the notebook.

"Keep that safe."

"But you've memorized it already."

He lifted his eyebrows briefly and smiled. "You know me."

Indeed, she did. She watched him walk swiftly over to answer the door and wondered at the twists and turns of her own life. Who would have thought that his present and her past would meet in a barn, perhaps the most unlikely place of all for anything besides grain and hay to meet the interesting end of a pony.

She came back to herself to find Acair collapsing next to her. He handed her a gilt-edged invitation.

"We've been invited to supper."

"What do we do?"

"One foot in front of the other," he said. "Hopefully there might actually be something decent to eat."

"What if it's a trap?"

He smiled, looking thoroughly unconcerned. "It always is, darling."

She suspected he would certainly know.

An hour later, she sat next to him at a remarkably fine table in a very large hall full of people who apparently wanted him dead. She supposed he was accustomed to it, but she wasn't sure she would ever be so. She smiled weakly when she realized he was looking at her.

"What?" she asked.

He reached for her hand under the table. "Bluster, darling, is our only hope."

"So says the grandson of a prince."

"So must say the future bride of the youngest grandson of Crui-hniche of Fàs, the most terrifying witch in all the Nine Kingdoms."

She smiled. "Are you the youngest?"

"Aye, which is why she spoils me with spells every time she sees me. Can you blame her?"

"You are charming."

"And you are lovely. Do you have your coins?"

She thought she might blush. "I didn't have any pockets, so I stuck them down the top part of this gown. I think they'll be safe."

"If anyone tries to filch them, there will be a murder tonight."

He was very gallant, which she supposed he knew, and look-ing rather more lethal than usual, which she wondered if everyone else knew. If he had casually inspected everything presented to them before he'd allowed her to touch it, perhaps no one could have ex-pected anything less. All she knew was that if she'd been the lord of the hall, she wouldn't have dared poison him.

She toyed with her food, wishing she could have been sit-ting in front of the fire in Acair's study, perhaps with her parents and siblings still alive, listening to her father—or step-father, as it were—read that dragon-filled tale—

"Léirsinn!"

He whispered her name, which she appreciated, and caught her wine glass before she dropped it and its contents all over her gown. She put on the best smile she could manage.

"Weariness," she said, hopefully loudly enough for those around her to hear.

"Of course, darling. An early night for you, perhaps."

She waited until she thought fewer eyes might be turned their way, then brought her glass to her mouth and leaned closer to him.

"I don't know if this means anything," she said slowly.

He had a sip of wine. "Do tell, just the same."

"After one of my parents would read that tale, you know the one."

"I do."

"There was always a final line we said, though my mother would never let us say it together. Each of us had a pair of words we would say in turn. Always in the same order."

He choked. She supposed he'd barely managed not to spew his wine all over the table.

"Do you remember them?"

"Of course."

"All of them?"

"Aye."

"Give them a little whisper in my ear, then."

She looked at him uneasily. "Will I bring the hall down around us?"

"I sincerely hope not," he said, with feeling.

She whispered them behind her hand into his ear. He smiled pleasantly and patted his mouth with his hand as if he might have been hiding a yawn. If that hand trembled, well, perhaps she was the only one who noticed. If he leaned over and pressed his lips against her hair, perhaps the company only thought him terribly besotted.

"I think," he murmured, "that you've discovered why he wants you."

She felt cold suddenly. Perhaps it had to do with wearing a gown that didn't cover her shoulders, or perhaps she'd had too much of the wine she'd hardly touched. All she knew was that she was very, very afraid.

"What now?" she murmured.

"We wait, and then we win."

She could only hope he was right about that.

She didn't want to imagine what would be left of the world if he wasn't.

Twenty-one

❧

If there were one thing to be grateful for, it was that he wasn't going to meet his end in a barn.

Acair pulled off his evening coat and handed it to Léirsinn to wear, partly because he hadn't had the foresight to bring her a wrap and partly because the cloth was black and she might blend into the darkness better that way. His own chemise was a brilliant white which might have the opposite effect, though he suspected that damned Sladaiche or Slaidear or whatever he was calling himself at present likely couldn't tell white from ivory with any success so perhaps the color of his shirt wouldn't make any difference.

Lesser mages, lesser spells. It was apparently going to be his lot for the evening.

Slaidear was waiting for them in the garden, on the far side of a crumbling fountain that was half full of putrid water. Unsurprising, but Acair honestly hadn't expected anything better. There were no ladders in the vicinity, however, which he thought might be a mercy for that fool there.

He stopped in front of that disgusting fountain with Léirsinn on one side and his wretched spell of death keeping watch on the other and wondered absently if it had been Slaidear to have created the beast that dogged his steps. Perhaps in the end, it didn't matter. Léirsinn would do what she could to contain it, he would slay the mage across from them, and the world would see sunrise free of one more villain.

He took a moment to appreciate the improbable nature of his current situation. Normally when someone wanted to slay him, that lad—and the occasional lass—took the time to engage in a proper exchange of written insults delivered via messenger. He was not usually the recipient of a terse *outside* scrawled on a grubby slip of paper that had been passed from hand to hand down a supper table until it reached him and the word disappeared after it had been read.

Vulgar, but he supposed that was the best that mage over there could do.

It was also very unusual to be in an altercation where he didn't have his full complement of spells available, nor had he ever fought a duel where he'd been far more concerned about a woman standing next to him than he was himself. Indeed, he couldn't remember the last time he'd fought a duel with a woman anywhere near him, especially one with magic she couldn't exactly control.

He glanced briefly at Léirsinn to find she had her hands in the pockets of his evening jacket. Assuming that meant she had transferred her coins from her bodice to where they would be more easily reached, he turned to considering the lay of the land. He was terrible at small talk, true, but he wasn't opposed to a bit of pre-duel chit-chat just to see which way the wind was blowing.

He turned a bored look on the mage standing some thirty paces away.

"What is it I should call you?" he asked politely. "Don't want to get the name wrong and call you *stupid* when *whoreson* will do."

Shards spilled out of Slaidear's mouth along with his curse. Acair had never seen anything like it and had to admit it was profoundly unsettling.

"Surely you're not too stupid to choose for yourself," he hissed.

Acair fought the urge to roll his eyes. "Very well. Given that

Slaidear is but a recent incarnation, we'll go with Sladaiche. Now, what exactly is it you want, *Sladaiche*? Besides my thanking you for pulling us away from a merely marginally edible repast, that is."

Sladaiche held up a loaded crossbow. Acair found himself surprisingly grateful for decades of yawning in the face of impossible odds because that was the only thing that saved him from gasping aloud at the moment.

"You shouldn't have left these behind," Sladaiche said with a sneer. "It might prove to be your undoing."

Damn it, he'd *known* that was going to come back to bite him in the arse. Bolts were one thing and easily countered, but those arrows there were enspelled with something that had slain mages in Fuadain's barn with terrible efficiency. He regretted not having taken the time to have a closer look to see what they were made from. He hoped he didn't pay the ultimate price for not having brought them along to keep them out of the hands of that man there.

He also wished he'd taken the time to discuss with Léirsinn the particulars of how she would need to contain that damned spell of death on his right, never mind exactly what she should do about fleeing if he fell. He didn't dare take his eyes off his foe to look at her, so he supposed he would have to rely on her superior ability to remain calm in the face of great, stomping steeds. She would do what she thought best and hopefully they would both still be standing in the end.

"Well," Acair said, turning back to the matter at hand, "better undone than knocked off a ladder by a child, wouldn't you agree?"

"You didn't knock me off!" Sladaiche shouted. "There was a flaw in the wood that gave way inopportunely."

"And you waited all this time to tell me that," Acair said with a disbelieving laugh. "How droll."

"I waited all this time to repay you for stealing that spell," Sladaiche snarled.

"I didn't steal anything," Acair said, shrugging carelessly, "I threw it in the fire. Why would I steal something worth so little?"

Sladaiche drew himself up. "I worked on that for centuries."

"Well done you, then," Acair said, clapping slowly, then he stopped suddenly and put on an exaggerated frown. "Wait. I heard you didn't create it yourself at all, but rather that you stole—"

"A filthy lie!" Sladaiche shouted.

Acair lifted his eyebrows briefly. "As you say, I suppose. It still needs a bit of finishing, though, wouldn't you say?"

Sladaiche pointed the crossbow at Léirsinn. "She has what I need. That is why she's still alive, but you . . . "

Acair very rarely found himself frozen in place, but he genuinely wasn't sure if he should leap in front of Léirsinn, pull her down behind the edge of the fountain out of sight with him, or take his chances with the spell next to him and go ahead and use his own magic.

Léirsinn pulled coins out of her pockets, but her hands were shaking so badly that a pair of them fell. Acair didn't stop her from bending to look for them in the dark. Better that she be out of sight when Sladaiche fired his bolt, which he did.

Not at Léirsinn, nor even at he himself.

Sladaiche fired the bolt through that damned spell of death that had first made an appearance not very far from where he stood at present, that same spell that had collected pieces of his soul and tried to kill him—

The spell shrieked and vanished with a keening that was so like the mages Léirsinn had slain in the barn that Acair staggered.

Or that might have been because he felt as if *he* had been the one shot through the heart. He patted his chest on the off chance that was the case, but found he was still safe and whole.

Or perhaps not whole. In truth, he felt a little . . . unwell.

Léirsinn caught him around the waist. "What happened?"

"Nothing," he said, forcing himself to straighten. "I'm fine."

And he was, for it occurred to him quite suddenly that there was now nothing preventing him from using his magic. He leaned closer to Léirsinn.

"We cannot risk another of those bolts."

"Distraction?"

"That seems fitting."

He watched that rather shiny coin he'd made for her leave her hand and had several things occur to him in such rapid succession that he wished desperately for time to slow that he might consider them all and sort them into their proper order.

First was that Sladaiche, for all his apparent lingering at the supper trough, was not an unskilled mage. He batted away the spell full of shadows Léirsinn threw at him and sent rats and snakes scattering away from him. Acair destroyed them with a word, but that cost him more than it should have, which led him to his second realization.

In destroying it, I destroy myself. He'd said those ridiculous words to Mochriadhemiach of Neroche as they'd been discussing that accursed minder spell that had been so determined to slay him for the slightest dip of his toes into magical waters. He hadn't meant them, of course, but that had apparently been a glorious miscalculation on his part.

For the first time in his life, he was afraid he didn't have enough of himself to work any serious magic.

Lastly, he wasn't exactly certain what he was going to do with Sladaiche's soul if he managed to drag it out of the man's body. He wasn't his father in more ways than one, apparently.

But it wasn't his life that hung in the balance and that made his decision far easier than it might have been otherwise.

He looked at his foe and spat out the spell Léirsinn had given him from her tale only to have Sladaiche laugh.

"You don't have it all!" he announced triumphantly.

"Don't I?" Acair drawled. "Well, allow me to give it another try."

He glanced at Léirsinn, the words *duck behind me, darling* on the tip of his tongue, only to realize he shouldn't have looked away. He heard the second bolt of that deadly crossbow be cranked home and fired before he managed to look back at his opponent.

Time chose that horrific moment to slow to a crawl. He saw the bolt coming toward him and knew that he might step aside, but it would still strike him.

What he hadn't anticipated was having Léirsinn leap in front of him.

He caught her as the bolt slammed into her chest.

He looked at Sladaiche. "You bloody bastard," he gasped.

Sladaiche started toward them, his face contorted in fury. "She must live. Give her to me!"

Acair sank to his knees, cradling Léirsinn in his arms. She groped for his hand.

"Hurry," she whispered.

Acair looked up and spat out his grandmother's spell of essence meddling at the mage stomping through the dregs of water left in that fountain. Sladaiche froze in place as surely as if a very useful spell of essence meddling had rendered him motionless. Even Cruih-niche of Fàs might have been impressed.

Acair looked down at Léirsinn and found her watching him with a faint smile.

"Stop dripping on my face," she whispered.

He blinked rapidly. "You talk too much," he said, his voice breaking. "Let's be about our work before you wear yourself out, aye? You can yammer at me later."

She smiled faintly, but closed her eyes. Acair ignored the flash of panic that swept through him, not for the world, or for the spell that required the woman in his arms, but for the possibility that he might, at almost a century, lose the very thing that he thought might make the rest of his years worth living.

He pulled himself away from that place of fear, looked at Sladaiche, and repeated the dragon's spell of soul thievery. He looked at Léirsinn. "Your turn, darling."

She coughed, then whispered four of the words, then paused.

Acair watched her eyelids close and thought he might have made a noise that sounded a bit like a howl.

And that had absolutely nothing to do with the finishing of that spell.

He felt hands on his shoulders, one on each side.

He looked up and found that red-haired gel from Eòlas standing on one side of him. A man sank down to his knees on the other. The man looked at him from eyes that were Léirsinn's.

"Ye gads," he wheezed. "Relatives."

"Hurry," the red-haired wench said. "She must wake and finish."

Acair had several thoughts about that, but the most unfortunate was that she was right. He leaned over and kissed Léirsinn's forehead.

"Darling," he said softly. "Two more words, my love."

Her eyelids fluttered, then she looked at him.

"Last two," he said with the best smile he could muster. "Then you can rest."

She nodded, and breathed out the final two words of the spell.

Acair watched as Sladaiche soul came out of him and slipped to the ground, forming a pool of shadow. He wondered briefly what he would need to do with the man's corpse, but the ravages of time and evil deeds had apparently been waiting to see to that. Sladaiche's form faded to ashes that slowly scattered into the night.

"Attend to his soul later," the red-haired woman said, "and heal Léirsinn now. We'll help you."

Acair wanted to ask her how the hell she thought she was going to do anything but watch him weep as he watched his love perish, but he was too distraught to do anything but nod. He felt their hands on his shoulders still, as if they were there to lend him their strength.

He thought, however, that the healing of the woman in his arms would require quite a bit more than moral support.

Léirsinn opened her eyes. "Is it . . . finished?"

He thought he might have made a different noise that was less like a howl and more like a sob, but perhaps he could slay the two on either side of him later if they noised that about.

"Aye, darling," he said. "'Tis finished and all the credit goes to you for it."

"That was six words."

"Indeed it was, my love. Well done, you. Now, close your eyes and rest. We'll see you made whole."

"Hurry," the woman said fiercely.

He watched the man take hold of the bolt, then he nodded sharply and used that same Fadairian spell he'd used on Léirsinn's arm at his house. The man pulled the bolt free as he spoke the last word. The wound was healed, he could see that through the rent in her shirt, but she didn't stir.

He did howl then.

He saw a different hand reach out and rest on her head. He looked up and found Soilléir of Cothromaiche kneeling there next to that flame-haired wench.

"Again," he said quietly. "I'll help. 'Tis the bolt, Acair, that has caused the damage."

"If I had more soul," Acair said, knowing he sounded as broken as he felt, "that wouldn't matter."

Soilléir nodded. "There is truth in that, but we'll see to remedying that later."

"I don't care about myself, damn you!"

"I know," Soilléir said. "You'll need to use your grandmother's spell this time. It will call to the magic in Léirsinn's veins and do what's required. Leave me room before the last word to add something of my own."

"I'll memorize both."

"Of course you will."

He realized that Soilléir wasn't waiting for him, he was already weaving something of his own over Léirsinn. He waited, not because he wanted the man's spell, but because he wanted the woman in his arms to be whole.

Soilléir looked at him expectantly, so he began his grandmother's spell of reconstruction. He felt the magics surrounding his heart leap through his hands to join his grandmother's spell in a way that left him, frankly, breathless. He paused for Soilléir to add his bit, then carried on and was rather grateful to have the prince speak the last word of his own spell along with him.

He saw after the fact exactly how Soilléir had turned his grandmother's spell into essence changing and wondered if that whoreson there knew what he'd revealed.

Léirsinn gasped as if she'd been struck, then let out her breath as slowly and peacefully as a babe. She breathed a time or two, easily, then opened her eyes and looked at him.

"I feel better."

He gathered her into his arms and added Soilléir to the list of people he would slay if they ever spread about the way he sobbed into the hair of the woman who had so thoroughly stolen his black heart.

He thought he might have wept for rather an embarrassingly long time.

It occurred to him eventually how uncomfortable she had to be, so he stopped smothering her and helped her sit up.

She looked around herself, then froze. Acair supposed that might have been courtesy of what was visible thanks to the werelight Soilléir so thoughtfully provided. He would have crawled to his feet and helped her to stand, but he found she needed no aid. She leapt to her feet so quickly, she almost toppled him over in her haste.

If she hauled him to his and almost knocked him into the fountain, he couldn't blame her.

She looked from the woman to the man and back.

Then she gasped out a hearty curse.

Well, that seemed to be the thing to do, apparently. He stepped back and watched as the three of them became one mass of weeping humanity. He wished heartily for a place to sit, but supposed the edge of the fountain was definitely not going to be his perch of choice. He looked at the pool of water there and found even just the sight of it to be profoundly disturbing. He looked at Soilléir.

"Any suggestions?"

Soilléir shrugged. "Mop it up?"

Acair started to tell him to go to hell, but found himself instead with a better idea. "I have just the thing."

He used Simeon of Diarmailt's spell to hasten the drying of ink and watched as the water simply disappeared. Unfortunately, the spell did nothing for what it left behind, which looked far too much like one of those damned pools of shadow for his taste.

He looked at Soilléir. "Your turn."

Soilléir considered, then silently turned the fountain into a birdbath.

Acair almost laughed. "You bloody bastard."

"At least I have a sense of humor."

"So you do. Enjoy it whilst you may because when I'm more myself, you will spend too much time fleeing from my wrath to find anything amusing."

Soilléir only smiled. "As you say. Oh, look, there is a bench. You should sit. You don't look well."

Acair was simply out of words, perhaps one of the more alarming states in which he'd found himself over the past year. He didn't, however, see any reason to shun a chance to recover a bit, so he shuffled over to that slab of stone Soilléir had fashioned out of nothing and sat with a deep sigh. He didn't protest when his primary tormenter joined him there.

"You have questions," Soilléir said slowly.

"I'll beat the answers out of you la—ah, damn it all. What next?"

Well, the king of the elves was what next, apparently. He wasn't sure why that bit of magick-making he and his lady had indulged in had attracted such an audience, but perhaps he would investigate it later. For the moment, he thought he might want to just concentrate on surviving the next quarter hour. Given the expression on Sìle of Tòrr Dòrainn's face, he suspected that might not be easily done.

Perhaps he had nicked one too many spells from the old elf and used them with a bit too much impunity.

He leaned over toward Soilléir. "Why is he here?"

"I believe Morgan sent him."

Well, that was something. He wasn't sure what he thought of that, so he decided bluster might be his only hope. Even if he'd been able to indulge in a bit of spell-making, it would have likely been only of the sort that allowed him to feint right, then dodge left. Sìle of Tòrr Dòrainn was a bit like the king of Durial, only with perhaps a tastier wine cellar. They were old, ill-humored, and sitting on a trunkful of spells he would have committed quite a few nefarious deeds to have a rifle through.

They were also two of the most powerful souls he knew and escaping the wrath of either would take more energy than he had at the moment.

Fortunately—or unfortunately, depending on one's perspective—that damned bit of Fadaire frolicking through his once satisfyingly wicked form had apparently recognized its sovereign and decided to flutter about in a bit of a salute. It was all he could do not to take a knee, as the saying went, and confess his love for all things elvish.

Soilléir leaned close. "You look unwell."

"You already mentioned that, thank you," he said grimly. "If you're curious, I also don't feel well."

"You look . . . sparkly."

He clutched his chest in profound alarm. It was a tremendous alarm, far greater than anything he'd felt before. He did heave himself to his feet, though, because he was no fool. Essence changers and elven kings were hemming him in, but his lady still might require a rescue from those two over there who had to be her siblings. 'Twas best he survive to see to that.

He noted that Soilléir had also risen to show the proper amount of deference. Handy, that, as he needed a bit of support. If he leaned harder on that damned meddler than was polite, he didn't suppose anyone could blame him.

Luck was with him, oddly enough, for Sìle paused to have a look at the trio standing next to the fountain. Acair sighed deeply. A reprieve, though he imagined it wouldn't last all that long.

"She won't be entirely as she was before," Soilléir murmured.

"I know that, damn you to hell," Acair said, dragging his sleeve across his eyes. "I will endlessly torment you because of it, rest assured."

"I would be disappointed in anything else."

"I would have traded you most of my soul for more years for her, you know," Acair said, because he couldn't not say it.

"You did."

He gaped at the man next to him. "What?"

"Tell her after the entire tale is finished," Soilléir advised.

He found himself distracted mostly because the king of the elves—the only ones who mattered, as Sìle himself would have said—had turned his sights away from that glorious woman and her siblings over there and had come to stand in front of him. He wasn't at all certain he wouldn't meet his end in a terribly uncomfortable way, but when a gentleman was facing the prospect of either bolting or remaining with the woman he loved, he didn't run.

Well, he might run later, when he was back to his old self and could swoop Léirsinn up and nip off the battlefield in dragonshape, but—

He straightened only to deeply regret it. He would have toppled over if he hadn't suddenly found a glorious horse miss at his side, pulling his arm over her shoulders and keeping him upright. Soilléir exerted himself to give him a shove when he almost lost his balance in that direction, but no more. He added that to the list of things he wouldn't be thanking the worthless whoreson for, then glanced at his love.

Her cheeks were wet, but her eyes were full of wonder. He smiled in spite of himself.

"Brother and sister, I assume?"

"Can you believe it?"

"Tonight, darling, I think I can believe quite a few things. Ah, and you remember His Majesty, the king of Tòrr Dòrainn?"

He wanted to listen to Léirsinn introduce His Maj to her brother and sister and he supposed he should have made note of their names, but all he could do was breathe and hope he wouldn't faint. Sladaiche was no more, apparently, and he supposed they now knew what the spell was he'd been looking for, but there was still the mystery of the shadows on the ground that perhaps might never be solved.

He had also lost something in the process, more than even a spell of death would have taken out of him.

There were odd things afoot in the Nine Kingdoms.

He realized that Sìle had taken Léirsinn's hand and gently placed a rune there, telling her that it would give her comfort and strength when she had a need for the same. He watched it glow with a golden hue so fiery that he wasn't entirely certain the damned thing wasn't made of fire.

Fitting.

Sìle glared at him. "Your hand as well."

All the tortures the elven king could place upon him sprang immediately to mind, tortures he imagined would reach new heights of misery thanks to that damned spell still lodged in his black heart.

"Ah," he managed, "thank you just the same —"

"Your hand, damn you!"

Acair studied the king and wondered how he might extricate himself from his current conundrum without either bolting or feigning an artful swoon. Unfortunately, there didn't seem to be any hope of escape. He held out his hand, not entirely certain Sìle wouldn't just lop it off for the sport of it.

Sìle looked at him from under bushy eyebrows. "I know what you did."

The possibilities were endless there, weren't they? If he felt rather than heard Soilléir snort, well, he supposed he deserved it.

"For my Mhorghain," Sìle clarified.

Damnation, the pollen was never ending in the south. Far past time to get himself back north where the chill might keep the damned trees and flowers from troubling him overmuch.

Acair cleared his throat. "It was, Your Majesty," he managed, "the least I could do."

Sìle grunted. "I daresay it was, but still. And so you know, she's the one who told me about it. Perhaps she thought I might encounter you on some deserted byway and decide the world might be a better place without you."

"Very kind of her—"

"Shut up," Sìle growled, "and hold still."

Acair found quite suddenly that there were still stars enough in the world to set up a wild and chaotic swirling about his head. The pain in his hand was blinding, but mercifully brief. He looked down at his hand—his skin was red as hellfire, to be honest—and watched as three separate runes flashed silver and gold, then faded. The skin on the back of his hand returned to its normal perfect coloration, albeit with those runes still faintly visible. He could still pinch the odd, priceless knick-knack without impertinent remarks about his grooming, thankfully.

He looked at the king. "Your Majesty?"

Sìle shrugged. "Figure it out yourself."

"Would my father know?"

"Go ask him. Take notes of his reaction and send word."

Acair was tempted to invite the irascible monarch to make the journey with him, but perhaps 'twas too soon. The old elf didn't look particularly chummy, but it had been a long evening so far.

Sìle looked at Soilléir. "My bit's done and my debt to this wee bastard paid."

"What did you gift him?" Soilléir asked.

"I vow I've forgotten already," Sìle said, seemingly stopping just short of scratching his head. "An irresistible impulse to endlessly go about doing good, or perhaps an inability to memorize any more spells. Can't say I remember at the moment."

Acair was certain of many things and none more than elves had very poor taste in jest. He listened to Soilléir and Sìle exchange the usual sort of pleasantries the moment called for and he should have participated in, but he found that all he could do was stare stupidly at the back of his hand at lines that were so beautiful he could hardly manage a coherent thought.

"What do they mean?" Léirsinn whispered.

"Haven't a clue," he murmured.

What he suspected was they were akin to those tangled spells his dam handed off to overeager youth who came to beg something intricate and mysterious from her. Those pieces of magic were nothing more than endless loops that ended where they began, leaving the mage unsatisfied and the spell worthless. His mother never failed to chortle as those same annoying yobs wandered off into the forest with their brows knitted and their faces fair buried against the spells in their hands. More than one lad had returned to his dam's house with a great knot in his forehead from where he'd encountered some immoveable object or other.

Sìle's gift was likely just the same. He would spend years trying to unravel the damned runes, sneaking into libraries where he shouldn't go, trotting off occasionally on the proverbial wild goose chase, only to find out after decades of the same that what he possessed was nothing more than directions to the king's most unkempt privy.

He wouldn't have been surprised.

He thought he might be wise to ignore the way that damned spell wrapped around his heart seemed to recognize a fellow coconspirator, calling to it with a sweet song of Fadaire —

"I believe he's cursed me," he wheezed.

Léirsinn put her arms around his waist and leaned her head companionably against his shoulder. "You do look a little green."

"I've had a long day," he said. "Worry over you, of course."

"You're an awful man."

"As I continue to remind you," he said with a deep sigh.

She only smiled. If she pulled his arm more fully over her shoulders and he leaned a bit harder on her than he should have, she didn't say anything.

It was weariness, that was all. He might have been fretting a bit over making a decent impression on her siblings after they'd seen him at less than his best.

He supposed he also might have been desperate for an hour of peace and quiet in which to contemplate that nugget Soilléir had simply dropped into the conversation without any warning at all.

He didn't protest when Soilléir suggested a retreat indoors to freshen up before perhaps thinking about where the events of the evening had left the world. Acair knew he had other things to see to still, but he wouldn't argue against half an hour of sitting in front of a fire with his love in his arms and absolutely no one wanting to slay him closer than the other side of a locked chamber door.

That was, he suspected, always going to be something of a rarity.

Twenty-two

Léirsinn looked at herself in the polished glass and wondered if having one's life completely turned upside down showed on the entire face or just in the eyes.

She turned away from the mirror, made certain she was buttoned and laced in all the right places, then pulled on her boots. One thing she could say about Acair of Ceangail: he had excellent taste in clothing. The other thing she could say about him was that he wasn't shy about using magic when the price for the same was no longer death.

She left the small bathing chamber and pulled the door shut behind her, then paused and looked at the man who had given her not only what she was wearing, but the ability to still breathe the same sweet air that he did.

He was sitting on the divan in front of the fire, sound asleep. She walked over to lean against the back of the chair across from him and simply looked at him. He was right, of course. She'd been lost the first moment she'd seen him.

What she hadn't expected, though, were all the things that had come into her life as a result, most notably siblings she'd thought were dead. Where they'd been and why they'd chosen the present moment to make an appearance was something she thought she might like an answer to.

She was beginning to see why Acair got himself into so much trouble digging where perhaps he shouldn't have.

She was half tempted to stick a pillow behind his head so he didn't wake up with a kink in his neck, but she supposed he'd woken with worse. At least he would wake again and so would she, though she wasn't sure her chest would ever not ache. She put her hand over the spot where not even a scar remained and thought she might definitely have a different opinion of magic than she'd had in her uncle's barn —

Her grandfather.

She caught her breath, then let it out carefully. She would let Acair sleep for a bit longer, find her siblings and hold onto them a bit longer as well, then she would see what could be done to save her grandfather before Fuadain did anything rash. There was still the mystery of what, if anything, he had to do with Slaidear, something she thought might be best to find out also sooner rather than later.

Ye gads, she was starting to sound like a certain black mage of her acquaintance.

She borrowed his jacket that he'd left lying over the back of a chair and made her way quietly from the chamber. She realized she had a destination in mind only after her feet led her unerringly back to the garden where she wasn't entirely sure she hadn't perished.

She walked through paths she hardly remembered having traversed previously and came to a stop in front of the birdbath that sat where a fountain had stood before. The crossbow and bolts were still there, the bolts lying where they'd fallen. She picked them up, then paused. The moon was still newish, but it gave at least a little light that fell on something that glinted faintly at her feet. She bent down and picked it up.

'Twas a rune that sparkled with a beautiful, dark richness that left her wondering if she might be holding onto a piece of someone's soul.

She had the feeling she might know to whom it belonged.

She pocketed it, then glanced at the birdbath. She had the feeling no bird would care to use it, but perhaps she was wrong. The water wasn't liquid, but instead something that greatly resembled a mirror if a mirror could have reflected anything but . . . well, she was going to say darkness, but that wasn't what she saw. There was no telling what Acair and Soilléir—an unlikely pairing to begin with—had decided to do with Sladaiche, but perhaps locking him forever in a pool of shadow had been fitting.

She realized, as she looked at herself reflected by the light of that new moon, that she had only seen herself, flaws and goodness and an elven rune that greatly resembled a dragon made of flames.

She also realized quite suddenly that she wasn't alone. She whirled around but found only Acair standing there, watching her gravely.

"Just me. Admiring our handiwork?"

She put her hand over her heart, mostly to convince herself that it wouldn't beat out of her chest. "Have you looked in it?"

"Will I regret it?"

She shook her head. "I don't think so."

He did, then shook his head and stepped back. "Soilléir's doing, not mine. I will say I am every bit as handsome as I always suspected, if not a little rough around the edges at the moment." He looked at the bow and bolts she held. "That was too close."

She held them out. "I don't think I want them."

He took them, then held out his hand. "Perhaps we'll gather up those damned horseshoes in the trunk at home, put them together with these, and send the whole lot to Soilléir to turn into something vile to leave under Droch's sofa. I can think of worse ideas."

She could too, but she imagined he knew as much. She let go of his hand and put her arms around his waist, avoiding things that had almost killed them both. "I found something you might want."

"Besides yourself?"

She smiled up at him, then kissed him and shook her head. "A little rune on the ground."

"Sìle's now losing things from his pockets?" he asked. "I'm intrigued."

"I don't think so," she said. She pulled it out of her coat—his coat, rather—then held it up. "What do you think?"

He gaped at it, then stepped away from her. He took several steps backward until he ran bodily into a bench, then he sat down abruptly. She walked over and sank down next to him.

"Well?"

He set the bow and bolts aside. "That's something there."

"A piece of your soul?"

"For all the good it does me," he said. "Why don't you hold onto it and we'll corner Soilléir before he scampers off. Perhaps he can open my chest and shove it in there with everything else rattling around in the vicinity of my heart."

She put it back in the pocket of his coat, then looked at him.

"I'm happy to have this all over with," she said quietly.

"You might be, but I've still relatives to impress. Speaking of, perhaps we should gather them up and go see about your grandfather."

She started to agree, then realized there were three people coming toward them. Acair heaved himself to his feet, then held down his hand for her. She rose, then looked at the siblings she'd thought had perished. She wasn't entirely sure what to say to them, but realized there was no need.

Her sister walked up to her and put her arms around her. She felt her brother's arms go around them both. She would have wept, but she was out of tears and too exhausted to go look for any more. It was enough to know she wasn't alone any longer—

Only she hadn't been anyway.

She stepped away and looked at the man who had changed that. She reached for his hand and pulled him over to stand with them.

"Acair, this is my sister, Iseabail. Iseabail, you perhaps know Acair of Ceangail?"

Acair made her a low bow that almost left him on the ground in front of them all. Léirsinn caught him and moved past that before anyone said anything untoward.

"Acair, my brother, Taisdealach. You might call him—"

"Or he might not," Tais said. He looked at Acair coolly. "I've heard tales."

"They're likely all true," she said cheerfully. "But I love him and he's kept me safe, so be good to him or face my fury."

Acair was apparently accustomed to that sort of reception, which she'd already known. He simply inclined his head at her brother and smiled politely.

"A pleasure," he said cordially.

Her brother scowled, but he didn't resort to any slurs so perhaps there was hope. She smiled at Acair.

"Where now? To Briàghde?"

"I think that might be best," he agreed. "Let's go fetch our gear."

"I'll meet you there," Tais said briskly. "Don't dawdle."

She watched her brother step back and simply disappear. She blinked, then gaped at her sister. "He has *magic*?"

"All of it," Iseabail said.

"How do you know? Did you know each other all this time? Did you know I was alive?"

She found her sister's arms suddenly around her. "Let's finish what we must, then we'll talk. And nay, I didn't know anything until a few weeks ago, but you can blame Soilléir for that."

Léirsinn looked at her as she stepped away. "But you have magic as well?"

Iseabail shrugged. "I have a bit. Well, I have a great deal, I just never know if it's going to do what I want it to." She looked at Soilléir and held out her hand toward him. "Will you help me shapechange?"

He took her hand and smiled. "With pleasure, my dear."

They disappeared without fuss.

Léirsinn stared at the spot where they had stood but a moment before, then looked at Acair.

"What did I just witness?"

"Something I wish I could unsee," he said with feeling.

"He's far too old for her."

"She's far too good for him. If it makes either of us feel better, he calls everyone *my dear*."

"He doesn't call you that."

"Darling, what he calls me isn't fit for a lady's ears." He picked up the bolts, then looked at her. "Let's hide these behind a planter, then fetch our gear and find our horse. I'm too tired to shapechange."

She thought that was odd, but it had been a long evening preceded by several longer weeks. She nodded and took his hand.

She decided it might be best not to mention that it was trembling.

He was tired, that was all.

W alking up the path toward her uncle's barn—her stepfather's brother's barn, to be precise—was one of the odder things she had experienced in a long string of unusual things. She had spent so much of her life there, most all of it that she could remember, but she felt as if she were viewing the place with a stranger's eyes.

The barn was smaller than she remembered, but tidy and useful. The house, however, was almost unimpressive.

No wonder Fuadain was such a miserable man.

She saw her siblings standing with Soilléir just outside the gates. The sight was so unexpected, she stumbled a bit, then found herself caught and pulled back so abruptly, she almost lost her balance. She looked at Acair in surprise, but he was only staring at a spot in front of her. She would have stepped right into that pool of shadow where shadows shouldn't have been if he hadn't stopped her.

"Would you make werelight, love?" he asked quietly.

She wondered why he didn't do it himself, but he likely had his reasons. She made a ball of werelight from the only spell she knew. Acair smiled at her briefly.

"Lovely light there."

"I'm a bit surprised I'm still able to do it."

He reached for her hand. "I haven't had the chance to ask you how you feel. Different? Those bolts were enspelled with I know not what, but I'm assuming Soilléir removed their poison."

"If magic was a deafening roar before, 'tis but a whisper now," she said, realizing as she said it that it was so. She looked at him. "I think I can bear it."

"I would have made you a jar of useful coins just the same, you know."

"I know," she said. "Thank you."

"You might be the first soul who has ever thanked me for my spells." He put his arm around her and stared at the ground in front of him. "I wonder about those shadows, though."

"I would have thought they would have disappeared with Sladaiche."

"As would I," he said slowly. "There's a mystery for you. Well, the sooner we solve it, the sooner we put our feet up. Do you have your coins?"

She looked at him in surprise. "I do, but why?"

He looked at her carefully. "I like to be prepared, Léirsinn. You never know when an extra spell in the right spot will be what turns the tide."

Given that he had a world full of spells at his fingertips, she couldn't imagine why he thought she would need hers. There was something amiss with that lad there, but she hardly dared ask what. She simply ducked under his arm and put her arm around his waist without comment. He could think what he wanted and she certainly wasn't going to make any comments about the fact that he wasn't entirely steady on his feet.

"It has been a long night," she said, because it had been.

He nodded with a sigh. "Let's be about finishing this. I would like to see your grandfather safe and whole. I might even greet Doghail over a shovelful of manure if all goes well."

"I would like to see him." she admitted.

He ushered her around the pool of shadow, then glanced at her. "Think he'd like a different view?"

"That might depend on how many Angesand ponies you're giving me as a wedding gift."

He smiled. "What a mercenary you are. To answer, I suppose as many as Hearn will let you have, no doubt with the understanding that I never get too close to them." He shuddered. "Horses. What have I done?"

"Nicked my heart and put it in your pocket on the way out of the barn," she said dryly. "Someone should have told you the trouble that sort of thing would get you eventually."

He lifted his eyebrows briefly. "We'll discuss that at length later. There is the rest of our party. You should go put yourself between Soilléir and your poor sister. His grooming leaves a great deal to be desired. I'm not sure even I, with my superior sartorial guidance, could possibly rescue him from his frumpery."

She would have poked at him for talking so much, but she could feel his hand occasionally trembling. She looked at him quickly and found that he was watching her.

"Weariness," he said with a shrug. "It will pass."

She didn't have any reason to tell him differently, but when he and her brother walked off together to investigate the insides of Slaidear's little house on the edge of the manor garden, she caught Soilléir by the sleeve. He looked at her and smiled.

"What is it, my dear?"

She frowned before she could stop herself. Perhaps he said that to every woman he met and perhaps every woman was distracted by the fairness of his face and the power she could see only the echoes of, much like a noon-day sun behind an immense cloud. He didn't look any older than she was, but what did she know? Acair didn't look any older than she was, either.

"Léirsinn?"

She pulled herself back to the present moment and fished about in the pocket of Acair's coat she was still wearing. The thin wafer she held out sparkled more silver than black in the werelight she realized was still hanging over her head. Soilléir studied it, then looked at her.

"His soul?"

"Some of it, at least. Can you, you know." She found herself fluttering her fingers in exactly the same way Soilléir's father had when talking about her family. "Put it back in him, that is. I think he doesn't feel well."

Soilléir considered for far longer than she was comfortable with, then looked at her.

"I think," he said slowly, "that you should hold onto it for a bit longer. He won't need it for this business, but he might need it later. Keep it safe."

That wasn't an answer, but she supposed she wasn't going to have better from him at the moment. She nodded and walked with him to Slaidear's house, but couldn't force herself to go in. She stood outside with her sister and found herself feeling unusually hesitant. She finally looked at Iseabail.

"This is strange."

"You're older," Iseabail said with a faint smile.

"As are you." She paused. "Where were you?"

"Do you know An Cèin?"

Léirsinn looked at her in surprise. "I know of it, though I've never been. Is that where you were?"

Iseabail nodded. "For most of my life."

"Where was Tais?"

"I honestly haven't had a chance to ask him. I just met him in Inntrig yesterday."

"That must be why Soilléir was there," she said. "He seemed a bit off-balance."

"Desperately trying to hide his tracks, rather," Iseabail said with a snort. She started forward, then stopped. "I'll hold you and weep later, if you'll allow it."

Léirsinn nodded, though she found she couldn't say anything. That she had siblings where she thought she'd had none before . . . she wasn't sure if she should have cursed Soilléir for knowing yet keeping them from her or not. She suspected he'd had his reasons, but she thought she might need very good ones indeed before she refrained from joining Acair on any quest to do damage to him.

"I don't think they found anything interesting inside," Iseabail said suddenly.

Léirsinn hardly had time to give any thought to what her sister had said before she found herself caught by the hand and pulled along with a surprisingly energetic black mage.

"House," he said briskly. "I think what we want is in Fuadain's solar."

She had no reason not to agree. She would have paused at the kitchen door to enjoy the sight of Fuadain's head butler at a complete loss for words, but she didn't have the chance. Acair pushed past the man without comment, pulling her along with him. She gave the man a casual shrug, then had to almost run to keep up with her companion. At least she hadn't had to scrape off her boots.

Acair ran up the stairs with her and strode down the passageway. She stopped in front of her grandfather's chamber, hardly daring to enter. Acair opened the door first, looked inside, then held it open for her. She moved past him, then hurried over to where Tosdach was still lying in front of the fire. He was breathing still, which she thought was something of a mercy.

"Fuadain first," Acair said. "We'll return."

She nodded and followed him back out into the passageway where she almost ran bodily into her siblings and Soilléir. Acair pulled the door shut and dropped a spell in front of it she imagined

Soilléir himself might have to make an effort to breach. She exchanged looks with her siblings, then followed Acair down the passageway to stop in front of her uncle's solar.

Acair banged on the door without any decorum whatsoever.

"Come!"

Acair looked at her. "I'll go first, so you're safe."

"And you?"

He shot her a look that made her smile.

"Very well," she said. "After you."

She followed him into her uncle's solar and had the oddest feeling of having done the same thing for so many years, yet having everything so changed. Fuadain looked at the five of them, slapped his hands on his desk, and rose to his feet. His expression was far less panicked than hers would have been in his place, but perhaps he knew things she didn't.

Things such as a spell of death that he threw not at Acair, but at her.

Acair caught it, examined it as if it had been a piece of questionable fruit, then tossed it into the fire.

"I wouldn't," he advised.

Fuadain blanched. She knew she shouldn't have enjoyed that as much as she did, but she thought she might be justified. And if her brother moved to stand in front of her and her sister, well, perhaps she shouldn't have expected anything less. She did manage to look around his shoulder, though, because she had spent the whole of her life that she could remember standing on that very carpet, biting her tongue, and she thought she might want to see that man behind the desk be on the receiving end of some well-deserved comeuppance.

"You're supposed to be dead," Fuadain spat. "As are those three!"

"Choose better assassins next time," Acair suggested. "Now, whilst my temper is still in check, show me where Sladaiche gathered the souls he took. It couldn't possibly have been something you managed all on your own."

"How dare you," Fuadain breathed. "Of course I managed it on my own!"

Tais held his hand out to stop her from moving, though she could have told him she had no intention of stepping in front of anyone else any time soon. Her chest ached abominably still.

"I find that difficult to believe," Acair drawled, "given the sadly inferior quality of your magic."

"Do you have no idea who I am?" Fuadain said haughtily. "*I*, unlike that barn worker Slaidear, can trace my ancestors back directly to Bhaltair of Mìlidh."

Acair looked at him, puzzled. "Who?"

"Mìlidh, you fool!"

"Never heard of it."

"It is *next* to Wychweald, to the east."

"Still not ringing any bells, old bean," Acair said with a shrug.

"It bordered Ionad-teàrmainn hundreds of years ago," Fuadain growled. "We were a warlike and fierce people, unlike those bloody horse lovers."

"Why the hell did you choose Sàraichte, then?" Acair asked, sounding genuinely baffled.

"Everything flows through here," Fuadain said, drawing himself up and looking down his nose. "Everything important, that is."

"I think that's a fanciful rumor begun by my great-aunt," Acair said, "but you obviously believe it. Is that why you thought you could draw all these souls here? Or was Slaidear doing all the true work whilst you wished you had better spells?"

Léirsinn listened to Acair poke at Fuadain and thought it might not have been his first time doing the like. He seemed to know exactly what to say to bring out the worst in her step-uncle, leaving Fuadain becoming increasingly red in the face.

Fuadain strode over to his sideboard and drew out a glass decanter. He glared at Acair as he slammed it down on his desk.

"They reside in here," he said haughtily. "I'm keeping them until Slaidear finds the proper spell and returns to give it to me."

Acair looked at him. "What was that spell meant to do? Or didn't he trust you with the details?"

"It was *my* idea!"

"I wonder," Acair said slowly. "Quite a powerful bit of business there for a lesser noble to be involved in. Perhaps he kept more from you than you suppose."

"How stupid do you think I am?" Fuadain snapped. "I wasn't relying on Slaidear entirely, something you couldn't possibly understand."

"Probably not," Acair agreed. "I'm obviously outmatched here."

"You are outmatched everywhere, especially in Beinn òrainn."

Acair smiled pleasantly. "Making bargains with Droch of Saothair, are you?"

Léirsinn wished she'd had a spot to simply sit and watch the entertainment. She was beginning to understand why Acair had earned so many powerful enemies.

"I sent him a horse as a gift," Fuadain said stiffly. "A small token to keep him doing my bidding, of course. I have the power to take these pieces of souls to myself, naturally, but I prefer to wait for the proper spell to be delivered."

"Naturally," Acair agreed. "What happens if we open this wee jar here?"

Before Fuadain could answer, Acair simply reached over and wrenched the lid off that glass container.

Fuadain shrieked. Or perhaps other things that weren't precisely visible made a noise that was absolutely unbearable to listen to. Léirsinn watched, open-mouthed, as shadows wafted up into the air above Fuadain's desk, then simply disappeared.

Acair rubbed his hands together. "I believe that takes care of things still lying about the world. If you four will excuse me, I believe I have a final thing or two to say to this man about his former treatment of my future bride."

She found herself ushered outside her uncle's solar before she could protest. Acair looked at her brother pointedly, putting his fingers briefly against his ears, then smiled at her and shut the door.

The screams that ensued were, she had to admit, hard to listen to.

Iseabail leaned closer to her. "He won't kill him, will he?"

"He certainly has the power to," her brother said. "Knowing what I know about him, however, I imagine he'd rather leave him alive to enjoy his nightmares for quite some time to come. And what does he mean, his future bride?"

Léirsinn took a deep breath. "About what you'd expect, I imagine."

"He hasn't asked my permission," Tais said pointedly.

Léirsinn realized she was sending him the same sort of look he was having from her sister and for some reason, that made her almost unreasonably happy. Iseabail elbowed her gently.

"We've done this before, I think."

"I think you might be right."

"And as usual, I have nothing to say about what you two combine," Tais said with a sigh. "Very well, wed him if you like. I'll still have a pointed conversation with him about your care and feeding. Over spells, if necessary."

"I'm certain he would enjoy that," Léirsinn offered.

"Are you suggesting I wouldn't?"

She would have warned him that such might very well be the case, but the door opened before she could. Acair came out brushing his hands off. He shut the door quietly behind him and smiled.

"Let's go see to your grandsire next, shall we?"

"To rescue him," Iseabail said slowly.

Acair blinked. "Well, of course. What else?"

Iseabail looked at him seriously. "You made Fuadain scream."

"Only once or twice."

Léirsinn found herself the recipient of a pointed look from that mage who loved her, so she took his arm and pulled him down the passageway with her.

"Thank you," she said simply.

"My pleasure," he said. "I have so little occasion to trot out things from my own nightmares these days." He put his hand over hers on his arm. "I would have done far worse, but I am, as I said before, trying to make a good impression on the relatives."

"How do you feel?"

He looked at her quickly. "Vindicated and in sore need of a holiday. But first things first. Let's see to your grandfather, then we'll decide how to fill the rest of our morning."

She put her hand in the pocket of his coat to make certain she had that piece of his soul, then walked beside him to her grandfather's chamber.

Nothing had changed except that Tosdach of Sàraichte was no longer her blood relative, though she supposed that was something Acair's mother and Soilléir's father could relegate to their histories of the Nine Kingdoms. She had spent so many years claiming him, she thought she might continue on. Besides, her siblings had no idea what the truth was as far as she knew. She would tell them eventually, but not at the moment.

They gathered to discuss Tosdach's condition, those souls with magic in their blood. Acair paused, then looked for her. He frowned, then crossed the room to take her hand and pull her into the circle.

She thought she just might have loved him for it.

"'Tis a very good spell," Iseabail said thoughtfully, "though not complicated."

"Agreed," Acair said. "I didn't look at it closely the first time I saw him. The magic the spell is made from—"

"Olc?" Tais asked grimly.

"A permutation of it," Iseabail said. She looked at Acair. "You're better suited to unraveling it than I am, no offense intended."

"I don't offend easily," Acair said with a shrug.

Soilléir snorted, which earned him a glare. He stepped back. "I'll leave this to you four and go put my feet up for a moment or two."

Léirsinn realized that whatever had been done to her by that enspelled bolt hadn't been enough to take away her sight. She watched her brother and the man she loved unravel the spell laid over her grandfather whilst her sister continually pulled threads from it until she simply snapped the last one in two.

Her grandfather blinked, then pushed himself up so he was sitting on the edge of his chair. He looked at them.

"Iseabail," he said in wonder. "Léirsinn. Taisdealach. Oh, my dears, you're all grown up!"

Léirsinn supposed the man might need to breathe eventually, but he didn't seem to mind having her and her sister choke him with fond embraces. He only laughed and reached out a hand to grasp Tais'.

She remained happily involved in a very sweet reunion until the moment came when she knew she needed air. She eased away from her siblings and grandfather and found Acair leaning with his shoulder against the wall by the doorway. He very casually opened the door and lifted his eyebrows briefly. She eased over, trying not to draw attention to herself.

"I love you," she murmured as she slipped out the door.

"How could you not?"

She waited, then realized he wasn't coming with her. She pushed the door open, took his hand, and pulled him out into the passageway.

"I thought you might want privacy," he said carefully.

"What I want is to run."

"We could shapechange."

"Or I could steal a horse."

He took her hand and walked quickly with her down the passageway. "This is what consorting with ne'er-do-wells gets a stable lass, I'm finding. Horse thievery? What next?"

"You'll be the first to know."

"Where are we going?" he asked.

"To find Doghail." She shot him a look. "Be prepared for an insufferably smug look."

"Did he predict our love match?" he asked politely.

"I'm afraid so."

"Smart man, that Doghail."

She supposed he might have been.

She walked with Acair through the house, back down the stairs, and out through the kitchen. She nodded to Fuadain's butler, thanked a chambermaid she recognized for her kindness, then walked out into the morning air and took the first decent breath she'd had in weeks.

She looked at Acair. "Thank you," she said simply.

He brought her hand to his mouth, kissed it quickly, then smiled. "Let's go see a man about a horse."

She smiled and walked with him to the barn.

Twenty-three

❖

Acair walked along the dusty road that led from the manor house at Bri̇àghde toward the port town of Sàraichte. He supposed he might eventually see his great-aunt, which would give him the chance to tell her that she was right about numerous things.

That he was trailing after Léirsinn of Sàraichte like a love-sick pup would assuredly be first on that list.

He watched his lady with her siblings walk in front of her grandfather who was sitting rather comfortably on a marginally well-behaved Sianach. Doghail had the pony well in hand, though Acair supposed that shouldn't have been surprising. He himself was bringing up the rear with an unusually taciturn Soilléir of Co-thromaiche, but perhaps the man was simply enjoying his last few breaths of easily obtained fresh air. That wouldn't last for long after he himself had recovered from the rather taxing amounts of spell-casting he'd done over the previous pair of days.

"You'll never manage it, you realize."

Acair would have slid the man a warning look, but he thought that might indicate that he had made even the slightest note of that protest, which he hadn't. He might not manage it, but that certainly wouldn't be for a lack of trying.

"Besides, you can't have answers if I'm dead."

"Stop stealing my best sayings," Acair grumbled, keenly aware of how often he'd said the same thing whilst in a tight spot, never mind how often others had said it to him, also whilst in tight spots. "You might be surprised what a body is willing to divulge on their way off stage, if you know what I mean."

Soilléir only refrained from comment. Too terrified to respond, more than likely.

"Very well," Acair said, setting aside thoughts of murder for the moment, "I'll have the entire truth now that I'm at my leisure to hear it. Let's start with that damned spell you sent to dog my steps. You remember, the one that almost slew me near Durial?"

"I remember."

"You said you didn't know who'd made it."

"I said the spell wasn't mine," Soilléir corrected. "I never said I didn't know who'd fashioned it."

Acair decided it was too early in the day to start gasping with outrage, so he forced himself to take a deep, even breath instead. "Whose was it, then?"

"Iseabail's."

Acair suspected that if he continued to take in the number of deep breaths the conversation was looking as though it might require, he would faint from too much breathing. He instead wriggled his jaw to keep from clenching it too tightly and nodded. "I see. Did she fashion this spell all on her own?"

"She might have had a suggestion or two from someone else."

"Of course. What was the magic?"

Soilléir took a deep breath of his own. Acair didn't hope for any fainting on the man's part, but he did spare a wish for a chair. He had the feeling he might need one.

"I won't bother suggesting that you might find it an amusing diversion to search for that answer yourself," Soilléir said.

"Wise," Acair agreed.

"The magic is Cnuacach, which is the magic of Ionad-teàrmainn, which is uncomfortably similar to Domhainn, which is the magic of Fàs."

"Why don't I know any of this?" Acair asked, dumbfounded.

"Because you were too busy looking elsewhere to notice what was in your back garden," Soilléir said, "if I might be so bold. The spell's main purpose was to keep you from using magic, for reasons I'm sure you can divine on your own. Its secondary purpose was to aid you in collecting pieces of your soul."

"You didn't send my mother a missive asking her to suggest that rot to me," Acair said, knowing he should have been appalled but finding himself not. "Did you?"

"We've discussed the idea before in a general sense."

"I don't want to know when."

Soilléir smiled. "I imagine you don't. And to answer, nay, our discussion didn't have anything to do with Sladaiche. I assumed you would find the answers you needed regarding him all on your own."

"Of course," Acair said, deciding 'twas best not to think about how closely he'd come to never having given that a bloody thought.

"Do you need to rest?"

He glared at Soilléir. "Do I look ill?"

"Pale, rather."

"I'm overcome by thinking about all the ways you could be deposited in a ditch in a desolate corner of some untraveled wasteland. All my strength is going to keeping myself from kicking up my heels and dancing a jig." He walked for a bit more, then frowned. "Did Iseabail know Léirsinn was alive when she fashioned that spell to make my life a misery?"

Soilléir sighed deeply. "Aye. I'm afraid I'm the one who told her—"

"Wait," Acair interrupted. He stopped and looked at his vexatious companion. "You need to start from the beginning. And before you do, I want you to admit that you *deliberately* put me in a position where I couldn't save Léirsinn if necessary."

"Not with magic," Soilléir said, "which I'll admit left Iseabail very concerned." He shrugged. "I wasn't."

Acair wasn't sure if he should be flattered or furious. "My reputation precedes me, then."

"It does," Soilléir agreed.

"I'm still tremendously offended by almost dying, but I'll try to put that behind me." He waited until their company had put a bit more distance between them, then he began to walk slowly again. "From the beginning, if you please."

"How far back do you want me to go?"

"*Beyond the range of my fists* would be my suggestion."

Soilléir only smiled. "I'll keep that in mind. Perhaps I'll start a bit in the middle with what happened to the children after Sladaiche—"

Acair held up his hand. "You don't need to say it."

Soilléir nodded. "Thank you." He sighed. "After they lost their parents. I'll admit that I, ah . . . "

"Made arrangements for them?" Acair finished for him.

"You know how that is."

Acair looked at him narrowly. "Did you beat that knowledge out of my sister or snoop all on your own?"

Soilléir only shook his head with a grave smile. "I loved Sarait, if you'll have the truth of it, so I was perhaps more interested in the happenings surrounding her than I should have been. Morgan didn't tell me, so you can justifiably accuse me of watching things I likely shouldn't have."

There was nothing to be said there. The fact that Soilléir had watched Sarait and several of her children be slain . . . well, whilst there were things he had to admit he occasionally envied about the lives of others with terrible spells tucked in their purses, he had just rid himself of that feeling about the man walking next to him.

"I saw to the children," Soilléir continued, "because I could. I also took the books of faery tales and hid them for safekeeping, because I needed to."

"You hid them in your grandfather's library," Acair said pointedly, "until you foisted one off on me thanks to whom—Ochadius of Riamh?"

"I need to be more careful about my messengers," Soilléir murmured.

"More afraid, rather, of what I'll do to you when I discover how extensively you've meddled, but go on. Where is the third one? You obviously don't know or you would be crowing about it."

"I don't," Soilléir agreed. "It has gone missing, but finding it is not my task."

Acair almost groaned aloud. If he had to listen to one more recitation of that one's vaunted code, he thought he just might lie down and bawl like a bairn.

"Let's press on," he said, hopping over the steaming pile of virtue his companion had tried to deposit there in front of him. "How did you know to rescue those children?"

Soilléir shrugged lightly. "I didn't."

Acair decided he would retrieve his jaw from where it had fallen to the earth later, when he also had a free moment to find the breath he'd just lost.

"How do you sleep at night?" he asked incredulously. "Lying like that."

"Let's say it was an educated guess."

"Let's not," Acair returned, "and instead you tell me the truth."

Soilléir looked slightly uncomfortable. "Perhaps we should look for somewhere to sit."

"That would be perfect," Acair said crisply, "for it would save me the effort of chasing you down to turn *you* into a birdbath. I have a pair of cousins who I can guarantee would plop you in their garden without a second thought."

Soilléir only smiled, which left Acair torn between admiration that he could so casually know there wasn't a damned soul in the whole of the Nine Kingdoms who could do anything at all to him and fury that he'd been used so thoroughly without so much as the slightest hesitance.

He revisited the thought that if Soilléir hadn't had his fingers in every pie from Tosan to Riamh, he never would have encountered Léirsinn of Sàraichte . . .

"I wouldn't say that."

He glared at him. "Stop that."

"You're gasping aloud and looking very green." Soilléir shrugged with a smile. "Another very good guess. As for other things, I knew Sladaiche—"

"Which you shamelessly lied about in that glade," Acair said bitterly. "Why didn't you slay him the moment he looked askance at the first horse in his charge? Nay, never mind. If I must listen to you blather on about your noble doings, I will cut off my own ears." He waved the man on to further details with a hand that was far less steady than he would have liked, but it had been that sort of morning so far. "You knew Sladaiche, allowed him to live, and then what?"

"I knew him," Soilléir repeated, "but there is always the possibility of redemption."

"You can't be serious."

"Very well, with some there is no hope, I'll admit. But it isn't my place to decide who lives or dies."

"If there were no evil, what would there be for good men to do, or whatever the rot is you sick up onto everyone you meet," Acair said, wondering if he might be soon indulging. Supper from the night before, what he'd managed of it, was definitely still lingering in a very unwholesome way in his tum.

"At this point you know most all of what you'd ever want to about him," Soilléir continued. "I have details about other things, though, that you might find interesting."

"Another turn in your granddaddy's solar is what I would find interesting."

"Library."

"There, too, but go on. Bludgeon me with the minutiae."

Soilléir, damn him to hell, only smiled and looked as relaxed as if he might soon be settling in for a pint or two at the local pub.

"What you likely would have discovered soon enough, but I'll tell you just the same," he continued, "is that the author of those wee books of faery tales is none other than Tosdach, Léirsinn's grandfather."

Acair knew he should have been surprised, but somehow he wasn't. "If you tell me that he's a powerful mage . . . "

"Nothing like that, I fear. Just a man with a love for a good story. As for your lady's family, I believe my father told you as much as he knew about the particulars. I can give you the details he doesn't know. Niall was slain by Sladaiche, though you may have guessed as much already."

Acair looked at him and for the first time in decades of knowing him felt a small stirring of pity. "It must be difficult," he said, finding the words sliding off his tongue whilst he could only stand there and watch them go. "To simply stand by and watch."

Soilléir walked next to him for quite some time before he stopped. He took a deep breath and looked at him. "Not many say that."

"They're too busy plotting how to have your spells."

"That might be true. But I appreciate the sentiment just the same."

"I'll deny it if you repeat it."

"I would expect nothing less." Soilléir walked on. "To continue, after a year or so, Saoradh met Muireall and proposed marriage. It was done out of love and the children were never told."

"Did he have magic?" Acair asked, trying to digest what he was hearing without a proper libation or a decent chair. "Léirsinn's true sire, I mean."

Soilléir considered. "They do in their line," he said slowly, "but their magic is a very capricious sort, far more unpredictable than what my family possesses. For the most part, the inhabitants of An Caol can trace their ancestors back to Ionad-teàrmainn. Léirsinn's sire is a direct descendent of the stablemaster that had Sladaiche banished for abusing the horses."

"I see."

"I imagine you're beginning to. Lord Tosdach had found great hospitality in An Caol. Being a lover of horses himself, making the journey back there often was, I'm given to understand, one of the pleasures of his life. When he felt he'd collected as many stories as he could, he bound them all into a trio of books."

Acair closed his eyes briefly. "Including, no doubt, at least one from Léirsinn's sire."

"One passed down from Léirsinn's paternal grandfather, actually, through her sire, but aye, you see where the tale leads."

"He collected the stories without having any idea what he was actually collecting, then Sladaiche followed his nose there and slew Léirsinn's father."

"Aye," Soilléir agreed, "only after having watched her father's father and grandfather, for reasons I don't need to give you. None of that line remains, as I said. I'm not sure their ends were quick and painless."

Acair rubbed his fingers over his brow, but found that a rather inadequate means of stopping the pounding there. "I won't tell her that bit, I don't think."

"Perhaps not now. She might want to know later, on the off chance Tosdach mentions it."

Acair nodded. "I'll remember that." He walked for a bit, then shook his head. "Why didn't Sladaiche just dig through their house and take the book when Léirsinn was a child?"

Soilléir looked at him steadily. "I don't think he even considered the books until after he'd slain the parents. I will admit I sent him off hunting things that didn't exist long enough to get the children out of the house. There was nothing left for him to find when he returned, not even the books."

Acair shook his head in disbelief. "Do you have any idea what sort of harm's way you put her in?"

"She wasn't unprotected," Soilléir said carefully, "and there were other distractions to draw Sladaiche's attention elsewhere. Your father was one."

"My *father*?" Acair echoed. "What in the hell does he have to do with any of this?"

"For that, we must go back many years. Sladaiche built a house next to your father's because he wanted your father's spell of Diminishing to use in completing what he'd taken from my grandfather's library, which was thankfully unfinished—"

"Wait," Acair said, stopping and looking at him. "We found the book, which I'm certain you already know, but the entire thing was gone, not just a single spell. Where are the innards?"

Soilléir shrugged. "No idea."

"You realize when you say things like that, I have to clasp my hands behind my back to keep them from resting where they so desperately want to instead. That would be *around your throat*, if you're confused."

"I wasn't," Soilléir said easily "As for the rest of the book, it likely rotted years ago in someone's compost bin, not that your grandmother couldn't rewrite every spell in there. I wouldn't worry."

Acair supposed he didn't need to point out that when Soilléir wasn't worried, the rest of the world needed to be terrified. He also wished with a desperation that left him a bit weak in the knees for a notebook and a pencil.

There was definitely no escaping it any longer. He had become his mother.

"When Sladaiche realized he would never have Diminishing from your sire," Soilléir continued, "he turned to others who might know it. Why do you think he left that spell on his mantel for you to find? You do realize, don't you, that none of your brothers who traipsed through his house could pull it down, much less unwrap it and cast it aside as dross."

"Well," Acair said, trying—and failing—not to feel a bit chuffed. "Well."

Soilléir smiled. "I believe though Sladaiche assumed you didn't know your father's spell, he thought you would have it soon enough. If he had been able to befriend you, who knows what would have happened? He might have persuaded you to tell him what he needed to know. There have been many who have watched your adventures with more than a passing interest."

"I'm certain I've kept *you* up at night."

"You have," Soilléir agreed, "and nay, you may not have any of my spells. That would require the seven rings of mastery and then tests I'm not sure you would care for."

"My heart is already broken," Acair said lightly. "Not sure you could do worse."

"I would break your soul, Acair."

Acair managed a look of loathing that didn't require all that much effort.

Soilléir only smiled placidly. "So to continue, the time came when Sladaiche turned his eye to the east and to your lady's family. I believe his thinking was the same with them as with you and your brothers. When he realized her parents couldn't give him what he wanted, he turned to the children. They were, of course, too young to be of any use at the time, but he was nothing if not patient."

"So you orchestrated the rescue of them."

Soilléir nodded. "I sent Iseabail and Taisdealach to other locales and arranged for Léirsinn to be sent to Tosdach. Sladaiche arrived the next day and because he feared what her grandfather might say, her grandfather was muted."

"Why not slay him instead?"

"I can only suppose Sladaiche thought he might know something. He of course rifled through Léirsinn's things but found nothing. But over the past pair of years, that patience had seemed to be on the wane. Fuadain was nothing more than a useful fool for him, but when I could see that ending badly, there was no choice but to act."

Acair shook his head. "But why me?"

"Many reasons. Your encounter with him when you were a child was one. You obviously have the power—"

"From my grandmother—"

"From your grandmother," Soilléir agreed, "which is something you might want to investigate later. Also, your house is built on the stables, as you now know, so he would have eventually razed it to the ground to look for what he thought might lie there."

"You put *me* in harm's way, without any power, putting Léirsinn's life in danger *now*, to face . . ." Acair found himself spluttering, but was at a loss for another way to express his astonishment. "What the hell were you talking about when you said I could walk where you could not?"

"What would you say if I said 'twas to walk within your own soul and find what lies there?"

"I would say that once I've had a decent meal and an equal amount of whisky, you had better have found someplace to hide." He snorted. "What absolute rubbish."

"The schools of wizardry are safe haven enough, I imagine."

"Do you know how many times I've slithered over those walls and put my feet up in Droch's solar?" Acair asked archly. "I've even had a wee skip about his bloody chess board and hobnobbed with the pieces too stupid to realize what his true game is."

"So you have," Soilléir said. "Next time you visit, come have a glass of wine at my fire. I'm sure we'll find much to discuss."

Acair rarely felt himself blindsided, but that someone would actually invite him in for simple conversation? 'Twas unsettling, to be sure. He fumbled about in the appropriate dresser for something nasty to say but found that particular drawer distressingly empty.

"I loathe you," he said, because 'twas simply all he had left.

Soilléir only laughed softly. "Anything else you'd like to know?"

"Actually, there is. You told me not to find a spell, but to steal it. That, Your Highness, is a bit more egregious than a simple white lie."

"I didn't think you'd be interested if I told you to go find something and use it for good." Soilléir looked at him gravely. "I misjudged you."

Acair waited.

"I apologize."

Acair looked about himself, then glared at the prince. "The world still stands, which is encouraging. But for that absolutely appalling mendacity, I believe I will require more than a simple apology."

When one had an essence changer cornered, there was no reason not to press one's advantage. He was quite sure his mother had said that a time or two, which led him to wonder if she'd had experience with the like.

Soilléir only smiled. "Seven rings of mastery, my lord Acair, then we'll talk."

"Can you imagine," Acair said with a snort, ruthlessly tamping down a little something that bubbled up in the vicinity of his heart over the thought. "Me, at the schools of wizardry."

"I can," Soilléir said. "Miach did it."

"He had time on his hands," Acair said loftily. "I, on the other hand, have a very full calendar."

"If you have an opening, you might consider it."

Acair set aside that appalling thought to perhaps contemplate after an inordinate amount of Durialian dark ale, then continued to walk in companionable silence with a man who had apparently been more involved in world events than he'd claimed to be. How those events had been a part of his own life without his having known a damned thing . . .

He thought he might have to walk on the shore near his house for quite a while before he managed to come to terms with them.

"One more thing."

He thought he might be able to guess what Soilléir was about to say, so he simply looked at him in silence.

"Her father's people have in the past lived decently long lives."

He took a deep breath. "I see."

"I may or may not have . . . meddled," Soilléir added. "With the both of you. For a bit longer than either of your souls would provide."

He was simply beyond surprise, to the point where all he could do was gape at the man in silence.

Soilléir only smiled and walked away to stand altogether too close to Léirsinn's sister.

Acair hung back as the company gathered itself together to discuss the gastronomic possibilities lurking inside *The Preening Pelican*. He watched Sianach toss off his equine shape with a snort and dart off into the forest with a yowl of feline hunger. Doghail staggered, but was caught quite handily by Lord Tosdach and ushered without delay inside. The rest of the company followed, chatting companionably.

He found himself in the end standing outside with Léirsinn. He was enormously gratified to have her put her arms around him and it had nothing at all to do with her keeping him on his feet. He supposed he would need to tell her about those things Soilléir had gifted the two of them, apparently, but perhaps later, when they were sitting in front of his fire at home and he'd had a decent amount of whisky.

He could only hope she wouldn't regret being saddled with him for as long as she likely would be now.

"No spot of shadow by the door," she said suddenly.

"Thankfully," he said, pulling himself back to the conversation at hand.

"I have that piece of your soul in my pocket, just so you know. Soilléir has thoughts on how we might put it back in you."

He could only imagine. "Whisky first," he said weakly.

"I suggested that."

He took her face in his hands and kissed her. "You are a sterling gel. You deserve a far better man than I."

"Should I keep looking, then?"

He blinked, then realized she hadn't released him. "Of course not. Just giving you one last chance to escape."

"Still not a proper proposal, Acair." She kissed him quickly, then pulled away. "You might want to work on that while we're working on you. Soilléir has a plan."

That plan, he discovered a half hour and four fingers of whisky later, involved a Cothromaichian spell of un-noticing cast over their company, Léirsinn's family's dragon spell spoken in reverse, and his charred soul and Léirsinn's hand placed on his bare chest over the scar Rùnach had so thoughtfully left behind to remind him how close he'd come to death before.

He gaped at the rune on the back of his lady's hand that blazed with fire in the shape of a dragon and snorted what felt like the fires of Hell directly into his flesh.

He looked around at the souls watching him, but none seemed to have the slightest bit of sympathy for the agony that was, he had to admit, mercifully brief.

He considered, frowned a bit, then looked at his love.

"I feel . . . better."

"You look better."

He flexed his fingers. "I might have to take myself out for a canter about the old place in a bit." He leaned closer to her. "I also might need to make a hasty journey in the direction of Angesand." He looked around him, but the rest of the company had somehow left him for a rousing game of cards with another group of locals. He turned back to his lady. "You know, in regard to that promise I made to Hearn."

She pushed a small coin toward him. "Soilléir said he went back to my unc—I mean, to Fuadain's study for a bit of a visit while you and I went to the barn."

"No doubt to make certain I'd left the man alive," he muttered.

"I think he cared far less about that than finding this, if you want the truth." She nodded. "He said you would need it."

He pocketed that very precious piece of what he assumed was

Tùr of Angesand's soul and decided that he might have to tender a decent thank-you for the same. "I don't suppose Seannair's youngest grandson also sent word ahead as well as leaving us directions on where to go?"

"I think he said something about not wanting to be too involved in things."

Acair looked for the barmaid and raised his finger. That comment was going to require another drink, but perhaps after that he would decide how best to accomplish the final task on his list.

"Will you tell me what we're actually going to do?"

He blinked. "Of course." He put his arm around her and leaned back against the wood of the bench they shared. "Hearn asked me to do a bit of, well, healing. For a change. With his son."

"Careful," she murmured. "You never know where that might lead."

"I know exactly where it will lead which is why I'll only do it this once unless you're involved, or perhaps one of our numerous children. But this is the final act of do-gooding for me. I'm looking for that old leaf and turning it back over."

"Of course."

He had to take a deep breath before he could look at her. "Frightened off yet?"

"Not yet," she said with a shrug. "And just so you know, you're terrible at this proposing business."

He met her gaze and realized she was looking as him as if she might very well have been rather fond of him. He ignored the choruses of *huzzahs* and other appropriate sentiments all the damn magics in his chest set up, and smiled faintly. "I might corner your grandfather later."

"Do you want me to come along and prop you up?"

He attempted a look of mock outrage. "Accompany me on my manly business? I think not."

Her smile faded. "Did it do any good?" she asked, sounding a bit wistful. "That magic of mine?"

"You can't truly mean that," he said, genuinely startled. "I couldn't have used that spell on my own. It needed you."

"Can you do this thing for Hearn's son with just me?"

"Of course," he said confidently. "I'll take Soilléir's place, you'll do what you do, and we'll see what happens."

"Soilléir did suggest that while you were wheezing."

"Of course he did," Acair grumbled. "The next thing I know, he'll be hiring me out to do his dirty work for him."

"He said that as well."

Acair leaned his head back against the worn wood of that sturdy pub bench and gave himself up for utterly lost. The next thing he knew, Soilléir was going to have him going round to every damned soul in the Nine Kingdoms to refill their cups, as it were.

He thought he might have to make a concerted effort to retrieve parts of his own black soul lest he never again be equal to carrying on the grand and glorious tradition of his parents.

Of course, he would have to find a way to balance that with the rather unexpected pleasure of having the woman he loved sitting contentedly next to him, stroking the back of his hand as if she might have a few fond feelings for him, and listening to the pleasant conversation of companions who had apparently tired of their gaming sport and returned to greener conversational pastures.

It was all very unexpected and unexpectedly pleasant.

Who would have thought that he might be adding to his list of favorite things?

Twenty-four

❖

L éirsinn stood just inside Sgath and Eulasaid's barn and looked at the sky that was threatening rain. She didn't mind rain, especially when she was able to stay inside and listen to it falling against a barn roof. Flying in it seemed a somewhat poorer way to enjoy it, but she supposed the hooded cloak Acair had given her might keep her dry enough.

She looked at the man in question who was also watching the sky and apparently considering whether or not the rain might stop.

"It was lovely of your grandparents to let us stay for a few days," she offered.

"They insisted," he said, "but aye, it was."

"What will you do now?" she asked.

"After I try to heal Hearn's son?" he asked, looking at her. "Or after I wed myself a gel with a rune on her hand and plans to acquire countless ponies?"

"The latter, surely."

He smiled. "Haven't a damned clue."

She leaned against the door and looked at him. "I never asked what you did to Fuadain."

"You don't want to know." He turned back to his contemplation of the sky. "He might not sleep easily for a while."

"Weeks?"

"I tend to operate in decades, darling. I did do him the very great favor of hiring a pair of lads from the pub to go look for his sons to come claim their inheritance since your grandfather didn't seem to be interested in remaining there. That was the very least I could do given that he likely won't manage anything past sitting in the corner and rocking for a few years." He turned toward her and reached out to tuck a lock of hair behind her ear. "What will you do now?"

"Have the people I love all in the same place," she said, finding the thought almost too lovely to contemplate. "Perhaps even my brother occasionally."

"He seems to have itchy feet, that wandering lad, but he'll always be welcome. We should absolutely offer your sister a safe harbor to keep her out of the clutches of that essence-changing madman. If you'd care to be in the same place with me, that is."

She looked at him pointedly.

He only smiled and reached for her hand. "Your grandfather likely needs a decent meal and a nap before I corner him to present my suit, giving us time to be off and doing. You don't mind coming with me?"

"As long you don't require anything from me that's longer than five words."

"Six, darling. You're up to six."

She didn't want to tell him that she had absolutely no desire to use any magic at all, mostly because she was appalled to find that might not be as true as she wanted it to be. She'd made werelight when she'd first come out to the barn and reached for that very handy spell of containment to avoid having to look for a broom not a quarter hour earlier.

"I'm finished after this time," she said firmly.

"Are you trying to convince me or yourself?"

She glared at him, though what she wanted to do was go into his arms and stay there for a bit.

But if anything could be said about that man there, it was that he wasn't oblivious. He smiled, then pulled her into a thoroughly comforting embrace.

"Use it or not, as it pleases you," he said.

"I might consider it if there were others who needed your help," she conceded.

"My help," he said with a snort. "Can you imagine?"

"I won't say a thing," she promised. "Wouldn't want word getting round about these new and unsettling sides of you."

He hugged her so tightly she squeaked.

"You do love me," he whispered.

"Almost as much as you love me," she agreed. She pulled out of his arms, then nudged him out of the way before he opened the stall door for Sianach. "I'll saddle him while you give that some thought. Are we riding or flying?"

"Let's fly, if Sianach will behave himself. Even on an errand of mercy, I don't fancy all morning spent out in the rain. Besides, I'd like to be back before Soilléir offends everyone so terribly that we lose our accommodations. Also, I have a grandfather to opportune."

She smiled and went to fetch Sianach's gear.

I t took only an hour or so to reach a little cabin on the edge of a clearing. She suspected they might have known they were in the right place by virtue of the enormous pastures nearby. If that hadn't been enough, the good lord of Angesand standing near the front gates, pacing, surely would have.

Sianach did them the very great favor of waiting until they were off his back before he slipped into his hell-hound guise, which only earned a brief smile of satisfaction from Hearn. He shook her hand companionably, then looked at Acair.

"You were successful?"

"The maker of those shadows is gone," Acair said, "and Fuadain of Sàraichte won't be making mischief either for a bit."

"What of Droch? I can understand why he wanted Falaire—who is mending properly at home—but he's not known for his interest in riding."

"Falaire was a bribe to keep him placated, or so I understand. Droch is still as he always was: looking for more power. I daresay he had his fingers in this stew, but he'll soon find there's nothing left in the pot. There's nothing to worry about from that quarter that I can see."

"You'll see to him down the road, no doubt."

"Your faith in me is gratifying."

Hearn looked a little green. "I'm honestly not certain what I have faith in at the moment, but I don't often find myself in this position."

Léirsinn cleared her throat. "Trust," was what came out of her mouth, though she certainly hadn't intended to say it. She was acutely aware of how difficult that had been for her when Mistress Cailleach suggested the same.

Hearn took a deep breath. "Follow me."

Léirsinn thought Acair looked as if he might rather do anything else, but that lad there didn't lack courage. He simply nodded once, then started after Hearn up the path to the house. If he caught her hand on the way and squeezed just once perhaps a bit more firmly than he'd intended to, she understood. She imagined Hearn wouldn't fault him if he couldn't restore his son to his proper state, but there were people a body simply didn't want to disappoint.

A woman was standing in the doorway, dressed as if she'd just come in from morning stables. Léirsinn supposed that was Hearn's wife, mostly because she could imagine that pair having had more than one spirited discussion about the horses in their care.

Hearn stopped a handful of paces away. "Marcachd," he said carefully.

"Hearn."

"How is the bay I sent you?"

"Eating," she said briskly. "Not ready to go back under saddle yet, but perhaps in another fortnight."

Hearn stepped back and nodded. "I've brought the company I told you about. Léirsinn of Sàraichte, my wife, Marcachd. Marcachd, you may already know Lord Acair, if by reputation alone."

Léirsinn was accustomed to the reception Acair generally received, so she wasn't surprised by the wary look he was enjoying at present. He simply stood there and left his hands in plain sight, no doubt in an attempt to allay any fears about his intentions.

Hearn's wife nodded once, then opened the door to allow them inside.

The house was full of the usual horselike clutter she was accustomed to—papers, bits of tack, boots in the corner—but what surprised her was the light. Perhaps she had spent too much time in Briàghde where the sun had shone relentlessly but with a harshness that had left her wanting to avoid it.

Or perhaps that had been her life before a black mage with terrible spells had stridden into her barn like a very unlikely Hero and filled her life with so many unexpectedly beautiful things.

What she knew was that whatever it was that left light streaming into Marcachd of Angesand's house—spells or perhaps simply pure mountain air—it made the woman's home a very peaceful, healing place. No wonder Hearn sent horses and sons to her.

A man sat just outside the back door, staring off across the pastures, unmoving. She stopped a few paces away with Acair and looked at him. He resembled Hearn so strongly she would have assumed they were kin even if she hadn't already known who to expect.

Marcachd moved to stand in front of her son. "I think you're mad to have brought this mage," she said to Hearn bluntly. "Had I not been so desperate, I would have forbidden it."

"The lad's powerful," Hearn said evenly, "regardless of how he uses it."

"What if he slays him?"

Léirsinn felt her heart break a little at the pain in Marcachd's voice, but she understood. If she had only known Acair by his foul reputation alone, she likely would have thought the same thing.

"Trust me," Hearn said. "And give this lad here a chance. 'Tis difficult to change when no one wants you to."

Léirsinn glanced at Acair to find him looking as if Hearn had just elbowed him in the nose. She squeezed his hand, but didn't dare smile. There was still a task in front of him that might very well be beyond what either of them could accomplish. It wasn't as if they'd been able to practice on anyone to perfect the art.

Trust.

She blew out her breath and waited for Acair to do his part, if doing could be done.

He took the piece of Tùr's soul that Soilléir had done him the favor of gathering, then looked at her. She nodded and felt a little silly, but 'twas too late to turn back.

Or at least she felt ridiculous until she watched Acair press that piece of soul against Tùr's throat and look at her. She repeated the six words she knew, backwards, then watched him as he reversed the rest of the spell from her own book of faery tales.

If he added a bit of the old *oomph*, as his mother might have said, from that piece of essence-changing Soilléir had used on him, she wasn't going to make any mention of it.

Tùr gasped, then opened his eyes. He blinked a time or two, then looked up at Acair.

"My lord Acair," he said, looking slightly winded. "Giving souls instead of taking them, eh?"

"You're confusing me with my highly skilled but morally destitute sire," Acair said faintly, "but aye, that does seem to be the case."

"A fine choice," Tùr said with a smile.

He stood up, shook himself off as if he'd just come in from the rain, then walked over and put his arms around his mother. Hearn stepped forward and put his arms around them both.

Léirsinn stepped away to stand next to Acair, then looked at him to find him shaking his head slowly. He looked at her helplessly. She smiled, nudged him affectionately with her shoulder, then decided they might have things to discuss later on when they had a bit of peace.

Marcachd of Angesand released her son and spun around. Léirsinn hardly knew what to expect, though she wouldn't have been surprised by either curses or a brisk invitation to find the front door. She *was* surprised to watch the woman throw her arms around Acair. She pounded him on the back exactly three times, leaned up and kissed him loudly on the cheek, then turned and flung her arms around her son again. If she wept, Léirsinn couldn't hear her and Hearn's enveloping hug hid her from sight.

Léirsinn looked to find Acair standing there looking as if he'd not only been elbowed in the nose, but kicked in the gut. He put his hand to his cheek as if he'd never touched his own skin before.

She wasn't sure she would ever not enjoy the sight of Acair of Ceangail off balance. He looked like a colt who hadn't quite found its legs yet, gangly and unsure.

It was one of the most endearing things she'd ever seen.

She supposed it didn't change who he was. She had seen him at what was arguably his very worst. Perhaps he'd shown Slaidear mercy, or perhaps he'd simply been the one to mete out the proper justice no matter how that looked. She imagined he'd left her uncle looking at horrors he would never unsee simply because he'd been able to. That might have been a bit much, but she was neither his judge nor his sanctifier. He would have to live with what he'd done.

So would she, she knew. That she could still light a fire with five words was proof enough of that.

"I didn't realize I'd come to visit, Mother," Tùr said. "I feel like I've been dreaming, but they weren't pleasant ones. Is there anything to eat?"

"We should go," Acair murmured.

She nodded, then found Hearn holding out his hand. She shook it, then he extended it to Acair as well.

"Thank you," he said simply.

"Thank you for the release from Uachdaran of Léige's dungeon."

"The price was worth it."

"I would have done it just the same, my lord."

Hearn slid him a look. "Careful, lad. Word will get around, you know. I do have that thank-you note you sent hammered into a barn wall. Someone might see it."

"I'll know whom to blame if they do."

Léirsinn supposed the world hadn't ended, but watching the two men in front of her exchanging pleasant words instead of curses was something. Hearn looked at her.

"He looks a bit shattered. Put him to bed for a few days, then have him shovel manure. He'll be back to himself before we're comfortable with it, I'm sure."

Acair only nodded without comment, which Léirsinn supposed was indication enough of how weary he was. She had a final look at Hearn's wife and son now walking off toward the pasture, then followed Hearn back through the house.

Hearn opened the front door. "Best be on your way before the morning is completely gone. Your lad can ride with you if you can stomach it."

Léirsinn walked out into the late morning sunlight, then stopped so quickly, Acair almost plowed her over. She caught him by his hands on her shoulders. Handy, as it gave her something to do until she found her tongue. She looked quickly at Hearn who had come to stand next to her.

"A decent pony," Hearn said mildly. "If you want him."

The Grey stood there, nibbling on Marcachd's flowers. He raised his head, nodded at her, then went back to his tearing of grass and bloom.

She supposed 'twas the burden of her non-magic that had rendered her so emotional. That was surely the only reason she was having difficulty seeing the lord of Angesand for her tears.

"I can't afford him."

"Didn't say you had to pay for him, now did I?"

"But—"

"I might occasionally send you other beasts to train. This one will no doubt drain your lad's coffers with feeding and housing him properly, so I'm repaid yet again." He nodded toward the horse. "Off you go, lass. I believe you're staying with Sgath. He likely has a stray brush or two."

"Thank you, my lord," Léirsinn managed.

Hearn shrugged, clapped Acair on the shoulder, then went back inside the house without further comment.

Léirsinn looked at the horse, then at the man standing there, barely, and wasn't quite sure what to say.

"Please don't make me walk to Sgath's," he managed.

She smiled. "We won't."

"He doesn't have a saddle."

"He doesn't need one. I'll give you a leg up, then you can just hold on and hope for the best."

He put his arms around her and held her for a moment or two. "Tell me he doesn't fly."

"Darling," she said, "I promise you won't know if he does. Just close your eyes and trust me."

She was fairly certain he'd muttered something that sounded a bit like a supplication, but she decided to ignore it. She gave him the promised leg up, then swung up behind him and gathered a bit of the Grey's glorious mane in her hands. She invited him to be gentle with her love.

He flew just the same.

S everal hours and a ride or two on that glorious horse while Acair napped in a pile of straw later, she was standing in a stall, brushing out a silvery tail. She finished, sighed, and considered weeping. She looked around to make certain no one would see, then jumped a little when she realized Acair was leaning on the stall door. His eyes were closed, though, so she imagined he hadn't watched her blubbering over a pony, no matter how perfect.

"Come to shovel?" she asked.

He opened his eyes and smiled at her. "Fetch you for supper, rather. I'll shovel later."

She thanked him for opening the stall door for her, handed off brush and curry comb to one of Sgath's stable lads, then brushed off her hands before she studied him.

"You look better."

"Another day or two and I'll be back to my old self," he agreed. "Decent food and lovely surroundings do wonders."

"It is very pretty here."

"The lake is beautiful. As long as I don't look all the way across to where Ruith is no doubt plotting my demise, that is."

"Perhaps Hearn will tell him of your recent escapades."

"That won't matter," Acair said cheerfully. "I can't charm everyone, so I'll just soldier on as best I can."

She walked with him back through the twilight and realized she was looking over her shoulder for something untoward. She looked at him and he shook his head with a smile.

"Safe enough, I daresay."

"Did you use magic to make sure of it?"

"The odd spell of ward comes in handy," he said. "But nay, I actually stirred myself to walk outside and have a look whilst you were fawning over that four-legged beastie. That and Sgath—"

"Your grandfather," she corrected.

He took a deep breath. "My grandfather Sgath has his own spells set, of course. And speaking of grandfathers, I had a wee chat with yours."

She looked at him. "Did you? About anything in particular?"

"Permissions," he said succinctly.

"And were they given?"

He nodded slowly. "With the appropriate warnings about seeing properly to the feeding of and caring for your own sweet self. I gave him my word I would do for you what you would allow."

"Interesting."

"I have one more thing to tell you, though."

She looked at him in surprise. If the odd note in his voice hadn't caught her attention, the rather unsure look on his face certainly would have.

"Changed your mind, did you?"

"I haven't," he said grimly, "but you might."

"Should I be sitting down?"

He looked, actually, as if he might be the one who needed to find somewhere to do just that. "I'm just going to blurt it out."

"I wish you would."

He took a deep breath. "Soilléir meddled."

"With my sister?" she asked in astonishment.

"With us," he said.

"How?"

He shifted uncomfortably. "It seems that he tossed our souls into the proverbial essence-changing pot, gave them a bit of a stir, then pulled them back out so they were of an equal measure. Or something very like that."

She patted the air around her, looking for somewhere to sit and found only the man in front of her looking solid enough for any sort of support. She took his hands that he held out and suspected that if she'd had any tears left, she would have used them all on him at that very moment.

"You gave me part of your soul," she managed.

He only nodded slightly.

"How long have you known?"

"A day or two."

She sighed deeply and walked into his embrace. She closed her eyes and decided that perhaps comfort and safety were things that might not be so terrible after all.

She supposed those things might be lasting a bit longer than she'd expected.

"Wed me?" he murmured.

"I might."

"I deserve that," he said with a bit of a laugh.

She smiled and turned to look out over the lake, realizing that she had stood in almost the same place several weeks earlier when she'd been trying to come to terms with what Falaire had been able to do. So much had changed, yet so much hadn't. Her life was full of horses and magic, Acair's life was full of magic and horses, and somehow, she imagined they might manage to meet somewhere in the middle and live out their lives together in bliss.

Very long lives, apparently.

"My grandparents offered us the use of their garden for a wedding, if you're interested."

She pulled back and looked at him. "I'm interested."

"Then let's go make a guest list. I promise to keep my hands in my own pockets."

"For the wedding."

"I think I might manage it that long."

She walked with him back toward his grandparents' house, supposing he just might.

Epilogue

❖

L ife was very strange when one was a black mage extraordinaire on extended holiday from evil-doing.

Acair had come to that conclusion over a handful of months spent walking along the shore with his shoes off. More often than not, he'd been joined by his wife — something he had honestly never thought to have, though she was the first to remind him that he was, as they saying went, robbing the proverbial cradle. His response was usually to remind *her* that she owned a decent bit of his soul which perhaps canceled any cradle-robbing on his part. If that was a discussion they would likely be having for centuries to come, he wasn't going to argue.

That such a thing would be possible was almost enough, he supposed, to allow Soilléir of Cothromaiche to sleep easily at night.

As far as others sleeping peacefully beneath his own roof went, he had been surprised to find himself entertaining the occasional guest. The first had been his grandmother who had arrived bearing her yearly Beltane letter. He had figured prominently in the space reserved for Relatives of Note, which he'd supposed was a far better location than where he usually found himself appearing. He had delivered the doily he'd secured, managed to keep her out of his private stash of port, and extracted a promise that she wouldn't slay him if he and Léirsinn made a visit later in the year to discuss spells and such. He couldn't have asked for more.

He and Léirsinn were fairly permanent residents, of course, as was her grandfather. Doghail refused a spot in the 'fancy hall,' as he termed it, but his quarters in the stables were almost as fine as what housed Sianach and that beautiful gray horse of Léirsinn's.

Léirsinn's sister had her own bedchamber, which she used more often than not. Her brother had come to visit exactly once thus far, but perhaps they could expect no more.

In the end, his life was full of things he had never expected and do-gooding had taken root in his soul. It was a sickness he would likely suffer from for the rest of his very long life.

He ignored the runes on the back of his hand given to him by an elven king which, he was damned certain, had mischief on their minds. That was likely the only mischief he would find himself enjoying any time soon, but a gentleman didn't complain overmuch.

He turned his back to the sea and surveyed his domain. The house he had already eyed with satisfaction. The stables, he had to admit, were equally spectacular, but perhaps he could have allowed nothing less. When one housed a steed or two—or perhaps more, he never could keep count and Léirsinn tended to offer rather vague and distracted answers when asked—with Angesand blood in its veins, well, one needed to make allowances. When one had already hosted the good lord of Angesand not a month earlier, one personally made damned sure the stalls were cleaned, the tack polished to perfection, and the floors were something one could eat from if necessary.

He frowned at the sight of that quartet of souls gathered near the house. That was Doghail, to be sure, and Léirsinn's grandfather. He was fairly certain that was his wife there as well.

The fourth was a mystery.

But given that Léirsinn had a spell or two in her pocket, Acair didn't worry.

Much.

He was who he was, though, and he'd accepted his fate as Second Most Loathed Mage in the Nine Kingdoms, directly behind his father. 'Twas vexing not to be First Horse, as the saying went, but there was little to be done about it. Perhaps in the fall he might give thought to knocking his father off his vaunted perch, but then again, perhaps not. An autumn spent admiring his very lovely wife whilst toasting his toes in front of the fire, penning the odd philosophical essay on the merits of doing good, drinking a respectable amount of various libations, aye, that might be just the sort of work for him.

But as he'd discovered, plans went awry at the most inconvenient times. He had the feeling he was running up hard against just such a time and that had everything to do with the look of that fourth soul there up the way. He put on his most useful look of utter boredom and strolled back over the dunes, prepared for the worst.

He presented himself to them with nary a fission of unease, gallantly kissed his wife's hand, made her grandfather a polite bow, then saluted Doghail with a hearty compliment on the state of the stables. He looked at the messenger and was rather more relieved than he should have been not to recognize the lad.

"Your business, good sir?" he asked.

The child couldn't have been more than a score if he were a day. He held out a gilt-edged missive with a hand that trembled badly.

"For your p-p-p-pleasure, my l-l-l-lord," he said, his teeth chattering. He dropped to his knees. "Please don't slay me, milord," he blurted out as if all the sundry demons of Hell had sniffed him and only him out and decided he would make a fine luncheon. Added to that, the poor fool looked as if he might soon burst into tears. "I'm only the messenger."

Acair took the missive gingerly. At least things were being delivered via humans instead of birds, though he wasn't entirely sure that instead of his boots being soiled with pigeon droppings, they wouldn't soon wear the contents of that lad's stomach.

Still, the written word had done him dirty in the past and he wasn't entirely sure that trend wasn't about to continue.

He pulled the boy to his feet and patted him on the shoulder.

"Not to worry," he said soothingly. "My best spell of death needed a wash and is now drying on the line. I imagine you'll manage to bolt off my land before I can reach it, don't you think?"

The lad wasted no time doing just that. Acair watched him flap off frantically, then turned to his companions.

Doghail rolled his eyes and walked off. Léirsinn's grandfather laughed and left to join him. That left just that red-haired vixen standing there, watching him with amusement.

"What of you, lady?" he asked archly. "No pleas for mercy?"

She snorted at him. "I have no fear of you."

"My plans for you went completely awry at some point," he said, reaching for her hand and tucking it under his elbow, "but I'll be damned if I can lay my finger on when or where."

"Too many maudlin sentiments, I imagine," she said mildly. "You've become tamed."

"Perish the thought."

"The truth can be painful, Acair."

He smiled in spite of himself because she was right. He looked at the missive in his hands, then at her.

"Do I dare open this?"

"It could be an invitation to a house party of some sort."

"After the last one we attended, I can see why such a thing would top our list of things to do right off."

She pulled her hand away and held it open. "Shall I read it for you?"

He handed the missive over without hesitation. "Please."

She broke the seal, then read. Her expression gave nothing away, but she was one of those horse people who managed great, biting, flying steeds without so much as a pucker marring their brows. That, and she lived with him. Her ability to simply watch, then shrug off the most appalling things was unmatched.

"An invitation?" he asked lightly.

She looked at him. "I'm not sure I would call it that."

"Then what would you call it?"

"A quest."

He could scarce believe his ears. "A what?"

"A quest," she repeated. She handed the missive to him. "I don't think this is a jest."

"If it is, 'tis in very bad taste."

He read. He felt the blood drain from his face. He quite happily planted his arse rather enthusiastically on a bench that seemed to find itself within sitting distance. He looked at the woman who sank down onto that same bench with him and found himself utterly speechless.

"Your reputation precedes you," she noted.

"A quest!"

Her eyes were watering madly. "Apparently so."

He waved the missive at her. "You're laughing at me."

She succumbed fully. He wasn't sure if he should have been offended or . . . well, offended.

Murder. Mischief. Mayhem. All such fond memories that seemed to be disappearing further and further out of reach.

He watched his wife remove the Parchment of Doom from his trembling fingers—he refused to think about how greatly they resembled those of the messenger—then continued to watch with profound unease as she turned it over.

There was scribbling on the back, but he could only assume that was a bit of added joy that would inform him that not only had he been called on an impossible quest he couldn't refuse, he was to go on said quest with naught but his charm, his good looks, and perhaps a pair of dressmaker's shears.

At the moment, he wouldn't have been surprised.

Léirsinn looked at him from those leaf-green eyes of hers. "There's more."

"So I see, and I'm afraid to ask."

"Just a few details," she continued mercilessly. "Location, of course. An opinion on the vileness of the miscreant in question."

"If you say *lost spells that only you can find, darling*, I will weep."

She smiled and handed him his gilded doom. "Read it for your-self, then." She pushed herself to her feet and headed toward the front door. "I'll go pack our gear."

"I didn't agree to this!" he exclaimed.

I don't think you'll want to refuse was what came floating back his way.

Well, he damned well would refuse. He was a vile mage of terrible power. He had spells to steal, priceless treasures to nick, a wife to continue to woo. He'd already begun to plot a way to slip inside Inntrig with pencil and paper and lurk in a wardrobe on the off chance Seannair of Cothromaiche talked in his sleep. One never knew what that sort of babbling might yield.

He also had been toying with the idea of a quick dash across the plains of Ailean to waft over the walls of the schools of wizardry and see just how far he would have to lower himself to earn those seven rings of mastery.

Of course, that might be unnecessary if whilst having a glass of wine with that essence-changing whoreson—if the man could be found actually laboring instead of flitting off on yet another holi-day—and if that wine might be tampered with, perhaps spells might be, again, blurted out in the midst of a nightmare or two.

That he might have to shelve those items labeled Nefarious Doings for a bit to see to things that numerous other, less devious mages could likely manage with perhaps unsatisfactory efforts—

"Acair, are you coming inside to pack?"

He sighed, suppressed the urge to fling the missive up in the air and hope it landed somewhere else—perhaps his grandmother's garden—and pushed himself to his feet.

A quest.

Ye gads!

To catch up on volumes One and Two
of Acair and Léirsinn's adventures:

The White Spell
The Dreamer's Song

To find out how it all began:

Star of the Morning

For a complete list of titles, visit
www.lynnkurland.com/books

About the Author

Lynn Kurland is the *New York Times* bestselling author of over forty novels and novellas. She can be reached through her website at www.LynnKurland.com.

CPSIA information can be obtained
at www.ICGtesting.com
Printed in the USA
LVHW041718110220
646575LV00003B/654